The Grey Gates - Book 2

Called

VANESSA NELSON

CALLED

The Grey Gates - Book 2

Vanessa Nelson

Copyright © 2023 Vanessa Nelson

All rights reserved. This is a work of fiction.

All characters and events in this publication are fictitious and any resemblance to any real person, living or dead, is purely coincidental.

Reproduction in whole or in part of this publication without express written consent is strictly prohibited.

For more information about Vanessa Nelson and her books, click or visit: www.taellaneth.com

For my very own hell-hounds, August and Neo
Love and head scratches for you both

Contents

1. CHAPTER ONE — 1
2. CHAPTER TWO — 13
3. CHAPTER THREE — 23
4. CHAPTER FOUR — 31
5. CHAPTER FIVE — 37
6. CHAPTER SIX — 42
7. CHAPTER SEVEN — 52
8. CHAPTER EIGHT — 59
9. CHAPTER NINE — 62
10. CHAPTER TEN — 71
11. CHAPTER ELEVEN — 79
12. CHAPTER TWELVE — 91
13. CHAPTER THIRTEEN — 97
14. CHAPTER FOURTEEN — 111
15. CHAPTER FIFTEEN — 120
16. CHAPTER SIXTEEN — 128
17. CHAPTER SEVENTEEN — 139
18. CHAPTER EIGHTEEN — 150
19. CHAPTER NINETEEN — 161

20. CHAPTER TWENTY	171
21. CHAPTER TWENTY-ONE	178
22. CHAPTER TWENTY-TWO	185
23. CHAPTER TWENTY-THREE	195
24. CHAPTER TWENTY-FOUR	201
25. CHAPTER TWENTY-FIVE	212
26. CHAPTER TWENTY-SIX	217
27. CHAPTER TWENTY-SEVEN	224
28. CHAPTER TWENTY-EIGHT	237
29. CHAPTER TWENTY-NINE	242
THANK YOU	251
CHARACTER LIST	252
ALSO BY THE AUTHOR	255
ABOUT THE AUTHOR	257

Chapter One

Max pulled to a stop at the junction and drummed her fingers against the wheel, staring at the roads ahead lit by the pick-up headlights and the orange glow of the street lights. There were three possible routes in front of her, and she wasn't sure which one to take.

In the short pause, with nothing else demanding her attention, her mind gave her a flashback to another night not that long ago when she'd woken to the feeling of hard, cold concrete under her, followed by the white-hot pain of a knife cutting through her skin and the too-cheerful voice of her would-be killer as he chatted away about his plans.

She shook her head, trying to clear the memory. She had survived, and that night contained just the most recent additions to a whole gallery of bad memories that she carried. In time, it would fade into the background with the others, taking its turn to invade her sleep with vivid nightmares. Right now, it was still creeping into her waking mind.

She had a decision to make about which road to take. She should focus on that. Not having a clear direction was an unusual feeling. She was used to having a purpose. But right now there was no one demanding her time or attention. In the two weeks since she had been attacked by the great, winged Strump and then kidnapped by the talkative killer, she had been either at home or on desk duties at the Marshals' offices, recovering from her injuries. No one particularly needed her to be at the offices. Her house and garden were tidier than they had ever been. She had found time to read through the pile of books she had been collecting, and gather more from one of the city's bookshops. She had even cleaned the house windows, inside and out. It had been a peaceful couple of weeks, with nothing and nobody trying to kill her, yet she could feel an itch building under her skin. She wanted to be working. She wanted a purpose.

She should go home. That would be sensible. Go home, get some rest, and plan what to do tomorrow. Or she could go to the Hunter's Tooth and see Malik, and whoever else she might know in the bar. Neither option really appealed to her. She was too restless to sit in a bar, or her clean and organised home.

Before she could decide on her next step, a pale flash at the edge of her vision made her groan. Not again. Her kidnapper had used a drug to keep her still, like his other victims. She had somehow managed to break free from the effects of the drug and had used magic to burn her attacker. Ever since then, she had been having moments of displacement when her senses betrayed her. Sometimes it was her hearing, sometimes her sight, and occasionally she had experienced phantom tastes in her mouth. She had thought the episodes were improving, and had managed to avoid talking about them with any of the health professionals who had been looking after her. The last thing she wanted was more needles and more tests and more scans.

She shifted her foot on the vehicle's pedals and felt the discomfort and tightness in her still-healing leg. Three different health professionals had told her that although the stitches were now all out, and despite the additional healing magic that had been applied, the underlying tissue was still weak and vulnerable to fresh injury. There had been twenty-eight stitches along her outer thigh from the razor-sharp claws of the Strump. It had been sheer luck the damage hadn't been worse, she knew. That didn't help heal her faster, though.

Another pale flash shot across her line of sight and she frowned. That wasn't in her head. There had actually been something crossing the road ahead of her. It had looked like a half-dressed woman. Even as she turned her head to follow the woman's path, a pair of men dressed in nothing more than jeans ran past the front of her vehicle.

Without thinking, Max turned the pick-up to follow them. Dealing with humans in trouble wasn't her job, but she couldn't stand by and let a woman be chased down by two men.

The pick-up caught up with the trio at the end of the next block. This was a business district, and all the buildings were empty at this time of night. The woman was cowering in the recessed doorway of an office building, pressed back against the red brick wall, the building's lobby dark, its glass doors locked for the night. It looked like the woman was wearing nothing more than a pair of jeans and a sleeveless top, short, spiky dark hair standing out from her head. The two men were looming over her. Max couldn't see more than their backs, but the tension in the men's shoulders and closed fists was clear.

Max left her engine running and got out. Even though she was off active duty, she was still dressed in her usual work clothes of a leather jacket and tough, flexible trousers, and she was armed. She pulled her badge out from under her jacket and drew her handgun, but kept the muzzle pointed to the ground.

The three people seemed to be having a low-voiced argument of some kind. The woman - no, girl - was pleading, tears streaming down her face. There was a trail of vivid bruising along both of her arms, shocking against her pale skin, as if she had been gripped by large hands, and one side of her face was swollen. She was trying to make herself as small as possible against the wall.

"Marshals' service," Max announced herself.

The men stiffened but did not immediately turn around. In the orange glow of the street lamp, Max could see that both were leanly muscled, and had intricate tattoos on their right shoulders, the trail of the tattoos' jagged, geometric designs extending down their arms.

"We don't need your help, Marshal," one of the men said. He half-turned towards her and she saw the hard planes of his face and the flicker of power in his eyes. Not quite human. That probably made him dangerous.

"Two men chasing a girl through the city at night? I'd like to hear an explanation for that," Max said, keeping her voice calm with an effort, trying to project confidence in her posture. It was difficult when she was keenly aware of the disadvantage of her human nature and the handicap of her injured leg. Her fingers tightened on the gun grip but she kept the weapon lowered. The girl was behind the two men, and Max didn't want to risk hitting her with a stray bullet.

"It's family business," the man said. His companion hadn't moved, still watching the woman.

"That's not an explanation," Max said.

"It wasn't meant to be." He fully turned to face her and she saw that the tattoo spread across the front of his shoulder, too. An old, intricate design, it made Max's mouth go dry. She knew that symbol of intertwined triangles. Everyone who was part of the city's law enforcement agencies - human or supernatural - would know it. It was the mark of the Huntsman clan, one of the Five Families that ruled the city. Unlike the other four Families, the Huntsman clan members were not related by blood or family ties, but rather gathered together a variety of non-humans in search of a home. They were also vicious criminals, although the power of the clan meant that very few of their members had ever been successfully convicted of a single crime.

The Huntsman clan fell in the murky ground between the Marshals' jurisdiction over supernatural creatures and the city's police, who dealt with more mundane human crimes. The Marshals' primary focus was on the creatures who couldn't pass for human, but they would make an exception for a rogue who caused injury to other city residents. As it was, the standing order from the Marshals' office was to avoid the Huntsman clan where possible, particularly where they were involved in any non-supernatural crime. The system was far from perfect, as far as Max was concerned, but taking on the entire clan would be tantamount to starting a war in the city and she honestly wasn't sure who would win.

Like all of the Families, the Huntsman claimed a stretch of territory in the city, and this wasn't it. As far as Max knew, this particular bit of the city didn't belong to any of the Families.

Max stayed where she was. She had had time to see that the girl huddled in the doorway didn't have any ink on her skin, so she wasn't one of the clan. Or not yet, at least. The Marshals' updates hadn't mentioned that the Huntsman clan were forcibly recruiting members, but it was in keeping with their reputation.

"Is she a relative of yours?" Max asked the man who was facing her. He was mostly human, she thought, with perhaps a quarter amount of something other in his make-up. Enough to give his face those hard lines and the power in his eyes. She suspected that most humans would cross the street to avoid him, even when he was wearing a full set of clothes.

"It's not your concern," the man said. "Now, go. Leave us be."

He lifted a hand and a wave of magic slammed into Max, taking her by surprise, lifting her off her feet. She flew back, hitting the side of her pick-up hard enough to knock the breath out of her before sliding to the ground.

The man raised his hand again, but before he could unleash whatever magic he had prepared, two dark shapes launched themselves out of the back of the pick-up. Max's shadow-hounds, Cas and Pol, reacting to an assault on their person. The giant hounds shifted into their attack forms mid-flight, landing on the man before he had time to react, digging in with their elongated claws, dragging him to the ground.

Max fought to get her breath back as the man tried to wrestle with her hounds. He was almost as strong as they were, but Cas and Pol were used to dealing with predators larger and stronger than they were. It was a matter of moments before Cas got hold of the man's throat in his jaws, effectively holding him still.

The other man snarled, advancing on Cas, just in time for Pol to slam into him, driving him away from the girl. Pol grabbed hold of the second man's arm and pulled him away from Cas and Max as if the fully grown man was a toy.

Max scrambled back to her feet. She had kept hold of her gun, which was one of the first things she had learned as a Marshall. Her chest hurt, lungs burning as she took a much-needed breath.

Before she could say anything, movement at the corner of her eye caught her attention. She turned, raising her gun, to find another three people coming towards her, two men and a woman. They all moved with the smooth grace of predators, and one of them was wearing a sleeveless t-shirt that showed the Huntsman clan marking on his shoulder.

The newcomers took in the situation with a quick glance, then charged at Max, ignoring the seven-pointed badge clearly visible outside her jacket. She fired, her bullets somehow missing the three completely. One of the men slammed into her, pinning her back against the truck, and grabbed hold of her wrist, squeezing so hard she had to let her gun go. He leant into her, baring his teeth, staring down at her with the promise of pain in his eyes, his breath hot on her skin.

Max brought her knee up, hard, catching him off-guard, and twisted out of his hold as he grunted with pain. She tried to reach for her gun, but the other two were waiting for her, a fist slamming into her face, a kick connecting with her ribs, and she stumbled back along the length of the pick-up. Away from her gun. Her heart thudded in her ears. It was three to one, and she had never been good at hand-to-hand combat.

Loud snarls announced the arrival of her dogs. They leapt on the closest attacker to Max, dragging the man away, giving Max just enough time to draw her back-up gun from the holster in the small of her back and fire point blank at the woman who was closing on her fast, a long knife in her hand.

The small calibre bullets barely made an impact on the attacker. She kept coming.

Max ducked to avoid the knife, rolled on the ground, crying out as the movement woke up bruises and sent a twinge through her barely healed leg. She managed to reach her handgun, its worn grip familiar against her skin, using the side of her pick-up as leverage to help her get up, firing as she straightened. The larger calibre bullets hit home, sending the woman staggering back. Max braced herself against the vehicle, ready for the group to attack her again.

A sharp whistle split the air, and the attackers backed away, turning and running into the night, moving too quickly for Max's eyes to follow them.

Max frowned after them, trying to breathe through the sting of her bruised ribs, wondering if she had managed to tear open the wounds on her leg. It was holding her weight, but sending waves of pain through her in counter-point to her pulse. Her hands were shaking as she put the gun away. That done, she turned to the girl only to find that the girl's throat had been ripped open, blood vivid red against her pale skin, her dark eyes sightless, staring up at the night sky. While Max had been fighting, one of the Huntsman clan had killed their prey.

A lump rose in Max's throat. She had wanted to protect the girl. And had failed. The guilt was a sick stab through her stomach. If Max hadn't been there, the girl might still be alive. Terrified and bruised and in the hands of the Huntsman clan, but perhaps still alive. Max had failed. Again.

Max took a step towards the body, eyes travelling over the girl's injuries, the weight of obligation pressing on her shoulders. She was responsible for this girl's death. The least she could do was remember the unnamed victim and what had been done. The girl was barefoot, wearing a pair of ragged jeans that had seen far better days, and what looked like a camisole. She was too thin, the bones of her collar bone forming deep shadows in the poor light. From the way she was huddled against the building door, knees drawn up, Max could see that her feet were bare and covered in scrapes and blood. The lump in Max's throat grew, accompanied with the first spark of anger rather than guilt. The Huntsman clan had chased this girl when she had been barefoot.

Between one step and the next, the world shifted. Max's vision went blue then yellow and red and green, the colours swirling and unsettling her stomach. The Huntsman clan might have chased the girl, but they had only killed her when Max intervened. The girl had not deserved to die.

Max's hands had been shaking, and her voice unsteady, when she had called the police to the scene. The girl seemed human, outside the Marshals' jurisdiction. The city's police would need to be the ones to take care of her and notify whatever family she had.

Max had gone back to her pick-up, leaning against the side with Cas and Pol pressing their weight against her, offering her their silent warmth and comfort while she tried to swallow the guilt and breathe through the various bruises she'd acquired. Her hounds had shifted back to their normal forms, looking like smooth-coated, dark coloured giant dogs, with gentle eyes and silky soft ears that she stroked, soothing both her and them. She had been fairly sure that the Huntsman clan wouldn't come back. The girl they had been chasing was dead, and the Huntsmans were unlikely to pick a fight with a Marshal outside their own territory.

It hadn't taken long for the police to arrive. The first officers on the scene were two who Max had met before. They asked her some questions, but seemed more concerned with keeping away from the body altogether when Max mentioned the Huntsman tattoos. That didn't surprise Max. No one wanted to risk annoying the Huntsman clan by getting involved in an investigation involving them.

With the members of one of the Families being involved, and a need for some diplomacy, the officers summoned a detective, and wanted Max to wait for more questions.

Tired and sore, Max agreed. It was the least she could do. The police and Marshals usually cooperated in their different roles as much as possible. She took a moment to send a message to Faddei Lobanov, the head of the Marshals' service. He would want to know that one of his Marshals had encountered the Huntsman clan outside their territory.

The arrival of a sleek vehicle made Max's heart sink further. Of all the detectives in the city, she had to get Ruutti Passila. It made a certain sort of sense, as Ruutti was connected with one of the other Families. But Ruutti set Max's teeth on edge. She was stunningly beautiful and used her looks and her natural magic, from her non-human nature, to get what she wanted.

The detective got out of her car looking as if she was ready for a fashion shoot, her finely boned face striking even in orange tint from the street lights, blue eyes vivid, short blonde hair a carefully arranged halo around her head, pale skin almost glowing in the poor light. Like a lot of the city detectives, she adopted a casual style with a leather jacket and jeans. Her clothes always fit her petite, delicate form perfectly and never seemed to stain. Max felt tall and clumsy by comparison with the detective, and was abruptly aware of the scuffs and marks on her own leather jacket and hard-wearing trousers. She lifted her chin, telling herself not to care. Her own reddish-brown hair was probably a tangled mess, shoved behind her ears, and her skin, far from being perfect, showed traces of scars to anyone who looked closely. The sharp planes and angles of Max's face hadn't come from her genetic heritage, like Ruutti's striking features, but from her past, which had burned away the softer shape of her younger face, leaving her with nightmares aplenty.

"Marshal Ortis," Ruutti said, her voice rich and warm, smiling with apparently genuine pleasure. "My, what have you been doing?" she asked. On the surface, her question was a simple enquiry, but nothing was ever simple with Ruutti. Along with the smile, the detective's blue eyes were sharp, assessing Max.

"I was trying to help," Max said, and went through what she had seen again.

Ruutti listened. She might look like a porcelain doll, but the detective had a sharp mind, and one of the highest clearance rates of anyone in the city. When she had heard Max's version of events, she asked questions. And more questions. And then some more questions, until Max felt that her brain had been drawn out through her ears and there was nothing left to give.

As Ruutti asked her questions, the street grew crowded with crime scene techs and a van from the medical examiner's office.

Only when Max had run out of answers did Ruutti nod and turn to the body and the other people gathered. The city's medical examiner had arrived in person, which surprised Max. The death of an anonymous girl didn't seem to warrant the chief herself. But Audhilde was there, her petite form smothered in a set of white coveralls matching those worn by the crime scene techs.

The sight of the coveralls and plastic face shields that the techs were wearing made Max shiver and press herself back against her vehicle again, hand going to her gun. She managed not to draw her weapon, but only just. Her mind filled again with the recent memory of waking up, lying on her back on a hard surface with a killer looming over her, wearing one of those white outfits, his ordinary face covered by a clear plastic shield. The man who had called himself John Smith had killed a number of people in an effort to complete a dark magic ritual, and if Max hadn't somehow managed to break free of the sedative he had used, she would have bled to death on that hard surface while he used her blood to complete a dark magic ritual.

The world slipped, the sharp contrast of the night and bright lights swirling into a mass of colours that all ran together and she had to flatten her hand against the side of the pick-up to stay upright, heart thumping. Three times in quick succession. Damnit. Far from getting better, the episodes were getting worse.

"Max, my dear, are you alright?" Audhilde's voice sounded too loud and too close in her ears.

She blinked, and the world righted itself. Audhilde was standing a few paces away, so not that close, stripping off a pair of bloodied gloves which she dropped into the bag one of the techs was holding for her before pulling off the paper cap, releasing her brown curls which bounced around her head. To most people, the medical examiner looked like a human woman in her thirties, barely older than

Ruutti or Max. Anyone with magic sensitivity would be able to sense her other nature and a hint of her true age. Audhilde was far, far older than she appeared.

"I was trying to help her," Max said. That didn't sound like her voice. But those were the words that had been running through her head since she had realised the girl was dead, and she had said them aloud more than once.

"She had a quick death," Audhilde said, "which is almost certainly kinder than what she'd have got with the Huntsman clan. They are vicious brutes."

The words were said with a quiet violence that made Max straighten, another tremor running through her. As well as being the chief medical examiner for the city, Audhilde was also one of the city's oldest and most powerful vampires. Her condemnation was not casual or hasty.

Audhilde glanced over her shoulder. The girl's body had been moved, transported to the medical examiner's van, so all that was left were extensive blood stains. An unpleasant surprise for whoever was unlucky enough to be first into the building in the morning.

"She's the fourth Huntsman victim I've seen in the past two weeks," Audhilde said, turning back to Max and Ruutti. Her normally warm manner was absent, anger clear on her face. "It needs to stop, detective."

"We're doing our best," Ruutti said, in a calm, professional voice that gave away nothing of her feelings.

"Not good enough," Audhilde said, with more of that quiet violence. "Four bodies in my mortuary. All killed outside Huntsman territory. And now they have also attacked a Marshal. If Max hadn't had her hounds with her, she might be heading to one of my tables now, too."

Max shivered, not just at the undercurrent to Audhilde's voice but also the realisation that the vampire was right. The only thing that had kept her alive had been having Cas and Pol with her. They had saved her life yet again. She would not have been able to defend herself against the first pair of Huntsman clan members she came across, let alone the total of five.

"Did you manage to identify the attackers?" Audhilde asked Ruutti.

The detective's normally pleasant expression slipped for a moment, frustration showing through. "No. We don't have a photo gallery for this clan. Their membership seems to change, and a lot of them take steps to alter their appearance as well. Max has given us a good description of the people she saw, though, which is something."

"But you have no clear suspects," Audhilde said, "and without a name or identity, the clan won't let you question any of their members." Max's brows lifted. She had known that the Huntsman clan was protective of its members, but hadn't appreciated the full extent of it. She wondered just how much the clan got away with by refusing to cooperate with law enforcement. And wondered, too, if the Huntsman clan knew quite how annoyed the chief medical examiner was. The Huntsmans might not care about a city official, but they would be stupid to ignore the potential wrath of a vampire of Audhilde's power and standing in the city.

"That's right," Ruutti said. She looked irritated. And no wonder. She liked closing cases. If the Huntsman clan didn't cooperate, she was unlikely to be able to find the killer and close this one.

"What about the victims?" Max asked, shifting her weight to ease the pressure on her injured leg. "Four victims. What do they have in common?"

Ruutti stared at Max with a flat, displeased expression. Impossible to tell what had annoyed her so much. Perhaps it was Max asking questions, perhaps the detective's lack of progress, or some other reason unconnected with the case.

"Not much, from what I can tell," Audhilde answered. Her anger was still there, almost visible in the night air. "I've seen two young men and two girls so far. They've all been around sixteen or seventeen. We have only identified one. The second victim, a young man. He was an orphan. No obvious connection with the clan."

"The victims haven't been reported missing?" Max asked, brows lifting. That surprised her. Most people across the city - particularly young people - had some kind of family or friend connection. Someone to worry when they hadn't been seen, and to report them missing. "Were they homeless?" That would make some sense, as the city's homeless population tended to keep to themselves and not involve outsiders. Another possible explanation was that the youngsters had been among the people displaced, forced to move from their homes and away from their communities when the Wild had surged forward, expanding into the outer edges of what had been the city's territory about a decade before.

"I don't believe so," Audhilde said. "Not homeless, at any rate. Their clothes were all worn and old, but clean and showed signs of mending. The first three were all well cared for, too. I can't speak for the latest victim so far."

"Were they all killed like that?" Max asked, her stomach twisting. The girl had been frightened. Had she known what was going to happen?

"No. This girl's death was far quicker," Audhilde said, meeting and holding Max's eyes.

Max ducked away from the vampire's gaze. Audhilde generally wore her power and her great age lightly, but there were moments, like now, when they showed through and Max had to brace herself against all that knowledge staring at her. The effort sent a tremor through her, her mind and body worn out from the events of the night.

"There's nothing to suggest anything for the Marshals to get involved in," Ruutti said, a certain edge to her tone making Max's brows lift. The detective had been all-too-willing, indeed eager, for her help not that long ago. And now she was trying to shut Max out.

With the girl's death still weighing on her, Max simply nodded, accepting Ruutti's dismissal. Investigating a murder wasn't part of the Marshals' jurisdiction, and her intervention might have made things worse for the dead girl. Whatever else she was, Ruutti was an excellent detective. There was nothing more Max could add to the investigation.

Still, she drove home with a sour taste in her mouth and the itch of unfinished business under her skin.

Chapter Two

Max woke the next morning stiff and sore, bruises a stark reminder of the night before and the girl she had failed to protect. Her nightmares had been full of the screams and death throes of the warriors she had also failed to protect, eight years before. Nine warriors of the Order who had surely deserved better than to be assigned to look after a barely competent apprentice. As their screams faded, her ears rang with the condemnation of the head of the Order telling her just how badly she had failed and that she was no longer welcome there.

She lay in bed for a moment, arms around one of her pillows, eyes closed, remembering that day. The head of the Order was generally quietly spoken and he hadn't raised his voice or shouted, just expressed his bitter disappointment in her failure. She had stood in front of his desk, the too-big clothes she was wearing rasping against her sensitive skin, still recovering from the fires of the underworld, disoriented from the unfamiliar feeling of air against her bare scalp as her long hair had burned off.

That day had been bad. She had been dismissed from the Order, accused of lying and sent away. But she had walked out of the Order into the care of the man who had found her, shivering and unable to speak and who had lent her the clothes she had worn and who, along with his wife, had given her a place in his house. Alonso and Elicia Ortis had provided her with safety and warmth. She might have got herself out of the underworld, but Alonso and Elicia had truly saved her.

Remembering the older couple, and the welcome she had received in their house, helped chase the bad memories away. The memory of the warriors' deaths wasn't the worst nightmare she had endured, but guilt and grief were leaden weights slowing her down as she forced herself out of bed and through the necessary steps to get ready for work. She wasn't on active duty, but being at the Marshals' headquarters was better than being home alone with her memories.

Catching sight of her reflection in the kitchen window, she saw that her face was swollen and bruised where the Huntsman clan member had hit her the night before, but she decided against taking a painkiller. The pain was a distraction. The wound on her leg had been angry and red when she had checked it, but seemed to still be healing, so she should be able to avoid another doctor's visit. That was something, at least. She had never liked doctors' visits. They made her far too aware of just how vulnerable she was.

She drank a mug of strong black tea and milk standing at the kitchen sink, looking out of the window, distracted by the sight of a dark shape moving across the sky. It was almost too far away for her to hear the engines, but she recognised the shape of a helicopter travelling towards the Wild. There was nothing between her house and the vast stretch of untamed land full of lush vegetation, an incredible array of animal and insect life, and natural magic that sang against her senses if she ever got close to its border. No humans lived in the Wild, and over the years it had reclaimed a lot of land once used by the city's residents. The last great surge, a decade before, had come seemingly out of nowhere, the tangled growth of the Wild taking over what had been houses and schools and shops and gardens within a terrifyingly short space of time, the residents having barely any time to pack up what they could and flee further into the city.

Max stared at the great trees that made up the border of the Wild and wondered if or when the next surge would come. She could lose her house, if the Wild chose to move in her direction. She didn't like to think about it, but it was possible. Luckily, she didn't have much she would need to take with her, and it would all fit in the pick-up. Really, all she would want to take were her dogs and some weapons. Everything else could be replaced or she could find substitutes.

The helicopter she could see dipped further towards the trees and she followed its progress. If she'd still been looking at her reflection, she would have seen a pinched, displeased expression. For some reason, wealthy people liked to charter helicopters from time to time to fly across the Wild, and over the past couple of weeks, Max had seen a few such flights. Never mind that most of the city was under restrictions in fuel usage as supplies were running low. The rules didn't seem to apply to the wealthy. So far none of the tourist flights had been attacked or caught by any of the extremely dangerous creatures that lived in the depths of the Wild, but it was only a matter of time. And then the Marshals would doubtless be called upon to try to rescue the idiots.

Cas and Pol frolicking around the garden in the early morning sun drew her attention back to the ground and brought a smile to her face, her bad mood lifting. Shadow-hounds were supposed to be fierce predators, but when her pair were off duty, they were giant comedians. They had found one of the old rope toys she had bought for them, and were playing tug and chase. As she left the house, the hounds abandoned the toy, rushing to her side. Max stopped to give them each a hug and a biscuit as they reached her pick-up.

Almost as soon as she turned the engine on, the pick-up flashed a low fuel warning at her and her gloomy mood returned. There was fuel at the Marshals' headquarters, but she wouldn't make it that far with what she had.

There was a small petrol station a few blocks into the city which was usually quiet, and only had four pumps, which meant she shouldn't have to deal with too many other people even if it was busy. As she turned off the street into the station, she passed the make-shift sign that proclaimed rationing was in effect and stifled a groan as she saw that there was only one free bay at the petrol station. As tempting as it was to drive on, she did need fuel, so she parked in the free spot.

She got out of her pick-up to the sounds of a loud argument and pushed down the urge to get back into her pick-up and drive on. Rationing had only been in effect for three days, but she remembered the last time it had been enforced, about five years before. There had been fights between drivers at petrol stations and more than one station had had to hire armed guards to protect both the fuel and their staff. Fuel rationing seemed to bring out the worst in people. She didn't want to get involved. But the Marshals' offices were too far away for her to walk, even if her leg hadn't still been healing.

She opened the fuel cap and drew down the allotted amount of fuel that all citizens were entitled to each day. More than enough to get her to work. As a Marshal, she could have over-ridden the limit, but the driver of the vehicle ahead of her was still shouting as she swiped her card to pay for the fuel.

Ready to leave, Max hesitated. Human arguments were not her business. She had tried to help the girl the night before, and that had not ended well. But the would-be customer ahead of her was yelling at the station attendant, using his greater height and bulk to loom over the slender attendant. The customer was dressed in what looked like expensive jeans and a crisp white shirt that suggested he didn't do any manual work. He was about the same height as her and powerfully built, while the attendant would barely reach her shoulder. Max listened for a moment, not surprised to find that the driver was demanding more fuel. The attendant seemed to shrink where he stood. He was wearing a body camera, the lens catching the light at his shoulder, staying silent under the rage.

"I'll wring your skinny neck!" the driver yelled.

There were two other customers at the station, both men, also out of their cars, and not even pretending to do anything apart from listen in. One of them was grinning, clearly enjoying the show. The other one grunted his approval as the shouting man voiced the threat.

Max decided enough was enough, with the possibility for violence thick in the air. The other pair of men had edged closer, the one who had signalled his approval clenching and unclenching his fists, looking as if he wanted to join in the confrontation.

With a sigh, Max pulled the seven-pointed star out from under her jacket so it was clearly visible, and took a step forward.

"What's the problem?" she asked, in her best calm-but-authoritative voice. She wasn't particularly practised at it, as most of the creatures she dealt with were not able to hold a conversation.

"Stay out of this, bitch," the driver snarled over his shoulder.

"Marshal," Max said, in the same tone she had used before. Perhaps she would get better with practice.

"What?" the driver said, glancing back at her. He was almost purple with anger, shaking with the force of it. He might tower over the young, slender forecourt attendant, but he couldn't look down at Max, which seemed to fuel his anger. "Marshal. Really? Why aren't you out killing the supes?" Ah. One of those who thought that the supernatural creatures that occasionally strayed into the city from the Wild just needed to be eliminated. Max's dislike of the man grew.

"We try really hard not to kill things," Max said, aiming for a conversational tone.

"Marshal, you're welcome to fill up," the attendant said. His voice was calm and pleasant. Not in the least intimidated by the much larger, shouting man. That surprised Max enough that she took a second, closer look at him, and had to hide a smile. She had thought she was intervening to stop the irate human from beating up an inexperienced youngster, but the youngster was actually a vampire and probably older than Max and the irate customer combined. The slender man could probably throw the burly, angry man clear across the street without any particular effort.

"I've got my ration, thank you," Max said, and turned back to her pick-up. Cas and Pol were leaning over the side, their short dark coats gleaming in the daylight, folded-over ears lifted in curiosity. They looked like perfectly ordinary giant dogs, and not the shadow-hounds they truly were.

"You're going to let her take fuel?" the customer said. "But not me?"

"Sir, you've had your weekly allowance already, and your vehicle is more than half-full," the attendant said.

Unseen by the angry man, Max rolled her eyes. It seemed that the pattern from five years before was repeating. Fuel rationing made normally mild-mannered and law-abiding citizens lose their minds. Considering they lived in a city with decent public transport links to all but the farthest-out places, and a good network of delivery services, she had never understood why so many citizens were so obsessed with having their own cars.

As she reached the front of her vehicle, there was a rush of movement behind her. A heavy hand grabbed her shoulder, dragged her around, a large fist heading towards her face.

She was almost too surprised to react, dodging just in time so that the fist grazed her face rather than slamming into her nose. She pivoted on one leg, grimacing as the nearly healed injury protested, twisting out of the grip on her shoulder, and drew her gun, holding it to the man's forehead. The fist had hit her existing bruises, her eyes watering at the sharp pain.

"Stop," she said. She wouldn't normally resort to one of her weapons. Not against a human. But she was sore and bruised from the night before, and didn't want to risk further damage to her leg.

The man stared at the gun, almost cross-eyed as he tried to focus on it, the purple anger fading to pale fright.

"You ... you ... you ..." he spluttered. "You can't shoot me," he said.

"Why not?" Max asked.

"I'm human. You can only kill things." His voice was higher than it had been.

"But I can defend myself, like everyone else," Max said, voice hard.

"Marshal, the police are on their way," the attendant said.

"Of course they are," Max muttered under her breath. She really didn't need this. It was another stupid frustration in what had felt like weeks of stupid frustrations. It had taken far longer than she had hoped for her leg to heal. The claws that had ripped into her might not have done any permanent damage, but they had caused deep wounds that had left her almost immobile for the better part of a week, her leg encased in bandages. The hospital had provided her with crutches, but she couldn't do her job on crutches. So she had been at home, or in the Marshals' office, for the past two weeks while she healed enough to walk without a crutch or a stick. And then, just as she was on the cusp of being back to something like normal health, she had got into a fight with the Huntsman clan.

And now this human had managed to land a punch on her existing bruises. It hurt. Far more than it should have done.

She looked at the human in front of her, his temper gone, and naked fear on his face. He may never have had a gun pointed at his head before. All the fury that he had shown in standing over the attendant had gone, and he was just an ordinary man. And she felt like a bully, holding the lethal weapon. She sighed, and put the gun away.

"You need to apologise," she told him.

"I'm s-sorry I tried to hit you," he spluttered.

"Not to me, you idiot. To the attendant. You were trying to bully him into giving you more fuel," Max said, voice clipped. "You know the rules, same as everyone else."

"The rules are wrong," the human said, anger flushing his face again. "We can't be expected to live like this."

"Live like what?" Max asked, glancing at his vehicle. It was one of the sleek, shiny cars that had probably never driven outside the inner city, or done any longer trips than travelling along the winding road that ran alongside the city green. Her own temper flared. "I'm guessing you live in the inner city. You can probably walk to most places you need to go. The car is a luxury, not a necessity."

"How dare you?" the man demanded, turning purple again.

As if on cue, a blue-and-white vehicle pulled up alongside Max and the angry man. A tall, dark-skinned woman in uniform got out of the vehicle.

"Marshal Ortis," the woman said, grinning. "It's good to see you."

"Sergeant Randall," Max answered, managing a smile. She had worked with Ellie before, and liked the police officer.

"What's going on here?" Ellie asked, turning to the attendant.

"Ma'am, this man was trying to get more fuel. The Marshal stopped by, and the man hit her," the attendant said. Max's brows lifted. It was a masterful summary, and one that seemed accurate.

"Looks like the punch landed," Ellie said, taking a closer look at Max's face.

"Yes, but the bruises are mostly from last night," Max said, her gloomy mood returning. She probably should have put some ice on her face.

"Still, he did hit you. Assault on a member of law enforcement. That's a serious matter," Ellie said, voice and face reflecting her disapproval as she turned to the purple-faced man.

"Oh, please, I barely touched her. And she was going to kill me. She has a gun," the man said. "I want to complain about that."

"Did she shoot you?" Ellie asked, with apparent concern.

"No," the man said.

"Then she wasn't going to kill you," Ellie said, and looked at Max. "But he definitely assaulted you."

"It's nothing. It'll heal soon enough. I'm happy to forget about it," Max said. She wished she had never stopped at this petrol station, had never intervened. In fact, while she was wishing, she wished she was back home and that this day had never started.

"Well, if you're sure," Ellie said slowly, with apparent reluctance. Ellie shared Max's dislike of bullies, and had a fierce reputation in the force for fairness.

"I am," Max confirmed.

"Still, you've caused quite a scene, sir," Ellie said, turning back to the furious man. "If you apologise to the attendant and to Marshal Ortis, I'll let you go with a warning this time."

The man stared at Ellie, his fists opening and closing by his sides. Caught in a trap of his own making. Max could all but see the calculation running through his head. He wanted to hit someone. Badly. But he now had a police officer and a Marshal to contend with as well as the forecourt attendant.

"I'm sorry," he said grudgingly, glancing at Max and then at the forecourt attendant.

"We'll be happy to serve you when you're due your next fuel allowance, sir," the attendant said, in the same pleasant, professional manner he had used all along. "For now, if you wouldn't mind moving along, I can see other customers waiting."

Max glanced behind her pick-up and saw that the vampire was right. There were two other cars waiting. Considering that she almost never saw a single other vehicle at this station, it had to be the effect of fuel rationing.

The man glared at the vampire, but to Max's surprise, said nothing, just got into his shiny car and drove off, almost running the attendant over on his way out.

Ellie glanced across the station to the other two men who had been watching. "Either of you have a problem I can help with?" she asked, in her most genial tone.

The two glanced at each other, then got into their own vehicles and drove off.

"You be careful," Ellie said to the attendant. "I know you've got him recorded, and you can look after yourself, but that one looked like he had a nasty streak on him."

"Thank you for your concern, Sergeant Randall. I can assure you I will be quite safe," the vampire said. He looked at Max. "Do you need more fuel, Marshal?"

"Not just now, thank you," Max said.

"Then, if you'll excuse me, I should get back to the office," he said, and made his way across the forecourt to the small shop and secure booth.

As he left, the waiting vehicles pulled into the spaces on the other side of the pumps. Max turned to Ellie.

"Are you seeing much of this sort of thing?" she asked.

"Too much," Ellie said, shaking her head. "It's escalating more quickly than it did before. The council's going to need to do something about the fuel supply before too long."

"I know," Max said. With the expansion of the Wild, the city had been cut off from a lot of its resources, including a source for more fuel, and the city's reserves were dwindling. Despite significant advances in technology, and alternative fuels, some things still needed old-fashioned fuel to run. The last time the city had run this short, the council had been forced to send a convoy into the Wild, to tap into the oil field that had been swallowed by the Wild. It had been a sign of how desperate things had become in the city that the council had even considered sending people out on such a dangerous task.

"As I've got you here, have you been hearing anything about missing people?" Ellie said.

"People? Humans?" Max asked, brows lifting.

"Yes," Ellie said, and shook her head again. "I keep forgetting to make that clear."

"I hadn't heard about people going missing, but then I wouldn't necessarily hear anything. It's outside the Marshals' jurisdiction," Max said. "I did come across a few of the Huntsmans last night and heard they have been killing youngsters."

"Yeah," Ellie said, face serious. "That's a bad business."

"What's been happening with the missing people?" Max asked, curious despite her best intentions to stay out of human affairs.

"You know the homeless warehouse, at the docks?" Ellie asked. "Well, word is that about a half-dozen people have gone missing from there in the past week or so. Perhaps longer, I don't know. It's not my case. I've just started hearing about it."

Max frowned. It had been a very long time since her job had taken her to the docks. There was a series of large, abandoned warehouses, one of which had been taken over by the city's homeless population, turned into a warren of make-shift shelters. Despite the wealth and prosperity which was so visible in the centre of the city, there were a lot of people who had been displaced by the expansion of the Wild, and put out of work as industries were forced to close due to lack of resources. And then there were the people who felt they had no choice but to flee whatever was going on behind the walls of their homes.

"Half a dozen people doesn't sound like a lot to go missing from there," Max said slowly. "Is it possible they have found homes or jobs?"

"That's been looked into, from what I hear, but no luck so far," Ellie said. She looked troubled.

"I'm sorry. Someone you know?" Max asked.

"No," the woman answered, "I just hate that we still have homeless folk. There are more than enough jobs and houses to go around."

"I know what you mean," Max said. "I'll let you know if I hear anything," she offered.

She said farewell to Ellie, gave Cas and Pol a pat before getting back in her pick-up and continuing her journey to work, wondering just how many other troubles would bubble to the surface over the coming days.

Chapter Three

The rest of the drive was uneventful, which was a relief. The shortest route to the Marshal's offices took her over the top of one of the shallow hills that gave the city an undulating shape. Between square, industrial buildings, Max caught a glimpse of the great sprawl of buildings and roads and green spaces that were hemmed into the available land between the Wild and the coast. She was always surprised by how big the city was, and how different its various districts were. As varied as its people. Most of the inhabitants were human, and many of them tried to ignore or steer clear of their non-human neighbours. The ever-present threat of the Wild made a lot of city residents uneasy enough without also having to think about or deal with the non-humans in the city's population mix. Max found the mix of peoples fascinating and frustrating in equal measure, even if she spent most of her working time in the outer districts of the city, the ones closer to the Wild and more likely to be affected by stray creatures.

The Marshals' headquarters was in a large, run-down industrial estate, the edge of the Wild clearly visible as Max made the turn from the road into the Marshals' complex. As soon as Max had parked on the cracked and worn concrete that surrounded the buildings in the Marshals' headquarters, Cas and Pol jumped out of the vehicle and ran off, heading for the science building and the Marshals' armourer, Leonda Parras. Even though she expected it, and was used to her dogs' love of Leonda, the dogs' obvious joy as they ran away stung as if they were abandoning her.

Telling herself not to be so silly, Max made her way to the Marshals' communal office, finding a few other Marshals there, settled in comfortable chairs and swapping tall tales over mugs of coffee. Not wanting to be alone with her thoughts, Max got her own coffee and settled in an empty chair, letting the bubble of conversation wash over her.

In a brief moment of quiet, one of the Marshals, Zoya, turned to Max, brows lifted. "I thought you were supposed to be on desk duty. I didn't know that staplers could fight back?"

Max grinned, taking the teasing in good part and relieved that Zoya was here at all. The other Marshal had been badly injured when Max had been supposed to be watching her back.

"I ran into some of the Huntsman clan," Max said, her shoulders hunching over, trying to avoid the surprised looks from the other Marshals.

"What happened?" Zoya asked, her teasing changing to concern. She was a compact woman, whose head barely reached Max's shoulder, made of muscle, with warm-toned brown skin and waist length hair which today was a pale pink colour, tied in a single, thick plait at the back of her head.

Max shoved her hair back behind her ear and winced as she brushed the newly sore side of her face. She told them, as briefly as possible, what had happened from seeing the girl to the conversation she had had with Audhilde and Ruutti.

"Four bodies?" one of the other Marshals, Yevhen, said, a frown gathering. One of the most experienced Marshals, he was sitting next to his wife, Pavla, both of them slender and tall with dark hair and pale skin.

"So far, yes," Max confirmed.

"That's not good news," Zoya said.

A shadow fell over the group and Max looked up to find the head Marshal, Faddei, standing nearby. With his broad shoulders and bald head covered in tattoos, he looked like he'd be more at home in a boxing ring than the office, but Max knew that his tough appearance hid a sharp mind. "I'd like to hear this story again, if that's alright," he said to Max. His gaze swept the others. "The Huntsman clan seems to be trying to spread their influence more widely. Be careful out there."

The other Marshals got up from their seats and gave their leader a variety of light-hearted acknowledgements from a mocking "ay, ay, sir" to a sloppy salute as they headed out, but Max knew that Faddei's warning had been heard.

When it was just her and Faddei left in the room, he sat in a chair opposite her, setting his own coffee to one side and favouring her with a direct look. "Tell me what happened," he requested.

So Max repeated the story. She was losing count of the number of repetitions, but the guilt was not fading.

"The Huntsman members. Would you recognise them again?" Faddei asked.

"Yes," Max said. "Why? I didn't think we had any galleries of them?"

"Not right now, no. But if the clan members are going to be beating up my team, that is going to change," Faddei said, looking and sounding determined.

He would have said the same thing to any one of his Marshals, or any one of the other dozens of people who worked for the Marshals' service. But Max's eyes still stung, and the tightness in her chest loosened a fraction. Faddei was the one constant she, and every other person who worked for the Marshals' service, could rely on.

"If you're free, I have an assignment for you," Faddei said. His tone and lifted brow made it a genuine question, not an order.

"All my reports are done," Max said, a welcome and unexpected smile pulling her mouth. She couldn't think of another time she had been able to say that.

Faddei grinned. "That's good. Leonda wanted someone to help test a new weapon. I thought you might be willing to help," Faddei said, a smile lifting his mouth.

"Happy to help," Max said, hoping she didn't sound too eager. She might not love the armourer quite as much as her dogs did, but she liked the woman, and anything would be more interesting than shuffling paper around the office for another day.

"Good," Faddei said, and grinned again. "Have fun."

Max finished her coffee in a large gulp then left the building, heading for Leonda's office with a spring in her step for what felt like the first time in weeks.

Working with Leonda and her team was just as much fun as Max had hoped, and far more exhausting than she could have imagined. They were developing a new handgun, designed to carry heavier weight bullets, and wanted to try different bullets, different grips, and all manner of other minor adjustments with a Marshal who would carry the new weapon out in the field, rather than in the controlled setting of their testing range. On the surface, the new weapon didn't feel all that different from her existing weapon, but it was somehow far more powerful. It had been fascinating working with Leonda and her team, seeing the care that the scientists took over every minor detail of the weapon. Leonda and her team had also peppered Max with questions, wanting to know how she would use the gun in the field, wanting to know about the recoil, reloading, and a dozen more things besides. There was no time for Max to feel the guilt of the unknown girl's death, or frustration at her still-healing wounds. She was absolutely absorbed in the project.

By the time the research team let her go, a whole day had passed. There had been a few short breaks, but Max had been on her feet for most of the day, her bruises coming to life as she left the building to find the sky darkening to night.

She paused outside the door, drawing in a breath, finding a smile on her face. It felt good to have been useful.

Cas and Pol crowded around her, demanding attention. The tests had been using live fire, so the dogs had been left in Leonda's office for most of the day. There were more than enough other people in the building to ensure they hadn't been lonely, but they clearly felt that they had simply been abandoned. Max scratched them behind their soft, silky ears and fed them treats from her pockets. As she dug into her pocket in search of more treats, she pulled out her phone and only then realised she had left it on silent for the day. There were a few missed calls from Faddei, Ruutti and a couple of numbers she didn't recognise, and the voicemail icon was lit up.

Brows lifting, as Faddei rarely called her directly, Max headed for the office building, dialling Faddei's number as she walked.

"Where are you?" Faddei asked.

"I'm just leaving the armoury, heading to the offices," Max said, brows lifting again at his tone. He sounded worried.

"Good. Don't speak to anyone else, and I'll meet you in the main office."

"Alright," Max said, the peace of the past few hours turned to apprehension, wondering what had happened. She ended the call and put the phone back in her pocket. Ruutti and the others would have to wait.

When she reached the main office, it was empty apart from Faddei, who was staring at something on his laptop screen. Max went to join him.

"You were looking for me?" Max said.

"Did you threaten to shoot someone this morning?" Faddei asked, voice carefully neutral.

Max blinked. She had almost forgotten the incident at the petrol station. "The guy grabbed me and managed to land a punch. I drew my gun, yes," she answered, and turned her face slightly to show the bruising that the other Marshals had noticed earlier. "He caught the old bruise. He just grazed me. Ellie was there. I didn't press charges."

Faddei ran a hand over his bald head and turned the laptop screen towards her. There was a video clip playing, the man saying *You can't shoot me*, and Max asking *Why not?* with her gun to the man's forehead. The clip was only a few seconds long and repeated over and over. It had been taken at a slight distance. One of the other drivers at the petrol station, Max guessed, cataloguing the angles and distance. She had been filmed without realising it.

"How did you get that?" Max asked, words clumsy in her mouth.

"It's on the internet," Faddei said dryly. "I've been fielding calls all afternoon from reporters asking if it's now Marshal policy to threaten to shoot unarmed civilians." He rubbed his head again. "And most people who've seen the video think you should be dismissed from service."

The ground was unsteady under her feet and her stomach churned, making her glad she hadn't eaten that day. Heat coursed across her skin, followed immediately by icy cold. Her face was on the internet. She glanced at the bottom of the screen and almost recoiled at the number of views the video had. So many people. She didn't want to be seen. She just wanted to live her life and do her job. And now thousands of people had seen her holding a gun to a man's head. She flinched from an invisible blow.

Then her ears caught up with what Faddei had said. People were calling for her dismissal. A wordless protest lodged in her throat. She needed this job. It was the only place she had ever felt accepted. Trusted. And it was probably the only thing she was qualified to do. "I'm sorry," she said to Faddei, mouth dry and lips stiff. Her eyes were stinging and she blinked, trying not to cry. "I didn't think," she said, voice harsh.

Faddei just nodded, saying nothing.

She drew a deep, shaking breath and realised something. He hadn't dismissed her. He had just said that other people wanted her gone. And she was still here. He hadn't asked for her badge. "That clip is just a tiny bit of what happened," she said.

"I've no doubt," Faddei said, sounding tired. "So, tell me, what did happen?"

Max had to swallow a lump in her throat before she could answer. He hadn't fired her. Not yet. Instead, he was listening. "Well. The guy was yelling at the forecourt attendant. I thought he was going to beat the attendant up. When I stepped in, he grabbed me and took a swing at me. Oh. The attendant had a camera on him. He should have a recording of the whole thing," Max said. "And then the attendant called Ellie. Well, not Ellie, but he called the police, and Ellie showed up." It was probably the worst verbal report she had ever given, tangled up and spoken in a rapid, too-high voice. Faddei just nodded when she had finished.

"Alright. I'll see if I can get the footage. Was the attendant hurt?" Faddei asked.

"No. I don't think he was even all that worried," Max said, shaking her head. "I didn't spot it at first, but he's a vampire."

"So you probably saved that man from something worse than having a gun pointed at his head," Faddei said, voice dry.

Max's eyes stung again. He hadn't fired her. A tiny sliver of hope wriggled through the chill that had taken over her body. Maybe she would keep her job.

He closed his laptop and tucked it under his arm. "I believe you. I'll make sure that the full story gets out to the right people."

Max had to lock her knees to stay upright. Cas and Pol crowded into her, sensing that something was wrong and offering comfort. Her eyes were still stinging, and she might even have tears on her face. She could always depend on her dogs. And Faddei, it seemed. Although he still had a serious expression on his face.

"But you want me to stay home for a couple of days?" she guessed, voice choked. She didn't blame him. Now that the shock was fading, and she realised she still had a job, she also realised that if she had been in his position, having to deal with reporters and outrage, she doubted she would have been so accommodating.

"If you could. Keep your phone on, though. I got your doctor's note earlier and you're cleared for duty again. Although that was before your run-in with the Huntsman clan," he added, frowning, "so a bit of extra time off is probably wise anyway."

Max wanted to protest. She wanted to say she was fit for duty, that she was ready to get back to work. But it wasn't her decision. And he hadn't fired her. "Alright." Max hesitated. "I really am sorry," she said.

To her surprise, Faddei grinned, shaking his head. "Don't be. This is mild, compared to some of the stuff I've had to deal with. Did you ever hear about the time that Vanko and Zoya chased a pair of Seacast monkeys into a gentleman's club? There was a strip show going on and half the council was in there. Apparently one of the monkeys tried to escape by climbing up the stripper's pole. That was some evening."

Max's urge to cry faded and she choked on a laugh. She could all-too-easily imagine the always cheerful Vanko and intense, dedicated Zoya chasing a pair of the enormous, carnivorous monkeys around a room full of half-dressed women and outraged council members.

The bubble of humour got her outside and into her pick-up. She managed to remember to turn on the ringtone before she put the phone into its dashboard cradle. She had spent long enough on the sidelines.

As she was driving out of the parking lot, her phone rang and she blinked, startled that Faddei or Therese had an assignment for her so soon. But the number on the screen was Ruutti, not the Marshals' service.

The detective was the last person that Max wanted to speak to then, but it was possible that Ruutti had more follow-up questions from the killing the night before. With a sigh, Max answered the call.

"Where have you been?" Ruutti demanded by way of greeting.

"Getting into a fist fight at a petrol station and then helping with weapons testing. How about you?" Max answered.

"What? Never mind. I need you to meet me," Ruutti said.

"I don't work for you," Max answered, the words almost falling over themselves to get out of her mouth. The last time Ruutti had dragged Max into police business, Max had ended up in an underground illegal fighting arena and had been injured by a Strump, the giant bird just one of the supernatural creatures kept captive for entertainment purposes. "And I'm still on leave," she added, stretching the truth a little.

"I don't need you to run and chase anything," Ruutti said, sounding impatient. "Have you heard about the missing people?"

"Just this morning. Something about homeless people missing from the docks?" Max said, frowning. "Why? What's that got to do with the Marshals?"

"We're running into dead ends," Ruutti said, and Max's brows lifted. The detective did not like to admit to failings. "A fresh perspective would be helpful." Max could hear the forced patience in Ruutti's voice and had to bite her lip to hide a smile, even though the other woman couldn't see her.

The smile faded almost at once as Max remembered the dead girl from the night before and the video clip Faddei had shown her. She had utterly failed to help the girl, and made matters difficult for her boss by pulling a gun on an unarmed civilian. The last thing she wanted to do was to get involved with another case working with Ruutti. Not least because the detective had taken all the credit for catching the talkative serial killer who had also tried to kill Max. Max had read the news headlines with disbelief. She didn't care about the publicity, but she did care that the detective had lied. Again.

"No," Max said, more bluntly than she had intended. "There are dozens of other detectives you could ask for input. Missing humans is your problem, and your world. Not mine." And she hung up before she could think better of it, pushing down the stab of guilt. It was perfectly true. Human crimes were Ruutti's business, not Max's. All Max wanted to do right now was go home, huddle on the sofa with her dogs and avoid the world before anyone else could ask for her help, or before she did anything else wrong.

Chapter Four

It was fully dark when Max finally arrived at the gates to her house and garden. The head-high gates were closed, as usual. She didn't think anyone would come out this close to the Wild to steal anything and, on days like today, she welcomed the solitude. But this close to the Wild it was possible that something would stray past the protective wards she had placed around the grounds. If she left the gates open, there was a strong possibility she would arrive home to find unwanted visitors grazing in her garden.

Tonight the gates were still closed, but there was a large, brilliant white envelope tucked just above the latch, where she couldn't fail to see it. In the glare of the headlights, she could see black writing on the surface. She stared at it for a moment before getting out of the pick-up to take a closer look. All her normal post went to the Marshals' offices as the postal service refused to deliver this close to the Wild, not wanting to risk coming across something that might have found its way out of the Wild. Which meant that the envelope had been hand-delivered, and she could not think of anyone who would go to that much trouble, not when the Marshals' offices were easier to reach.

The only package that had been delivered to her in the last couple of months had contained replacement ammunition for the rocket launcher that the Marshals' service didn't know she had. It had been used against a Harridan, and she had wanted to resupply the case before she returned it to her Vault. The arms supplier had been willing to get a courier to deliver the package, for a fee. Max had paid, wanting the rocket launcher out of her house and back into its place in her Vault. Marshals might be allowed to carry handguns off-duty, but she didn't think Faddei would turn a blind eye to her keeping a rocket launcher under her sofa. Even though putting the rocket launcher case back into her Vault had taken most of her energy for a whole day, it had been worth it. The Vault as an organisation provided secure storage for magicians, and asked no questions about what was stored there. Not even the council could get a list of magicians holding a Vault, let alone what was inside. Max only had hers because every apprentice of the Order was given one, and it was coded to her and her alone, so even Kitris, as the head of the Order, hadn't been able to take it back when he had dismissed her.

But that delivery had been planned. This envelope was unexpected. She frowned at it, unable to think of anyone who would make the effort to drive here to deliver it. She couldn't sense any magic on it, so she picked it up. The envelope was addressed simply to Max Ortis, and there was no return address, but there was the faint impression of a seal on the closure. She broke open the envelope and found a rectangle of thick paper inside, a faint scent like old roses reaching her nose. There was handwriting on the card in old-fashioned joined-up letters that had certainly been made by a fountain pen, and a simple message.

"Dearest Max, you did a great favour for one of my household earlier today. To express my thanks, I should like to invite you to afternoon tea, at the date and place below. I look forward to seeing you there. Warmest wishes, Audhilde."

Max's fingers tightened and she forced herself to relax, not wanting to damage the heavy and doubtless expensive paper. She liked Audhilde. The vampire was professional and knowledgeable, with a warm manner that belied the grim nature of her work. But this wasn't work-related, Max knew, and she held in her hand an invitation from one of the city's most powerful vampires to an afternoon tea, which had a specific meaning within a vampire household that Max did not fully understand.

Max read the message again, trying to work out what favour she had done, realisation creeping over her. The vampire at the petrol station. He must be a member of Audhilde's household. Max didn't know precisely how vampire households and hierarchy worked - it was a closely guarded secret - but clearly Audhilde felt that Max had done something special. And even though Max didn't consider it to have been particularly worthy of thanks, there was no possible, polite way to refuse Audhilde's invitation. She would risk offending Audhilde, which was not something she wished to do. Which meant that at the appointed time, Max would need to go into a vampire's house and put herself into the care of one of the most powerful beings in the city.

One of the dogs whined, letting her know she had been standing for too long. They knew that they were due to be fed when they got to the house.

"Sorry," she said to them. She put the message back into the envelope and pushed open the gates.

It was only when she was making sure that the gates were locked behind her, the dogs running around the garden, that she realised she had a far more basic problem than offending one of the oldest and most powerful vampires in the city by not turning up: she wasn't sure she had any suitable clothing for afternoon tea with avampire.

The next day, Max took herself and her dogs to the one place in the city she knew she would always be welcome, and where she might find answers to the conundrum of what happened at afternoon tea with a vampire. And perhaps also some sympathy for her unfortunate rise to fame on the city's media channels. She had fielded a half dozen calls from reporters wanting answers from her to a series of questions, the most prominent of which were whether she was in the habit of threatening innocent humans, and whether she had ever shot a human on purpose.

To her relief, she had solved the problem of clothing by digging through every item in her wardrobe and finding clothes she had forgotten about, relics of some impulse buying from her early months in the Marshals' service, almost eight years ago, when she had been overtaken with the heady sense of freedom and having her own money to do with as she pleased. She remembered spending a small fortune in a boutique that Malik had recommended, and it seemed that shopping trip was finally going to be useful. So that was one problem solved.

The Hunter's Tooth bar didn't look like much from the outside, but she didn't care. As she walked through the front door, Cas and Pol bouncing ahead of her like over-excited puppies, she drew in what felt like the first easy breath she had taken since she had seen the video clip.

The bar's owner and operator, Malik, was in his usual spot, mixing drinks. He glanced up as she came in and favoured her with one of his generous, welcoming smiles. It had been a long while since they had been anything but friends, but Malik's smile still warmed her all the way through. It didn't matter that he had that effect on nearly everyone, or that his particular magic meant he could make this bar feel like the safest place in the world. Everyone was special to Malik, and all were welcome at the Hunter's Tooth.

Max settled at one of the stools by the bar and waited while Malik finished serving a group of what looked like university students. He gave them another one of his smiles, and Max had to bite her lip to hide her grin as she saw the effect it had on the group. Malik was undeniably beautiful, with mid-brown skin and curling black hair and a facial structure that could have earned him a modelling career if he had possessed any real vanity. Doubtless the students would be vying for his attention before long. Max didn't blame them, although she was tempted to tell the girls not to bother. Malik did not tend to favour very young women. But it was not her business who he kept company with, and not her place to interfere.

"Max," he said, leaning over the bar and kissing her cheek. "It's good to see you. Are you healed?"

He didn't mean the bruising on her face, she knew. It didn't surprise her that Malik knew about her injury. Although he never seemed to leave the bar, he knew most of what went on in the city.

"Almost good as new," she told him. "Back on active duty."

"But not today," he noted, glancing at her outfit. Apart from the leather jacket and heavy-wear trousers she wore for work and the clothes she had re-discovered on her hunt the night before, she had a limited wardrobe. She was wearing jeans and an over-sized, faded purple sweater that hid the back-up gun she had tucked into her belt. Like all Marshals, she was allowed to carry weapons even off duty.

"No. Faddei, er, suggested I take some time off." Heat rose up her neck and face. She had never wanted to be famous, and certainly not for holding a gun to an unarmed human.

"I saw the clip," Malik said, voice full of sympathy, "and the longer version. The man was lucky you didn't actually shoot him."

"I think you must be the only person who's seen the longer version," Max said sourly. "I've had reporters on the phone this morning who clearly hadn't seen it."

"It's spreading more slowly, but it is spreading," Malik said. He put a mug of coffee in front of her, half-full of the dark liquid he preferred, and set a milk jug next to it. "It will be yesterday's news soon enough," he added.

"I hope so," Max said, trying to smile. He was trying to be helpful. And she knew it was true. She had watched stories come and go from the news cycle often enough. It felt different when she was the story, though. She ducked away from his perceptive gaze, topping the coffee off with milk and cradling the mug between her hands. Malik's coffee was far too strong and bitter for her liking, but mixed with enough milk it was a perfect drink. "I could have used your calming influence," she said lightly. "Both for me and the man."

Malik smiled in response, but it didn't reach his eyes. Max had never known him to leave the property, which was saturated with his magic. People seemed to find him when they needed him. Not for the first time, she wondered if he *could* actually leave the property. She didn't know enough about his kind to be sure. She did know that Ruutti and Malik were the same type of non-human, and when Ruutti and Malik had first met, Ruutti had seemed to imply that the males of their species couldn't move around freely. Ruutti certainly could. But then, Ruutti used her magic and influence to question people in her role as detective, not to keep a bar full of people from breaking out in fights.

"So, if you're not working today, what are you planning to do?" Malik asked.

"I was hoping you could help me out with some-" Max began, then scrubbed a hand through her hair. "I've been invited to Audhilde's house for afternoon tea. And I don't know what that means." Her nose wrinkled in distaste.

Malik's eyes crinkled at the corners, but he didn't openly laugh, just nodded, leaning one hip against the bar and taking a sip from his own mug of coffee. No milk for him.

"Afternoon tea ..." He took another sip of coffee. "It's a great honour to be invited, particularly to so old a house as Hilda's. Traditionally, it's a time for the household to gather and exchange news over refreshments. Some houses are more formal than others, but that's the core of it. There may actually be tea involved in Hilda's house."

Max breathed out, relieved. That sounded fairly simple, and something she should be able to cope with. Far different from the potential for some dark ritual that she had been imagining. "Thank you. I knew you'd be the right person to ask," she said.

"Any time," Malik said, smiling. And she knew he meant it. She had asked him for information or help many times over the years, and he had never turned her away. Not once. Not even after she had broken up with him, realising that he wasn't what she needed or wanted.

"It seems busy in here today," she commented, not looking at the group of students. "For a mid-week day, I mean."

"One of the university courses has just finished. Apparently they would normally have tried the Sorcerer's Mistress, but they were worried about being savaged by wild beasts," Malik said, his voice soft enough to carry only to her, his lips twitching and eyes bright with laughter.

"Well, the Marshals' service cleared out all the non-human beasts," Max said lightly, "but I'm glad you're benefiting from the extra trade."

"All are welcome," Malik said. It was his motto for the bar, and one he lived by. Even having known him for years, and seen his philosophy in action, Max could still not imagine being so accommodating. But Malik would not turn anyone away, no matter who they were or what they had done. They just had to keep the peace on his property, that was all. On very, very rare occasions a visitor had been encouraged to leave. But somehow even the angriest, most combative person in the world would find themselves soothed and calm within this building, under the influence of Malik's magic.

Chapter Five

Max came out of the Hunter's Tooth into daylight, feeling relaxed and almost happy for the first time in what felt like weeks. She should have come to see Malik long before now. But she hadn't wanted to visit while she was sore and feeling sorry for herself, and between hospital visits and trying to be useful at the Marshals' offices, she hadn't had much free time. Or so she told herself.

Cas and Pol crowded against her, looking up at her with hopeful expressions. She gave them each a pat and reached into the back of the pick-up, delving into the lock box there. Along with weapons and ammunition, there was also a large tub of dog biscuits.

As Cas and Pol were chasing biscuit crumbs around the cracked concrete ground, Max's phone rang. She answered without looking, assuming it was Faddei. It turned out to be another reporter and Max hung up without speaking.

Cas and Pol had stopped chasing the crumbs and were focused on something behind her. She turned and saw a familiar figure walking towards her along the front of the Hunter's Tooth. Bryce. One of the senior warriors of the Order. She had last seen him in the aftermath of her kidnapping. She had managed to kill her would-be killer, and Bryce had turned up. He had looked after her with an impersonal professionalism that she had not been in a fit state to appreciate at the time. She had thought she would never see him again, and wondered what business he had here.

As he kept walking straight towards her, she tensed. It seemed he was looking for her and she could not imagine why. They had had an odd conversation when she had been huddled on the ground, waiting for medical assistance to arrive. The bad memories she had of him from her time in the Order - when he had thrown her across the room in an unarmed combat training class, and then denied her access to the room when she had turned up the next day - had been eased, the sharp edges taken off them. As far as Bryce was concerned, at least. She had learned that she should not have been sent to his combat training in the first place. He hadn't wanted her back in the room because it was dangerous. It hadn't been his fault. Or hers. It had been the senior apprentice who had told her to go to his class who had been at fault. Someone who had taken delight in tormenting her. She shut her memories down before she could think too much further, lifting her chin as Bryce approached. Even if she and Bryce were on neutral terms, she had hoped she was done with the Order.

The Order of the Lady of the Light was entrusted with ensuring compliance with the Lady's edicts against the use of dark magic within the city, and with the protection of the daylight world from the underworld. Although the city's various agencies - the Marshals, police and the Order - did work together from time to time, it was rare for the Order to work with the other agencies. After all, the Order contained not only skilled magicians in the form of the Guardians, but also highly skilled warriors. They could manage their assigned role without outside assistance, and were reluctant to get involved in other city matters. So Max had managed to avoid them since her dismissal until very recently.

"Good afternoon," Bryce said. Taller than she was, he moved with the quiet grace and coordination of a trained warrior. He was dressed, as usual, in hard-wearing, casual clothes accessorised with body armour and weapons and a badge with the symbol of the Order - a double-headed axe. His close-cropped dark hair had grown a little since she had last seen him, topping a face that had been in more than its share of fights. There was a distinct bump in his nose from a previous break.

"Er. Hello," Max said, aware she sounded graceless and ill-mannered, but the almost-friendly greeting was not what she had expected. She took a quick look around the street, trying to work out why he was here, and then remembered the blanket he'd given her when she had been injured. "Oh. Do you want the blanket back? I've washed it," she said, reaching for the passenger door of the pick-up, stopping as he raised a hand.

"No. You can keep that. I'm glad to see you're healing," he said.

"Yes," Max said. "Em. This isn't your normal neighbourhood. Was there something you needed?" she asked. She could not imagine why a warrior of the Order might seek her out, but he was here.

"I was heading for the bar," Bryce said, tilting his head towards the building.

"Oh. Of course," Max said, face heating up. He wasn't here to see her. Why had she imagined he was? And why was she disappointed that wasn't the case?

"I was going to ask Malik if he knew how to find you," Bryce said, mouth tilting in a smile. Max's stomach filled with butterflies and she held herself still, wondering what he wanted. He shifted his weight, hands in his pockets. "I've been hearing rumours of people going missing."

"I've heard rumours, too. From the docks," Max said. The butterflies were fading and she tried to push her disappointment aside. He was here for business, that was all. And what else would it be, she asked herself. Their paths had barely crossed when she had been in the Order, and she was out of it now, and held in disgrace by its leader.

"One of our trainees was down there last week, and he swears there was dark magic painted on one of the walls," Bryce said. He wasn't quite looking at her.

"Oh?" Max asked, not sure what else to say.

"I don't have proof, though. I wondered if you would be able to take a look?"

"Me?" Max could not have been more surprised if he'd asked her to go back to the Order with him.

"None of the Guardians are interested. They don't believe a trainee warrior could recognise dark magic," Bryce said, face tight. "And I'm not sure the apprentices would know what the spell was."

There was a lot underneath the plain words he spoke, and Max could only imagine how frustrating he had found it that the Guardians hadn't listened to him. The Order was supposed to combat dark magic, but it had a rigid division between its warriors on the one side and the Guardians and their apprentices on the other. None of the Guardians would follow a request from a warrior - that was not the way the Order worked. The only apprentices who might be prepared to go on a field trip with Bryce at his request were the very junior ones, who almost certainly wouldn't recognise dark magic, or be able to tell what the spells were for. Max remembered the two apprentices she had met recently - Alexey and Sandrine.

The twins had been assigned to assist the Marshals in what Max guessed had been a punishment by their teachers, rather than a genuine effort at co-operation between the Order and Marshals. The twins were powerful and almost certainly knowledgeable enough to recognise dark magic, but she could understand why Bryce wouldn't want to ask them for help. The pair were as arrogant as their apprentice-master, and had acted as though the warriors were beneath them.

With all that in mind, it made sense why he had sought her out. She was the only living former apprentice that she knew of outside the Order, and a logical person to approach to ask about dark magic.

For a moment, she was tempted. It was not good news that people were going missing, and the potential for dark magic being involved was even worse news. Dark magic practitioners were usually intent on inflicting pain and suffering and gathering power for themselves, not caring who they might hurt or what damage they might do. In the most extreme cases, the practitioner might use ritual sacrifice to try to gather more power. But like all borrowed power, it wouldn't last, and the dark magician would need more sacrifices before long. If there was any possibility that a dark magician was using the missing people in his rituals, that needed to be stopped, and stopped at once. She wanted to help. But her face was already all over the city's online media, and the last time she had tried to help, someone had ended up dead. A knot tightened in her stomach.

"I'm sorry," she said. "I don't think I can help. If it's dark magic, Kitris will want to know." It was the Order's job to monitor and police dark magic in the city. And Kitris' job, as the head of the Order, to care about such reports, even if they were rumours.

Bryce stared back at her. She couldn't read the expression, but thought it might be disappointment.

Before he could say anything, the world slid sideways and she slumped against her pick-up, her vision going red and yellow and white and black, all the hard lines and edges of the world swirling together. She closed her eyes against the sickening, twisting shapes and breathed lightly, trying to persuade her stomach to settle. After a few breaths, she opened her eyes cautiously, finding that the world was back in its proper shape, and Bryce was still standing there, frowning.

"Are you alright?" he asked.

"I'm not sure," Max said. Her hands were shaking, knees weak.

"Have you eaten today?" he asked her.

She choked on a laugh. It was the sort of question he would ask one of his trainees, making sure they remembered to take care of themselves even while they were expected to work and train hard.

"I can't remember," she said, frowning. "Perhaps not. I did have some coffee with Malik."

"Malik's coffee? No wonder you're off balance," Bryce said, corners of his mouth twitching in what might have been a smile. That sounded like the voice of experience and she choked on another unexpected laugh.

She was feeling almost back to normal, so she straightened away from the vehicle. "I'm sorry I can't help," she said.

"Don't worry about it. I'll speak to Kitris," he said. He tilted his head to her and turned and walked away.

Leaving Max to slump against the pick-up again, wondering what had just happened, or not happened, and trying to wrestle with the guilt she felt about not being willing to help the Order or the police tracking missing people that were not any part of her job description. Missing people and the potential for dark magic were both serious concerns. And she couldn't help, she told herself. She couldn't. She'd made too many mistakes in the past few days. There were other people who were perfectly capable of dealing with the issues. It didn't need to be her.

Chapter Six

Audhilde's house was among the few remaining grand old houses that still stood in its own, walled garden. It was accessed from the road by a pair of tall iron gates that swung silently and smoothly open to admit Max's pick-up as she drove up. The wide gravel driveway led to a large, open area in front of the house. There were no other vehicles there, but she knew that her battered pick-up did not match the house. She spared a moment to be glad of Malik's advice and her long-ago shopping spree. She had swapped her normal battered clothing and heavy boots for a deep red wrap jumper, black tailored trousers and plain black, flat shoes. She was as confident as she could be that she wouldn't look out of place inside such a grand house.

Out of habit, she parked the pick-up with its nose pointing out, ready to drive away, and got out, putting her gun in the locked box in the back of the pick-up. The vehicle looked empty without her shadow-hounds, but she had left Cas and Pol at home, judging that Audhilde's invitation had not extended to them as well. It was an effort turning away from her weapons to head for the house. She felt almost naked. But she didn't want to insult Audhilde by turning up armed. This was supposed to be an afternoon tea. Besides, she had a feeling that if Audhilde wanted to harm her, there wouldn't be much Max could do about it.

As she walked towards the front door, she got an idea of the sheer scale of the place. The garden grounds were vast. She could see an orchard to one side and a large pond to another side. The house was built of faded red brick, rising three storeys high and stretching out to either side.

Max made her way up the shallow front steps to an enormous door painted a vivid cobalt blue. Before she had a chance to look for a doorbell, the door opened and the vampire who had been working as the forecourt attendant at the petrol station appeared. He smiled at her.

"Marshal Ortis. The lady will be so pleased that you were able to join us," he said. "And may I take this opportunity to thank you personally for your actions the other day?"

"You are welcome. Although I didn't really do much," Max said, entering the house as he stepped aside. "I think you had the matter well in hand."

"That is kind of you to say so, but I am grateful nonetheless," the vampire said, closing the door behind her. "It's this way," he said, and began walking across the entrance hall.

Max tried not to gape and stare too much as she followed him along a long, patterned rug that ran across the polished wooden floor of the entrance hall. It was without a doubt the most opulent house she had ever been inside in her life. The walls were hung with fabulous paintings that looked to be originals, ranging from what looked like an old portrait of the house to a far more modern canvas that seemed to be nothing but swirls of different coloured paint, but which nonetheless drew Max's attention as she walked past. There was a great double staircase rising over their heads, and doors leading off to either side of the entrance hall.

In the archway formed by the staircase was a low, dark wood table with a long, shallow silver dish filled with clear water and a brilliant gold sphere settled in the middle of the dish. It was a deceptively simple design, but anyone in the city would recognise it as an altar to the Lady. The sight of it, so prominently displayed at the centre of the house, settled some of Max's nerves. She had a far plainer altar in her own garden, a simple metal dish filled with water which the local birds liked to use as a bath from time to time. Audhilde's beautiful altar and Max's far plainer one served the same purpose. A focal point for the house and its inhabitants. A reminder of the presence of the Lady in all things - if the priests and priestesses were to be believed. For Max, it was a reminder of the serenity she found within the Lady's temples, as if nothing bad could ever happen within the Lady's House.

She tilted her head to the altar in a reflexive gesture of respect as she followed the vampire around one side of the staircase and through a doorway into a very large room with wooden panelling to about Max's shoulder height, and more paintings hung on the walls above the panelling. The room had what looked like an entire wall of windows which overlooked the gardens, sunlight spilling in.

The end of the room where Max had entered was set up as a dining area with a rectangular table that could comfortably seat more than a dozen people. At the other end of the room, chairs and people were gathered in front of a fireplace that would fit Max and both her dogs and have room left over. The people were a mix of humans and vampires, Max realised as she made her way across the floor. Mostly human. The inner workings of vampire households were a closely guarded secret, but from what little Max had been able to pick up over her life about vampire tradition and culture, it seemed that powerful, old vampires like Audhilde operated a system of patronage whereby they provided accommodation for humans in return for regular offerings of blood. It had never tempted Max, but she could understand why some humans might be drawn to the arrangement.

She had a moment of displacement, crossing the floor towards the group, the sound of her footsteps swallowed in the plush rugs underfoot. This wasn't her, or her life. This quiet, genteel and evidently wealthy building and group of people were so far removed from her day-to-day living it was as if she had stepped into another world.

Then Audhilde was on her feet, smiling. The vampire was dressed in one of her deep blue outfits. It seemed to be a favourite colour.

"My dear, I'm so glad you're here. Welcome to my home," Audhilde said, holding out her hands. Max took them, returning the gentle squeeze and then letting go as Audhilde stepped back. The vampire was far more graceful than Max, but then she had had several human lifetimes to practice.

"Thank you. Thank you for inviting me," Max said. There was doubtless some proper protocol that she didn't know about. And as she was faced with the reality of Audhilde and the gathered people, an awful thought occurred to her and she blurted out the first thing that came to her mind. "I'm so sorry. I didn't bring anything. Was I supposed to?"

"No," Audhilde said firmly, managing to still smile while being absolutely definite. "You were only to bring yourself, that is more than enough."

"Oh, good," Max said, feeling her face warm at her unchecked words. She had been told often enough growing up that she didn't have any good manners. It was unpleasant to realise that was still true.

"Come, sit," Audhilde said, indicating an empty chair next to her own.

"Thank you," Max said, and took the chair. It was an old-fashioned wing chair, a twin of the one Audhilde was using, but had been re-upholstered in vivid colours.

As Audhilde took her seat again, one of the humans brought a large tea cup and saucer across and set it on a tall table next to Max's elbow. She realised then that there were small tables scattered between the chairs, and a dizzying variety of cups and saucers and a few tall mugs as well as plates of what looked like sandwiches and small cakes.

The same human came back a moment later with a small milk jug and a plate of sandwiches and cakes.

"Let me introduce you to my household," Audhilde said.

For a moment, Max wanted to run, faced with a sea of unfamiliar faces. She drew a breath and concentrated as Audhilde named the people around the room. Despite Max's first impressions, there were only six people apart from her and Audhilde. Four humans and two vampires, including the one who had met her at the door. They were dressed in a variety of colours and styles that Max didn't recognise, but she knew enough to realise that they had all made an effort with their appearance for this afternoon tea, and was glad again she had found some more appropriate clothes.

The forecourt attendant's name turned out to be Lukas. The other names and faces swam in Max's head, indistinct no matter how much she tried to remember them.

After the introductions were made, Audhilde turned to Lukas.

"What have you been doing since we last gathered?" she asked the younger vampire. It was said in a gentle, questioning tone.

Lukas smiled, apparently pleased to be selected for attention, and gave an account of his past couple of days, including the incident at the petrol station. Max was quite sure she had not been nearly as heroic as Lukas made her out to be, but stayed quiet.

Audhilde went around the rest of the gathered group in turn, listening intently to the answers that were given, putting in a word here and there. Max found the whole thing fascinating. The other vampire and two of the humans lived and worked in the house and grounds. Given the size of the place, Max was not surprised that it needed full-time staff. The rest had jobs outside the house.

It was a family, not just a household, Max realised. The humans ranged in ages from a young man barely into his twenties to an old woman dressed in a deep pink dress, sitting with a straight back, who was most likely into her seventies at least. But they all treated each other with evident affection and respect, including Audhilde.

As they all shared their news, Max couldn't help wonder what afternoon tea might look like in another vampire's household. The only other vampire who Max had met who might match Audhilde in age, and certainly in power, was Lord Kolbyr. Like Audhilde, he only had one name, but one was all that was needed. Even just remembering him sent a chill across her skin. The ancient vampire was a master of dark magic, and Max could not imagine him sitting on equal terms among his household as Audhilde was here, or taking an interest in what each person had been up to. Lord Kolbyr was also fond of games, on his own terms, and Max was quite sure he would find subtle and not-so-subtle ways of reminding his household who was in charge. Sitting in a room with him would not be this relaxed affair, with laughter from time to time.

When every member of the household had been given a chance to speak, Audhilde settled back in her chair.

"Thank you, my dears. Now, if you don't mind, I'd like to talk to Max alone. No, leave the tea and food, please. We might need some more," she said.

The other members of the household got up almost at once, all of them making a point to pass Audhilde's chair on the way out and touch the older vampire whether it was a pat on her hand, a touch on her shoulder or a gentle squeeze of her arm.

When they had all gone, and the door had been shut behind them, Audhilde turned to Max, smiling.

"Not what you were expecting?" she asked, mischief in her face.

Max was startled into a laugh. "No. But I didn't know what to expect."

"And came into the house unarmed, anyway. I am honoured by your trust in me," Audhilde said.

"Well, I didn't think my back-up gun would do much good," Max confessed.

Audhilde laughed. "Here, do have some more tea. And that lemon cake is a particular favourite of mine."

"Thank you," Max said, getting up and serving herself at Audhilde's urging. "Can I get you anything?"

"Not just now," Audhilde said, and waited until Max had taken her seat again. "It's kind of you to indulge me with your visit," the vampire said.

Max's brows lifted. That was not the sort of statement she expected from Audhilde. The other woman was normally very direct. It hadn't been a question, and Max didn't know what to say, so she sat back in her chair and let the silence settle around her. It was a comfortable silence, warm and welcoming like the rest of the house, and she found she was in no rush to break it. Despite the evident wealth on display, this felt like a home.

"You must be wondering why I invited you," Audhilde said.

"Well, yes," Max said candidly. "I don't think that Lukas actually needed my help."

"But you did help him, and I did want to thank you. But, no, that's not the only reason I wanted to speak to you," Audhilde said.

For the first time that Max had known the vampire, she seemed hesitant. Unease prickled across Max's skin and she set down her cup, facing Audhilde. "Tell me," she said.

"The other night, you had an episode," Audhilde said. "A moment of ... let's call it displacement. Where things weren't quite as they should be."

Max stilled, ice creeping across her body. She had avoided talking to anyone about the episodes, as Audhilde called them. Even though they had been worrying her. But Audhilde had noticed.

"What is it?" Max asked, face stiff. It was only after she had asked her question she realised it had not occurred to her to lie, and try to pretend everything was fine. If anything, it was a relief to have the conversation forced on her. "What do you think the, er, episodes signify?" Audhilde was a medical doctor as well as the medical examiner. Max's mind turned on the worst possible outcomes that

Audhilde might reveal. Some kind of tumour. Seizures. Some terrible illness Max had no name for, but which could cut her life short. She wasn't ready for that. She felt she had barely begun to live.

"I think you are coming in to your magic," Audhilde said, before Max's mind could conjure up any more terrible scenarios.

"I already have magic," Max said, startled, her mind turned away from medical possibilities.

"The little tricks you do? No, those are nothing. There's great potential in you, but you've never been able to use it," Audhilde said, leaning forward slightly in her chair.

"How did you know?" Max asked, astonished. She had never told anyone about the sensation she had whenever she used magic, that there should be more.

"I'm old," Audhilde said, mischief in her face. "I've learned a thing or two along the way." The mischief faded and Audhilde propped her hand on her chin, looking at Max. "It's very common for magicians to develop their powers slowly. Far more common than you might think, in fact. And not everyone uses magic the same way. You keep trying to use magic like the Guardians, for example."

"That's the way I was taught," Max said, trying not to flinch. She hadn't thought that anyone outside the Order and Faddei knew that she had been an apprentice. But Audhilde seemed to have been paying far closer attention than Max had realised.

Audhilde sighed and shook her head. "Kitris and his formulas. He has been teaching his methods and insisting that it is superior magic for far too long. He is incredibly narrow-minded for someone who has lived more than a century."

That was surprising enough that Max laughed. She had often thought that Kitris was extremely stuck in his ways and it was refreshing to hear someone else say so. Within the Order, it was simply accepted that his word was law. And outside the Order, he was almost as revered. Kitris' position as head of the Order made him one of the most powerful people in the city, equally as powerful if not more so than the heads of the Five Families, or the High Priestess of the Lady's temples, and certainly more powerful than the individual members of the council who seemed to spend most of their time arguing with each other. Max remembered him as a fairly ordinary-looking, seemingly human male who had enjoyed the power and prestige of his position while also working hard to ensure the smooth running of the Order. It had been one of the things she had respected about him, that he worked as hard as everyone else.

Audhilde smiled, as if lost in memories of her own. "I remember when he became head of the Order. It had been far less disciplined, with the Guardians being far more, er, creative. He decided that it was chaotic and a new regime was needed. Well, he has got his wish."

Max was fascinated despite herself and almost asked a question, stopping the words just in time. Even though she had just been thinking about Kitris, she didn't want to talk about the Order. She would prefer to forget about them entirely. Instead, she played Audhilde's words over in her mind. "You are suggesting that there's another way to use magic," Max said slowly.

"I am," Audhilde agreed. "Many more, in fact. And I am sure that there's at least one other method that will suit you better than the mathematics that Kitris teaches."

"I've no skill for maths and formulas," Max confessed, wrinkling her nose in distaste. It had been a constant source of friction with her teachers over the years, and she had been told she was both stupid and incapable of learning more than once. But equations made no sense to her, the lines and symbols blurring in front of her eyes.

"Very few people do, at least to the extent that's needed to follow Kitris' version of magic. I swear he makes things complicated on purpose," Audhilde said. "Come, I have some books I can lend you which I think may help." She stood up and headed towards a door Max hadn't noticed before, next to the great fireplace. Curious, Max followed.

The door opened to a room half the size of the one they had left, but with its walls covered from floor to ceiling in shelves of books from hefty, leather-bound tomes to slimmer, brightly coloured paperbacks. There were several comfortable-looking chairs arranged around the space, some of them gathered in front of a fireplace that mirrored the one in the other room.

Max turned around slowly, looking at the vast collection. There was a heavy-duty rail running around one of the upper shelves, and a set of ladders that Audhilde took hold of, pulling them around the room to a particular set of shelves.

"You have a very beautiful home," Max said, still staring. She had never seen so many books in one place before. Not even in one of the city's libraries.

"Thank you. This house, and this room in particular, has been a refuge for many years," Audhilde said, taking a few steps up the ladder. "Ah. Yes. Here," she said, drawing a book out of the shelves and holding it out to Max. "That should be a good one to get started," she said.

Max moved across and took the book, reading the title: *A History of Magic*. She couldn't help smiling. That did, indeed, seem like a good place to start. The book was reasonably thick, the hard cover heavy in her hands. She looked up in time to see Audhilde drawing out another two books.

"These are a little more specific, but will give you some other things to work on. Possibly," Audhilde said.

Max took the other books she was handed and glanced at the titles. They were a little more obscure, but still made her smile. *A Treatise Against Mathematical Theory*, and *Witch or Wizard?*

"Keep them as long as you need to," Audhilde said, coming back down the ladder. "And I can find some more reference materials if you need them."

Max stood with the three books in her hands and looked at the ancient vampire. "Thank you," she said, meaning it. "I don't understand, though, why you would trust me with your books?" That wasn't quite the question she wanted to ask, but it seemed rude to outright demand to know why Audhilde was helping her.

Audhilde looked up at her, the vampire barely reaching Max's shoulder, and smiled slightly. "I'm not entirely sure why, either. But I have lived long enough to trust my instincts. And my instincts tell me that we may have need of you and your magic soon enough. I haven't felt magic quite like yours before."

Max ducked her head to look at the books again, both to hide her surprise at Audhilde's frank confession and her resistance to the idea that she might be needed. She had done her duty. She had fulfilled what had been required of her by the Order. She did not owe the world anything more. But the words wouldn't come, stuck in her throat, and she simply nodded.

"You should not have any more difficulties with reporters trying to contact you," Audhilde said, moving back towards the door they had entered.

"Oh, really?" Max asked, going after the vampire.

Audhilde glanced over her shoulder with more than a bit of mischief in her smile, but didn't say anything. She kept walking through the house to the front door. It was still daylight outside, but only just.

"I hope that you will visit again," Audhilde said. "We have afternoon tea at the same time every day, and you will always be welcome in this house, no matter if I am here or not."

Max managed to say thank you, caught off guard and aware that she was being offered yet another honour by the old vampire. She said goodbye and took the borrowed books to her battered pick-up, glancing in her rear-view mirror as she drove away and seeing Audhilde standing in the open doorway, other members of her household gathered around her. Max had the sense that she had just been granted something special with the open offer to visit, and that Audhilde had meant it. Max could turn up to her house the next day, and the day after that, and receive the same welcome. And Max knew she would be tempted. The house had felt like a true home, with a true family inside it. She had only had that feeling once before, when she had been staying with Alonso and Elicia, and had been too hurt to fully appreciate it then.

As she drove out of the gates, she shook her head, mouth twisting into a smile. Her life was strange indeed that she was considering a vampire's home as a place of peace and safety.

Chapter Seven

Max found her direct route home blocked by a protest. There were cars parked in the streets, their drivers standing beside their vehicles, shouting their anger at fuel rationing. It seemed a silly way to protest as far as Max was concerned, using their limited fuel to drive to that street. A few of the protesters had brought crude, home-made signs, although they didn't seem to be able to agree on their message. Some of the signs wanted more fuel. Others demanded the resignation of this or that member of the city council. Someone was even holding a sign saying *Take Back the Wild*, which was a theme Max had only rarely come across. Oddly enough, the few people she had seen or heard on the city's news media who seemed determined to *Take Back the Wild* didn't have any firm plans as to how that could be achieved, but just insisted that *something* should be done. Presumably by someone else, Max thought sourly.

The mood in the street was sharp-edged and ugly, the various protesters with their various slogans and chants making each other even more angry. Most people liked to live their lives without thinking too much about the city's isolation and limited resources, but the smarter ones knew that the Wild could move forward again at any time, and the city's population had nowhere to go if that happened. A lot of land had already been lost to the Wild.

Max turned away before anyone could see the Marshals' symbol on her windscreen, reassured by the sight of a few police officers tucked away down side streets. The police were aware, and keeping an eye on things. That was probably as much as they could do just now.

The new route that she took brought her closer to both the docks and Huntsman territory but, crucially, not into Huntsman territory. She did not want to meet any more clan members, and certainly not on their own ground.

As she slowed to a stop at a set of traffic lights, she saw a man putting up a poster on the pillar that supported the lights. It was the sort of littering that the police mostly turned a blind eye to. But the man looked familiar and, as he turned to look down the street, Max's breath caught in her throat. She hadn't seen that face for a long time, and he had more grey hair, but she did know him. She pulled over and parked haphazardly on the corner, getting out as the man was walking away.

"Alonso," she called, leaving her pick-up. She still had the Marshal's sticker on the windscreen, so no one should try to give her a ticket or tow the vehicle.

He stopped at once and turned, the familiar face breaking into a smile she remembered so well.

"Max!" he cried, and came towards her, arms open.

She let herself be enveloped in a powerful hug that lifted her off her feet, swallowed by familiar scents of soap and herbs, finding her face wet with tears when he set her down.

"It's been such a long time," she said, not wanting to let him go.

"Yes, it has," he said, still smiling at her.

He had aged. He had already been elderly when she had first met him eight years ago. She had been shivering with pain and reaction, not quite sure she could believe that she had escaped the underworld and was back in the daylight world. She had been flung back into the world in the middle of a lake, the water around her boiling with the heat she brought with her, and had swum to shore through shoals of dead fish, finding an old, crusted tarpaulin to wrap herself in.

Alonso Ortis had found her there, her teeth chattering, her head bald as her hair had burned off. He had been there to fish, but he had taken one look at Max and the lake full of dead fish, and instead had given her a large blanket from his truck that was far softer on her damaged skin than the tarpaulin had been. With her wrapped in kindness and warmth, he had taken her back to his home. He and his wife, Elicia, had taken Max in with no questions asked. She had been given her own room, with a narrow bed and an altar to the Lady, a set of clothes to wear and food and drink. It had been two days before she had been able to speak to say thank you, or to tell them her name.

She might have survived the underworld, but Max knew that she would not have survived her return to the daylight world if it hadn't been for Alonso and Elicia. They had housed, clothed and fed her and refused to take any money in exchange. And despite his dislike of driving in the city, Alonso had driven her into the heart of the city to meet with Kitris. And then, when Kitris had dismissed her, he had driven her back to his and Elicia's house and let her have a day or so to grieve before they had given her a gentle but firm push towards the Marshals' service. One of Alonso's relatives worked in the Marshals' compound, and knew that the service took on all sorts of people. It had been a long time before Max had fully appreciated just how unqualified she had been to exist in the world outside the orphanage and the Order.

Alonso and Elicia had saved her. Max wanted to hug him again, and find Elicia and hug her, too. She had never found a way to properly thank them for the help they had given her.

"What brings you to this part of the city?" she asked. The last she had seen him, a few years before, he and Elicia had still been living on the outskirts of the city, in the small house that had been theirs through their whole marriage, with a large garden packed full of edible plants.

His smile faded and she realised that he looked exhausted. And heart-sick.

"It's Nati," he said. "She's missing. And her daughter Ynes too."

Nati was the Ortises' daughter, Max remembered. It had been her room that Max had stayed in at their house. Which meant that Ynes was their granddaughter. A new addition to the family since Max had last seen them.

"Missing? I'm sorry," Max said at once. "Come, sit, tell me about it," she said. There was a set of wide stone steps leading up to an office building nearby and she drew Alonso over to sit on the steps before he fell down.

Alonso settled on the stairs and put his head in his hands, crumpling one of the paper fliers he was holding. Max gently took it from his hands and smoothed it out as she sat next to him, reading it through. There was a photo of Nati and a young girl that must be Ynes, with a plea for information and a phone number.

"Do you know what happened?" Max asked Alonso.

He put the rest of the fliers down on the step between them, smoothing them with his hand. He had tears on his face, his eyes bloodshot. Not the first time he had cried that day, or probably in the past few days. Alonso Ortis was probably somewhere around sixty years old, as tall as Max, broad and strong. He and his wife were the kindest people Max had ever met, and her heart ached to see him so distressed.

"There was a boyfriend. We didn't like him. He kept Nati away from us. Took her to his people. We didn't find out about Ynes until she was nearly six months old," Alonso said.

Max reached across and put her hand on his arm. He covered it with his own, holding tight as he continued.

"We didn't like him. Not at all. But Nati insisted she was fine. She was happy. Everything was alright. And then Elicia stopped by to see her and saw bruises," Alonso said, his voice cracking. "And Nati chased her away. Told her not to come back. That was a week ago. We went to the police, and they went to check on her. Gone. The boyfriend said he didn't know where she was. The police said there was nothing they could do." Alonso squeezed Max's hand. "So I am looking for her. And so is Elicia. We're doing what we can."

"Does she have any friends she would go to?" Max asked, a chill settling in her middle. An abusive boyfriend, with his girlfriend and child missing. She could imagine a lot of bad endings to that story.

"We checked. Her school friends said they got the same thing as Elicia. She didn't want to see them. Shut them out. They were all worried, too."

"What about the temples?" Max asked. They were not just places of worship, but some also provided temporary refuges for desperate people.

"No," Alonso said, his face twisting. "The boyfriend has some kind of connection with the temples. Or so he said to Nati. She wouldn't go there."

Max let him squeeze her hand tight enough to bruise as he drew a shaky breath, more tears flowing. "How long have you been looking?" she asked.

"Four days. Five. I don't know. My poor girl," Alonso said, covering his face with his free hand.

"I'm sorry," she said, her own voice choked. She squeezed his arm, wishing she had better words to give him. She had met Nati, once, when she had been staying with Elicia and Alonso. The girl had been beautiful, a younger version combining the best parts of Elicia and Alonso. Long, silky black hair, an infectious smile and a warm heart to rival her father's. Nati had been newly independent then, only recently having moved out of her parents' house for a job in the city, excited to have her own apartment and to be meeting new people. Max could not imagine the vibrant young woman she had met with bruises and a child, turning her parents and her friends away.

"We can't find her. Not any trace of her," Alonso said.

Max looked down at the faces again. "Do you have the original photographs?" she asked, reaching into a pocket for her phone. "Can you send them to me?"

"What? Why?" Alonso asked, straightening, and reaching for his own phone.

"I am a Marshal," she reminded him. "And I work with the city's police from time to time. I may be able to get some more information," she said. Even as she said that, she remembered the missing people that Ruutti was looking for. It was a long shot, but it was possible that a desperate woman might take her young daughter into the warehouse at the docks. Nati might be hiding, rather than any of the worse alternatives that Max could think of.

"I could not ask it of you," Alonso said.

"You didn't ask," Max said, a smile pulling her mouth despite the awful circumstances. "I am volunteering. You and Elicia helped me so much before. Let me see what I can do for you both, and for Nati and Ynes now."

"Oh, Max," he said, and hugged her again. She could feel the damp from his tears against her shoulder. "Thank you," he said, voice muffled.

He sat up and opened a photograph on his phone. The original of the picture on the poster. Max gave him her number and he sent the picture across, along with a half dozen others for good measure. She took down the boyfriend's name and address as well. Ivor Costen. She didn't recognise the name, but the address was on the outer edge of Huntsman territory. She didn't hesitate or flinch from the idea of going there, even in her mind. This was Alonso and Elicia's daughter and granddaughter.

By that time, a uniformed officer had spotted her badly parked pick-up and was approaching it, his notebook in hand. Max watched as he read the licence then the Marshal's sign in the window. He shook his head, looking like he was muttering something under his breath before he turned away.

"Let me take you home," Max said to Alonso. "You look exhausted."

"I must get Elicia first. She was going down the next street. Oh, there she is," Alonso said.

Even with his daughter missing, his face lit up when he saw his wife. They had been married nearly forty years by now, Max remembered, and they still loved each other. She turned to follow his gaze and saw the familiar figure of Elicia making her way through the crowds. Nati's mother looked as exhausted as her husband, but she managed a smile and a wave for him, pausing in her stride when she saw that Alonso was not alone. Then Elicia recognised Max and her face broke into a smile to rival Alonso's. She came forward and met Max with open arms and a hug almost as fierce as her husband's.

"Oh, my darling girl. It is so good to see you. It's been too long," Elicia said.

"Yes, it has," Max said softly, returning the hug. It had been perhaps three years since she had seen the Ortis family, and that had been more accident than anything else, in a crowded, busy place with no time to talk. She had told herself it was easier to cut off ties with them, that they couldn't possibly want to see her. They had a vast circle of friends, and their own family to care for. But now, with their warmth around her, a hollow place began to fill in her chest and she realised how much she had missed them. "I'm sorry. I should have visited."

"She's still a Marshal," Alonso said, as if he was proud of Max's achievement.

"Oh. That's wonderful. I'm so glad you've settled to that, found something that suits you," Elicia said, and hugged Max again for good measure.

"Alonso was telling me about your trouble," Max said.

"And Max is going to see what she can find out for us," Alonso said.

"Yes. I will. But for now, can I take you home? It's getting dark, and I know you don't like to be away from the house after dark," Max said. She also remembered that the pair of them didn't like to drive in the city where possible - they had most likely come into the city on the bus, and it could be a long wait for the next one.

"You remember so well," Elicia said. She looked at the corner and Max's battered pick-up. "Is that the same vehicle?"

"Yes," Max said, laughing. Elicia had been utterly disgusted with it three years before, and it seemed her opinion had not changed one bit.

Despite the circumstances, with all of them crowded into the cab of Max's pick-up, it was a merry journey across the city to the Ortises' home. Max refused their invitation to join them for dinner. With copies of the fliers with Nati and Ynes' picture, the photos and the information both Alonso and Elicia had provided, Max wanted to get started looking for the missing mother and child. She wanted to question the boyfriend, but first she needed to get her dogs. She suspected that a boyfriend who beat up his girlfriend might not be quite so ready with his fists around her shadow-hounds.

Chapter Eight

It was evening when she made it back home, and even with Cas and Pol for back-up, she didn't want to venture into Huntsman territory after dark. Early morning would be better, and she stood a better chance of catching Nati's boyfriend off guard with a morning visit.

Which meant she had another evening at home ahead of her. Cas and Pol greeted her with the sort of enthusiasm that suggested they hadn't seen her for weeks, and that they were starving. For her part, Max found she had missed them, too, in the few hours she had been away. And she was pleased to find that her dogs had managed not to destroy any furniture in the time they had been left alone.

Despite the fuel rationing, the city's infrastructure was still working, so Max spent the early part of her evening with a notebook and the city's internet, sifting through the publicly available information about the boyfriend and the other missing people. It wasn't much. The boyfriend, Ivor Costen, didn't have any criminal record and had been smart enough to stay out of the news.

Even though the police were concerned about the missing, the city's media didn't seem to be as bothered. The missing had all been homeless. Until Nati and Ynes. Assuming they were missing, and not hiding in the docks. Max could understand why Alonso and Elicia were worried. They were living in the same house and yet their daughter had not tried to reach them. There were a few possibilities as to why that could be, and none of them were particularly good. The worst possibility was that Nati and Ynes were already dead, their bodies still undiscovered. But they could also be injured, or trapped somewhere, unable to call for help. Compared to those options, hiding at the docks and being too afraid to contact Nati's parents was a better option.

When she had researched as much as she could from the limited access she had at home, and thought of a lot of bad outcomes for her search for Nati and her daughter, Max was itching to move, to get started on her search but dawn was still many hours away.

She was too restless to sleep straight away and instead turned her attention to the books Audhilde had lent her, starting with *A History of Magic*.

Despite the dry title, the book was fascinating, and even before the end of the first chapter, Max felt as if she had learned more about magic than she had in her lifetime before. She had never been taught that there were different types of magic, even though it made perfect sense. After all, a lot of supernatural creatures possessed some magic and they couldn't use the same formulas that the Order's Guardians used. And witches were often self-taught, at least when they started out, relying on instinct rather than mathematics.

Thinking of other types of magic also reminded her of her encounter, not that long ago, with a full-fledged demon. One of the beings from the dark lord's court in the underworld, somehow prowling the daylight world. If the Lady was light and joy, Her darker brother spun pain and deceit, and the demon had been no exception. Queran had been wearing a human shape, but she had been able to see through that to his demon nature. He had worked magic, too. Foul, dark magic that had spun into a shadow-hound that had then tried to kill her. Even though she had been fighting for her life at the time, she couldn't remember seeing the same formulas or spells in Queran's magic that she had been used to at the Order. But then, he had been a demon, so perhaps the daylight world rules didn't apply to him.

The teaching of the Order, and the magic used by most magicians across the city, relied on having a framework for spell-casting that was constrained by mathematics. And Max had never been good at mathematics or formulas. She could still remember the cold sweat across her body as she tried and tried and tried to memorise even the simplest spell. She had had to study late into the night, writing and re-writing the sections of the spells until they were committed to her memory and she could use them. Even then, she had never been able to use the spells all that well.

She had spent her years in the Order, and a lot of time since then, feeling frustrated at the apparent disconnect between her feeling that she had magic within her, and her inability to use it in the way that she was being taught.

And here was a book, written quite some time ago, which suggested that all that struggle had been unnecessary. That there were other ways she could have tried to access and use the magic she sensed within her. As she read on, learning that some magicians could use staffs as focal points, and still others could speak their magic into a potion, a hot spark of anger lit in her chest. She had spent years being told she was stupid. She had been sneered at and told she was defective more than once. And it turned out that it was possible that she had simply been following the wrong method. That there might be other ways she could access her magic and use it. Like the moments when she had been half-naked and vulnerable, at the mercy of a killer who wanted to use her blood as part of a dark magic ritual. She had broken free of the drug he had used on her, and had burned him, using magic. But the magic had not been brought about by any of the formal spells that the Order had taught her. Instead, the defence had come from a place of desperation and instinct. And it had worked.

She didn't ever want to be in the hands of a killer again, but she couldn't help wondering if there was something there she could use. And wondering, too, what else she had been taught that was wrong.

Chapter Nine

Somewhat to her surprise, between her worries for Nati and Ynes and her anger at her former teachers, Max slept through the night. She was so used to being dragged from sleep by nightmares that when she woke to the sound of her alarm in the morning she blinked at it, not comprehending what the noise was. A decent night's sleep was a rare and treasured thing.

Even more surprising, she had no more calls from reporters as she got ready for the day, then made her way into the city and couldn't help wondering just what Audhilde had done to make that happen. She stopped for fuel at the same petrol station where she had been filmed, a little apprehensive that she would find reporters waiting, but the only person there was an attendant that she didn't recognise. Relieved, she filled her pick-up with her fuel allowance and paid for it before heading further into the city, Cas and Pol settled in the back of the pick-up. Their ears lifted and she saw their heads appear in the rear windows as she called Faddei to let him know she was following up on a favour for a friend.

To her surprise, Faddei didn't ask any questions, but he did sound cheerful as he said that the reporters had stopped calling.

With one less thing to worry about, Max parked on the street where Nati's boyfriend lived, just inside Huntsman territory. Not everyone who lived in the territory was a member of the clan, and Max was hoping for a half-awake human male who would be co-operative. She wasn't sure she would find him home, but wanted to try anyway.

Cas and Pol were delighted to be out of the vehicle, and in a part of the city where they hadn't been before. The street was made up of small houses, probably three or four rooms at most, with small patches of garden and chain link fences around each property. Most of the gardens showed some signs of neglect, with an old sofa or kitchen appliance sitting outside.

The address that Alonso had provided led to a house that stood out from the others as the garden was well-tended, the grass cut and the fence intact. The house was in need of painting, like many of its neighbours, but the windows looked clean. There was a black car on the street outside, the sort of car Max had seen many young men driving. It would make a fearsome noise when the engine was on. And doubtless used a lot of fuel, which might explain why it was sitting unused.

She opened the gate from the street and Cas and Pol kept to her sides as she made her way up the short path to the front door, then knocked. There was no obvious security in place, and no magic that she could sense.

She was dressed for work in her old leather jacket and hard-wearing, close-fitting trousers, gun ready in her thigh holster and the seven-pointed star of her Marshal's badge on display. Nati was fully human, but Alonso hadn't been able to say if the boyfriend was.

Sounds of grumbling and footsteps inside the house told her that someone was home, at least.

The door opened to reveal a man dressed in a wrinkled, sleeveless t-shirt that might have been white a long time ago, and jeans. He rubbed a hand across his face, seemingly half asleep, not looking at her. The movement drew attention to the tattoo across his right shoulder.

Max registered the tattoo before she recognised him as one of the Huntsman clan who had attacked her. Not one of the original pair who had been chasing the girl, but one of the later arrivals. She drew her gun before he could react, levelling it at his face while Cas and Pol both growled low in their throats.

"Ivor Costen?" she asked. It always paid to be certain.

"Bitch," he answered.

"I'll take that as a yes. Is there anyone else in the house?"

"I don't need to tell you nothing," he said, lip curling. He had gleaming white teeth. He wasn't human, not quite, but she wasn't sure what type of creature he was. It was difficult to tell properly with his surly expression, but she supposed he could be handsome in most circumstances. Handsome enough to draw the attention of Elicia and Alonso's warm-hearted daughter, at any rate.

"Cas, Pol. Search the house," she told her dogs.

The hounds slipped past the man, prompting a cry of protest from him.

"Hands up. Back into the house slowly," Max said. She hadn't seen anyone else on the street, but that didn't mean they weren't being watched. And Ivor wasn't just some bully human, but a member of the clan.

Somewhat to her surprise, he complied. She moved into the house and nudged the door shut behind her with a foot, listening for the click to let her know it was shut and she didn't need to worry about someone else coming up behind her.

As soon as the door was shut, the man lunged sideways, grabbing a length of wood that had been leaning against the wall. She had time to recognise it as a sporting bat before he was swinging it at her. She ducked and stepped sideways. The blow meant for her landed on the wall instead, the man cursing.

Before Ivor could gather himself for another swing, Cas and Pol were there. Pol grabbed the arm holding the bat and set his weight against the man's, Cas seizing hold of his other arm. Between them, the dogs pulled the man to the ground without difficulty. Cas put his heavy paws on the man's chest, pinning him while Pol kept hold of the arm with the bat.

"Help. Get them off me," the man cried, fury gone into fear.

"Drop the bat," Max told him. She still had her gun in hand, but didn't want to shoot if she could help it.

The man let go of the bat. Max risked a step forward, kicking the weapon out of the way. It thudded against the wall beside the door.

Max stepped back, out of reach of his fists if Ivor decided to be difficult, and took a quick look around. They were in the main living area of the house, which smelled of stale beer, old pizza and sweat. The furniture was in good repair and neatly arranged, but had an overlay of a discarded jacket, with old pizza boxes and beer cans littering the coffee table. It looked like someone had been keeping up the house until recently.

"Get up, and go and sit on the sofa," Max told the man. "Cas, Pol, get off him and keep watch."

Her dogs moved away from the man as he got to his feet and shuffled over to the sofa, planting himself on it. He reached for one of the beer cans in front of him, scowling when it proved empty.

With rage clear on his face and in the glitter of his eyes, Ivor Costen looked exactly like the sort of bully who would beat up his girlfriend, Max thought. He had lost all of his swagger and bravado when her dogs had taken him down, but he was glaring up at her, despite the gun.

"What do you want?" he asked, sullen.

"Who was the girl you were chasing the other night?" Max asked. "The one your friend killed."

"Why do you want to know about that piece of meat?" he asked, lip curling again.

"Do you want my dogs to take hold of you again?" Max asked. He didn't seem worried by the gun, but he had definitely reacted to her dogs. He flinched. "So, tell me, who was the girl?"

"I don't know," he asked, still surly. She believed him. He didn't seem to care about the girl or her death.

"Why were you there, if you didn't know who she was?" Max asked, trying to keep the disgust off her face.

"For the clan," Ivor answered, a savage light gleaming in his eyes. "For my brothers and sisters."

The ones who had chased a girl through the city, and then killed her. Max's disgust was now mixed with anger. She drew in a breath, trying to keep hold of her temper. She hadn't come here for the girl. But now she had a name and an address to give to Ruutti for the detective's investigation. "Where's Nati Ortis?" she asked instead.

Finally, she had found something he did care about. He stiffened, face tightening, then glared at her again. Anger. A lot of it.

"What's it to you?" he demanded.

"Really, we're going to go through this again?" Max asked, her finger tightening on the trigger. Guns were dangerous in more ways than one. She was sorely tempted to use it. Instead, she put it away and folded her arms in front of her, glaring back at the man. Cas and Pol were more than capable of dealing with him if he tried to hit her again.

"She's not here," Ivor said, not looking at Max.

"I can see that," Max said. Cas and Pol might have run back from their search to grab hold of Ivor, but they would have alerted her to anyone else in the house. "Where did she go?"

"Dunno," he said, still not meeting her eyes.

"So she just left, is that it?" Max asked, voice cool. "Just took off, and you don't know where she is?"

"Ungrateful bitch," he answered, grabbing another beer can, then swearing and throwing it across the room when it, too, proved to be empty. "She had a house. A roof over her head. Lazy cow."

It was a good thing Max had put away her gun. Even so, Cas and Pol made low sounds in their throats. They might not understand all the words, but they knew tones of voices, and they were better at reading body language than Max was.

"You think she left you? You didn't make her leave?" Max asked.

"I told her to stay. Told her what would happen if she didn't," Ivor said, lifting his chin and glaring back at Max. "You uptight bitches don't know your place."

Max let her mouth curve into a hard smile. "Is that so? So, you tried to keep her in her place. But she had a mind of her own. And she left you, is that it?"

He half-rose from the sofa, hands clenching to fists, and froze as both Cas and Pol growled and took a step forward, lips curling up to show the tips of their white fangs. Ivor sank back onto the sofa, eyes glittering with his other nature, whatever that was.

"Did she take her belongings with her? For her and for Ynes?" Max asked.

"No," he answered.

For the first time, Max didn't believe him. He was looking away from her again.

"So, she did take some of her things. And some for Ynes, too," Max guessed, and by the glare she got in return, the guess was accurate. "But not everything," she added. Another glare.

That made sense, if Nati was running away. She would only have taken the things she could carry.

And it also made sense, now, why she had not gone to her parents. She would have known that Ivor was one of the Huntsman clan. And would have known the dark reputation that the clan had. She would not have wanted to put her parents or her friends at risk.

Looking at Ivor, defiant and surly, Max realised she wasn't going to learn anything else from him. Still, she had more information than she had started the day with, and something to work on. There were only so many places where a desperate mother and daughter could seek refuge in the city.

Max left Ivor sitting on his sofa, surrounded by empty cans and smelly pizza boxes, and headed out into the fresher air of the city. She had work to do.

The police precinct where Ruutti worked hadn't changed much since Max's last visit. The officer on the desk gave her a cautious greeting, probably wary of Cas and Pol. The dogs immediately put their front paws up on the reception desk, giving the human officer their version of a grin. Max had to hide a smile at the officer's reaction. Perhaps eager to get the giant hounds with their gleaming white teeth away from her, the officer promptly directed Max to where Ruutti Passila was, without asking Max's business.

The detectives' section of the building was mostly open plan, but part of it had been sectioned off with whiteboards surrounding a long table covered with papers. Max could see Ruutti in front of one of the whiteboards, making a note of something.

The detective turned as Max came through a gap in the whiteboards.

"Marshal Ortis. And your hounds. Please tell them not to touch anything," Ruutti said, as if she had been expecting Max.

The detective's quiet assurance set Max's teeth on edge, but she waved Cas and Pol to settle themselves on an unoccupied part of the floor.

"I've got a name for one of the Huntsman clan who was involved in the girl's death," Max told Ruutti.

"Oh?" Ruutti had not been expecting that, her brows lifting. "Do tell."

"Ivor Costen," Max said, and gave his address and a brief description.

Ruutti wrote down the information, her eyes narrowing as she looked back up at Max. "You seem very well informed."

"I've just been to see him. I was there on another matter, but thought you'd like the information," Max said, turning away from Ruutti's prying eyes to look at the whiteboards. There were eight of them in total, each with a photograph or sketch at the top left corner. "These are the missing people?"

"The ones we've identified so far, yes," Ruutti said. She took a step back and leant against the table. "I thought you weren't interested?"

Max didn't answer at once, making her way along the row of faces and names. None of them even remotely matched Nati and Ynes' descriptions. Which didn't mean much. Nati hadn't been away from her home long enough to have settled into the homeless town. The people there might not realise she was gone, assuming she had ever been there in the first place.

"Ivor's girlfriend and their daughter are missing," Max said, pausing in front of the last picture. A young man, smiling up at the camera, a gap between his front teeth. Barely eighteen, she saw from the description on the board.

"You think there's a connection?" Ruutti asked.

"I don't know," Max said honestly, turning back to the detective. "Ivor was abusing her, and it seems to me that she probably ran away. Her parents have been trying to get answers. The police didn't seem to be that helpful."

Ruutti grimaced. "An adult woman and her daughter leaving an allegedly abusive boyfriend. Unless we have an actual report of violence, it's not easy to follow up. Do you know which station it was reported to?"

"No," Max said. She pulled one of Alonso's fliers from her pocket, and flicked her phone screen to a picture of Nati and Ynes.

Ruutti took the flier and looked at the photo. Max had to give the detective credit, she took a long, careful look, as if memorising the details.

"Nati Ortis." Ruutti's brows lifted. "A relative?"

"Not exactly. Her parents, Alonso and Elicia, are friends of mine," Max said.

Ruutti gave her a long, hard look but didn't say anything, to Max's relief. She didn't want to try and explain the sense of obligation she felt to the older couple, or the fact she had chosen their second name as her own as a daily reminder of their generosity, and who she owed her new life to.

"Can I keep this?" the detective asked, holding up the flier.

"Yes. I can forward you the photos if you want, too?" Max offered.

"Alright," Ruutti said.

Max sent the photos to the detective's phone, then put her own phone away. "Any leads?"

Ruutti lifted a perfectly arched brow. "Now you want to help?"

"If it's connected to Nati and Ynes, yes," Max said.

"There's no evidence of that," Ruutti said, and glanced past Max's shoulder. "I'll ask around about the Ortis woman and her daughter," she said in a rapid, low voice. The change in manner made Max's brows lift. The detective was almost furtive, and it was not something Max had ever seen from her before.

"Marshal," a man's voice said, calling Max's attention to the area outside the whiteboards. "How did you get in here?"

Max's brows lifted again, both at the sharp tone and the presence of Evan Yarwood, the chief of detectives, in this station. She had thought he would be at the central police station in the middle of the city, close to the council. Her dogs rose to their feet, attention going to Chief Yarwood. By the gleam in their eyes, they hadn't liked his tone.

"I walked in," she said, trying for an easy, friendly tone, waving Cas and Pol to stand back. The last thing she needed was for her dogs to decide they really didn't like the senior detective.

He stared at her, doing the thing that a lot of human men tried - attempting to stare down at her. Like many men, he was confounded by the fact she was at least the same height as him. As far as Max could tell, he was entirely human. He was dressed in a similar way to Ruutti, with a leather jacket and jeans and had pale skin and reddish-brown hair. She couldn't remember speaking to him directly before now - the last time she had seen him had been outside one of the Lady's temples not far from the body of a young woman. He was the youngest person to ever reach the rank of chief of detectives, and had been unchallenged in his post for several years as far as Max was aware. That suggested he had a hard core of ambition. And managing the interaction between the city's detectives and the occasionally sensitive cases they had to deal with required some political skills. So while he might look like an ordinary human, Max knew he was anything but.

"You shouldn't be here," he told her. "Detective Passila has more than enough work to do."

"I came to give the detective some information on an assault," Max said, still trying to stay calm. She wasn't used to so much open hostility from law enforcement. "But I've done that, so I'll leave," she said, waving Cas and Pol to follow her. "Detective," she said to Ruutti by way of goodbye. Ruutti nodded, a glint in her eye suggesting she was seriously displeased by something. Max didn't think it had anything to do with her.

Chief Yarwood didn't move as she approached, so she was forced to almost brush past him to get out of the ring of whiteboards, Cas and Pol at her heels. He was holding himself as upright as possible, chest puffed out, full of something like anger. Or possibly resentment. Forced to pass him more closely than she would have liked, she caught a hint of a rich scent around him, the sort of heavy perfume a woman might wear, and wondered just where Chief Yarwood had been to pick up such a scent.

Max made her way out of the building without incident, spending a brief moment wondering just what had so upset the chief of detectives before deciding that she didn't care to know. She had gained a little bit of information. Neither Nati nor Ynes had been reported missing. And searching the docks was the best lead she had in trying to find them.

Getting information from anyone at the docks was going to be a tough ask, she knew. She had only been there a couple of times before and, after her first visit, had made sure not to arrive empty-handed, wanting something to give to the people there who had nothing. And also now, when she wanted to ask questions, she needed something to give in exchange. She needed to go shopping.

Chapter Ten

With a heavy backpack over one shoulder and her Marshal's badge tucked out of sight, Max left her vehicle in the last public parking lot before the streets gave way to the docks. There was an industrial workshop across the street and the city's buses didn't run to the docks, so the car park was half-full of the workers' vehicles, most of the cars older models with a few dents and scratches in the side. No one wanted to bring their sleek city cars here. During the day it was generally safe, but the street represented the line between Huntsman and Raghavan territory and trouble was common after dark. Max wasn't heading for the workshop, but away from it, through the parking lot, to the rough concrete surface, bulky machinery and buildings that were a legacy from a long-ago busy sea port. The port had not been active since long before Max had been born.

The bright, vivid daylight of the city faded as she walked further into the permanent mist that shrouded the docks and she shivered, chill seeping through her clothes. It was impossible to see far in any direction, her footsteps muffled by the fog. As she kept walking, the backpack heavy and awkward on her shoulder, she caught the first scent of the sea, salt strong enough to taste, dampness in the breeze against her cheeks. She wondered what the sea might look like if the fog lifted. She had seen paintings of seascapes, but had never actually seen the ocean itself. No one in the city had. She wondered, too, just how far the fog stretched and what might be out there. Every now and then someone attempted to go off the end of the docks, into the mist, to explore. No one had ever returned. Max's skin chilled. The city and the Wild were real things that she could see and touch. There could be a whole other city out in the fog. A whole other Wild.

The speculation and thought slid out of her mind as she kept walking. There was the city and the Wild. Those were real. Nothing else. The fog was the edge of the world.

A great, dark creature loomed out of the mist in front of her and she checked in her stride, hand going to her gun before she realised it wasn't a creature at all. Instead, it was one of the abandoned shipping cranes that had serviced the docks when they had been busy. No one in the city could remember those days, but it always unsettled her that there was evidence here that there had once been something beyond the fog. Beyond the edge of the world.

Thick, metal legs rose high over her head, the top of the crane hidden in the fog. To one side she could hear the gentle lapping of water against the concrete dockside. She had found one of the mooring points for the container ships that used to visit the port, offloading their goods. There must have been a time when the fog wasn't there. She knew that. And yet, she could not remember that time. And no one else in the city seemed able to remember it, either. Before she could think too much more about it, she remembered that the fog was the edge of the world. There was nothing else. Just the city and the Wild.

With her heart rate slowing back to normal, she moved further along the dockside and didn't react as she saw another giant shadow loom out of the fog. This time, the shape was in the water. A medium-sized vessel, it was still larger than any land-based vehicle. It sat next to the concrete dockside, moored by long, heavy chains that were showing signs of rust. She caught a glimpse of open doorways and windows on the vessel as she went past. The ship had doubtless been robbed of anything useful, including its windows and doors.

On her other side, inland, the first building appeared. A long, low dark shape in the mist, it stretched into the distance, the end of it hidden by fog.

Cas and Pol made low sounds in their throats, alerting her to something wrong. She paused, looking down at her dogs. They were both focused on the next crane that was just appearing out of the fog ahead of them. There was something besides the leg of the machine coming into view. Max slid her arm through the other strap of her backpack, settling it across her shoulders so it was more secure and balanced, and drew her gun, making sure it was set to single fire. She might need to defend herself, but she didn't want to kill anyone.

As they drew closer, Cas and Pol fanned out, but stayed in their dog forms rather than shifting to their attack forms, which told Max they didn't think whatever it was ahead was a direct threat. She kept her gun pointing down and made her way forward.

She was about twenty paces from the bottom of the crane when she realised that the object next to the crane leg was a person. No. Three people.

Muttering a curse, she slowed down. The only people who had business on the docks were members of the Raghavan Family, a sprawling conglomerate of families and businesses that occupied the vast tract of land between the city and the unseen sea. With the expansion of the Wild a decade before, the Family had lost much of its land and jealously guarded the territory it did have left. She had hoped to avoid meeting any member of the Family on her visit here, as they could be difficult to deal with.

The three people turned as one, as if finally sensing her and her dogs' presence, and the one on the left lifted a hand in greeting. She stopped, startled and relieved. Not members of the Raghavan Family. Instead, the one on the left was Bryce. The other two - a man and a woman - she didn't recognise, but by the way they carried themselves, and their proximity to Bryce, she guessed they were also Order warriors.

It said something about how prickly the Raghavan Family could be that she was relieved to see members of the Order here. She put her gun away as she approached the trio. Cas and Pol moved a few paces farther out to either side, keeping their attention on their surroundings. They had worked together long enough that the dogs were staying on watch without her asking.

"A surprise to see you here," Bryce said, brows lifting. She felt heat rise on her face. He had asked her to visit, and she had refused. And yet, here she was.

"I could say the same," she answered, glancing at the other two. Definitely warriors. And, like Bryce, probably not entirely human. It was very subtle, but something in the way they moved suggested some *other* nature mixed in with their mostly human heritage. It was the sort of gracefulness that Max's wholly human body would never be able to manage. "What's up?"

"We were just making a patrol," Bryce said, in a too-casual manner. Max's brows lifted. The Order's warriors did not just do patrols, and particularly not in territory closely guarded by one of the Families. Before she could ask any questions, he turned slightly. "This is Khari and Joshua," he introduced the other two. A couple, Max realised, by the way they stood together. And she had guessed right that they were warriors - they each wore the Order symbol on their right shoulders. A double-headed axe. The woman had pitch-dark skin that seemed to absorb the light, her black hair done in intricate knots tied at the back of her head. The man was almost her opposite, with cool, pale skin and strawberry blond hair in soft curls around his head. Despite their superficial differences, they were both about the same height as Max, so tall for humans, and each had an athletic build that was well-suited for their profession. Like Bryce, they had an air of quiet confidence that Max associated with highly trained, highly proficient warriors. "This is Marshal Max Ortis," Bryce told the others.

Max exchanged nods with the couple, conscious of a wave of relief that Bryce was using her new identity. She didn't remember the couple at all from her training days, and hoped they hadn't heard enough about her to make a connection.

"Did you find something?" Max asked.

"We think so," Khari said. She pointed to the base of the crane. "Neither Josh nor I have training in magic, but we are sensitive to it. And there's been some magic here."

"You're right," Max said. Now that the warrior had pointed it out, she could feel the brush of unfamiliar magic against her senses. It had almost blended in with the lapping of the water and the dampness of the fog. Either the magician had managed to disguise their spell, or it was not very powerful. Max's guess would be on the first option. She couldn't imagine a weak magician wasting their power in an out-of-the-way place like this, and in Raghavan territory, too. Her mind skipped back to the speculation she had when Bryce had told her about the possible dark magic, connecting it with the reports of missing people, and unease slid through her. The Raghavan Family were fiercely protective of their territory. She could not imagine a magician, even one steeped in dark magic, foolish enough to challenge them by setting up his spells on their grounds. Which either meant the magician was powerful enough that he didn't care about the Family's anger, or the Raghavan Family knew about his work. Neither of them were good options, as far as Max was concerned.

As she approached the crane leg, she saw markings on the metal. Someone had drawn a spell there with what looked like dark paint. If it was dark magic, though, it might well have been drawn in blood. And her guess had been right. Powerful magic.

"That's dark magic," she said, drawing her small torch so she could get a better look at the spell against the rusting metal. She hadn't studied enough dark magic to know exactly what it was, but it looked like some kind of protection. "Which direction did you come from?" she asked the others.

Bryce pointed further along the dock. The same direction Max and her dogs had travelled.

"I think this is supposed to prevent people going that way," Max said, pointing ahead, along the dockside. Not towards the warehouse, its silent bulk almost invisible through the mist. "It's been here a little while."

"A few weeks, we thought," Joshua said. "No, we can't read the magic. We were looking at the tracks and the fading of the paint."

Max shone her torch down to the ground, unable to see anything that might even resemble tracks. Still, she trusted the warriors. They had the same air of quiet self-assurance as Bryce.

"What happens if we go that way?" Bryce asked.

"Something bad, would be my guess," Max said, turning her torch off and returning it to its pocket. "You should tell Kitris," she told Bryce, remembering that had been her advice to him the last time they had met.

"I did," Bryce said, his face tight. "He said it wasn't worth the Order's time."

Max stared at him, turning the words over in her mind. Bryce looked full of tension, from his tight jaw to his fixed shoulders and the white knuckles of his hands, clenched into fists by his side. She wondered if that had been the first time that Kitris had not listened to Bryce. And then her brows lifted. Even though Kitris had decreed that this wasn't worth the Order's time, Bryce had still brought two other warriors with him to the docks to investigate further.

"You don't agree with Kitris," she said slowly.

"No," Bryce said, the word bitten off. "There shouldn't be any dark magic in the city at all."

"Kitris has been short-tempered for weeks, and even less open to suggestions or new ideas than normal," Khari said, her nose wrinkling. It was said in a matter-of-fact tone that suggested Khari had a very clear understanding of Kitris and his flaws. Despite the circumstances, Max had to bite down a smile, warming to the other woman. "Not sure what's got him so worked up, but he's definitely concerned about something," Khari added.

"Well. There was a serial murderer trying to open the Grey Gates not so long ago," Max pointed out.

"That would do it," Joshua agreed.

"We heard about that," Khari said, focusing on Max. "Rumour is that one of the Marshals stopped him."

"Is that the rumour?" Max asked, wanting to duck away from the woman's assessing stare.

"Can you tell us anything more about this spell?" Bryce asked, before Khari could speak again.

"No, I'm sorry. It's not my specialism," Max said. "But if you go that way, just be careful. That's been done by a skilled magician and probably packs a punch."

"Noted, thanks," Bryce said.

"Alright. I'm going this way," she said, pointing to the warehouse. "Good luck," she added.

"You aren't curious why someone would want to stop people going along the dock?" Bryce asked before she could move away.

Max started to say she wasn't interested, but paused. Something about Bryce's direct question prompted her to be honest. "It's not that so much as this is Raghavan territory. They don't like trespassers, and it's most likely that they're trying to keep prying eyes out of their business." It wasn't common practice for any of the Five Families to use dark magic to protect their properties, but it had been done before. Anything was possible for a price.

Not thinking there was anything more to say, and wanting to escape more questions from Khari, Max turned and headed towards the warehouse. It had been a long time since she had been here, but this warehouse was most likely empty, with the one behind it being occupied.

She hadn't gone far when she realised that the three warriors were following her. She stopped and turned, lifting a brow at Bryce.

"You didn't tell us what you were here for," he said, in response to her silent question.

"A friend asked for my help," she said. "His daughter and granddaughter are missing. It's possible they came here."

"They must be desperate," Khari said.

"Yes," Max answered, hesitating before going on, "The daughter's boyfriend is a piece of work. I think she's run away from him, and didn't think it was safe to go to her parents. The boyfriend is with the Huntsman clan."

"Do you have a photo?" Joshua asked, surprising Max. He was quite serious. "We can help to look. More eyes, better chance of finding them."

"Josh's younger sister also ran away from an abusive boyfriend," Khari explained, voice soft. She exchanged looks with her partner and touched the back of his hand in silent sympathy. "We didn't get there in time for her, but perhaps we can help this young woman."

"I'm sorry," Max said to Joshua. "Some help would be welcome," she added. Trying to search through the warren of the warehouse for two people who didn't want to be found was a daunting task. She opened the photograph on her phone. "The woman's name is Nati Ortis. Her daughter is Ynes." She dug into her pocket and pulled out one of the posters Alonso had prepared. "Here. Nati's parents made this."

"She looks young," Khari observed, looking at Max's phone as Joshua took the poster.

"Three years old," Max confirmed, throat and chest tight. That Ynes was so young just told her how desperate Nati must have been. She held her breath, waiting for someone to comment on the fact she shared her last name with the missing woman, but no one did. Instead, Bryce nodded, as if coming to a decision. He took a look around. They were close to the first warehouse, which had both its side doors open, showing a shadowed and empty interior.

"Alright. We'll cut through here. The homeless are in the next warehouse, and we should use the small doors at the ends, not the main doors," Bryce said. "Josh,

Khari, why don't you take the landward end, and Max and I will head to the seaward end."

The couple agreed, and started walking again. Not sure whether to be amused or offended at having decisions made for her, or grateful for the extra help, Max fell into step beside Bryce as they passed the threshold of the empty warehouse. There wasn't as much fog in here to dampen sounds, and their footsteps echoed off the metal roof high above. Glancing up, Max saw that the roof was intact. It said something about the Raghavan Family's power that they had managed to keep so much metal away from the city processors. There was always a demand for metal, no matter how dented or rusted. The city's engineers had gotten very good at reusing old materials over the years.

She was about to turn her attention back to the ground when a spark of red in the roof caught her eye. She stopped, frowning.

"What is that?" she asked.

Bryce glanced up but it was Khari who answered. "Cameras," she said, grimacing. "The Raghavan Family likes to keep watch on what goes on."

Max stared up at the lens far overhead. "I wonder if they keep track of the homeless," she said, speculating aloud.

"I doubt it," Khari said, voice flat. "They are more interested in protecting their property."

That was more than consistent with what little Max knew of any of the Five Families. She turned back to the path and they kept walking, the back of her neck itching with the idea that someone might be watching them. She tried to set that aside, concentrating on the task ahead of her. The extra, and unexpected, help was welcome and a dangerous little sliver of hope grew in her. Hope that they might find Nati and Ynes safe and well.

Chapter Eleven

The first thing Max noticed when they went into the side door of the next warehouse was the smell. It was an almost visible trail in the air, a mingling of the odour of unwashed bodies, damp, rot, and other smells that Max didn't want to think about. The weather was cooling in anticipation of winter, and she couldn't imagine how bad the smells must be in the height of summer. It said something about the plight of the people living here that they saw this as their best option.

The next thing she noticed was the damp. The air was sticky and humid against her skin. Looking ahead, she could see the whole internal space had been divided up with blankets, bits of cardboard, the occasional piece of chain link fence, and other odd shapes such as an old shopping cart missing its wheels and what looked like an internal door from a house. The divided spaces she could see were mostly barely big enough for a single person to lie down in. And they all showed signs of occupation, from makeshift beds to clothing, and the occasional person sleeping.

Even though there had been no city planners involved, the people here seemed to have organised themselves so that the spaces were set back to back, with corridors running between the fronts. The corridors were not straight, curving in random directions, but there was a definite organisation to the layout.

Over the smell and damp was the noise. There were people everywhere, giving rise to the babble of conversation that filled Max's ears, overwhelming after the quiet of the outside.

Not far away from where she and Bryce had come into the building, there was a group of people settled on ragged blankets and bits of cardboard, tin mugs in their hands. They were all dressed in mismatched layers of clothing dulled by use. The group looked around as Max and Bryce appeared, the attention sharpening as Cas and Pol came into view. Max had thought about leaving the dogs outside, but with the presence of dark magic on the docks, and not knowing what she might find inside, she had kept them with her.

"Doggy!" a child's voice announced. A small, too-thin child ran from between the adults and, before Max could react, dashed up to Pol, throwing both arms around the great hound. Pol stood stock still, looking as utterly confused as Max had ever seen him. She choked on a laugh. Her dogs were used to far more respectful treatment. As the child hugged her dog, Max realised he was a young boy, perhaps ten years old, hair matted with dirt, wearing a sweatshirt several sizes too big for him. The boy looked up at Max, eyes shining. "What's his name?" he asked.

"That's Pol," Max said. "And this is Cas," she added.

"Oh, another one!" The boy let go of Pol and ran across to Cas. Cas gave Max an expressive look over the stranglehold that the child had on him. Her dogs were definitely not used to such casual treatment.

"Matthew, come away," a frantic voice sounded from the group, who were all now getting to their feet. "They might be dangerous," the woman added, coming forward. She didn't want to get too close to the dogs, Max realised, her eyes wide as she looked from one to the other, frightened for her son.

"The dogs won't hurt him," Max said, and signalled Pol to come closer to her side. He twitched his ears, dignity still ruffled by the child's embrace, and pressed himself against her, as if she would protect him from further hugs. "Matthew, is it? Can you let go of Cas and go back to your mother?"

"Can I keep him?" Matthew asked instead, still hugging Cas's neck. He was barely taller than the dog.

"No," the mother said, horrified by the idea. Max could only imagine how difficult it was for the mother to keep herself and her son fed. Adding a giant dog was impossible, even if she had wanted to.

"I'm sorry, no," Max said more gently.

Matthew let go of Cas with evident reluctance and went back to his mother. She snatched him away, huddling back into the crowd of people gathered.

"What do you want?" one of the older people asked. A grey-haired woman with warm-toned, deep brown skin and a scar running down one side of her face. From the way the others were standing around her, she was some kind of leader, or at the least a person they respected.

Max looked around the group. She didn't see Nati anywhere. She hadn't expected to. If the Ortises' daughter was in the building, she would likely be hiding, not sitting near one of the doors.

"I'm looking for a mother and her daughter," she said, sliding her backpack off one shoulder. It seemed to have grown heavier in the short journey here. "They might have come here about a week ago. The mother probably had bruises."

"A lot of people come here with bruises," the grey-haired woman said, chin lifting.

"I can imagine. I'm sorry," Max said, keeping her voice gentle.

"Why should we help you?" Matthew's mother asked, arms wrapped around her son. "Coming in here to look down your nose at us."

"That's not my intention," Max said, embarrassment crawling under her skin. "I know her parents and they are worried about her. I just want to know she's safe."

The group stared back at her, mulish expressions on their faces.

"I brought some things I hope will help," Max said, taking a step forward, setting the backpack down and unzipping it. After the first time she had been to the docks, she had resolved to never come back without something to give. She had consulted with the only homeless shelter in the city and put together packs with socks, wet wipes and palm-sized, high-calorie meal-replacement bars.

"Stop," the grey-haired woman said, as one of the group twitched, making a move for the backpack. "Think you can bribe us?" the woman asked, lifting her chin and staring at Max.

Max took a step back, frustration and more embarrassment warring within her. For some reason, she hadn't anticipated meeting resistance to the questions she had to ask. That had been foolish of her. The people here owed her nothing. After all, she had ignored them, like the rest of the city. "No," she said, "the backpack and its contents are yours whether you help me or not. I know it's not enough," she added, and then bit her lip. It wasn't enough, but she hadn't meant to say that part aloud.

The woman looked down at the backpack and her face tightened. She was also struggling with conflicting emotions, Max sensed. The woman spoke well, and held herself tall and straight with pride. She had not started her life here, and probably had never imagined she would end up in this warehouse, crammed in with so many others.

"We don't want your pity," one of the men in the group said. He was barely a head taller than Matthew, with sallow skin and great dark circles under his eyes. He had the jerky, uncoordinated movements that Max associated with drug users.

Max stayed quiet, skin prickling in discomfort. She hadn't meant to be insulting, but she wasn't sure how to mend the situation.

"We'll make sure this is shared around," the grey-haired woman said, taking a step forward and picking up the backpack. Her brows lifted as she settled it on her shoulder. "There's more here than I thought."

"It was as much as I could carry," Max said, conscious of Bryce standing a pace or two behind her. "Do you mind if I look around and try to find Nati and her daughter?"

"Show me pictures," the woman answered. She was still holding the backpack. Not willing to let it go to someone else in the group, Max suspected. Definitely some kind of a leader.

Max pulled out her phone. It was an older model, with a protective rubber case to try to stop it from being damaged. Ruutti would not have been seen dead with such outdated technology, but the group paid close attention to it and more embarrassment prickled across Max's skin. She took her phone for granted, but the people here might have one phone between them, if that. Max ignored the stares and pulled up a photo of Nati and Ynes, taking a step closer to show it to the woman.

"I've not seen either of them," the woman said, after glancing at the pictures. "You can look, but I doubt you'll find them."

"Thank you," Max said. She wondered how Khari and Joshua were getting on at the other end of the building, and whether they had met as much cooperation. She didn't move, the faces on Ruutti's whiteboards coming to mind. "I'm told that people have been going missing from here. Eight people? Maybe more?"

The woman stared back at her, expression flat. Impossible to tell what she was thinking.

"The police are looking into it, but if there's anything you can tell me, I'd like to hear it," Max said.

She hadn't wanted to get involved. Not at all. But here she was, even if she had been answering a call to help Alonso and Elicia. And now that she was here, she couldn't ignore the people in front of her. Much of the city might like to pretend the warehouse and its occupants didn't exist, living in a fantasy that the city had full employment, and every resident had a home. The city council saw the warehouse as a problem. Max's feelings were far more complicated. She could so easily have ended up here. When she had come back from the underworld, after Kitris had rejected her and dismissed her from the Order, there had been nowhere for Max to go. She was too old by far to be taken in by one of the orphanages again, and the only shelter in the city was always full. It was only the big hearts of Alonso and Elicia that had kept her safe, and steered her onto a path that had ended with a job and housing, rather than here, just one more exhausted face among many.

She wasn't sure what she could do to help the people here, but she knew that they deserved to feel safe. Perhaps, once she had found Nati and Ynes, she could consider that further and what she could do.

"More than eight," the woman said, not meeting Max's eyes. "We don't exactly keep a register, you know?"

Max nodded. "Alright. Do you have any idea how many others are missing?" she asked.

"No," Matthew's mother said, still clinging to her boy. She was frightened, and it was no longer about Cas and Pol. "But there's something bad happening."

It was on the tip of Max's tongue to ask if there was anywhere else the group could stay. She held the words in. If they had somewhere else they could go, she was quite sure they would already have gone. So she nodded instead and glanced at Bryce to make sure he was paying attention. She needn't have worried. He was standing a pace or two behind her, all his weapons tucked away, still and quiet but taking everything in.

"Can you tell me a bit more about that? Something bad? Do you mean people? Magic? Creatures?" Max asked, turning back to the group.

She wasn't sure what she had said, or if it was how she had said it, but it was as if she had opened a door. Floods of words came out of the crowd around her, all of them talking at once, telling her about strange lights, cold drafts, red eyes, green smoke, bad feelings, and a sticky sensation against their skin.

She listened, not wanting to stop them, trying to take it all in. The torrent of words slowed until only one or two people were talking at a time. There were empty places near the warehouse's main door that used to be full. Quite a few of the missing had gone from there. The spaces were still empty. No one else wanted to go there. They had managed to close and bar the main doors at the front and back. The side doors were only open when there were people there to keep an eye out. The grey-haired woman's face tightened as she said that they liked to have the doors open during the day to let some fresh air in.

For some reason, that small detail made Max's heart constrict in her chest. The people were living in the most awful circumstances she had ever seen, and wanted to have a bit of fresh air now and then. It was such a simple wish. The constriction was swiftly followed by anger. None of them deserved to be here. There were rows and rows of abandoned houses on the outskirts of the city. More than enough to accommodate all of the people here with solid walls and roofs and green space outside and running water and electricity. The city could afford a small army of people to take care of the city green, the stretch of open land that ran through the wealthier part of the city, and maintain vast greenhouses to supply the public buildings with fresh flowers and exotic fruits. Supporting basic services to abandoned buildings wouldn't even make a dent in their budget. But she knew that idea would be dismissed out of hand by the council.

She was distracted by her anger and almost missed one of the group mentioning a strange figure that they had seen more than once, outside the warehouse, on the docks. This figure had been seen a few times during the space of weeks that people had been going missing. No one had got a good look at it, or got close to it. The group couldn't confirm if it was human or something else. Or even if it was the same figure each time. The only thing that the people around Max agreed on was that it was very tall, and no one wanted to get near it.

Which reminded Max of the dark magic that the warriors had found on the docks. She glanced back at Bryce again and he nodded, confirming he'd noted that detail, too.

With her ears ringing from the information she had been given, she thanked the group. She and Bryce headed further into the warehouse, making their way through the makeshift village, Cas and Pol trailing after them. She checked every sleeping space she came across, but didn't find Nati or Ynes, and no one she asked had seen or heard of a mother and daughter seeking refuge in the past couple of weeks.

By the time they reached the middle of the warehouse and saw Khari and Joshua coming towards them from the other half, Max was feeling hopeless as well as frustrated and still angry. Neither Khari nor Joshua had found any information, either, but they had only covered one corridor in the warehouse, and there were many more to go.

Cas and Pol had picked up on her unsettled feelings and were keeping close to her, hyper-alert. Max tried to take a deep breath, to ease her tension. Her dogs were well-trained, but all it would take was for one frightened person to throw something at her, or at them, to start a bloodbath.

Pol's low growl had her turning, hand going to her weapon.

The warehouse was a long rectangle. She and Bryce had entered at one of the short ends, Khari and Joshua at the other. In the middle, where they were now standing, there were great floor-to-ceiling rolling doors that had been wedged shut. Even as Cas and Pol both turned to face the huge doors at the back of the warehouse, something large and heavy thudded against the metal doors, leaving a large dent.

"Get back," Max called to the people around them as she drew her weapon, facing the door. Her warning wasn't needed. The space between the rows of living spaces was abruptly empty, the entire warehouse falling into an eerie quiet.

Whatever-it-was thumped against the doors again. The metal groaned under the impact. A low, snarling sound reached Max's ears, raising the hair on the back of her neck. That sounded like a predator of some kind. And she had left her shotgun and heavier ammunition in the pick-up, not wanting to frighten the warehouse occupants.

"Khari, Joshua, on the left," Bryce ordered. "With me," he said to Max.

She opened her mouth to argue, but decided against it when she saw the weapons they were carrying. All the warriors had produced heavy-duty automatic weapons from somewhere, far more powerful than her handgun. And they were all highly trained warriors. So she pointed her gun to the ground and meekly followed Bryce as he headed for the right hand side of the doors. Cas and Pol stayed with her, both of them on alert.

As they drew closer, the thing hammered at the doors again. The dents were about head height, which suggested a large creature. She tried to work out the shape of it and what the creature might be from the dents, but the damage was distorted and made no sense to her eyes. Something big and angry, that was all she could really tell. She was keenly aware of the warehouse full of people around her, none of them with the skills or equipment to stand up to whatever was on the other side of that door.

There was a small door set into the larger doors, just big enough to allow a single person to enter or exit. Bryce pointed towards it and gestured Max to stay behind him. She frowned at his back, but stayed where she was. Not only was he better armed, she would also bet he was wearing body armour, something that hadn't been in the budget for Marshals. As a general rule, if a Marshal got close enough to a creature to need the protection of body armour, things had gone very badly wrong. Marshals preferred to deal with their targets at a good distance, and with powerful tranquillisers wherever possible. The creatures they hunted generally had claws or teeth that could tear the Marshals apart, but didn't fire back.

Bryce slipped out the door with minimal fuss and Max followed him, the dogs with her.

The shock of being outside in air saturated with sea salt rather than the stench of the warehouse made her dizzy for a moment.

Then something huge and dark swept out of the fog, an enormous spike bigger than her head swinging towards them. Max yelled a warning, but Bryce was already moving, rolling on the ground and coming up to a crouch, weapon ready. Khari and Joshua poured out of the door they had used, Joshua kicking it shut behind him.

There was no time to worry about the warehouse as the creature in the fog shifted again. It was walking on all fours, its body close to the ground, the long, flexible tail swirling the mist behind it. It lifted its head and tasted the air with a forked tongue, eyes turning to them. It gleamed shimmering blue and green in the poor light. It was beautiful and terrifying.

"Holy Lady, that's a Galdr," Max said, voice high and shaking. She had never seen one in person before. "It shouldn't be on land," she added.

"How do we stop it?" Bryce asked, voice tight.

"Bullets will work, but I want to know what it's doing here," Max said. "They don't usually come inland. And they aren't usually aggressive," she added, earning a sceptical look from the others. "No, really. They look fierce and will attack if provoked, but they are renowned for being very calm."

"We're not really inland," Bryce commented. He sounded almost terrifyingly calm.

"Watch out for the tail," Max said. "If it's going to attack, that's its only weapon."

"Tail. Got it," Khari said, voice tight. "Orders?" she asked.

For a moment, Max thought that the warrior was talking to her.

"Stay still and quiet. It might go away," Bryce said.

"Oh, really?" Joshua muttered, sounding sceptical. But he and Khari stayed exactly where they were, barely breathing.

Cas and Pol were on either side of Max, huddled down to the ground, both in their attack forms, but not making a sound, eyes fixed on the creature ahead of them.

The Galdr held its position, tail swirling again, and Max frowned. It had battered the doors of the warehouse as if it wanted to get inside, but was now just sitting still. It didn't make sense.

She shifted position slightly, moving her weight to one side. Its eyes flicked to her, but it didn't move. Interesting. And now she had a moment to breathe, she could feel a trail of magic in the air. A bit like the dark magic that the warriors had found on the crane.

"It's got dark magic on it," she told the others.

"For what purpose?" Bryce asked.

"I don't know," she answered honestly. "It's around its neck. Looks like a collar," she added. "I have an idea," she said. "Can you cover me?"

"Go ahead," Bryce said, not moving.

Max put her gun away and put her hands together in front of her, palms touching in a posture that all magicians learned along with basic spells. Her idea was instinct rather than anything she had been taught, and an unconventional way to use magic, but as Audhilde had pointed out to her, there were lots of different ways to use magic. She created the smallest of sparks between her hands and stared ahead at the dark magic around the creature's neck. Now that she was focusing on the magic, she could see marks on the creature's flesh where the dark magic had dug in. The creature twisted, shaking its head as if trying to get rid of the magic. No, the collar. That's what it was.

The little spark of magic in her hands faded as she poured an unravelling spell into it. She was too far away to deliver the spell, though. She took a step forward.

The Galdr's head snapped round, eyes focusing on her, and its tail lifted, the great spike at its tip looking even more lethal as Max got closer.

"I need a distraction," Max said to the others. "I'm going to send my dogs one way and try to deliver the spell," she said. She closed one of her hands, hiding the bit of magic, and used her free hand to send her dogs out. They didn't want to go, but they moved as she asked.

The creature's eyes followed the pair of shadow-hounds and Max ran forward, jumping up and throwing the bit of magic at the creature's neck, high over her head.

She was so focused on her task that she forgot to pay attention to the tail. It whipped around, the flat side of the spike catching her and sending her spinning through the air until she slammed into the side of the warehouse. A low, snarling sound filled her ears as she landed on the ground. Her dogs.

But no gunfire.

"Hold fire." Bryce still sounded way too calm. "Max, are you alright?"

She tried to speak and managed a moan. Hurt hurt hurt. Everything hurt. Her ribs, back, hip, leg, arm, head. Ouch ouch ouch. She managed to push herself to an almost-sitting position and shook her head slightly to try to clear her sight. Mistake. The world spun and she threw up on the ground beside her.

Large, dark shapes appeared beside her. Cas and Pol, standing watch.

"What's happening?" she asked, voice croaking. At least, that's what she tried to say. It came out as incoherent noise, but Bryce seemed to understand.

"It's just standing there," Bryce reported. "Can you get up?"

"Gimmemoment," Max said. She tried moving and almost threw up again. She had definitely hit her head. Hard. Too slow. Forgot about the tail. Stupid. She managed to get onto her hands and knees somehow and then, wobbling, onto her feet. She rested her hands on Cas and Pol's shoulders, the dogs moving closer to help support her. "Up," she reported to Bryce. The world was spinning in nauseating circles. Hurt hurt hurt.

Now she was on her feet, she remembered that she had a painkiller patch in a pocket. Somewhere. Pocket. Which pocket? No. That was her torch. That was her phone. Ah. There. It took three tries, but she finally got the patch onto the bare skin at her neck and almost cried as blissful numbness spread through her body. She still hurt, but she could move, and her vision was clearing.

The creature was still standing where it had been, as Bryce had said. The dark magic around its neck was gone, leaving a raw and angry wound.

Max took a step forward, closer to Bryce, and the Galdr turned to look at her, tongue flicking out again. It opened its mouth, a low sound emerging. It ground through the bones of Max's head, making her wince. She put a hand to her face and it came away with blood on it. Head wound. That explained a lot. Oh, wait, she had already realised she had hit her head.

She sank to the ground a couple of paces away from Bryce. Sitting down seemed like a very good idea.

The creature took a step forward, head lowering. Max could sense the tension in the warriors, but they stayed still. The creature breathed out. Warm, salt-laden air brushed over Max's face. There was magic in the warmth, bright and laden with sea salt and full of life. As the breath ran over her, she felt power trail across her skin, lifting all the pain away, easing every bruise. As the warmth faded, she was left with a sense of light filling her. She laughed, getting to her feet, the movement easy and free. She touched her head. No blood.

"Amazing," she said, taking another step closer to the creature. It moved closer to her, too, its head still low. On impulse, she put her hand up. It butted her hand with its nose, reminding her of Cas or Pol demanding a pat, and she laughed again. "This creature is full of magic," she told the others.

"We can see. You're glowing," Khari said, sounding bemused.

"I am?" Max asked, and looked down at her hand. Khari was right, her skin was luminescent. She laughed again. She couldn't remember the last time she had felt so good. "Thank you for the healing," she said to the creature, even though she was fairly sure it wouldn't understand her language. She touched two fingers to her heart. "The Lady's light be with you."

The creature ducked its head, then turned away, heading along the docks.

As it moved, Max remembered the dark magic. "Wait. There's a trap that way," she said, alarmed, as the creature disappeared into the thick fog.

Chapter Twelve

Max ran after the Galdr, heart thumping in her chest. She didn't know what lay ahead, but the dark magic protection had not been put there by accident or on a whim. Someone had wanted the rest of the docks protected from casual passers-by.

Cas and Pol were dense shadows in the fog on either side, both of them still in their attack forms, either reacting to her tension, or sensing something ahead that she couldn't see yet.

The fog lifted a little and she caught sight of the Galdr ahead of her just as an explosion shook the ground under her feet. She managed to stay upright, drawing her gun and continuing on at a walk, her dogs matching her pace. The creature had stopped, shaking its head, its tail lashing behind it. Max gave it a wide berth. She didn't think that it would deliberately harm her, but it would defend itself.

More figures moved in the mist, forming into humans as they came closer. Armed humans. They were all wearing the deep purple that she associated with the Raghavan Family. She bit back a curse. So much for avoiding the Raghavans. There were at least a dozen armed men and women who formed a loose semi-circle in front of the creature, blocking its path forwards. At Max's end of the semi-circle, two more people appeared. A man and a woman. They did not appear to be armed, but were dressed in draped fabrics in shades of purple and red. They moved almost as one, of a similar height and build, both with mid-brown, warm-toned skin and silky black hair that they wore loose, hanging below their shoulders.

Max's heart sank even further. The Raghavan siblings. Of all the people she had to run into, it was two of the highest-ranking members of the Family. A slight stirring in the air brought with it the salt tang of the unseen sea and a richer scent that was tantalisingly familiar, although she couldn't remember where she had come across it before.

She put her gun away. There were enough weapons on display already. She pulled out her badge, the seven-pointed star gleaming in the light, reacting to the magic around them.

"Marshal," the woman said. Shivangi Raghavan. The elder of the twins. She was a striking woman, with perfectly formed arched brows over dark eyes surrounded by thick lashes. She looked as if she was ready to be photographed, her beauty captured for all time. Max couldn't help feeling scruffy by comparison, and wondering just how long it had taken Shivangi to get ready for the day. She looked Max up and down, lip curling. "You have no place here. Leave. Now."

"I found this creature with a dark magic collar," Max said, keeping her tone even. "You are well aware that it is illegal to keep supernatural beings, and that dark magic is also illegal."

"That is not your concern," the man said. Hemang Raghavan. He not only shared the same striking looks as his sister, but had all of his sister's arrogance, too. "You are on our territory."

"Does your mother know that you've been keeping a Galdr trapped with dark magic?" Max asked. The elder Raghavan ruled her family with an iron grip. She had been known to skirt the law more than once, but Max had a hard time believing that she would condone keeping a Galdr, or such blatant use of dark magic.

"Our mother is dead," Hemang said, voice flat. Impossible to tell how he felt about that.

"The Family is in our hands now," Shivangi added.

"I'm sorry for your loss," Max said, trying for an even tone while her heart sunk further. Damayanti Raghavan might have been able to keep control of her children. But if she was gone, there would be no one who could restrain them.

"That is of no matter to you," Hemang said, staring at Max with flat eyes. "You are on our territory. You are not welcome. As my sister has said, you will leave. Now."

Max stood her ground, folding her arms, and pointedly not reaching for her gun. The Galdr was standing still, its tail raised. But it seemed to know that the armed people between it and the sea were a threat to it. Or perhaps it had encountered them before, Max realised, cold sliding across her skin. After all, someone had put a dark magic collar on the creature. Not the Raghavan twins themselves. Neither of them had enough magic of their own to have done that work. So there was a dark magic master in the Raghavans' employment.

"You are in violation of the city's codes and laws," Max told the Raghavan siblings in the same flat voice that they had used.

"We did not agree to those laws," Hemang said, chin lifting, a small, pleased smile playing around his mouth.

"No?" Max asked, voice hard. It wasn't the first time someone had said that to her, but she doubted that Hemang had thought it through. "So you don't want the clean water or electricity or sewerage system? You don't want access to fuel for your vehicles? Or for the roads in your territory to be repaired? You don't want access to emergency food rations if needed? You don't want the police to patrol your territory, or for the Marshals' service to clear out crow spider nests or remove Seacast monkeys?" She paused, watching the smile fade from Hemang's face to be replaced by fury. His sister was tight-faced, eyes narrowed with what looked like rage. "If you are declaring your territory to be outside the law, then you will also not benefit from anything that the city provides," Max continued. It was the one hold that the council had over the Five Families, the one thing that kept them - almost - in check. Even though they were powerful, the Families generally lacked the resources and skills to make up for the things that the city organised and provided.

"Those things are ours," Shivangi hissed between clenched teeth.

"They are provided by the city council, which makes the laws," Max said evenly. "And if you do not want to obey the laws, there will be consequences to that."

"You seek to insult us?" Shivangi said, jaw still locked.

"By no means. But you are in clear violation of the city's laws by having this creature on your territory, and in having allowed dark magic to be performed. You need to let the creature go."

"You have no proof we permitted dark magic," Hemang said, still furious. He would likely be considered handsome in most circumstances - and likely spent as much time arranging his hair as his sister spent on her flawless make-up - but Max would wager that most people would also agree that his sister was definitely the brighter of the two.

"Oh?" Max said. "I've found not one but two examples of dark magic in your territory. Are you telling me that you don't know what goes on in your territory?"

"This is pointless," Shivangi said, turning her shoulder on Max. "Kill her, and restrain the creature," she told the armed men and women.

The semi-circle of Raghavan soldiers hesitated, their weapons still more-or-less pointed at the creature, and not at Max. She felt an unexpected smile on her own face. She would wager that not one of the soldiers would have paused before obeying an order from Damayanti Raghavan. Hemang and Shivangi might have inherited the Family, but they had yet to win the respect of their people.

"Why are you not firing?" Shivangi asked the nearest soldier, her anger clear.

"She's a Marshal," the soldier said. Interesting. He didn't use any term of respect when addressing his head of Family. Most heads of Family insisted on something like *sir* or *ma'am* or even, in the cast of the Forster Family, *my lady*. It was an almost reflexive courtesy for all Family members, and the lack of it made Max wonder just how bad the divisions in the Family were.

"And she has shadow-hounds with her," another soldier said.

"Not to mention there were warriors of the Order about earlier," yet another said. Max tried not to react to that. She wasn't quite sure where the warriors were, and couldn't rely on them for support in what was now a matter for her to deal with - the Galdr fell squarely into the Marshals' jurisdiction rather than the Order's.

"So, if we kill her, we'll also have to try and kill her hounds before they kill us," the first soldier said.

"And the Order warriors, too, if they are still about," the third soldier agreed.

"Cowards and fools, the lot of you," Shivangi said, and grabbed at the gun held by the nearest soldier. She made an inarticulate sound of fury when the soldier held on to it. "Give me your weapon. Now."

"No," the soldier said. "Damayanti would never have ordered us to kill a Marshal."

"Or restrain a Galdr," the second soldier said.

Shivangi slapped the first soldier across his face, the crack of it ringing loudly in the sudden hush. Max stared in shock, frozen to the spot. The violence had come from nowhere, almost casually delivered by the beautifully dressed woman.

"Never mind, I'll do it myself," Shivangi said, and pulled a small gun from under her luxurious robes. She raised the gun, pointing it in Max's direction.

Cas and Pol surged forward as one, Cas getting there a fraction ahead of his brother, jaw clamping around Shivangi's wrist, his momentum and weight carrying the woman to the ground. She fell with a loud thump and a scream of fear and fury combined. She tried to twist out of Cas' hold, but he didn't let go. He must have tightened his jaw because she dropped the gun, the metal clattering on to the concrete. She shrieked again, reaching into her robes with her free hand and pulling out a long, curving knife. The faint light caught against the blade as she drove it sideways, aiming for Cas.

A single shot rang out, a precisely aimed bullet hissing through the air past Max and into Shivangi's arm at the shoulder, causing her to fall back, dropping the knife with another clatter.

Bryce came forward, his weapon raised and ready to use. He stopped beside Max.

Hemang's face twisted into a snarl and he reached into his robes, too. Before he could produce another weapon, Pol tackled him, body-slamming the man behind his knees so that he fell forward, landing on the ground with as little grace as his sister had.

With both heads of the Family on the ground, and her dogs watching them, Max turned to the soldiers.

"Will you step aside and let the Galdr pass, please?" she asked.

"Marshal," the first soldier said, the term of respect more than he had offered to either of the twins. He turned and gestured to his fellows, and all of them melted back, leaving a gap more than big enough for the creature to go through.

It lowered its head towards Hemang and Shivangi, the twins still lying on the ground, Shivangi whimpering in pain. She glared up at the creature as it blew a breath over them both. Not the healing breath it had used on Max, clearly, but something else. Both twins tried to scramble away, going still almost at once at low growls from Cas and Pol.

Then the Galdr turned to Max, and she thought she saw something like a smile crossing its face before it surged forward, moving as quickly as it had before, heading for the sea that Max could hear and smell but not see. The bulk disappeared into the fog and there was a quiet splash. The Galdr was gone.

Chapter Thirteen

There was an awkward pause, the soldiers all trying to avoid looking at the Raghavan siblings, Shivangi moaning in pain and Hemang glaring at Max as if he would like to kill her with his bare hands.

Now that the creature was gone, Max knew she should call her dogs back. That would risk either or both of the twins trying to kill her again, but she didn't have a right to keep them pinned to the ground any longer.

As she opened her mouth to call her dogs back, a trail of magic slid through the air, carrying with it the stench of rot and decay. Dark magic. It had the same flavour as the magic that had been around the Galdr's neck. Max reached for her gun on instinct. Bullets were unlikely to do much against magic, but she felt better having the weight of the weapon in her hands.

On the ground, Shivangi's moans of pain turned into almost manic laughter. "Did you think the Galdr was our only protector?" she asked. "Now, at least I will have the satisfaction of seeing you die."

The mists behind the twins swirled, something large and slow-moving gradually taking shape. Another creature. A dark figure. This one walking on two legs, with broad shoulders and great, muscled arms that seemed distorted in the fog. Max remembered the vague descriptions that the people in the warehouse had given her. The Galdr had not fit that, but this creature did. It was almost human in shape, and at a distance the details of its appearance were disguised by the ever-present fog.

As the creature came closer, Max recognised its outline and her stomach flipped.

"A Darsin. Seriously?" she asked, voice too high, setting her gun to automatic fire and raising it to point at the newcomer. "What in the dark-blighted world were you thinking?" The old curse slipped out before she had time to think about how appropriate it really was in the circumstances, with the dark magic of the Darsin tainting the air around it.

"He's really quite loyal," Shivangi said, a savage smile on her lips. She might still be pinned to the ground by Cas, but she had recovered her confidence.

"Loyal?" Max repeated, voice still too high. "Cas, Pol, with me," Max said, moving away from the others. The soldiers had just been following orders. They didn't deserve to be caught up in whatever-it-was that the twins were involved in. The Darsin followed her unerringly. As she held her gun in front of her, she realised that she was still glowing from the Galdr's magic.

The Darsin paused, huffing out a breath, as if assessing its foe. Max returned the favour. Even a short distance away, it towered over her, built of muscle and covered in a toughened hide that she didn't think her bullets would penetrate. Its arms were enormous and arrayed with spikes that looked as sharp as knives. It was wearing a simple leather loin cloth. Above the broad shoulders its head looked like a lion, if a lion had dark purple-and-red skin and a mane of tangled black hair. Its lip curled back, revealing gleaming white incisors.

But the most dangerous thing about the creature was not its teeth or its spikes or its great strength. It was one of the most intelligent creatures that humans had ever come across, able to use its natural magic with stealth and cunning.

"I am a Marshal charged with defence of this city," Max said, trying to sound calm. "You and your kind have agreed to leave the city alone. Your presence here is in violation of that agreement." There. That sounded full of authority. Faddei could have done better, and while Max wished the head Marshal was here, she had to work with what she had.

The Darsin looked at her with unblinking eyes for a moment, then its lips peeled back again and a low, dark sound emerged from its throat that Max identified as a laugh.

It said something in reply. The voice that emerged from its thick throat and vast chest was deep and full, the words heavily distorted by its lion mouth. Max was so shocked by the fact it was talking to her that it took a moment for her ears to catch up with the words.

"Stupid human laws. Not my laws," it said. It waved one of its arms. "Go."

For a moment, Max was tempted. Even with Cas and Pol, she was no match for a Darsin. But then she remembered the soldiers, and the warehouse crammed full of desperate people not that far away. She couldn't leave them. She had a fair idea of what the Darsin would do to them if it was left to roam.

"No," she said. "Why are you here?" she asked.

"Bargain," it answered, revealing teeth again in another smile. "Little treats. Big magic."

Max's lips formed the words, trying to make sense of them, and a chill ran over her skin. Little treats. There was a reason that Darsins were banned from the city. They had a horrific diet.

"What did the Raghavans promise you?" she asked, lips stiff. She feared she knew, but she needed it confirmed.

"Human meat," the Darsin said, and gave another dark chuckle. "You tasty."

She heard shocked gasps from the soldiers. Perhaps they hadn't known what the twins were keeping on the docks, or hadn't realised what bargain the twins had made. Darsins could survive on any kind of meat, but they had a distinct preference, and the twins had used that. Human flesh in return for the Darsin's service. Max's mouth was dry, throat tight.

"Not happening," she said, forcing the words out.

"I agree," Bryce said from just behind Max. "You can leave now, and you won't get hurt."

Max glanced aside to find the three warriors lined up, their automatic weapons raised and aimed at the creature.

"Ah. Demon spice in human meat. Delicious," the Darsin said, eyes travelling across the three warriors.

Max wanted to be sick, but it seemed that the Darsin was done talking. It grunted, and came forward. A direct attack. It was so much bigger than she was, it probably didn't think it needed to be subtle.

Max fired. Her bullets bounced off the creature's hide, rattling onto the dockside.

The warriors fired as well, their heavier weapons and bullets striking home.

The Darsin roared, the spikes on its arms lifting, the mane around its head spiralling out. Shadows gathered around it. Magic. Foul magic.

It flung that magic towards them and Max was flung into the air for the second time that day, landing a good distance from where she had been standing, sliding across the rough ground, cracked concrete tearing at her clothes until she slid to a stop. The thump of hitting the ground rattled every bone in her body, forcing the air out of her lungs. She couldn't breathe, mouth open, scrambling to try to get to her feet, knowing there was still danger.

She managed to get to one knee and breath rushed into her lungs, searing pain across her chest. Her leg hurt where the newly-healed wound had been. Ribs hurt again. Hands hurt. No time for that.

She had managed to keep hold of her gun, at least.

As she forced herself up from her knee and to a standing position, she realised she was alone in the fog. No sign of Cas or Pol, any of the warriors, the Raghavan siblings or soldiers. Or the Darsin. And she couldn't hear anything, her ears full of the roar of her own pulse and harsh, laboured breathing.

Not good. She took a step in the direction she thought she had come from, almost falling again as pain shot through her leg. She'd done some damage to the wound there. She set her jaw and forced herself to take another step forward, bracing for the pain. Noise assaulted her too-sensitive ears. Gunfire. Screams. And a low, menacing growl that made her want to turn and run the other way.

Then a pair of low growls that she knew well. Her dogs were there. Somewhere in the fog ahead of her.

She kept going towards the cacophony of noise, and had to duck a moment later as something flew out of the fog towards her. It looked like part of a human body, but was moving too fast for her to be sure.

As she pushed forward, the mist cleared enough for her to see the Raghavan soldiers lined up, firing at the Darsin. The twins were hiding behind their soldiers. So much for the Darsin's loyalty. To one side, the three warriors of the Order were methodically firing at the creature, their bullets having a far greater impact than the soldiers'.

Even as Max watched, the Darsin reached out, grabbed one of the soldiers, lifted him into the air and tore him apart. Max could feel a scream lodged in her own throat, but she didn't have the breath to let it loose.

Somehow, the Darsin sensed she was back. It turned towards her, lips peeling away from jagged teeth that were going to give her more nightmares. Its muzzle and teeth were covered in blood. Its body was marked with bullets, but it was still standing, and still coming towards her.

Max shoved her gun away and put her hands together, trying to pull on her own magic. She'd used magic earlier, with the Galdr, but she had had some time to think and prepare. There was no time now. Her mind went blank. What was the spell for light? What was it again? Something curve something subtract something linear. Hells, she couldn't remember. She just needed some light to counter the Darsin's darkness. The Lady's light. Where was a priest when she needed one?

She found her lips moving in an old prayer, something all children learned, calling on the Lady for the blessing of Her light even as she struggled to draw on her power. Blinding, brilliant light formed between her hands. She stared at it in shock. She hadn't performed any spell or recited any formal words. The magic had just come into being.

The ground shook as the creature charged forward and there was no more time to be shocked. She turned her hands, pushing the magic away from her with her palms.

The light flooded out and slammed into the Darsin, stopping it in its tracks. It swayed where it stood, looking down at its midsection where the light had hit home, confusion clear on its face. Then it sank to its knees with a thump that shook the ground again and slowly fell sideways, its eyes staring ahead at Max.

She fell to her own knees, her strength giving out, and watched in horrified fascination as the life went out of the creature's eyes. It was dead. She was sure it was dead. She hoped it was dead.

Which left her kneeling in the sea mist, not far from a group of terrified soldiers and the furious Raghavan twins. There was blood on the ground. A lot of blood. And more bits of bodies. A shaken, bitten-off sob met her ears and she realised she was crying. She dealt with supernatural creatures day in, day out. But not ones like this. Not ones that walked and talked and used magic and *ate people*.

She pushed her fist against her mouth, trying to stop more sobs or tears. Now was not the time to cry.

"Nice work."

Bryce's voice was right beside her. She looked up, feeling tears on her face, and saw he was holding a hand out, offering to help her up. She took the hand and leant on his strength as she got to her feet. The ground didn't feel quite steady, and her leg didn't want to work properly, but she managed to find her balance and let go of him.

Nice work. She knew he meant it as a sincere compliment, but as she looked at the dead Darsin, she couldn't think it was anything other than awful. And it was the second time she had killed using magic without really knowing what she was doing.

"You killed it, you bitch," Shivangi said, shoving her way through her terrified soldiers. She had found time to tie a scarf around the wound on her shoulder, Max saw. And recover her rage. "You had no right to interfere."

"You made a bargain with a Darsin," Max said, voice flat. "Which is another violation of the city's laws. You promised it human flesh in return for its service." The words were terrible in her mouth, heavy and foul. "If I shot you now, I would be doing the city a favour."

"Favour? You talk of favours," Shivangi hissed. "You close-minded bit of filth. My family has owned this land for generations. This is ours. Ours. You don't get to tell us what to do."

For the first time in her career, Max wished she had a body camera on her. She would have loved to have a recording of Shivangi. This was not the face that the woman would want the world to see.

"The bargain," Bryce said. He was still standing near Max, gun held in front of him. The muzzle might be pointing down, but he could lift it at any time. "Does your bargain have anything to do with the missing people?" he asked.

Max thought she had reached the depths of horror for the day, but it seemed she was wrong. Even though she knew what the Darsin had been promised, and had earlier wondered whether there was a connection between the missing people and dark magic, it had not occurred to her that the Raghavan twins would have let it simply take what it wanted from the homeless population.

"Who's going to miss them?" Hemang's lip had curled into a sneer. He looked far less handsome with that expression, Max noted.

"How many?" Max asked, her face frozen.

"Why do you care?" Hemang asked, still with that disdainful expression.

"Because they are people." Far from being cold, Max found herself burning with rage. "You had no right to use them as bargaining chips. So I'll ask you again. How many?"

"I don't know," Hemang answered, turning his shoulder on her. He didn't care, she knew.

"Where was the Darsin's nest?" she asked him. The creatures were known for dragging bits of their prey back to their nests. There might be answers there.

"This is our territory," Shivangi began.

"I am fed up with you and your attitude," Bryce said in a quiet, dangerous voice.

Max glanced across to find all three warriors with their weapons raised and pointing at the twins.

"You will answer the Marshal's questions, or we will kill you," Joshua added. He meant it, too.

"You have ten seconds," Khari added. "Ten, nine-"

"It's in the old machine shop," Hemang said, jerking his chin to indicate the direction. "You won't be able to miss the smell."

"I suggest you leave right now before we do decide to shoot you," Bryce said, in that same voice.

Shivangi lifted her chin, face set in a stubborn expression.

"Wait. Before you go. Why was the Darsin here? What was it doing for you?" Max asked.

Hemang and Shivangi stared at her with almost identical expressions of disdain. They didn't answer, but turned away. If they had thought to find support from their soldiers, they were disappointed. The soldiers wouldn't look at the Family heads, not moving as the twins walked towards them.

"Actually, I'd like the answers to those questions, too," the nearest soldier said. It was the same man that Shivangi had slapped earlier. Although he had survived the Darsin attack, his uniform was blotched with dark stains and there was spatter across his face. He had just watched at least two of his fellow soldiers killed by the creature that his commanders had brought to the docks and bargained with.

"Me, too," another soldier said, the refrain echoed among the rest of the armed group.

"Get out of my way," Shivangi said, waving her good arm to try to clear a path in front of her. The soldiers didn't move. "You have no right," she said.

"Did you offer up our lives to the Darsin?" the first soldier asked, lifting his head and meeting her glare.

"Just because you were Damayanti's favourite does not give you the right to question us," Hemang said, jaw tight.

Max's ears pricked up at that. She had wondered why a Raghavan soldier was so bold in defying the head of the Family. If he had been a confidant of the now-dead matriarch, that made sense. From the way they were all glaring at each other, it seemed that the three of them had a long history. The argument could go on for hours.

"Look, I don't care about your Family politics," Max said, taking a step forward, careful to brace her injured leg to hold her up. "I just want answers."

"It's not your concern," Shivangi said, and shoved her way through the soldiers. They didn't move out of her way, but they didn't stop her, either. Hemang followed.

The soldiers stayed where they were, weapons lowered.

"What can we do?" the first soldier asked, turning to Max. Beneath the blood spatter, she could see a face similar to Hemang's. They were like enough to be brothers. It was entirely possible that they were related somehow.

"We'll need to have a guard posted on the Darsin's body. It's definitely dead, but I don't want anyone taking souvenirs. Then you can show us the way to the machine shop," Max said. She pulled out her phone. "And I'll need you to escort the Marshals, police department and forensics team to the place as well."

"Marshal," the soldier acknowledged her order with a dip of his chin.

Max dialled the preset number.

"What?" The Marshals' dispatcher, Therese, answered with her usual sharp tone.

"It's Max. There's a dead Darsin on the docks. We need a clean-up crew for that. Then call Audhilde and Detective Passila. We need a forensic team to go through the Darsin's nest to search for human remains, and some of them may be connected to the case that Ruutti is working on. There will be some Raghavan soldiers waiting at the driving entrance to the docks to guide the teams to the body and the nest site," Max said. She paused. Therese normally just hung up, but she had a feeling that this time the dispatcher might have questions.

"A Darsin," Therese said, sounding shaken. "Right. Do you need back-up?"

"No," Max said, and hung up. She looked at the Raghavan soldiers and lifted her brows. "Alright, make sure there are people waiting for the Marshals and the others. I've a feeling they will be here soon."

"Marshal," the first soldier said. He issued orders in a lilting, beautiful language that Max didn't understand. Two of the remaining soldiers took up posts on either side of the Darsin's body. Another four jogged away into the mist, heading in a direction that Max thought was back inland. The remaining soldiers, all four of them, turned and looked at Max for orders.

"The machine shop, please," Max said.

The nest was every bit as awful as Max had feared it would be. She could smell the decay before the door was opened, and left Cas and Pol outside. Their noses were far more sensitive than hers, and they would be more useful keeping watch.

In the shadowed interior she saw parts from at least two different people before she turned away. Just for a moment. She didn't want to deal with any more horror that day, but knew she had to look. Someone needed to make sure there had only been one Darsin, and that all of its victims were dead. So she got out her torch and shone the bright light on the remnants that the Darsin had left.

The soldiers had all taken one look inside the building and turned and run, most of them throwing up in the patch of weeds and dirt that bordered the side of the building.

The warriors hid their feelings behind tight expressions and went through the building with her, making sure there was nothing alive before they went outside into the comparatively fresh air of the fog. They were further along the docks here, and visibility was even worse.

As Max exited the building, walking away from the open door and the stench coming out of it, she saw the first set of flashing lights approaching and heard the low hum of a vehicle. She moved a few more paces away, out of the direct line of the door and the awful smell, and Cas and Pol joined her, pressing their big, warm bodies against her. She scratched them behind their ears, noticing white showing around their eyes. They didn't want to be here any more than she did, and this close to the building their senses would be overwhelmed. She gave them a final pat and waved them further away from the building and its dreadful contents.

As her dogs moved away, the vehicles drew closer, becoming visible in the fog. She was somehow not surprised when the mortuary van and a sleek city car, carrying police lights, pulled to a stop together, Audhilde and Ruutti getting out of their very different vehicles at the same time. Audhilde was already in her overalls, a pair of white-suited technicians coming with her. She paused as she got within a few paces of Max, her nose wrinkling in distaste.

"A Darsin. Really?" Ruutti asked.

"Shivangi and Hemang Raghavan had made a bargain with it. They provided human flesh, and it provided dark magic," Max said, her voice flat.

Even in the poor light, Max could see Ruutti pale. The normally assured detective seemed to shrink where she stood. "The Raghavan twins themselves? Not their underlings?" Ruutti asked.

"Yes. They informed me that Damayanti Raghavan has died, and they are now joint heads of the Family," Max said.

"That's above my pay grade, thankfully," Ruutti said. Which meant she would need to refer it to the chief. Even if she didn't like him, Max didn't envy Evan Yarwood the task of dealing with the Raghavan twins. But, to borrow Ruutti's phrase, that was above her pay grade, too.

"The politics are the least of our concerns," Audhilde said, an edge to her voice. "I can smell decomposition from here. What do we have?" she asked Max.

"It's ugly," Max said. "The Darsin had made its nest in the machine shop, which is that building. There are, er, human parts."

"I've heard about people going missing in this area. You're concerned that the bodies inside may be the missing homeless?" Audhilde asked, eyes narrowing.

"I am," Max said, her throat closing up.

"Did you find the mother and daughter you were looking for?" Ruutti asked.

"Not yet," Max managed to say, then couldn't speak for a moment. She had been trying not to think about Nati and Ynes in the whole awful process of looking through the machine shop. "Do you mind if I stay out here?" she asked them, her voice small, almost as if asking permission.

"Not at all. We will work best uninterrupted," Audhilde said in a matter-of-fact voice. She took a small container out of her pocket and smeared paste under her nose, passing the container to the other two technicians, who did the same. "That means you, too, detective. You will need to see the scene, but then you can leave." Audhilde took the container back, pulled her coverall hood up and fitted a clear plastic visor over her face before heading into the building with her two technicians.

Ruutti followed a few paces behind, looking every bit as reluctant as Max was sure she felt.

Max moved away. The pain in her leg had dulled to a fierce ache. She didn't think she had ripped open the old wound, but the Darsin throwing her had definitely done some damage. There was another building nearby and she went to stand in its shadow, wanting the comfort of something solid at her back. It was only then that she realised Joshua and Khari had moved away from the machine shop as well. They seemed to be talking on their phones. Reporting in, Max assumed. The Order, and Kitris in particular, would want to know about the existence of dark magic and the presence of the Darsin.

Bryce had moved with Max to the other building. He was standing near her, not looking at her directly. Even though she didn't know him that well, she had a strong sense he had something to say.

"What's wrong?" she asked. She felt as if she'd just survived three days without sleep, and had no energy for patience or subtlety.

That surprised him into looking at her, meeting her eyes for a brief second before he looked away again.

"The Darsin recognised that I, that we, are not human," he said, hesitantly.

"Yes," Max agreed, frowning.

He did look at her then, brows lifting. "You knew?"

"Well, yes," Max said, still frowning. "Is it supposed to be a secret?" she asked, wondering if she should have pretended that she hadn't noticed. Some people could be very sensitive about their *other* natures, preferring to keep them hidden.

"No. Well, not exactly," he said. He seemed utterly confused. "But you knew?"

"Yes," Max confirmed again. "What's wrong?" she repeated.

He was staring at her, still looking as if he'd been hit by a truck. "You don't mind?"

"Well, no," she said, confused in turn. "I'm not sure why you think it should make a difference?" she asked.

"You hunt non-human things," he said, a touch of colour on his face.

"I hunt things that are hurting the city's population," Max corrected, an edge to her tone. "I don't just go around killing things for the sake of it. Are you planning to run amok around the city and just randomly shoot people?"

"No," Bryce said, lips twitching.

"Well, then," Max said. She leant back against the wall to ease some of the weight off her leg and winced as one of her bruises woke up. "Where's a Galdr when you need it?" she muttered. The healing it had given her had not survived the Darsin's attack. She was tempted to use another painkilling patch, but she'd used one earlier, and one was all she was supposed to use in a day. Besides, she wasn't sure how her body would react to another patch with different magic after the Galdr's healing.

"I've got brandy," Bryce offered, pulling a flask out of a pocket.

"Order brandy?" Max asked, staring at the offered flask. She had only tasted it once or twice, and the memory lingered.

"It's the best," Bryce said.

"Yes, it is," she agreed, taking the flask. The liquid slid down her throat, warm and honeyed, the taste filling her senses. She thanked Bryce and handed the flask back, tempted to have more, but that one drink was plenty. It might not affect him or the warriors as much, given their partly non-human natures, but she could feel her whole body relaxing.

"Here," he said, holding something else out. A protein bar. She looked at it as if it was a grenade primed to go off.

"You're being nice to me," she commented, taking the protein bar. She noticed he had one for himself, too, and that Khari and Joshua had finished their phone calls and were likewise taking in some food.

"Not really. It's been a rough day. We've got a lull at the moment, but the day's not over yet," he said.

"No," Max agreed. She knew it wasn't rational, but she didn't want to leave until Audhilde had examined the remains in the building. And she wanted to see if she could find Nati and Ynes. Which reminded her of the stories the homeless had told. "You remember the people in the warehouse telling us about a dark figure? I'm thinking that was the Darsin," she said.

"That makes sense," Bryce said easily.

"At least partly," Max said, scowling into the growing dark. "We'll need to see how many bodies are in there."

"At least eight people missing from the warehouse," Bryce commented.

"They might not all be here," Max said. She emphatically did not want to find that there was another Darsin on the docks, or other supernatural guardians that the Raghavan twins had forced or bribed into helping them, but she knew she couldn't rule it out. "Someone needs to search the whole area and see what other surprises the Raghavan twins have set out."

He'd already thought of that, she saw. Which might be why he and the other warriors were still here. That sort of thing was what the Order was supposed to do, not the Marshals' service. Unless they found any more supernatural creatures, of course. Max scrubbed her hands across her face. It was going to be a long, long night.

Khari and Joshua came across before Max could ask any more questions.

"There's an Order mage and more warriors on their way here," Khari said, addressing both Bryce and Max. Max's brows lifted, wondering why the warrior was telling her this. "They want to look at the dark magic."

"Finally," Bryce said, with a dark edge to his tone. He glanced at Max, brows lowered. "They weren't interested before."

"Well, news of a Galdr held by dark magic, and a Darsin loose on the docks got their attention," Khari said cheerfully. "Kitris is taking a team to speak to the Raghavan twins. He wants to know if they've made any other deals. He'll join us here after that," Khari said.

"We've been ordered to give the mage our support," Joshua said, addressing Bryce, somehow making it clear that Bryce was also included in that instruction.

"We haven't finished clearing the docks," Bryce said.

"The mage is aware," Khari confirmed. Her lips twitched. "Apparently he thinks it could be fun."

Max shook her head slightly. She wasn't sure who the Order was sending, as she couldn't remember anyone who would be described as a mage rather than a Guardian, but it sounded like they had a death wish.

Then her ears and her brain caught up and she realised that meant that there would soon be another team of Order warriors, and a mage, who she may or may not know on the docks. Followed, at some point, by Kitris himself.

She was moving away from the wall, and the warriors, before she knew what she was doing, the urge to get away so strong.

"Where are you going?" Joshua asked. "The mage will probably want to speak to you."

"I have things to do," Max said, voice tight. She saw Ruutti emerging from the building, the detective looking unsteady on her feet, and headed for her. Dealing with the aftermath of the Darsin's bargain was an awful prospect, but didn't carry the same emotional weight as dealing with yet more members of the Order.

Chapter Fourteen

Ruutti was standing a short distance from the machine workshop, her hands braced on her knees, breathing heavily, when Max joined her.

The detective glanced up, saw Max, and resumed her breathing. She had what looked like some of Audhilde's paste smeared under her nose. Something to combat the stench, Max guessed, although it didn't seem to be working well, if Ruutti's pallor was anything to go by.

"Audhilde says it's going to take her days to sort out the remains," Ruutti said, still looking at the ground. Her voice was tight. "But her best estimate at the moment is there's at most four sets of remains."

"Four," Max repeated, a chill running over her. "And you've had, what, eight missing person reports?"

"Eight identified. Ten in total. So far, yes," Ruutti said, straightening. "So we still have some people unaccounted for. Is it possible the creature had another nest somewhere on the docks?"

"I don't know," Max said honestly. "From what I know of Darsin, it's unlikely. It may be worth asking the Raghavan soldiers. They should be familiar with the area."

"Do you think they knew what was inside?" Ruutti asked.

"No," Max said at once. "I don't think they knew the bargain that the twins made."

"That's something, I suppose," Ruutti said. She hesitated, glancing sideways at Max as if she had bad news and wasn't quite sure how to deliver it.

"You'd rather I stayed out of your way?" Max asked, caught by an unexpected urge to laugh. She did laugh when Ruutti's brows lifted, surprise clear. "I want to go back to the warehouse and let the people there know what's been happening," Max said. "And I still haven't found the people I was looking for."

Ruutti stared at her, a frown gathering. "You're really just going to walk away?" she asked.

Max paused, turning Ruutti's words over in her mind. "There's nothing more I can do here. The Order is sending a magician along with more warriors to look at the dark magic, and probably search the docks. Audhilde is at work with the bodies. You and your people are going to start asking questions. The head of the Order is speaking to the Raghavan twins. There's really nothing more for me to do," Max finished, trying to shove the guilt aside. It really wasn't her job, and the people now involved should be more than capable of dealing with the aftermath of the Darsin's activities.

Ruutti was still frowning. "The head of the Order? You mean Kitris? He's here?"

"I don't know. I was told that he's going to see the twins and make sure there are no more bargains in place," Max said.

"And you don't want to stick around and see him?" Ruutti asked, head tilting. "He almost never leaves the Order's premises."

"No," Max said, answering the direct question. "I have other things to do. I'd appreciate it if you would let me know if you find the mother and daughter, though."

"Likewise," Ruutti answered, frowning again.

Max turned and left before the detective could ask more questions. Ruutti was sharp and smart, and Max didn't want to be under her scrutiny any longer than she had to be. Besides, as she had told the detective, there was nothing more she could do. Not for the dead people that Audhilde was looking at. But she could speak to the living, and see if she could bring some peace to Alonso and Elicia.

It was late into the night when Max finally emerged from the warehouse again, out into the fresh air and darkness. There were no external lights on the buildings at the docks and the moonlight reflecting off the ever-present fog barely gave a faint, diffuse glow. Once she had waited for a few moments to let her eyes adjust, she could pick out her route without needing a torch. She headed back through the empty warehouse, noticing that the red eye of the camera was still active, and kept going towards the parking lot where she had left her car, her whole body aching with bruises and tiredness. None of the people in the occupied warehouse would admit to having seen Nati or Ynes, although everyone she had spoken to seemed more than willing to try to help. When they said they hadn't seen the mother and daughter, she had believed them.

She was light-headed with the close confines and smells of the warehouse, and lack of food. The protein bar Bryce had given her had been many hours before. Her leg was sore, too, and she was walking with short, halting strides. She hadn't been able to examine the wound and see what damage had been done, and wasn't looking forward to that experience. For a brief moment, she was tempted to find her way back to the machine shop and see what progress Audhilde and her team were making. A twinge through her leg and the ache from bruises across her body stopped the impulse before it could fully form and she kept heading for her pick-up. Besides, she reminded herself that it wasn't her case. And if Audhilde had news, Max trusted that she would call.

She had given a summary of events to the people in the warehouse. The grey-haired woman she had spoken to earlier had come to meet her and listened in silence while Max spoke, then thanked her for the information. There were a few questions, which Max had answered as best she could. And then there had been nothing more for her to do there. The greatest threat to the people in the warehouse was gone, with the Darsin's death, and there was nothing Max could do to undo the damage that had already been done.

Cas and Pol fell into step on either side of her as they left the shadows of the empty warehouse, heading across the open space that led to the parking lot. As she left the shadow of the building, she saw a group of people clustered near several large, dark vehicles, of the sort commonly used by the Order. Max checked in her stride. She emphatically did not want to speak to anyone from the Order.

Not now, not ever. She changed course to avoid them, heading for the fence that bordered the docks and would eventually lead to the parking lot and her pick-up.

She had been spotted, though. She saw a few faces turn towards her. She ignored them and kept walking, her dogs on either side.

Soft, rapid footsteps drew her attention. Bryce had left the group of people and was on his way to meet her. She stopped. She had been seen, and she was quite sure that the warrior could outrun her if need be. It was easier to stop and see what he wanted. Cas and Pol's ears lifted, eyes on the running man approaching them.

"Kitris wants to see you," Bryce said, not even a little bit out of breath as he stopped a few paces away from her.

"No," Max said. It was a visceral response, dredged up from the soles of her feet, ringing through her. Seeing him would just put a cap on the horrible day. She had nothing to say to the head of the Order. And didn't want to hear any words he might have for her, either. He had said quite enough eight years before. "He can refer any enquiries to Faddei."

"He's over there," Bryce said, lowering his voice as if worried Kitris might hear Max's sharp words.

Max's eyes strayed past Bryce to the group of people gathered near the vehicles. They were mostly warriors, from what she could tell at this distance, but she recognised the reddish-brown hair of the head of the Order on one, and the dark robes of a Guardian on another. Not just Kitris, but one of the Guardians, too? *No* was too mild a response. She wanted to run away. She stayed where she was. Running would make her look weak, and that was the last thing she wanted where Kitris was concerned.

"I don't work for him," Max said, words tight.

"He wants to see you," Bryce said again, face grim. He didn't move, but seemed to loom in front of her and she became aware of the weapons he carried, and the fact that he was far stronger and better trained than she would ever be.

Max glared at him, and heard a low, dark sound from one of her dogs. She wasn't worried, more annoyed. There was no way that even Bryce, with all his skills, could get her across the open space if she didn't want to go. Not with two shadow hounds on her side.

"Why?" she asked.

"I don't know," Bryce said. She believed him. Kitris probably hadn't told him. The warrior hesitated, then said: "He was annoyed to find the dark magic traps in place."

"You mean he was annoyed to find the dark magic that you had told him was there?" Max asked, a sarcastic edge to her voice.

Bryce's lips twitched. "Yes," he answered.

"That's nothing to do with me," Max said, voice a snap.

"I know," Bryce said. He was still standing in front of her, waiting. No longer looming. Perhaps she had imagined it.

"I'm tired and sore," Max said, hearing the whine in her voice and not able to do anything about it. It was the truth. "It's been a long and grim day. I'm heading to my pick-up. If he wants to speak to me, he can find me there," she added, and turned on her heel, stalking away. It was petty of her. And it would annoy Kitris almost beyond bearing that an underling had dared to disobey his wishes, but she didn't care about that. What she did care about was the stash of snacks she had in her pick-up glove compartment. She needed something to settle her stomach before she dealt with the head of the Order.

It wasn't far to her pick-up. It was sitting on its own in an otherwise deserted parking lot and was still in one piece, which was a relief.

By the time she had given the dogs some food from the locker in the back of the pick-up, and swallowed half a chocolate bar in one giant bite, she heard more footsteps. This far from the docks, the fog had lifted. There were no street lights here, and the bit of moonlight that had lit up the fog before was now hidden behind dark clouds overhead. She turned the vehicle's side-lights on, so she could see a little better, the harsh white-toned beams highlighting the group of people approaching her. There were warriors, most of whom she recognised, including Bryce, Khari, Joshua, and a pair of unarmed men in the middle. The two unarmed men didn't need weapons to be dangerous, though. She knew both of them well.

The taller man with the reddish-brown hair, pale skin and sneer was Kitris. He was dressed in his usual head-to-toe black, not a single emblem or symbol about him to signify that he was one of the most powerful men in the city. To anyone who was magic-blind, he looked disappointingly ordinary. To anyone with magic sensitivity, he carried a wealth of power with him. Max was tired enough that Kitris' aura grated against her senses. The shorter man, in the dark robes of a Guardian, had close-cropped black hair liberally sprinkled with grey and a tight, disapproving expression. Orshiasa. The Guardian who had taken her on as an apprentice. The only one willing to do so, according to Kitris.

Kitris waved a hand at the warriors, commanding them to stay where they were, and he and Orshiasa kept walking forward. The warriors obeyed without question, standing still. A couple of them were carrying their weapons ready, muzzles pointed to the ground. Not aimed at her. Not yet, anyway.

The chocolate bar was not settling well in her stomach. She left the other half on the passenger seat, wiped a hand across her mouth to make sure it was clean, and then took a step away from the vehicle, waiting for the two men to come closer.

"Your manners have not improved and you still lack respect," Kitris said in a voice that could cut diamonds. Annoyed that she hadn't obeyed his wishes without question, she guessed. The harsh glare of the side lights showed her that he had not changed in the eight years since she had last seen him. He seemed to be entirely human and yet he'd been head of the Order for at least a hundred years. He looked like he could be anywhere between thirty and forty, and carried himself with a certain self-assurance that had always made her wary.

"I don't work for you," Max answered. The comment about respect hit home, but she would not let him see that. She might not ever have liked him, but she had respected him until he had sent her to her death and then dismissed her for daring to survive.

"Obviously," Kitris said, the sneer more pronounced. "I only allow competent people in the Order."

It should not have stung. Not after such a long time. Not when she had actually completed the task he set for her. And not after the grim discoveries of the day. But his words opened up old wounds, internal scars that she thought had healed over long ago. The trails left by his open, bitter disappointment in her poor performance and her lack of skill when it came to using magic.

At least, using magic the way he had insisted it be used, she realised. She could almost feel the weight of Audhilde's books in her hands. She hadn't got far in her reading, but the little she had managed to take in had planted knowledge that there were other ways of using power in her mind. She had already known that Kitris wasn't perfect. She hadn't realised that his close-minded arrogance had extended to the use of magic as well.

She had faced a Darsin earlier in the day. Had reached in desperation for light and had brought forth more power than she had ever managed before. She might not know how, but the knowledge that she had done it made her stiffen her spine and stare back at Kitris. He was trying to look down his nose at her, despite being shorter than she was. It gave him a pinched expression and highlighted fine lines at the corners of his eyes.

"What do you want?" she asked. She had tried, over the years, to never let him see how much his disdain had hurt her. Kitris would see that as a weakness. And he did not respect weakness.

"I did not believe it was true," Orshiasa said, surprising her. He had yellow-toned sallow skin, but he looked as if he had paled in the poor light. He stared at her, pale eyes glittering. "You failed in the most egregious way. And yet you are still alive. Have you no honour?"

Max's insides were trying to turn themselves into knots. There had been a time when she would have done nearly anything to earn Orshiasa's approval. He had been a hard task-master, perpetually disappointed in her efforts no matter how hard she tried to learn the lessons he taught. He was one of the oldest, most powerful and most respected of the Guardians and she had been reminded, almost every day, what an honour it was that he had accepted her as his apprentice. The reminders hadn't come from the man himself, but from the other apprentices, their teachers and instructors and Kitris. Even though the Guardian was barely as tall as her shoulder, she had always felt small and unworthy next to Orshiasa, the familiar feeling creeping over her even now. She forced herself to stand square and tall in front of the pair of them. She remembered Orshiasa's lessons about honour. Failure was the worst possible outcome. According to his personal code, when she had failed in the mission that Kitris had sent her on, she should have ended her own life.

She lifted her chin, staring back at him, words and memories crowding her mind. If she had truly failed, she would have been dead long before she would have had any chance to fulfil Orshiasa's code of honour. She had not failed. She had completed the task that Kitris had set for her. Instead, it was Kitris who had no honour. He had dismissed her and, it seemed, lied about what she had done. And even though old hurt and anger were a sharp spike in her chest, there was no point in telling Orshiasa the truth. He would not believe her.

"What do you want?" she asked Kitris again.

"You have nothing to say to your former master?" Kitris asked, voice tight.

Max glared back at him, more words crowding her mind. She had too much to say. But if she started talking, she might never stop, and it wouldn't do any good. They both believed they were right. They always had. "You told me he had set me aside, when you dismissed me from the Order," she told Kitris, voice tight. "There's nothing more to say. Now, for the final time, what do you want?"

His pale blue eyes lit with fury and power, and ice crawled over her skin. Kitris might spend his time strutting around and giving orders, but he was a powerful magician in his own right, and not above using his power on other people. She lifted her chin again, staring back at him. She would not run. She would not cower. He had wanted to speak to her, not the other way around. And she didn't believe that even Kitris just wanted to spend time insulting her. He had a purpose to this awkward reunion.

"I want to know who set the dark magic traps on the docks," he said, jaw tight.

"I don't know," Max said, startled. She had been one of the least competent magicians the Order had ever seen, at least according to both Kitris and Orshiasa. She couldn't imagine why either of them would want her opinion on the dark magic, which had been created with considerable skill. "I assumed they were the work of the Darsin."

Kitris stared at her with a displeased expression. She was very familiar with that look, and his disappointment. "You assumed," he repeated, a sharp edge to his words.

"The Darsin said it had made a bargain with the Raghavan twins. Magic in return for meat," Max said, trying not to think about what that had meant.

Kitris continued to stare at her.

"And you killed the Darsin?" Orshiasa asked. His clear and absolute disbelief might have been funny on a less awful day.

Max stared back at him and pressed her lips together. He wasn't her apprentice master any longer. She didn't owe him any answers or any explanations. And even with the little bits of knowledge gained from Audhilde's books, she would be hard-pressed to explain what had happened in any event. She could remember her near-panic as she tried to form the light spell in her mind, and then the surge of power that had flowed through her and into the Darsin. It had not been the magic of the Guardians, or the way she had been taught. But it had been effective.

"Was that it?" Max asked Kitris. "You wanted to know what I knew about the dark magic? I have told you what I know."

"That's all for now," Kitris said, still wearing that displeased expression. "But I may have more questions."

"Any questions you have can be referred to the Marshals' office, which handles all external enquiries," Max said, holding his pale blue eyes. It seemed that eight years had made a difference, after all. She had never been able to face him like that before. Or perhaps it was the weight of all the memories she carried. The task she knew she had accomplished, even when he told her she was a liar. She had been broken and wounded when she had seen him last, and had accepted his dismissal. That had been eight years ago. She wasn't sure she would be quite so meek now.

She turned, ignoring the indrawn breaths from both men as she walked away from them, around her pick-up to the driver's door, waving Cas and Pol into the back. She settled into the driver's seat, turned on the engine and backed away from the still, silent group.

It was only when she was driving into the city that she realised she hadn't put the headlights on and her hands were shaking. Her whole body was trembling, in fact. She had faced down both Kitris and Orshiasa. Both of them. She had held her ground and not backed down. It had cost her almost all the energy she had. And she suspected she now had a new nightmare to add to all the others. The disapproving, disappointed stares of Kitris and Orshiasa, with an audience of silent, staring warriors of the Order.

Chapter Fifteen

The first thing she had done when she had got home was to peel off her damaged trousers and check her aching leg. It was bruised and swollen around the old wounds, but she couldn't see anything more sinister. Ordinary painkillers and ice-packs had helped reduce the ache enough for her to sleep. At least for a short time. Fresh nightmares dragged her back into the waking world more than once. Giant figures coiled with dark magic and speaking in Orshiasa's voice. *Have you no honour?*

Heavy-eyed and still sore, she made her way to the Marshals' offices the next morning. Faddei would want to know about the Darsin and the Galdr, and the twins' bargain.

On her way, she had to skirt around a group of angry-looking people gathered at a petrol station. They had placed their cars around the site so that no one could get in, and had also managed to trap a few vehicles inside. Max saw the usual hand-made signs demanding an end to fuel restriction, and another one of the *Take Back the Wild* signs. The protesters were loud, and from what she could see, were simply shouting with no threats of violence. Not yet, anyway. There were more than enough police there to deal with the protesters, but she couldn't help wonder how many other demonstrations were taking place across the city. The news on the radio was that the city council was having to consider reducing the rations for citizens in order to keep essential services running. The radio host commented that the mood in the city was getting angrier, and suggesting that people avoid the city centre if possible.

The almost-visible anger and the shouts echoing in the air reminded Max of the escalation that had happened five years before, just before the council had been forced to send an expedition out into the Wild to gather more fuel.

Some of the more far-sighted members of the council had suggested trying to establish a permanent relay to the oil field. It had seemed to gain some favour, until the council realised just how many resources would be needed to carve a road through the Wild and keep it protected. Another proposal to try to establish a pipeline from the city to the oil field in the Wild had encountered the same issues, only more acute as the council and the city would need to fund and resource protection for the entire length of the pipe and the access roads that would be required.

Max made a mental note to fill up her pick-up at the Marshals' site. As one of the arms of law enforcement, they had their own supply of fuel, and would get priority while the rationing continued. But the council's rationing couldn't magically increase the fuel stocks. The council was going to need to find a way to break the stale-mate, and soon.

So she was in a glum mood when she turned into the Marshals' site. The space around the Marshals' buildings had a lot more vehicles than she was used to seeing. Cas and Pol bounded away, weaving between the battered pick-ups and vans on their way to find Leonda. It looked to Max as if most of the Marshals were on site, and not out around the city. It happened from time to time, so she didn't think too much of it until she went into the main office and found a group of other Marshals huddled around one of the desks, watching something on a large monitor. Her stomach sank, wondering if the video clip of her holding a gun to an unarmed man was still doing the rounds.

A few faces turned towards her as she came in, with expressions she couldn't read. They didn't seem disgusted, though, which was a positive sign.

"Hey, Max, there you are. Wow, a Darsin?" Vanko said, waving her over. "Old Raymund is beside himself with excitement." Vanko's eyes were gleaming with mischief, as normal. He was a medium-height human male corded with muscle, similar in build to Faddei to the point where Max had wondered if they were related. Except that Vanko had an abundance of tousled, blond-streaked brown hair and a smile that hid a quick mind.

Max went across to the group and saw that what they were viewing was not the viral video clip, but rather images from one of the Marshals' examination rooms. There were two rooms equipped with extendible examination tables and scientific instruments to allow the Marshals' science team to carry out their own versions of the autopsies that Audhilde carried out in the city mortuary. The rooms had video surveillance to make sure nothing was missed.

This particular examination room held a familiar, charred body. The Darsin. There were a few people moving around the room, including the tall, slender figure of the Marshals' chief scientist, Raymund Robart. The time stamp at the corner of the screen told Max it was a live feed. The scientists were wearing coveralls and face shields as a precaution, and over the monitor Max could hear a lot of quiet, rapid conversation.

"I've never seen one in real life before," one of the other Marshals said. He looked up at Max. "Is it true that they can speak?"

"Yes. And use magic," Max said, her voice and throat tight. "It was terrifying," she said honestly. It felt strange admitting it out loud, but if there were any people in the world who would understand just how disturbing that had been, it was the Marshals around her.

"Is it true that it had a nest and had been eating people?" Zoya asked, looking at Max. The question was quiet, serious. Max could feel the interest of the other Marshals. They might not have seen a Darsin before, but these were the sorts of creatures that the Marshal service had been formed to deal with.

"Yes," Max said, and her throat closed up. She had to swallow before she could go on. "Audhilde and her team were examining the remains. Last I heard, they think there were at most four people." She left unsaid that the body count could change. No one around her needed that spelled out to them.

She looked at the screen. Even dead and charred, the Darsin was an impressive creature. And she didn't want to look at it anymore. She turned away and headed for her shelf, her movements stiff and awkward, pretending to be interested in whatever messages might have been left for her.

There was one paper slip on her shelf. A request to see Faddei as soon as she got in. He had anticipated her visit, it seemed, otherwise he would just have called.

When she turned back from the shelf, the monitor was off and the rest of the Marshals were gathering their belongings, heading out for their assigned patrols in pairs. Marshals always worked in pairs. All of them. Except Max. When she had joined the Marshals' service, still feeling broken, it had been one of the promises she had extracted from Faddei. She didn't want the responsibility of looking after a partner. He had frowned, but he had honoured her request. She and her dogs worked alone.

As the other Marshals passed her, she got hands on her shoulder, pats on her arm, and quiet, heartfelt words. *Well done. Good job. Stay safe.*

By the time the room was empty, her eyes were stinging. The support and understanding was something she had never experienced before coming to the Marshals' service. But they had all faced things that would give most people nightmares, and did it day after day. She might work alone, for reasons of her own, but she was one of them. They had accepted her, without caring who she was or where she had come from. It was enough that she wore the badge and did the job. The warmth of it enveloped her. Before she had joined the Marshals' service, she hadn't realised that it was possible to feel so connected to near-strangers.

Before she could give in to the tears that were gathering, she heard footsteps. She headed for the coffee, and was unsurprised to see Faddei coming into the room when she turned, mug in hand.

"Are you alright?" Faddei asked, with apparently genuine concern.

Max's brows lifted and she paused with the coffee halfway to her mouth. She lowered the mug, frowning. "Yes. Or, rather, mostly. I've bruised my leg again, and it's a bit sore," she said. The bruising had been deepening to vivid colours when she had woken up that morning. "And I've got some other bruises, but otherwise I'm fine."

That answer didn't seem to satisfy her boss, but he didn't say anything, getting his own coffee and waving her across to the comfortable chairs. She took her drink and joined him, wondering what was bothering him. As far as she knew, she hadn't done anything wrong. Well, apart from pulling a gun on an unarmed man. But Faddei already knew about that.

He settled with his own coffee and took a sip before setting it aside and looking at her. "A Galdr and a Darsin. That's a big day for anyone. And you weren't even supposed to be on duty," he said, lifting a brow at her. She couldn't read his expression.

Max's fingers tightened around her mug, apprehension creeping over her, realising she had perhaps done something else wrong. She hadn't officially been on duty. But she had been wearing her badge, and using her Marshal's authority. She wondered if she was about to be suspended again.

"Tell me what happened," Faddei said.

Max put her coffee to one side and told him, starting with meeting Alonso. She kept the story as brief as possible, and Faddei just listened, not asking any questions until she was done.

"Did you find Nati and Ynes?" he asked, when she had run out of words.

"No," she said, throat tight again. She picked up her coffee, finding it tepid. "I gave Alonso an update this morning." That had not been a pleasant conversation, made worse by Alonso's gratitude for her efforts so far. She hadn't brought him or Elicia any peace, and was running out of ideas of what to do next. "I'm not sure where else to look," she said. She couldn't bring herself to say that she needed to wait for Audhilde's examinations to be completed to learn if Nati or Ynes or both were among the dead in the Darsin's nest. She hadn't told Alonso about that particular, terrible, possibility. He and Elicia were worried enough.

"I had a call from Kitris," Faddei said.

"Oh?" Max said, looking at the surface of her coffee in an attempt to hide her expression. Standing in front of him and Orshiasa the night before had probably not been a wise move. She seemed to be making a lot of bad choices lately.

"He said that you disturbed an Order operation," Faddei said. There was an undertone to his words that caught Max's attention. He wasn't annoyed with her, that much she could tell. But something had annoyed him.

"Not true," Max said flatly. "From what Bryce told me, Kitris himself had refused to investigate the possible dark magic on the docks. I thought that the three warriors were there on their own time."

"There seems to have been a lot of that going about yesterday," Faddei said, lips twitching. He seemed more amused than anything else, Max realised. That was something, at least. He sobered. "I thought as much. I reminded Kitris that supernatural creatures are our jurisdiction, so you had as much right to be there as the Order did."

"Thank you," Max said, not trying to hide her relief. It didn't seem as though she was going to be suspended again, at least. Faddei saw it as a core part of his job to stand up for and support his Marshals, but she never took it for granted. After all, she had been apprenticed to Orshiasa for several years and he had turned away from her.

"Kitris was not happy that you referred all questions to me," Faddei said, the quirk of his mouth turning into a full grin. "I reminded him that as the head of the Marshals' service, that is the proper process. I told him not to contact you directly."

Max was glad she didn't have any coffee in her mouth as her jaw dropped open in surprise. "I'm sure that went well," she said, voice faint, trying to imagine Kitris' reaction. Not only had she openly defied the head of the Order in their encounter the night before, but the head of the Marshals' service hadn't cooperated with him, either. Kitris would at least respect the authority of Faddei's position.

Faddei's grin grew broader. "Not in the least," he said cheerfully. "But he couldn't really argue. After all, the Order didn't actually do its damned job and look into the reports of dark magic."

Max hid a smile. It was true, but of course Kitris wouldn't see it like that. "Do you know what the Raghavan twins had to say?" she asked.

"Well, that's a good question. Having a Darsin on their docks, and making a bargain with it breaks at least a dozen city laws." Max nodded in acknowledgement. The Marshals might be called in to deal with the creatures and contain them, and the Order should deal with any dark magic, but the enforcement of the laws and any prosecution would be handled by the city's police. She didn't envy them the task. Faddei sounded grim as he went on. "Lots of people want answers. Apparently they can't be found. None of their people know where they are, either. It's causing a bit of a stir," Faddei said. His grin had faded, but his eyes were still bright. He had borne the full fury of the city council more than once, and it must be refreshing to have their anger directed to someone else.

"Really?" Max asked, surprised. She sat a little straighter, thinking over her encounter with the twins. The family's power was concentrated in the docks, and doubtless they had hiding places there to use if they needed. But from the way Faddei had spoken, it sounded as if they were genuinely missing rather than hiding. "Shivangi was injured. Did they seek medical treatment?"

"No. I spoke to Evan Yarwood earlier. He was summoned to the scene." Max remembered the chief of detectives' foul mood the last time she had seen him.

Getting called to the Raghavan territory was hardly likely to have pleased him. Faddei was frowning, relaying the information he had been given. "There were some signs that they'd been into their residence and treated Shivangi's wounds - bloodied bandages and such - but no sign of the twins themselves. All their possessions were still there, as far as the police could tell. It's a mystery," Faddei said. "I haven't been to the council yet, but I can only imagine the speculation that's running wild. I don't suppose you've got them stashed away somewhere?"

Max laughed. "No. I would be glad to never see them again." Then she tilted her head. "The chief of detectives was called to the docks? Is he taking over the investigation from Ruutti?"

"I don't know," Faddei said. "I doubt it, though."

"He didn't seem happy to see me at the police station the other day," Max said.

"Politics," Faddei said, nose wrinkling in distaste.

"I could not do your job," Max said, shaking her head.

"Oh, you could. You'd just need to take Cas and Pol everywhere with you. They could stare everyone down," her boss answered, grinning.

"If you ever need to borrow them, just let me know," Max offered.

"I'll keep that in mind," Faddei said. He finished his coffee. "There's a council meeting today and the word is that they are going to order a convoy into the Wild to collect more fuel to restock the city reserves."

"I've been noticing more protests," Max commented, wrinkling her nose. "Apparently the people really, really like their cars."

Faddei gave a short laugh. "That is true. Someone actually set their car on fire outside the council building yesterday to prove just how much they needed their car for transport," he said, a sharp, sarcastic edge to his voice.

"Were you on the last convoy? What was it, five years ago?" Max asked. She had been a relatively new Marshal then and hadn't been involved with the convoy itself. Along with the other few Marshals who had been left in the city, she had spent the week rushing from one creature sighting to another, all of them trying to do the job of three or four people.

With the expansion of the Wild, the city had been cut off from a lot of natural resources, including the oil field that had provided fuel for the city. But the machinery was still there, surrounded by the Wild. A strong enough convoy should be able to break through the Wild and get more supplies to keep the city moving. It was an obvious solution to the current fuel shortages. If they couldn't reach the oil field, the city's reserves would run out sooner rather than later. And then the sleek city cars would all be abandoned, unable to move anywhere. The city's law enforcement - from the police to the Marshals - had some extra reserves but it wouldn't be long before they, too, were forced to abandon their vehicles and look for alternative means of transport, or alternative fuel sources. The effects would be devastating from the mundane effects of people being unable to get to work to medical teams unable to reach people in need. And the Marshals wouldn't be able to get to emergencies. A lot of people around the city would die. So although Max didn't have much sympathy for the city dwellers who just wanted to drive their cars, she did care about the people who needed the police or paramedics or Marshals to turn up and help them.

"Yes." Faddei's face was grim. "I can't see an alternative. We were almost overrun more than once last time, so we're going to need to take a lot more fire-power with us. That means almost all the Marshals and a lot of law enforcement being co-opted for the convoy. We'll need you, Cas and Pol. As soon as the convoy is confirmed, I'll let you know. Leonda and Raymund are preparing extra ammunition and other supplies for us." He hesitated, then gave her a direct look. "I want you to go and get checked over today. Get that leg looked at before we head into the Wild."

Max wrinkled her nose, wanting to disagree, but knowing he was right. The Wild was no place for anyone carrying an injury. There were no magical barriers to hide behind to stop and rest. "Alright," she said reluctantly.

"Let me know what the doctor says," he told her.

Max nodded, getting up as Faddei rose. He was as serious as he had ever been. Going into the Wild was not something to be undertaken lightly. But a lot of the city infrastructure, such as electricity and its water supply, depended on oil fuel to keep running, or as emergency back-up in case the newer power sources failed. If they couldn't get to the oil field and replenish the supplies, the lack of petrol for their vehicles was going to be the least of the citizens' worries.

Chapter Sixteen

The journey had been quiet so far, which was making Max's skin itch. The jungle around them seemed to be empty of large predators, and she didn't trust that. Not one bit. The last convoy that had gone into the Wild, several years before, had ended up losing two tankers and half a dozen people.

Max braced herself against another jolt and bounce of the truck's cabin, trying not to wince as a stab of pain travelled up her leg. The medical team had spent what felt like an eternity the day before running tests she had no name for then poking and prodding the bruises on her leg, stirring up enough pain to bring tears to her eyes, before declaring that she didn't seem to have opened up the wound or done any further damage beyond the bruising. She had been cleared for light duties, with evident reluctance, the senior doctor insisting that he would talk to Faddei directly.

Max wasn't sure what the doctor had said to the head Marshal, but Faddei had called her in the afternoon, letting her know that she was included in the convoy going to the Wild, but only because they wanted Cas and Pol. She hadn't managed to speak to Faddei face to face, so just had his slightly terse tone on the phone call to go by and the knowledge that if the convoy hadn't needed the shadow-hounds, she would have been left behind. It was something of a miracle that the injury hadn't been worse, she knew. That didn't help with the pain, though, as the vehicle bumped over another rough patch of ground.

She bit back a curse. She hated the thought that she might be the weak link in the team, making the others vulnerable. She'd added self-cooling ice packs and conventional painkillers to her bag when she had been packing the evening before, as well as collecting extra painkilling patches from the Marshals' armoury when she had stopped in for her ammunition and other supplies. Leonda had been personally supervising the roll-out of the ammunition, her usual warm smile looking a little worn, dark patches under her eyes. She and her team must have been working through the night to get everything ready.

Max hoped that Leonda and her team were getting some well-deserved rest now, even as she braced herself against another bump of the truck. There was a sliver of pale blue sky ahead of them, but otherwise they were surrounded by different shades of green, yellows and reds from the varied and vibrant plant life that inhabited the Wild. Giant trees rose impossibly high to either side, their dark reddish-brown trunks barely visible through the smaller trees and shrubs competing for daylight and space. With every breath, Max drew in the mixed scents of the plants around them, a heady mix of sharp, acid-edged tones and softer, juicier smells that suggested there was ripe fruit somewhere not far away.

"Man, if this is a decent path, I'd hate to be on a rough one," the driver said, breaking into Max's glum thoughts. He wrestled with the wheel as the truck tried to spin away from the path ahead of them. It was a crude cut through the green of the Wild, little wider than the truck itself, and Max did not envy him the task of keeping them moving forward across the uneven surface and chopped-down plants.

Max grunted an agreement, keeping her eyes on the area around them.

They were one of the middle vehicles in a ten-truck convoy of tankers making their way through the Wild, heading for the nearest oil field. All of the trucks were hauling giant, empty tanks with their drivers, and everyone else in the group, under strict instructions from the city council not to come back to the city until all the tanks were completely full.

As the truck jolted again, Max thought sourly that she would have more respect for the council's order if even one of the council members had volunteered to come along with the group to see the situation for themselves. But the council was more concerned with the unrest they could see around them in the city streets rather than the distant, unseen dangers of the Wild.

So all the members of the council were safely back in the city, guarded by the magical barrier holding back the Wild and the less magical but still potent protection of the remaining Marshals and other law enforcement officers around the city.

A branch slapped against the truck's windscreen, temporarily blocking out forward vision. A muffled cry came from behind Max and the driver, reminding her of the passengers. The passengers had been spread through the convoy and were an odd mix. Most of them were wiry-looking workers making up the crew who would be responsible for making any repairs and then getting the oil drills working again after several years of being dormant. The rest were scientists who had wanted the chance to study the Wild up close, and perhaps gather more samples. There were plants in the Wild with incredible healing properties, apparently. Or so one of the scientists sitting behind Max had told her at great length when they had started this journey. Without looking back, Max knew that it had been one of the two scientists who had cried out, startled by the branch.

She kept her eyes on the outside, still. That was what she was here for. To keep watch. Protect the trucks and the people.

The convoy was following an old road that had led to the oil field when it had first been constructed, a few decades before. The road had been built to city standards, wide and smooth and robust enough to take the heavy industrial traffic that was needed. The Wild had made a mockery of the effort that had gone into the construction of the road, smothering it completely. The oil field, like a lot of the city's industry, had been abandoned ten years before when the Wild had surged forward, reclaiming a lot of the land that the city had occupied. Most of the oil crew had been on the last convoy and remembered the road being fairly overgrown, but passable. It seemed almost unbelievable that the dense tangle of undergrowth that the convoy was making its way through could have sprung up in only a few years, but the Wild was saturated with magic and that tended to have odd effects on both animals and plant life.

The magic outside the vehicle hummed against Max's skin, threading into the air around them. Anyone with magic sensitivity would be able to feel it. It was distracting, meaning that she had to concentrate harder than normal on what was around them to ensure she didn't miss any threats.

And she was lucky. Thanks to her aggravated leg injury, she had a seat in one of the trucks rather than riding on a cabin roof. Each of the trucks had a pair of powerful guns mounted on the roofs, manned by Marshals, specialists from the city's police department and warriors from the Order. It was an odd mix of different folk, and Max was delighted that she was not in charge of co-ordinating them all. That honour fell to Faddei. He was in the lead truck, staying in radio contact with the rest of the convoy. As Max's view forward was restricted to the Wild and the rear end of the truck in front of them, it was reassuring to hear Faddei's calm, measured voice on the radio from time to time, checking in on everyone. The rounded end of the tanker in front of them was their guidepost along the road, something tangible and real to follow.

Ahead of Faddei was a ferocious-looking vehicle that Vanko had nick-named the Chomper. It was an old, heavy-duty tractor fitted out with whirring blades in front that were cutting a path through the undergrowth wide enough for the rest of the convoy to pass. There was evidence of the Chomper's work all around, not just in the cut-up vegetation the trucks were driving over, but in the severed branches clinging on to the lower limbs of trees to either side and the sharp smell that was something like cut grass only much stronger and untamed.

There was a pair of Marshals settled on the Chomper, too, along with more heavy guns. This was the Wild, after all. Many of the things that lived here thought of humans as food and as little as the Marshals might like to kill creatures, they would defend themselves and the others if necessary. And after the losses on the previous convoy, no one was taking any chances.

The council spokesman who had briefed the team in the pre-dawn gathering had told them that the council would not accept any losses this time, a statement which had made Max want to put the entire council onto the roof of the Chomper and have them lead the charge into the jungle. From the expressions on the faces of other Marshals, she thought they may have had the same idea.

It probably hadn't occurred to the council members in their city suits that none of the Marshals, at least, were here because of the council's order or because the city dwellers were furious that they couldn't drive their cars as much as they wanted. No, the Marshals were here because the city needed the fuel. Even with strict rationing, and the advances being made in alternative fuel-sources, a lot of critical infrastructure still needed old-fashioned oil for power and the city's reserves were dwindling. The Marshals wanted the radio towers to keep working, to allow easy communication, to keep the power stations working so that the lights stayed on and the taps kept running with fresh water, among other things.

Max wasn't sure how many council members were aware of just how fragile the city's infrastructure was. Their primary concern seemed to have been the protests and the possibility of them being voted out at the next election. They wanted to look good to the population and let them fill their cars for pointless journeys. None of the council members were ready to face the hard truth that they needed to find a way of not relying on oil.

Right now, though, oil was needed. And for some outlying homes, like Max's own house, heating oil was also required. She remembered struggling to get the tank filled last winter, when there hadn't been any shortages. This year was going to be worse. She had used some of her recovery time to phone around various contractors. No one wanted to come to her house, so close to the Wild, even if they had fuel to sell her. She'd been forced to rely on her back-up electric generator for hot showers for the past few days, but that wasn't a long-term solution, and didn't help heat the house. Winter was on its way.

Another bounce focused her on the here-and-now. The truck slid sideways, the driver cursing as he wrestled it back onto the track.

"It'll be easier coming back," he said. "The weight will help." He was an older human man, and from his mannerisms Max could tell he knew what he was doing. He might be barely as tall as her shoulder, but he was made of lean muscle and intense focus, similar to many of other drivers. No one wanted inexperienced or easily frightened drivers for this convoy. The one less-experienced driver, a woman about Max's age who looked like she would single-handedly take on anything that came at her, was in the vehicle behind Max's, and all the other drivers had been keeping a check on her without trying to make it too obvious that was what they were doing.

As the truck bounced back onto the path, Max hoped he was right and the return journey would be smoother. Not only was the constant jolting aggravating her wound, but the unsteady movement was making her feel queasy.

A large shadow moving in the trees near her made her sit up, lifting the shotgun and grabbing the radio handset from the console.

"This is truck five. I've got movement in the trees to the left. Anyone else see that?" she asked. It was an open line, meaning everyone could hear her and she could hear everyone else.

"This is Vanko on truck six. I see it too. Can't tell what it is yet." Vanko and Zoya were manning the guns on the roof of the truck behind Max.

"Truck seven. We see something. No idea what it is either," an unfamiliar voice came in. Probably one of the law enforcement personnel on that truck.

"On the right," came over the radio. The voice was high-pitched, and Max didn't recognise it.

"This is truck seven," the unfamiliar voice said again, calm and firm. "Simmons, get a grip. Where on the right?"

"Sorry. Truck four," the high-pitched voice said.

Max glanced to her right, and saw another shadow moving. Through the trees, she couldn't make out what it was, only that it was big, and keeping pace with the trucks. She checked that the bag of spare ammunition was still in place, hung from the vehicle dashboard in front of her, its mouth open to allow her easy access to reload.

"What the heck is that?" came another stranger's voice over the radio.

"This is truck one." Faddei's voice was clear and firm. "No chatter. Business only."

Max could hear the tension in his voice, and knew he would be frustrated that the threat, if it was a threat, was behind him where he couldn't do anything about it.

She shifted in her seat, her leg protesting as she tried to put her weight on it to give her a better position to brace for firing the shotgun. She muttered a curse, lost in the noise of the vehicle engines.

The whatever-it-was in the trees on the left side was closer now. She had a fleeting impression of a humanoid shape with broad, malformed shoulders and long, ragged hair, its head far higher than the roof of the tankers. She cursed again, more loudly, and grabbed the radio again.

"Truck five. The thing on the left looks like a full-grown Behemoth," she said. Despite Faddei's reminder to stick to business, she heard curses over the radio.

"Truck one here. Any update on the thing on the right?" Faddei asked.

"Truck four. No. There's still a shadow. Can't tell what it is." The high-pitched voice was fractionally calmer, then lost composure completely as it added: "A Behemoth, really?"

"Truck six here. Behemoth on the left confirmed. Another Behemoth on the right. Sighting confirmed," Vanko's voice was steady, a much-needed dose of calm for the non-Marshals. Max would bet that the other Marshals were, like her, mentally reviewing everything they knew about Behemoths and possibly also wondering just how many tranquilliser rounds would be needed to take down such a large creature.

"This is Bryce on truck ten. Reminder: do not fire unless they attack." The voice cut through more curses, speaking with the same authority as Faddei. The senior member of the Order's warriors, Bryce was right at the back of the convoy. Despite the gossip and speculation Max had overheard when they had all been setting up that morning, she didn't think the separation of Faddei and Bryce was because they wanted to be as far apart as possible. Rather, it was because they each recognised the other as a leader of their people and it made logical sense to have the front and back of the convoy manned by experienced people.

There were more mutterings through the radios, too indistinct for Max to catch, but no one fired.

Her palms were damp on the shotgun's grip as she held it ready, straining her eyes to the left and then the right, trying to keep track of the Behemoths. She had never seen them before, only heard rumours and sat through more than one of Raymund's lectures on the creatures. The Marshals' lead researcher on supernatural creatures had a vast wealth of knowledge and enthusiasm for his subject that often led to him getting carried away. Very few people interrupted, though. The information that Raymund Robart gave them had saved lives more than once.

Max briefly closed her eyes, trying to recall Raymund's lecture on Behemoths. It had been quite some time ago. Even as she tried to remember their behaviour patterns and weak spots, another voice cut across the radio.

"Truck nine. We have something else on our right." The voice was terse. One of the human law enforcement agents. They were more accustomed to dealing with violent humans than supernatural predators, but they were also the best trained of anyone outside the Order warriors and Marshals.

"Truck ten. I see it. Looks like another Behemoth," Bryce's voice cut through more rounds of curses.

From behind Max, in the cabin of the truck, she heard a quiet whimper. One of the scientists, she thought. Probably regretting their decision to join this convoy, however excited they had been to get into the Wild and explore.

There was no time to reassure them, and no reassurance that she could honestly give. One Behemoth would be difficult enough to deal with, but it seemed as if they had three. A family group? Max frowned as she tried to remember what Raymund had said. Something about nests and territory and young. She made another grab for the radio, almost losing hold of her shotgun.

"Truck five to truck one," she said, "have you seen a nesting site ahead of us?"

"Truck one. Nothing so far. Why?" Faddei asked.

"Truck five here. Didn't Raymund say something about Behemoths having transient nesting sites and defending them? I'm wondering if we've strayed into their new territory," Max said. She heard some muttered agreement over the open radio, other Marshals confirming what she had remembered.

"Truck one. All stop. I repeat. All stop," Faddei said. "Dog handlers out of the trucks, everyone else stay put and keep watch. And no firing unless we're attacked."

Dog handlers included her. Cas and Pol had been disgusted at the idea of riding in the truck's cabin. They were somewhere on the roof, having managed to scramble up the ladders put there for the humans, no doubt having a grand old time with the fresh scents and sights of the Wild around them. As the truck drew to a halt, Max gathered her ammunition bag, slinging it across her body. She picked up the portable radio unit and clipped it to her belt, then turned to the driver.

"There are still two people with heavy guns on the roof," she reminded him. "Keep the windows and doors shut until I get back."

"Yes, ma'am," he said, nose wrinkling as he looked across her into the forest. There were enormous shadows in the trees on either side of them. More than three, Max thought.

She got out of the truck, grateful for the iron steps to help her manage the distance to the ground, and looked up at the cabin roof. Cas and Pol were leaning over, looking at her, eyes bright, tongues out, looking for all the world like overgrown lap dogs rather than the superb predators they were.

"Come on, we're needed," she said, settling the radio earpiece in place. Her dogs slid down the side of the truck, ignoring the steps. She could only hope they didn't scrape the paintwork too badly on their way down. Once on the forest floor, they bounced in place. Happy to be off the truck, and happy at the prospect of working. They were absolutely silent, though, eyes travelling to either side and the great shadows in the giant trees around them.

"Dog handlers, comms check." Faddei's voice sounded in her ear. Far clearer and louder than over the radio.

"Max here," she responded.

"Aurora here." Max would know that deep, warm voice anywhere. Aurora and her partner Ben had helped Max train Cas and Pol, and had a pack of shadow-hounds of their own. Despite the circumstances, it had been a welcome surprise to see both of them earlier.

"Ben here." Ben's voice was lighter than his wife's, but still full of warmth.

"Sirius here." The one that Max didn't know as well. Aurora and Ben had brought him along. The small, slender, dark-skinned man had been quiet, but his hounds were devoted to him, and that was usually a good sign in Max's experience.

"All present, good," Faddei said. "Can everyone move to the front of the convoy and keep an eye out for nesting activity?"

"I've got more shadows in the forest around me," Max said, beginning to walk forward. Cas and Pol came with her. As far as she could tell, the Behemoth shadows stayed where they were.

"Me too," Aurora's voice confirmed.

"Ay, here too," Ben's voice followed.

Faddei spat a curse that had Max raising her eyebrows, and drew a spurt of laughter out of the others.

"Your grandmother did what, old man?" Aurora asked, still chuckling.

"Never you mind," Faddei said, laughter clear in his voice. "Positions, please."

"I'm just past truck two," Aurora answered.

"Right behind you," Ben said.

"Just at truck three," Sirius said.

"Just passing truck four," Max said, glancing up at the cabin high above her as she made her way around the vehicle. There was a big black number 4 on the cabin's side, and there would be one on the top of the tanker, too, in case anyone needed to try to find them by air.

She saw a pale face peering down from the top of the cabin, a tight expression suggesting that the gunner was holding his nerve, but only just. That must be Simmons. She remembered him from the briefing that had been held before dawn that morning. A heavily muscled human man somewhere in his early forties, he had been confident and sure of himself. All his confidence seemed to have gone. She didn't blame him. The Wild had a habit of affecting even the bravest and best-trained fighters. So she gave him a brief nod, one warrior to another, and got a terse nod in response, but saw his shoulders relax a fraction. She wondered who else was on the roof with him, and hoped they would keep each other calm.

"Which side of the convoy are you on, Max?" Faddei asked.

"Left side," she answered. "Do you want me to move?"

"No. I can see Ben and Sirius on the right. Any movement from our guests?"

"Nothing," Max confirmed. "They stopped when we did."

"That's something, at least," Faddei grunted.

Max silently agreed, and sent up a prayer to the Lady that the Behemoths would stay quiet and still and out of the way, and that the convoy wasn't heading straight for a new nest. Based on the briefing they had been given, and the rough map she had been trying to follow, she thought they were still a good hour's journey from the oil field. And that assumed that they could follow the old road. If they had to divert around a Behemoth nest and hack a new path through the Wild it could take them another day to get there, which would mean travelling overnight through the Wild. Even though she was sure that some of the law enforcement team would have night-vision lenses, trying to move at night would make them far more vulnerable to the supernatural predators that tended to hunt at night and were perfectly adapted to their environment, unlike the ungainly trucks and their passengers.

Her vision shifted, another perspective overlaying hers, the world going black-and-white, then shades of red for a moment, one area to her left lighting up like a beacon. She muttered a curse, stumbling as she tried to keep her balance.

"What's up, Max?" Faddei asked.

"Sorry. I tripped," she said through stiff lips, heat scorching her face. She hated to admit a weakness. They needed her dogs, not her. If it hadn't been for Cas and Pol, she would still be back at the Marshals' offices and not out here.

Faddei said nothing, which was almost worse than if he had tried to reassure her or even criticise her for being clumsy. He was missing the lower part of one leg and fingers from one hand, and he was still managing to move through the forest, she reminded herself, biting her lip to hold in a sigh.

The Behemoth to her left shifted position slightly. She stopped, Cas and Pol halting with her. Through the trees and the dense undergrowth, the enormous creature seemed to be looking straight at her. And behind the Behemoth, further into the forest, she could sense something. Not another Behemoth, as she couldn't sense them with anything but her eyes, but a tangle of magic and life.

"Faddei, I'm just at the back of truck three. There's something off in the forest to the left here. Behind the Behemoth. There's magic there," she said.

"Can you get a closer look?" Faddei asked.

"I'll need to break out of the line," she said, and waited, mouth dry, heart rate picking up. That was not in the plan. They were all supposed to stay in visual contact with at least part of the convoy.

"Go ahead," he told her. "Aurora, can you go ahead of the convoy a bit, make sure we're not about to run into anything?"

"Sure can," Aurora said.

"Leaving the convoy now," Max said. She took a deep, steadying breath, made sure her dogs were with her, and then took a step off the path the trucks had made and into the Wild.

Chapter Seventeen

Between one step and the next, the world changed. The background hum of the truck's engines, the creak of the vehicles as they settled into place, all vanished and she was swallowed by a silence so profound it roared in her ears. She glanced down, finding Cas and Pol close by, their ears laid back, bodies tucked in closer to the ground. Something had upset her hounds.

The magic she had sensed was a beacon pulling her forward, through head-height bushes with leaves that stuck to her clothing as she ducked under the lowest branches of a young tree, the sapling long and spindly, reaching for the limited light. She moved around the huge expanse of trunk of an ancient tree, its canopy somewhere far, far overhead.

Now that she was out of the noisy metal truck, and off the path that the Chomper and trucks had ripped through the jungle, there should have been life moving around her. The Wild was full of living things, from the plants to the great Behemoths standing close by. It was never quiet. There should be rustling of creatures in the undergrowth, the chatter of primates nearby, branches shifting, wings flapping, leaves stirring in the slight breeze. And her footsteps and her passage through the jungle should also be making a sound. But there was nothing. Just the roaring quiet in her mind.

With nothing for her ears to follow, she had to rely on sight and scent and the feel of the air against her face and hands. There was a dark, earthy smell from something large and warm nearby. Probably the Behemoths. For all their size, they were reputed to be peaceful creatures and almost exclusively vegetarian. Like the Galdr she had encountered at the docks, they had a reputation for being gentle, but could be ferocious when provoked, or when defending their territory.

Her vision lit up in shades of red again between one step and the next. She stopped, shaking her head, trying to clear her sight. She remembered Audhilde's theory that she was coming into her magic, whatever that meant. But the displacement was still worrying. Max had almost asked for a medical assessment the day before, held back by the new information Audhilde had given her. And the knowledge that if she admitted to another medical problem, Faddei would have practically chained her to a desk until it was thoroughly investigated. So she didn't want to seek medical help. Not yet. The little bit of information that Audhilde had given her and that she had managed to read suggested the medical profession might not be able to help. She set her jaw as the red shades swirled, regretting her decision to stay quiet, fear making her breath quicken. What if something happened while she was in one of her episodes? It wasn't just her life at risk out here. Her dogs, and the convoy she had left, were depending on her.

Her sight returned to normal, the pull of the magic stronger and closer. It had moved towards her. That didn't seem like a good thing.

The earthy scent had also grown stronger. She looked over her shoulder and saw that one of the Behemoths was standing next to the great tree she had just skirted around. The giant creature was looking down at her, watching her. From her perspective, so close to it, it seemed nearly as tall as a three-storey building, clad in long, ragged fur in varying shades of brown, allowing it to blend in with the shadows under the trees. Its hands, hanging by its sides, were bigger than she was, three fingers and a thumb with curving claws at each end. She noticed that one hand hung lower than the other, thanks to the creature's misshapen shoulders. It was standing slightly hunched over, as if not used to being upright. And although she had not heard or sensed it moving towards her, now that it was close by she could sense the quiet, earth-toned magic it carried. Nothing survived the Wild for long without having some magic.

Max's breath caught in her throat, instinctive fear holding her still. The thing was huge. And it had followed her without her knowing. But the creature did nothing. Just stared. And as her pulse slowed a fraction, Max realised that the creature was not staring at her with anger or hate, which she might have expected. Instead, it looked like it was in pain. She had the impression that its gaze was pleading with her to do something, although she had no idea what. Something like guilt shot through her, even though she wasn't sure what she had done or what she was supposed to do. But to see so enormous a creature in such obvious pain drew an answering response from her. She could not help wondering why the Behemoths had sought out the convoy, and whether the rest of the group was also in pain.

The beacon of magic she had been moving towards pulsed, as if demanding her attention. The Behemoth twitched in response, as if it, too, could feel the other magic. Max tensed, waiting for the giant to move.

When the creature did nothing apart from stand and breathe, she turned away. She couldn't do anything for the afflicted creature just now. And there was a potential threat somewhere in the jungle. Not far away. She needed to deal with that. And then perhaps she could see what could be done for the Behemoth.

She pushed through another tangled bush, getting more leaves over her jacket, and stopped.

There was a small clearing ahead of her. It didn't seem natural. Every other part of the ground in the Wild was covered with living or dead plant life. This was a patch of bare earth, soft light catching motes of dust or magic in the air.

In the midst of the clearing was a figure in the grey robes of one of the Lady's priests, hood drawn up over his head. He was standing with his back to her, apparently watching something on the other side of the clearing.

Max raised her shotgun and took a careful step forward. Her toe nudged the bare earth and she heard the creak of the leather of her jacket, the harsh sound of her breathing, and low growls from both Cas and Pol as they focused on the figure in front of them. Her dogs had more or less ignored the Behemoth she had just encountered, but were completely focused on the stranger ahead of her.

"I'm a Marshal and I'm armed. Turn around slowly, please," Max said. Her voice was odd, flattened by whatever magic was in the air around them. It had an almost-familiar flavour, now she was close to it, even if she couldn't place it just now. She stayed where she was. The stranger might actually be a priest, in which case she should be polite, even if she could not imagine what a priest was doing out here in the middle of the Wild and surrounded by magic. The Lady might be present in all things, but all of Her Houses were in the city, not out here.

"Dearest Miscellandreax," a familiar voice said. The figure turned and pushed back its cowled hood, revealing the too-tanned face of Queran. He looked like a human man somewhere past his middle age, with dark hair going grey at his temples. His eyes gave him away. They were full of smoke and hints of darkness and pain, showing his true nature. A demon. One who had taunted her through her childhood, then reappeared a couple of weeks ago, leaving her a dark magic shadow-hound to contend with.

No wonder the magic had seemed familiar. Dark magic spun by a demon.

Max's finger tightened on the trigger, but she didn't pull. Not yet. The demon was here in the Wild for a reason. Now that she was closer to him, she could sense the power rolling around him. He was far more powerful than she was. He had jumped off a building and landed on the ground several storeys below without any apparent injury. The tranquilliser cartridges in her shotgun were unlikely to have any effect.

"You look tired, my dear," he said, sympathy thick and sugar-sweet in the air. "Bad dreams, my child?" he had given her plenty of those as a child, introducing her to the concept of monsters long before she had met any in real life.

"What do you want?" she demanded, stowing the shotgun in a loop on her trousers and drawing her handgun instead, making sure it was set to automatic fire. At least her smaller weapon was loaded with bullets designed to kill, not incapacitate. It might not do any good, either, but she felt more comfortable with it in her hands, aimed at the demon.

"Such hostility. Dear, dear me." The demon lifted a hand, inspecting his fingernails with close attention. "You are a long way from your home."

"So are you," Max answered, trying not to think about the demon's home, which was the hell-scape of the underworld.

"That is very true. Very true indeed. At least here - what do you call it, the Wild? Yes. At least here, in the Wild, there's a chance of a decent fight," Queran said, baring teeth that should have been human but which looked wrong to Max's eyes.

"Is that why you are here? To fight?" Max asked, not really expecting a straight answer. Dealing with demons did not fall in the Marshals' jurisdiction. Demons were creatures of dark magic. Any demon sightings should be reported to the Order, and they were supposed to deal with the unwanted visitor above ground.

She had not got to that part of her training before the Order - no, Kitris - had sent her to face the Grey Gates.

"In a way," Queran said, surprising her with an almost-direct response.

Max fractionally lowered her gun, mind working through the sudden appearance and strange behaviour of the Behemoths and Queran's arrival. Max did not believe in coincidences. She could not believe that the Behemoths were working with the demon. A hazy memory from a long-ago lesson suggested that the Behemoths' ancestors had been one of the Lady's first creations. "Why are you wearing the Lady's robes?"

"The Lady's? Really? They are mine, you know," he said, turning in a circle as if to show off his outfit, hands spread out. "And so very comfortable. I think that robes would suit you."

"No, thank you," Max said, her voice a definite snap. A lot of children from the orphanages grew up to be priests or priestesses or otherwise serve in the Lady's Houses. It made sense, as the temples and their grounds became home and the people there a family of sorts for many of the unwanted children that the priesthood took in. Not Max. Put there by parents who hadn't wanted to raise her themselves, she had never felt at home. Unwanted, still, even in a place where all should be welcome. "You're here for a reason. What is it?" she demanded.

Queran looked at her long enough that she had to grit her teeth against the dissonance of his presence. His shape was human, down to the dark hair greying at his temples, and the too-tanned skin. But he was definitely not human. Everything about him was wrong, from the way he moved to the magic grating against her senses. "Something has happened," he said at length, still focused on her. "You've changed."

Max's throat closed up and her finger tightened on the trigger. She forced herself to relax, to try not to openly react. There was no possible way that he could know about the changes in her, changes that she did not understand. "And you haven't changed one bit," she said. "You are still not answering my question."

"As if you have a right to answers," he said, sneering. "I am far older and more powerful than your limited imagination could ever conceive."

"And yet you are here. Stuck in this world," Max said. It was a guess, as she didn't think he had any way of getting back to the underworld with the Grey

Gates closed, but it seemed she had been right. His face tightened, a hint of something *other* crossing his face.

"I serve at His will," Queran said. It sounded like a rote saying, but one that carried more than a hint of honesty. "Though I do long to see His face again." That last bit had sounded like the bare, unadorned truth.

"A servant of Arkus dressed as a servant of the Lady? Thinking of changing sides?" she challenged him. Part of her was terrified. This was a demon, the air saturated with his presence. Another part of her - which seemed to be in charge of her mouth - was furious. He had caused her so much misery when she had been a child. She had hoped to never see him again, and yet here he was, evading her questions.

Queran rounded on her, all pretence of humanity stripped away, eyes glowing red, the bones of his skull standing out in his face. "You will not speak His name," Queran roared, the sound louder than the silence before. He lunged towards her, hands outstretched, fingers turning to claws.

Max fired. Half a magazine's worth of bullets tore into the grey robes, which spun under the force of the attack, cloth shredded and falling slowly to the ground.

Ground which was all of a sudden covered like the rest of the forest, rather than the bare earth that Queran had been standing on.

Max cursed, turning in a circle, her hounds moving with her, searching the forest around her. She could still see the towering shadow of the Behemoth, but couldn't feel the magic any longer. Queran seemed to have gone, leaving nothing but the bullet-torn robe behind. And she still wasn't sure why he had been there in the first place.

Movement in the undergrowth made her turn again, weapon raised, Cas and Pol on alert to either side.

A black-clad man shoved his way through the final thicket of bushes before the small clearing Max was in. She couldn't help noticing that the leaves didn't seem to be sticking to him. He stopped when he saw her, frowning as if he didn't recognise her, and then looked past her, and looked shocked.

"You shot a priest?" he demanded.

Max was tempted to fire on him. So tempted. This day was just getting worse and worse. Of all the people to turn up in the middle of the Wild. Radrean. A fellow apprentice in the Order when she had been there. A friend, and more than a friend. Or so she had thought. Only to learn it had all been a lie. All tricks and deceit.

Seeing him again after the better part of a decade made something in her chest crack. At first glance, he looked almost the same as she remembered. A little shorter than she was, with paler skin, dark eyes and dark hair that he was wearing slicked back from his face. She had thought him handsome once. Before he had turned on her. Old hurt and old humiliation broke through an inner scar and bled into her heart. He had tormented her, when he had realised she was no longer fooled by his charm. Sent her into Bryce's unarmed combat class, as one of his milder tricks. And his reward for his torment was to be elevated to the status of Guardian, while her reward for her unquestioning loyalty and service to Kitris and the Order had been dismissal.

She lowered her gun with an effort. It wouldn't be wise to shoot at a Guardian. Besides, the demon might come back and she would need all her bullets for him. The demon was a much bigger threat than Radrean ever would be.

"It was a demon wearing a priest's robe," Max said, voice flat. At least all the hurt she was feeling was contained inside, none of it showing on the surface.

"Don't be ridiculous," Radrean said. She remembered another magician of the Order saying that to her not that long ago. That one had been Alexey, one of Radrean's apprentices. Now that she had seen the original, she could see that Alexey had perfectly copied his master's tone. "How could you possibly recognise a demon?"

Max lifted her chin. The contempt in his voice was almost visible, even though he didn't seem to recognise her. Perhaps he spoke to all Marshals like that. Or perhaps it was just women.

Before she had time to answer, more movement in the undergrowth alerted her to another arrival. Bryce. Naturally. The senior warrior of the Order had left his post with the convoy. Not for her. She had no illusion about that. He was here to keep watch over the Guardian.

"You really shouldn't stray from the convoy," Bryce said to Radrean. He frowned slightly at the bullet-ridden robes. "There was a priest here?"

"A demon wearing a priest's robes," Max said, even though the question hadn't been addressed to her. She lowered her gun still further, down to her side. Bryce would not like having a raised weapon in close proximity to a Guardian. The Order's warriors were charged with the protection of Guardians, and took that obligation very seriously. "Does Faddei know that there's a Guardian in the convoy?" she asked Bryce. The briefing that morning had included Marshals, warriors of the Order, members of law enforcement, the oil field crews, drivers, dog handlers and scientists. She did not remember any mention of a Guardian, or indeed any other magician, and she was sure that she wasn't the only one who had noted that absence. Although most of the Marshals could work some limited magic, having a more powerful magician along would have been helpful. She wasn't sure if the lack of it meant that the council hadn't asked for it, or hadn't been able to persuade any of the city's magicians to go with the convoy.

Even if his presence on the convoy had not been official, Radrean hadn't been at the meeting. Despite having been barely half-awake and without enough coffee, Max was absolutely sure she would have spotted her former bully.

The warrior's face tightened, giving her all the answer she needed.

"You need to tell him," Max said to Bryce. She would have liked an explanation for why Radrean was here, but couldn't bring herself to face him to ask the question.

"You will say nothing," Radrean snapped, glancing over his shoulder at Bryce. Max's brows lifted as she saw the expression on Radrean's face. It seemed his contempt was more universal than she had imagined. "And you will keep silent, too," he added, turning to Max.

"You don't get to give me orders," Max told him and turned away, heading for the robes. Queran had pulled an impressive vanishing act, but it was possible he'd left something behind. She picked up the fabric, finding it warm to the touch, the warmth sliding over her skin, making her want to drop the robe and burn it. As she lifted it from the ground, a trail of dark spice floated past her nose along with a hint of magic. A heavy, glittering object fell out of the robe onto the ground and she holstered her gun, bending to pick it up. A crystal the size of her palm, it was almost too hot to hold in her hand, a trail of red winding through its depths, reminding her of the colour that Queran's eyes had turned. The crystal was full of the demon's magic. She frowned, wondering why he had left it behind when he vanished. And then wondered if he had truly vanished, or if he was somewhere close by, unseen.

The crystal heated in her hand until it was too uncomfortable to hold. It was mounted as a pendant on the end of a long, glittering silver chain, so she held the chain instead. The ornament reminded her of the smaller crystals that a lot of human magicians wore. Outside the Order, some magicians used crystals as focal points. Max's teachers had scornfully dismissed the idea, but she had seen enough magicians wearing them to know that was not a universal opinion.

"Why was the demon here?" Bryce asked. He wasn't looking at her, his attention on the jungle around them.

"He didn't say. In fact, he made a point of not saying," Max answered, also looking around, trying to extend her senses to see if she could find Queran's trail. He had evaded all her questions, but there had to be a reason he was here, in the Wild. And a reason he had been carrying a crystal saturated with his magic.

"There was no demon," Radrean said, sounding scornful. "The idiot woman shot at a priest's robes. Probably scared of her own shadow."

Max's fist closed around the fabric in her hand and she made herself take a breath before she spoke, holding on to her temper.

"Why did you leave the convoy?" she asked Radrean, forcing herself to look at him. When she had known him, he had liked his comforts. Shoving his way through a jungle wasn't something he would generally choose to do. Assuming he hadn't changed that much.

"That's none of your concern," he told her, turning his shoulder to her and glaring at Bryce. "You. Take me back to the convoy."

Bryce didn't move, frowning down at Radrean. "Not yet. Answer the Marshal's question. Why did you leave the convoy?"

"I thought I sensed dark magic in this direction," Radrean answered, impatience clear. "But it's gone now."

"Really?" Max asked, startled. Both by the fact that Radrean had actually left the safety of the convoy to follow a trail of dark magic, and also that he was now unable to sense the dark magic. She had always assumed that he was a more powerful and capable magician than she was. She held up the chain with the crystal dangling from it. "You don't sense this?" she asked. Queran's magic seeped out from the object.

"No," Radrean said with a snap, barely looking at the crystal. "A lot of priests wear crystals. They capture the Lady's light. It's not dark magic."

Max opened her mouth to disagree, then thought better of it. The only crystals she had ever seen in or around the Lady's temples had captured bright white light, not the angry red in this crystal. He could hardly have missed the different colour, but there was no point in arguing with him.

"I think the demon might have done something to the Behemoths," Max said, addressing Bryce. "I felt the same magic when I walked past one of them."

"That's the stupidest idea I've ever heard," Radrean said.

Bryce ignored the Guardian and turned his frown on Max. "Why?"

"There's something wrong with them. The one I walked past looked like it was in pain. And they aren't behaving normally. Do you know if the dogs found anything ahead of us on the trail?" Max asked.

"No," Bryce said slowly, turning his gaze to the nearby Behemoth, just visible through the trees. "The others are doing exactly the same thing. Just standing still."

"We need to get back," Max said, gesturing for her dogs to move out. "Find Faddei," she told them.

Cas and Pol moved ahead and Max started after them.

She was halted after only a pace by Radrean's hand on her arm, his grip tighter than necessary.

"I didn't say you could leave," he told her.

She stared at him, seeing the fine lines around his mouth, no doubt from the sour expression he usually wore. With the closer study, she could see that the years had not been kind to him. His hair was a uniform colour, suggesting he was using dye to maintain the sleek, black shade.

"I don't answer to you," she told him, twisting out of his grip and striding away. Cas and Pol had stopped, waiting for her.

"I didn't say you could leave," he repeated.

She felt magic gathering behind her and paused, looking over her shoulder. He was staring at her, hints of red in his eyes. Before she could say anything more, Bryce stepped between them. The warrior had his automatic weapon pointing at the ground, but still seemed to tower over Radrean.

"The Marshal has a job to do. Let's get back to the convoy," the warrior said.

Max tucked the priest's robe under one arm, keeping hold of the crystal, and drew her gun in her free hand before she headed out, trusting her dogs to find the way. As she moved, the nape of her neck prickled at having Radrean and his ill temper behind her. She almost stumbled as she realised that she wasn't worried about Bryce. Just the Guardian.

She couldn't worry about him now. She had to get back to the convoy and warn the others about Queran and his meddling.

Chapter Eighteen

Cas and Pol led her around an enormous tree. She thought it was one she had passed before, but couldn't be sure. She was completely lost, far more used to being in the city, where even the sprawling suburbs and industrial areas had roads and there were usually street signs she could follow. Out here in the Wild she could not see much beyond Cas and Pol in front of her, her view to all sides blocked by plant life from the bushes she was pushing through to the great trees she was walking around. And every now and then she caught sight of a head-height, thick spike of a plant with what looked like delicate pink petals at the top. Carnivorous plants that had been known to attack humans before now. She gave them as wide a berth as possible. She just wished she had been able to do the same for Queran. Even though the demon was not visible, she caught a trace of his magic now and then, and suspected he might be close by. She didn't know enough about demons to know if he needed a physical form to have an impact on the world, or if he could just exist as thought and still wield his magic.

Just past the tree, the great shape of one of the Behemoths rose high over her head. She couldn't tell if it was the same one she had seen before. It was facing her, its shoulders hunched over, that expression of pain on its face.

She paused, wanting to say something or do something. She hadn't seen a Behemoth in the flesh before, but she was quite sure they were not supposed to look like they were in agony.

Before she could act on her impulse, the crystal she was carrying flared brilliant, blinding crimson, sending sparks of red out into the air around Max, Queran's magic almost choking her. The pulse of magic it released flew outward, cascading through the jungle.

The first thing it hit was the Behemoth. The creature shifted its feet, opening its mouth and letting out a cry that sounded like fury and pain combined. It lifted one of its hands, its fingers curling into a fist, and aimed at Max.

The creature was far slower than anything Max had fought before, and she ducked to one side. The crystal was still glowing red, dark magic seeping out into the air. She tried to hold it, thinking she might be able to use her own magic to command it to stop. It seared her hand and she dropped it with a curse, still holding on to the chain. Trying to look into it with her own magic got her nowhere. Queran's spellwork was too powerful, and it continued to seep out of the crystal. She could see the lines of the spells sliding through the air, tangling around the nearby Behemoth, and snaking off into the jungle. The spells were too tangled for her to read, but confirmed that Queran had definitely done something to interfere with the great creatures.

Even as she tried to find a way to stop Queran's magic, she heard answering cries from the other Behemoths in the forest, no doubt as the trail of red-hued magic hit them as well. Their deep voices were followed by high-pitched chatter that might be Seacast monkeys, and rapid gunfire. Her heart rate picked up. The convoy was under attack. And she wasn't there to help.

She started forward, heading for the sound of fighting. The crystal bumped against her leg and she stopped, staring at it. That flare of red magic seemed to have started the attack. If she could stop the magic from flowing, perhaps the attack would stop, too.

She couldn't use her own magic. She lacked the power and skill. No. She needed to destroy the stone. She looked on the ground, trying to find a rock or, better still, a pair of rocks that she could use to crush the crystal. All she could see were dead leaves and tangled roots, but she kept looking.

A whiff of an earthy scent warned her of the next Behemoth attack. The creature had its lips drawn back from blunt, yellow teeth in a grimace that suggested it was struggling. Perhaps fighting against whatever command Queran had given it. It was moving almost comically slowly, giving her plenty of time to avoid its swing.

Max huddled down on the ground by the trunk of the enormous tree, out of reach of the Behemoth, searching among its exposed roots for a rock or something she could use to destroy the crystal. Nothing.

She could try shooting it, but there was more of a risk that her bullets would ricochet and perhaps hit one of her dogs. Or the Behemoth which was even now approaching her, both its hands clenched into fists.

Movement nearby announced the arrival of Bryce and Radrean. The Guardian sneered down at her, huddled among the tree roots, apparently not seeing the Behemoth nearby.

"I had heard Marshals were cowards," he said.

"Do you have a whetstone?" she asked Bryce, ignoring Radrean. "I need something to break this crystal. I think the magic in this crystal is affecting the Behemoths. It flared just before they attacked."

"Yes," Bryce said, sticking a hand into the pack at his front and bringing out a small slab of rock. "Here."

"Thank you." Max took the stone, placed it on the ground with the crystal on top and then drew one of her knives. The one with the heaviest handle. Thumping the knife handle against the crystal had little impact, only a tiny fragment of it breaking off. Still, it was a start.

"Our comms have been cut off," Bryce said, crouching down in front of her. He had a heavy-handled knife of his own ready. "Here, let me try."

Max sat back without a word, put her own knife away and pressed the button on her earpiece. She had almost forgotten she had it, as it wasn't something she was used to carrying. Nothing. Not even static. "Queran must have jammed the comms somehow." She glanced up at the Behemoth, wondering what in the world the demon was up to. Drawing her away from the convoy, setting the Behemoths up to attack and cutting off the comms? He must have a plan.

"That demon is trouble," Bryce said, hammering his knife onto the crystal. He touched the crystal, to move it to a better position, and hissed in surprise, snatching back his hand. "That's hot."

"Yes," Max agreed. "Keep going. I think it's starting to crack."

"We don't have time for arts and crafts," Radrean said, as Bryce set to work on the crystal again. "The convoy is under attack, and that creature took a swing at me."

Max glanced up, seeing the Behemoth towering over Radrean, still with that awful expression on its face. "I don't think it wants to attack. I think it's being forced to."

Bryce didn't even look up, focusing on the crystal he was trying to destroy. On his next blow, the thing cracked in two.

Max let out a cry of relief as the red magic faded, along with the sense of Queran's presence.

The Behemoth standing nearby, its fists raised to try to thump Radrean again, shivered from head to toe. It lowered its hands, uncurling its fingers, then flexed them and rolled its misshapen shoulders before breathing out a sigh that sounded like the weight of the world had been lifted from its shoulders. It looked down at Max and Bryce, still crouched by the tree, the broken crystal between them. Its face smoothed out, then its lips curled into what might have been a smile. It tilted its chin towards Max and put its hand on its chest, where a heart would be on a human.

Max straightened, and copied the gesture, putting two fingers of her right hand over her heart in the Lady's salute that she had learned along with the simplest of prayers as a child.

The Behemoth dropped its hand, turned and headed off into the jungle. All around them, Max saw the other great shadows moving away as well. The giants were leaving.

But the fight wasn't over. She could still hear gunfire.

She scooped the broken bits of the crystal up, shoving them into an evidence bag from one of her pockets along with the pendant chain, and handed the whetstone back to Bryce. "Thank you," she said. She still had the priest's robes under her arm. Cas and Pol were waiting for her, and she headed after them, gun in hand, not stopping to see what Bryce or Radrean might do. The convoy was still under attack and she had a responsibility to help them.

She finally reached the convoy at the side of truck two, finding it overrun. There were at least two dozen creatures swarming over the vehicle, using their long fingers and toes to grip the slick surfaces, their grey-blue fur rippling with their movements. Seacast monkeys.

For a moment, she just stared, trying to work out what the monkeys were doing. Then one of them ripped off the nearest door of the truck and screams came from inside the vehicle as the monkey reached in and dragged out the armed person riding shotgun. One of the law enforcement professionals. Someone who had probably never seen a Seacast monkey before. The man screamed. Max was too far away to take hold of him and try to fight off the monkey. She couldn't shoot the creature without risking the human, so she shoved her gun away and pulled out the shotgun, firing at the back of the monkey.

Her tranquilliser cartridge hit home, but didn't stop the monkey, which seemed to be trying to pull the man apart with its bare hands.

Rapid gunfire nearby startled her. She glanced sideways to find Bryce standing there, his assault rifle at his shoulder, grim-faced as his bullets tore into the monkey. He had a better angle, and managed to kill the monkey without shooting the human.

With Bryce's arrival and the death of one of their own, the monkeys turned away from the truck and instead turned their attention to Bryce. They paused, two dozen sets of red-rimmed eyes staring at the warrior, before swarming towards him.

The monkeys stopped short of Bryce as if they had run into an invisible wall. They shrieked in fury, jagged claws scraping at the unseen barrier.

Behind Bryce, Radrean had a hand flung forward, a look of intense concentration on his face, and with a moment to breathe, Max could feel the faint trace of Guardian magic. Radrean had stopped the charge. Finally doing something useful.

It looked like a heroic act on his part, but the Guardian was standing just behind the warrior, and if the monkeys had attacked Bryce, Radrean would have been next.

Other armed law enforcement offices gathered, staring open-mouthed at the sight of the monkeys held suspended mid-air.

"Well, don't just stand there. Shoot them. I can't hold them forever," Radrean snapped.

Before Max could say anything, or protest, more rapid fire cut through the air and the monkeys, held suspended in the air, were efficiently torn to shreds. The invisible barrier stopped the blood and viscera from scattering over Max, Bryce and Radrean, but the truck was not as lucky, nor were the other people who had moved in from either side to finish off the creatures.

It was all over in seconds.

As the echo of the last shot faded, Radrean dropped his magic and the bodies of the monkeys slid to the forest floor. Max wanted to be sick. She hunted creatures, but only killed them where necessary, and never like that. Never when they had been held immobile, unable to move, unable to do anything as bullets tore through them.

She turned away, gut churning, and headed for the front of the convoy. She still needed to find Faddei.

Behind her, she heard at least one person being sick, and at least another pair of people whimpering, probably shocked to their core by what they had just witnessed.

She didn't have to look far to find Faddei. He was standing next to the cab of the first truck, face grim as he stared back along the convoy at the carnage.

"So, there's a Guardian in the convoy," he said, as Max came up to him. He looked as if he was holding on to his temper with difficulty.

"So it seems," Max answered.

"What happened out there?" her boss wanted to know.

"The demon was there. He was dressed as a priest," Max said, and held up the robes. "He had this," she added, tucking the shotgun under her arm and holding up the evidence bag with the split crystal. "He was using magic to control the

Behemoths. I thought he was also controlling the Seacast monkeys, but maybe not," she added, avoiding looking back at the remains of the creatures.

"You shot at a priest?" Aurora asked. The human woman was standing a few feet behind Faddei, her pair of shadow-hounds just behind her. She grinned as she looked at the robes. "That's a nice grouping of shots."

"A demon pretending to be a priest," Max said wearily, wondering if anyone would actually believe her. "Queran," she added, for Faddei's benefit. "He wouldn't tell me why he was here."

Faddei made a dark, angry sound. He believed her. But then, he had already known about Queran. "Probably doesn't need a reason beyond making trouble." He glanced over his shoulder, up at the cab of the truck. "Tina, can you throw my bag down, please?"

"Sure thing." The light voice belonged to the driver of the first truck, a petite woman who looked far too delicate to be in charge of the enormous vehicle. Most people probably didn't realise that she wasn't entirely human. Part-ogre, if Max had to guess.

Faddei's bag, a large, heavy sack, landed on the ground by his feet. He bent and unzipped a side pocket, producing a large clear plastic bag, which he then held open for Max to drop the robe into.

"I'm sure Raymund and his team will want to look at this," he told Max. "Can I take the crystal, too?"

"Of course," she said, handing it over. "Bryce managed to break it in two, which seems to have stopped the Behemoth spell. But I can still sense something coming from it, so there might still be some other magic."

"Understood," Faddei said. He dug into his bag again, and this time came up with a heavy black velvet pouch which he dropped the crystal into. As soon as he closed the drawstrings on the pouch, the crystal disappeared from Max's senses. She raised her brows. She hadn't realised that Faddei carried a nullification pouch with him as standard equipment. He put the bagged robe and crystal away in his luggage. "Do you know the Guardian?" he asked her, in a low voice not meant to carry to anyone else.

"Radrean," she told him, trying to keep her voice and expression neutral. She hadn't told Faddei much about her time with the Order, and so the name might not mean anything to him. "He was an apprentice when I was there," she added. She didn't want to tell him anything else. To his credit, Faddei had never asked for much detail from her, and he didn't now.

"Wasn't it his apprentices you dealt with recently?" Faddei asked, frowning.

"It was," Max confirmed.

Faddei rubbed a hand over his bald head, scowling. "Right. We need to clean up that truck and get moving. We're going to lose the light if we stay here too much longer."

Max glanced up at the sky and it was her turn to frown. "It's late afternoon," she said, startled.

"You've been gone about two hours," Faddei said. "And we couldn't move forward, not until we knew what was happening with the Behemoths."

A cold trail worked its way over Max's skin. Two hours. She had lost time in stepping into the jungle and talking with the demon. She swallowed. If it hadn't been for the Behemoths, Faddei would have ordered the convoy to move forward and counted her and her dogs as a loss.

She hadn't had any supplies with her beyond extra ammunition, she realised, another chill running over her. She had come close to being stranded in the Wild with just her dogs and guns for company. It was possible - just barely possible - that with Cas and Pol's help, she could have followed the convoy's trail through the jungle. But it would have been the three of them against everything in the Wild, and she wasn't sure they would have made it.

Even so, she would not have blamed Faddei or any of the others for leaving her. They had a job to do, and fulfilling that was far more important than trailing through the jungle looking for a lost Marshal. Even if she did have shadow-hounds with her.

"Get back to your post," Faddei said, in a gentle tone. He picked up his bag and handed it to Tina, then turned back to Max. "We'll organise the clear up here. And I suppose I should introduce myself to the Guardian," he added.

Max couldn't speak past the lump in her throat, so just turned and walked behind Faddei as he made his way along the length of the first truck to where Bryce and Radrean were still standing, a cluster of law enforcement gathered around the remains of the monkeys.

"-never seen anything like it," one of the law enforcement officers was saying as Max came into earshot.

"I've heard stories about these things," another one said, "never thought I'd see one."

They were staring at the churned-up bodies with fascination, weapons held in front of them, muzzles down.

Radrean was standing beside Bryce, a sneer on his face. But he hadn't moved away, Max noted. Doubtless he was expecting to be thanked for his efforts. He would be disappointed. She suspected that Faddei had a lot of things to say, and thanks wasn't one of them.

Rather than looking at Radrean, she turned her attention to the man who had been dragged out of the truck. A pair of the drill crew who she didn't recognise were settled to either side of them, a large medical kit beside each of them. Max moved away from Faddei and went to the small group, crouching down by the man's head.

He was still breathing. That seemed a miracle in itself, given a Seacast monkey had taken hold of him.

"Is there anything I can do?" Max asked.

"Not right now," one of the drill crew said, sounding harassed. "We're not sure what to do," he admitted, in a burst of honesty that had an edge of desperation to it. "He had a dislocated hip and shoulder. We've set them back. He's not waking up. We're not sure what other damage he has, or how to treat it. We're not equipped for this sort of thing."

"You're the first aiders for the crew?" Max asked.

"Yes. We usually deal with broken bones or cut injuries," the other man said. "We can give him painkillers, and keep him comfortable, but I don't know if we're missing something."

"And we're out of comms range for the city," the first one said.

"Alright," Max said. She leant back on her heels, wincing at the pain in her leg. She should have stayed on her feet. "Faddei," she called. The head Marshal was squaring off with the Guardian. Max had been deliberately ignoring whatever those two were saying to each other.

The head Marshal turned at once on her call, and came across with brisk strides. "What's up?"

"Tell him what you told me," Max said to the first man. "Faddei has a healing gift. He might be able to help."

"He might," Faddei agreed, and shook his head. "Damn. I'm sorry I didn't come across earlier. I just assumed he was dead. He's still breathing, at least."

The first aider gave Faddei the same summary as he had given Max.

"Alright," Faddei said. "Well, we can't get him back to the city, but we can hopefully keep him comfortable and alive until we get back. Max, can you find Vanko for me?"

"Yes," Max said, getting to her feet.

She made her way back along the convoy, Cas and Pol trailing behind her. Vanko had been on the roof of the truck behind hers, she remembered. He was still there, attention on the forest around them.

"Hey, Vanko. Faddei is asking for you," she told him. "Can you switch out with someone else?"

"Sure," Vanko said, sliding out from behind the roof-mounted weapon. "Is it as bad as it sounded?" he asked quietly as he landed on the ground beside her, his normally cheerful manner absent.

"Awful," Max said, and couldn't say anything more for a moment. "There were about two dozen Seacast monkeys swarming truck two. They pulled the shotgun guy out. The Guardian held the monkeys in place with magic while some of the others shot them." She was going to be sick. She knew she was. "It's a blood bath."

Vanko had paled, but he nodded. "The man is dead?"

"No. He's injured. I don't know how badly. Faddei is with him," Max said. "He just asked me to send you. I'm going back to my post."

"Are you alright? You were gone a while," Vanko asked.

"I met a demon wearing a priest's robes," Max said, and shook her head. "I know. That sounds strange."

"It's the Wild," Vanko said, with a hint of a smile. "That sounds perfectly reasonable." He winked at her and headed off towards the front of the convoy.

Max went back to her truck, stopping and leaning against one of the large front wheels, Cas and Pol pressing against her, seeking pats and reassurance. The demon's presence had unsettled them, and the scent of blood was thick in the air, even here.

Just as she was feeling marginally more settled, and about to get back into the truck, Bryce and Radrean approached, heading for the back of the convoy.

She ignored them, keeping her focus on her dogs and their silky soft ears, until Radrean halted as he reached her. She looked up. He was staring at her, eyes travelling up and down her body in a way that made her want to slap him.

"No wonder I didn't recognise you," he said. "Miscellandreax. You used to be almost pretty. But you were always a useless magician. Some things never change."

Max clamped her jaw shut. Radrean's lip curled in disgust but he moved on.

She stared after his back. *Almost pretty* should not have stung. She had never had illusions about being a great beauty. But he had told her different things, all those years ago.

Cas lifted his head and looked up at her with his soft eyes and she sighed as she petted him some more. A demon, Behemoths and Seacast monkeys, and they hadn't even reached the oil field. She didn't want to think about what might be waiting for them there.

Chapter Nineteen

*T*HE WORDS AND SYMBOLS *on the blackboard made no sense, melting together into a swirl that looked almost familiar, if she could just get her eyes to focus.*

"You see, don't you, why it has to be this way?" The voice came from somewhere behind her. It was a woman speaking, and Max thought she should know the speaker. Except there was a blank where a name and face should go. And she didn't like having anyone standing behind her.

"Pay attention, child." Another woman's voice. This one a snap, and someone she was familiar with. One of the orphanage's teachers, who had tried and tried and tried and failed to teach Max the mechanics of mathematics she would need for spell working.

Max swallowed, hard, against the tightness in her throat and the stinging in her eyes, and tried to focus on the blackboard again. It still didn't make sense, no matter how hard she tried.

"Are you ready, Marshal?" Another voice, not one she could place immediately.

She opened her mouth to say that no, she wasn't ready, and yet another voice sounded, directly into her ear.

"This is truck one. We're just arriving at the site now. Aurora, Ben and Sirius, can you help the rest of the Marshals, law enforcement and warriors set a perimeter? Max, can you come to the building and do a sweep with Cas and Pol?"

Vanko. That was Vanko's voice. He was riding in truck one as Faddei had stayed with the injured man in truck two.

Max jolted out of her doze and into the real world. The truck was still moving forward, but the ground underneath was solid, firm. Concrete. They had reached their destination. She scrubbed a hand across her face and listened to Aurora, Ben, and Sirius confirm their orders in her earpiece. When they were done, she cleared her throat.

"This is Max. Copy. Give me a few minutes to get to you." There. That sounded professional, not like someone who had been mostly asleep moments before.

"I can drop you here, if you like," the driver said.

Max blinked and looked outside. It was pitch dark, the night lit only by the headlights from the convoy, which bounced and jolted as the vehicles kept moving. Just ahead of her vehicle, there was a large, dark blot against the night sky. That must be the oil field's main building, which they had been hoping to use as their base while they were here.

"Yes, thank you," Max said. She had been limping quite badly when she had got back to the truck, her leg aching. No one had mentioned it, but it seemed that the driver had noticed. The trucks had all been given pre-assigned parking slots, and her vehicle was to park closer to where the oil wells were, and not closer to the building.

"No problem," the driver said. The truck slowed smoothly to a halt. He grinned at her. "I could sleep for a week. Make sure there aren't any bugs in there, will you?"

"I'll do my best," Max promised, managing a smile for him. He had saved her a walk, and she was grateful. She could only imagine how worn out he and the rest of the drivers were. They had endured a long day driving through the Wild, struggling to keep the vehicles moving forward. She glanced back at the passengers. The two scientists were sleeping, heads resting together. The three members of the work crew were leaning forward slightly, trying to get a look outside. "Remember to stay within the perimeter, please," she said to them, then grabbed her ammunition bag and personal bag from the space at her feet and left the truck, waving another thank you to the driver before she closed the door.

Cas and Pol came down from the roof at her call and the three of them headed across to the dark bulk of the main building.

As the last remnants of sleep faded from her, Max took a look around. The night was full of the noise of vehicle engines and chattering voices. After the Behemoths and the Seacast monkeys, the tension had been almost visible. But they were at journey's end, and she could hear the relief in a lot of the voices around her. They thought the worst was likely to be over.

None of the Marshals or warriors were joining in the relief. They knew that the worst was probably ahead of them.

Max spotted Vanko standing outside the dark building. He had a crowd of people around him, and was giving directions in a patient voice worthy of Faddei. He waved the others away as Max came up to him.

"You have the layout?" he asked her.

"Offices, laboratories, kitchen, washrooms and a couple of large communal rooms on the ground floor, sleeping quarters on the two upper floors. Main entrance at the front, but there's a back door and a side entrance," Max said promptly. "Anyone gone inside so far?"

"No. There are warriors walking a patrol around the building so they'll keep an eye on the doors," Vanko answered. He glanced over his shoulder and dipped his chin to someone behind them. "I've asked Pavla and Yevhen to go with you. There's a team working on the generators, but there's no power just now, so Pavla and Yevhen are going to assist with some lighting spells. They'll stay back and let you and the hounds work."

Max looked across to see the pair of Marshals coming towards them. They were both carrying their shotguns and bags of extra ammunition, like Max, ready to deal with whatever they found inside.

"Good, thank you. Are we going to use the upper floors, do you think?" Max asked Vanko.

"We'll need to see what condition they're in," he answered, "but I think Faddei had planned that we'd bunk down on the ground floor. Easier to keep an eye on everyone. The canteen area should be big enough." And once they got the water going, there would be enough facilities for all of them to use, Max knew. The building and the oil field around them had been designed to cater for far larger numbers than they had brought.

"Got it," Max said. She set her personal bag down next to Vanko's on the ground, then slid the strap of her ammunition bag over her shoulder so it was sitting across her body and clipped her torch to the top of her shotgun. Cas and

Pol waited beside her, ears lifted. "I'll stay off the radio unless I find something," she told Vanko.

"Right," he nodded, and waved Pavla and Yevhen to come forward. The only married Marshals, the pair always worked together and were an experienced and reliable team.

"We'll watch your back," Pavla told Max. She was tightly focused, ready to work. "Light spells are ready to go."

"Good, thank you. Let's go," Max said, and waved Cas and Pol ahead of her.

The building had lost both its front doors at some point in the years since it had been abandoned. The space loomed ahead of her, the light from her torch not penetrating far as she drew closer.

"Light coming through now," Yevhen said from behind her.

A soft mist surrounded her, wafting forward on an unseen breeze into the building itself. As the mist spread out, gentle light grew in the building, letting Max see the open space of what had once been the building's reception area. There was a wide staircase rising up to one side of the area. It was shrouded in darkness after the first turn.

"Let's clear the ground floor first," Max suggested. A lot of creatures didn't like climbing stairs, particularly not the sort of open tread that she could see here.

"We're with you," Pavla said.

"Cas. Pol. Search," Max said.

The instruction was more of a formality than anything else. The shadow-hounds knew what they were doing. They moved to the left hand side of the open space and worked as a pair, going into every corner, including behind the large and heavy-looking reception desk. When they were satisfied that the space was clear, they moved to stand at the pair of doors on the other side of the reception area, waiting for Max to join them.

They worked through the rest of the ground floor, finding evidence that creatures had been inside the building, but not as many as Max would have expected. Most of the doors had been opened, many of them destroyed, and there was very little furniture still in one piece. But there was nothing alive on the ground floor apart from the three Marshals and pair of hounds.

There was a second staircase in the middle of the building, this one much plainer than the one in the reception area. Cas and Pol surged forward, ahead of the light that Pavla and Yevhen were providing.

"They've got a scent," Max told the others, following her dogs up the stairs with caution, making sure to shine her torch overhead as well. There was another storey above this one. The narrow beam showed her a plain ceiling. No predators waiting to jump down onto the Marshals.

As she set foot on the upper floor, a thrum of magic wriggled under her foot. She cursed.

"Did you feel that?" she asked the others.

"Something. Not sure what," Pavla answered. Max didn't need to look around to know that the others would be standing with their weapons raised, slightly turned away from Max to make sure that they had full view of their surroundings.

A sharp bark from the darkness ahead made Max's body tense. Her hounds had definitely found something. And something that required a warning to her. She took a step forward and sensed Pavla and Yevhen moving with her. The three of them would be in the path of whatever it was that Cas and Pol had found. Max's chest tightened. She hated having other people with her when she went into danger.

"Can you hold back a bit?" Max asked. It would give the other Marshals more time to react to a threat, and keep them out of immediate danger.

"Sure," Yevhen answered.

"We'll send some more light forward," Pavla added. As she spoke, Max felt a swell of magic behind her and more of the pale mist seeped past her, providing a little more light.

"Thank you," Max said, and moved ahead. The magic provided a more diffuse light than her direct torch beam, showing her a wide corridor with doorways at regular intervals along either side. Most of the doors were open, blackness beyond.

The trail of magic she had felt when she set foot on the floor was still there, getting stronger as she moved along the corridor. A lot of creatures of the Wild had magic, and some even left trails of it.

Cas and Pol were standing outside the last door on the left, both of them on full alert, in their attack form with longer hair, sharper claws and fangs, their eyes glowing as they kept watch on whatever they had found.

Max made her way slowly along the corridor, flicking her torch into each room she passed, just to be sure. Whatever Cas and Pol had found would be the greater threat, but there might be smaller creatures hiding away. She didn't see anything.

As she approached the door, she caught a sharp, acrid scent that burned into her nose and made her eyes sting. It wasn't anything she'd come across before.

Then between one footfall and the next, the world shifted, her vision swirling into black and red, then back to normal, and a familiar, unwelcome magic coated her from the tips of her boots to the top of her head. Queran. She could almost taste the demon's signature as she struggled to lift one foot off the ground to move forward.

Then her vision cleared and the magic faded and she was left looking at her dogs facing into the room at the end of the corridor. And then backing slowly away.

A chill ran down her spine and the world seemed to slow around her, everything focusing on the slow, careful movement of her dogs. She had never seen her dogs back away from a threat. Not once, not in all the years they had worked together and all the creatures they had faced together.

Even as she stared, mouth dry, pulse thudding, her palms damp on the grip of the shotgun, a great, jagged black tentacle appeared through the door, edging out into the corridor, followed by another one. No. Not tentacles, Max realised. Legs. Jointed legs that belonged to an enormous creature.

She could not move, could not breathe, everything frozen.

The pair of legs braced against the door frame and a bulbous head with too many eyes and a great, open mouth with more teeth than any one creature would need appeared. The head was larger than Cas.

Another leg appeared, followed by the start of the creature's body. Dark, iridescent blue.

Mammoth spider, Max's brain told her, even as her body couldn't move. Rare. Venomous. And vicious.

It was too close to her dogs, who were still backing away from it. No wonder. Shadow-hounds were immune to most toxins, but the venom in a mammoth spider's bite could kill them.

That got her moving. Finally. She shoved the shotgun away and pulled her handgun. She needed real bullets, not the tranquilliser cartridges. She aimed for the open mouth and started firing.

The creature screamed a protest, the sound making Max want to huddle down on the ground. She emptied the magazine, ejected it and loaded another, firing again even as the creature sprang forward, its enormous body taking up most of the width of the corridor, legs braced against the floor and walls and ceiling as it scuttled towards her.

Cas and Pol ducked under it and grabbed a leg each, trying to drag the creature to a halt, ignoring the risk from the spikes on the legs. They barely slowed it down. Her dogs were protecting her, utterly fearless, and it terrified her. She did not want to lose them.

Max unloaded another magazine into the creature's mouth. She could see blood mixed with saliva and broken teeth as the creature bore down towards her, another scream splitting the air.

And then the thing was on top of her. She ducked, trying to roll away from the gaping maw and hitting the side of the corridor, flinging up a hand to brace against a reaching leg. She scrabbled, managing to reload her gun and fired into the creature's underbelly. Some of her bullets bounced off. A few hit home. Enough that the creature pulled back, a pair of legs reaching towards Max.

Max scrambled away, along the floor, reloading again.

It was only with the tiniest bit of space between her and the creature that she realised she was the only one firing. She hadn't heard anything from Pavla or Yevhen.

She put one hand on the floor to brace herself to get up and felt Queran's magic crawl against her skin. She remembered the barrier she had passed through. The demon had somehow set this up. It was possible that neither of the other Marshals could see the nightmare bearing down on them. The creature could kill them, and they wouldn't be able to defend themselves.

Acting on instinct, Max *pushed* magic out of her, through her hand, against Queran's magic on the floor. It wasn't anything she had ever been taught, but she needed to break whatever spell Queran had laid.

The creature was still coming forward and she fired again. She heard cries of alarm from behind her and more rapid fire joined hers. Pavla and Yevhen, followed by a frantic-sounding call from Yevhen.

"Vanko, there's a mammoth spider on the first floor. We need back-up. Now!"

With three sets of bullets slamming into the creature it finally, finally, slumped to the ground, oozing foul-smelling, dark blood over the floor.

Max slowly got to her feet, reloading her gun for what felt like the tenth time. She had run out of magazines against her back and pulled more from her bag. Her hands were shaking, pulse thumping in her throat.

"Cas. Pol," she called, voice too high. She couldn't see them. The shadow-hounds knew to stay out of the line of fire, but they could still have been injured. And it would only take one bite, one scratch, for the lethal spider venom to get into their bodies.

A disgruntled snort sounded from one of the open doors next to the fallen creature. Two heads poked around the door jamb, ears lifted.

"Good boys," Max told them, her voice shaky with relief.

"Where the hells did that thing come from?" Pavla demanded, her voice too high as well.

"We lost sight of you," Yevhen added. "We were waiting for back-up-"

Whatever else he might have said was drowned by heavy footsteps running up the stairs behind them. All three Marshals turned as one, weapons raised, and a trio of warriors came into view, all of them carrying heavy-duty automatic weapons ready to use. Max didn't recognise the first man, but the other two were Khari and Joshua. The warriors paused under the raised guns, coming forward when Max and the others lowered their weapons.

"Sweet Lady above us, that thing stinks," the warrior she didn't know said, nose wrinkling. He was a dark-skinned man with grey in his tightly curled black hair. "You took it down? That's good shooting."

"We haven't finished clearing the floor," Max said, her voice still too high. She glanced into her ammunition bag. She still had plenty of spare magazines, but they had been supposed to last the duration of the trip, not just one night.

"We'll follow you," the warrior said.

"Alright," Max said. She glanced at Pavla and Yevhen. They gave her tight nods in response, so she turned to go forward again.

The stench was one of the worst things she'd ever experienced. It was almost suffocating and she tried not to breathe at all as she edged her way around the massive body of the spider.

"Watch out for the leg spikes," she called over her shoulder. "The whole thing is toxic to people." She remembered her dogs grabbing its legs and shivered. Luckily, it was just the spider's bite that was deadly to shadow-hounds.

"Got it," the unnamed warrior answered, sounding tense.

Once she was around the dead body, Cas and Pol came out of the doorway, their ears laid back, doubtless suffering even more from the smell.

As she moved beyond the corpse, a chattering sound met her ears.

"There's something else here," she called over her shoulder.

A few muffled curses assured her that the warning had been heard. She gestured for Cas and Pol to go ahead and followed them, weapon raised.

The doorway that the mammoth spider had come out of was a dark hole, the sounds coming from inside.

She grabbed the torch from the mount of her shotgun and shone it into the room.

A writhing mass of legs and bodies met her eyes.

"Back!" she yelled to the others, taking her own advice. "Back, back, back!"

The others were sprinting away, a few paces ahead of her. Cas and Pol were with her as she came up to the adult spider, and hurdled the dead body with ease, leaving Max and her stiff, sore body to pick her way around the spread out, jagged legs.

Just in time.

As she cleared the corpse, a mass of legs and bodies swarmed out of the room.

"What in hells?" Joshua asked, even paler than he normally was.

"Baby mammoth spiders," Pavla answered, voice grim.

"Just as venomous as the adults," Yevhen warned.

"Fire," the unnamed warrior said, and followed his own command.

The warriors' heavier weaponry tore into the smaller spiders. Max took a step back, giving them a clearer path, and focused on picking off the one or two smaller spiders that got through the warriors' blanket fire.

Max's ears were ringing when the guns eventually fell silent, the corridor full of the stench of spider blood and gun smoke.

Her whole body was vibrating with the force of the fire power that had been unleashed around her, fear twisting along with revulsion as she took a step sideways and leant against the wall for a moment. She hated showing weakness. Hated it. But she wasn't sure her legs could keep holding her up. Not right now.

She briefly closed her eyes, scrubbing a hand over her face only to immediately straighten away from the wall, her eyes snapping open when one of her dogs growled.

There was no creature coming towards them, just a Guardian making his way up the last few steps, Bryce at his flank.

Radrean paused at the top of the stairs, lip curling as he looked at the carnage.

"The building isn't clear yet," Max said. She didn't think Radrean would listen, but she knew the warriors would. "We've cleared the ground floor and that half of this floor so far."

"Sheer incompetence," Radrean said, eyes flicking to Max and then away. "And a ridiculous amount of mess."

Max clamped her jaw shut before she could say anything hasty, such as suggesting that the Guardian clear the rest of the building on his own while the rest of them put their feet up downstairs. Instead, she double-checked the magazines in her gun and shotgun and turned her shoulder on the Guardian, looking at Pavla and Yevhen. "Ready?" she asked them.

Chapter Twenty

The rest of the first floor was an anti-climax, just rooms filled with dust and broken furniture. Cas and Pol did their jobs while Max felt a knot of tension growing between her shoulder blades. Her dogs went first, with her following, and then Pavla, Yevhen, the warriors and Radrean. Far from taking Bryce's suggestion to leave, Radrean insisted on staying and favouring them all with comments about how long this was all taking.

No one else said a thing, but the air was almost vibrating with tension by the time the rest of the floor was clear. They had ended up at the front of the building, with the open-tread staircase leading down to the reception area.

Max turned her light upward. There was still one floor to go, and she wanted to check the roof, too. Cas and Pol went up the stairs two and three at a time, ears lifted, eyes bright.

"I think they've sensed something," she told the others, lifting her shotgun and beginning to climb after her dogs.

"We'll send some more light when we're at the top," Pavla promised.

"You *think* they have sensed something?" Radrean asked. Max could hear the sneer in his voice even with her back turned to him. She clamped her jaw shut and kept going, Pavla and Yevhen a few steps behind her.

As she reached the top of the stairs, the diffuse light that the Marshals had been providing slid past her, through the open door into the corridor beyond. Cas and Pol were a few doors along the corridor, systematically going from one side to the other, noses down. They were following some kind of a trail, but didn't seem concerned, just interested.

Max stepped into the corridor and followed her dogs, shining her torch into each open door as she passed. More dust, more broken furniture, but no predators to concern them. She saw a spider's web in one of the rooms and paused, but it was a normal-sized web. No more mammoth spiders crawled out of the dark towards her.

As she made her way along, she could hear the others following. The warriors and the Marshals moved quietly, used to the need for stealth. Radrean's footsteps were heavy on the carpeted floor.

"Why is there no more light?" the Guardian asked after a moment.

"We're providing light to work by," Yevhen answered him.

"I can barely see," Radrean complained.

"This is how we search. A lot of predators do not react well to bright lights," Pavla told him, in a tone that suggested she was holding on to her temper with difficulty.

"But you have torches," Radrean said, then cursed. "This is ridiculous. I can barely see to walk."

Max felt a gathering of power behind her and stopped, half-turning to protest. Before she had time to do or say anything, a brilliant, blinding white light filled the corridor, scorching past her and down the length of the building. She flung up a hand, trying to shield her eyes. It was too late. Her sight was overwhelmed by the light and she was blind. She heard cries of protest from the others, low growls from her dogs, and then a chattering sound that made the hairs on the back of her neck stand up.

"Cas, Pol, to me," she called, turning back to face the corridor. The light stabbed into her eyes, producing tears which didn't help. She blinked, trying to see. The light that Radrean had created was harsh, white and blinding, far too strong for the confined space of the corridor. She could barely make out the shapes of her dogs coming back to her. As they came up to her, they were shaking their heads, their eyes narrowed to slits in an effort to shut out as much of the light as possible.

Someone bumped into the back of her and muttered an apology. Max glanced over her shoulder and saw Pavla there, the other Marshal's eyes also streaming and narrowed to try to counter the blinding light.

The chattering noise came again and Max's skin crawled. There had been one mammoth spider on the floor below. What if there were more up here? And the spiders far preferred the dark. They would not react well to Radrean's light.

"Everyone stay where you are," Max said, voice harder than it needed to be, coloured with her irritation at Radrean. "There's something in the corridor ahead of us." She took another step forward, straining to see, but all her eyes would register was blinding white and a few hard angles that she assumed were the walls and doors of the corridor.

"Well, what is it?" Radrean demanded.

"I can barely see anything, you idiot," Max snapped.

"This is why we don't use bright light on a hunt," Yevhen added, tone almost as sharp as Max's. "It compromises our vision."

"Turn it off," Pavla added, matching her husband's tone. "Now."

"Oh, very well," Radrean said, and muttered something about ungrateful fools under his breath that Max pretended not to hear. Max felt the gathering of his power again and the light died as if he had turned off a switch.

Max blinked, blind again, unable to see for long, awful moments, the absence of the blinding Guardian light leaving her in what felt like pitch darkness. A few muffled curses came from behind her, and ahead of her both Cas and Pol grumbled, low sounds expressing their own displeasure.

The chattering sound came again. Much closer. Acting on instinct, Max tucked herself against one of the walls.

"Everyone watch your backs," she said, "there's something coming."

"Can you see what it is?" Pavla asked. She and the others had stayed where they were, a few paces behind Max.

"Not yet," Max said, voice grim.

A rush of movement ahead of her was all the warning she had before far too many black, spiked legs came into view. Her eyes hadn't adjusted well enough for her to make out the detail, but she recognised the shape.

"Mammoth spider," she yelled, throwing her shotgun to one side and drawing her gun, firing into the thing that was on top of her.

"Get down," Bryce ordered, voice booming in the tight space. Max dropped to the floor, calling for her dogs to take cover, and the corridor filled with the sound of automatic gunfire, the heavy weapons carried by the warriors ripping into the mammoth spider as it surged past Max and her dogs. The spider screamed, but like the one in the corridor below, it was no match for the warriors' weapons.

Bits and pieces of spider flew into the air, splashing against the walls, raining down on Max. She tried covering her head with one of her arms, hoping to avoid the worst of it, her mouth and nose full of the putrid stench of the thing. It smelled far worse dead than alive. At least she didn't have any scratches or open wounds for its poison to seep into. A small blessing.

At length, the gunfire died.

"Max?" That was Bryce's voice, sounding distant after the roar of the guns. "Are you alright?"

She made a sound that might have been agreement and got off the ground, using the wall to steady herself as her still-healing leg protested. Bits and pieces of dead spider slid off her onto the ground. She looked around, not seeing Cas or Pol in the dim light.

Before she could panic, a soft sound nearby drew her attention and she saw the two of them poking their heads out of a room further down the corridor. Apparently they had been more sensible than she had, and taken shelter out of the path of the bullets and pieces of spider.

"Lady's light, that stinks," Max said, shaking an unidentifiable piece of the spider's guts off her arm, then bending down to retrieve her shotgun. The ammunition bag was still slung over her body and, like the rest of her, covered in spider debris.

"Have you got cleaning spells?" Pavla asked, ever practical.

"A few, yes. But we should clear the rest of the corridor first," Max said, stepping around a still-twitching severed leg as she made her way along the corridor. She glanced back. Everyone else was on the other side of the spider's carcass. "You can wait there, if you prefer."

Pavla and Yevhen were already moving, though, picking their way through the debris. They were Marshals, after all.

Max turned to face the way ahead. Cas and Pol were out of the room, working their way along the rest of the corridor without her having to tell them. She held her shotgun up, the torch providing additional light, and followed them. The other spider had created a nest full of young. She could only hope that this one hadn't had time. Or that it was a male, with no young to look after. She didn't know enough about mammoth spiders to be able to tell male from female. And the bits and pieces littering the corridor would be hard for even an expert to put together.

Cas and Pol found the spider's nest at the end of the building, in the room above the other one, but there were no baby spiders, or even any eggs that Max could see. Still, she tossed in one of Leonda's special grenades, which would scour the room with magic and make sure that there was nothing harmful in the space.

That done, she finally dug out a pair of cleaning spells and doused herself twice, almost crying with relief as the bitter, pungent stench of dead spider faded and her clothes and person were clean.

When she was clean, she discovered that the warriors and Guardian had also joined them. Radrean was still wearing a pinched, displeased expression. It seemed to be his normal look. The warriors were standing with their weapons held ready, keeping an eye on their surroundings. Pavla and Yevhen were unharmed, and seemed to have avoided being coated in bits of spider.

"Let me check the roof," Max said. They were at the end of the building, with a fire escape door nearby that led to the night air.

"Go ahead," Radrean said, waving his hand. "There's nothing there."

Max set her jaw and left the building, sending Cas and Pol ahead of her up the fire escape stairs. The roof was a flat expanse of a sticky, rubbery substance that her dogs hated walking on. The night sky gave her enough light to see that there was nothing else alive up here. She wasn't sure if Radrean had known that, or if he had just been guessing. And she wasn't going to ask him.

Before she turned away, ready to head back into the building, a distant flicker of light caught her eye. It was far into the distance, well beyond the perimeter of the oil field. She stopped, wishing she had some binoculars with her. The light was steady, and deeper into the Wild, suggesting someone else was in the vast expanse of wilderness apart from them. As she was frowning at it, it faded. But she was sure of what she had seen.

She went back down the stairs and rejoined the others.

"Nothing out there," Max reported, keeping her tone light. Vanko and Faddei would need to know about the light she had seen as soon as she could get a private word with either of them, but it was far enough away that it wasn't an immediate danger.

"Told you," Radrean said. From the expressions around him, Max wasn't the only one with an urge to smack the smug Guardian.

Max keyed her radio, opening a channel to Vanko. "The building is clear, although I recommend we just stay on the ground floor. There are dead mammoth spiders on both of the upper floors," she told him.

"Is everyone alright?" Vanko asked immediately.

"Yes." Her leg was aching, but that was not worth mentioning. And no one else had been injured, which was something of a miracle.

"Good. Good job. Come back down. I'll get some of the crew to put barriers up to block off the upper floors," Vanko said.

"Good idea," Max said, nose wrinkling as the stench of dead spider drifted down the corridor to her. "Although we should do some clean up here first," she suggested.

"Isn't there a Guardian with you?" Vanko asked. Over the radio she couldn't read his expression or fully catch the tone of his voice. He sounded like his normal, cheerful self. With perhaps a bit of mischief thrown in.

"There is, yes," Max answered, and looked across the corridor to Radrean.

"What? You expect me to clean up your mess?" he said, lip curling.

"We're all going to be staying in this building for a few days at least," Pavla said. "It would be nice if it didn't stink of rotting spiders."

"Not to mention the risk of drawing in more predators," Yevhen pointed out. From the expression on Radrean's face, it was clear that had not occurred to him. But then, he had spent his life first in the inner city, born to wealthy parents, and then moving to the carefully managed halls of the Order. Far away from the dangers that Marshals were used to.

"Agreed," Bryce said, and looked at Radrean. "You wanted to come on this journey. We all need to earn our place. Consider this your contribution for today."

Max ducked her head, hoping to hide her smile. She hadn't heard that particular tone from Bryce before. He and the other warriors were normally so careful to be respectful and deferential around the Guardians. But perhaps he had had enough of Radrean's sneering. Or perhaps he also didn't want to spend the next few days with a backdrop stench of rotting spider and the risk of more predators being drawn to the building.

Radrean didn't say anything, but turned away and flung a hand out along the corridor. His magic poured out. A complicated cleaning spell unravelled, far more detailed than was needed, reducing the bits and pieces of dead spider to piles of ash on the floor. It was the sort of spell that Max had never managed to master, and never would.

"Good, let's go," Max said, and headed down the stairs.

They all waited on the next floor for Radrean to repeat his performance, and then headed to the ground floor where the air was mercifully clear and there was a hub of activity taking place with the scientists and oil crews helping to bring the luggage in from the trucks to set up makeshift sleeping quarters in the canteen area, with the games room - the other communal room - being turned into a dining room.

As Max and the others reached the ground floor, the lights came on and a ragged, relieved cheer went up around the room. At least they would have electricity for lights and for cooking. And to spot any more giant predators who might wander into the building.

Chapter Twenty-One

Much later in the night, Max was awake and restless. Whether by accident or design, the scientists and oil crew had included some truly skilled cooks in their number, so the entire party had eaten far better than she had expected. Everyone had seemed worn out from the long day, most people heading for their beds as soon as the meal was done. The warriors, Marshals and law enforcement officers were all on a watch rota, with Max not due to be on shift until the next day.

Most of the conversation over the meal had centred on Radrean, who had revealed himself to the group as a whole when the meal was served. Very few people got to see one of the Guardians in real life, let alone share a meal with them. Max had kept out of his way, trying not to listen as he bragged about his heroics in clearing the building, and trying not to get annoyed as he lapped up the open adulation of many of the other members of the group.

She tried to give him the benefit of the doubt, aware that her past history with Radrean made her ill-disposed towards him. Unless something had changed significantly since she had left, he would be the youngest, most junior Guardian and therefore surrounded by far older and more experienced magicians who most likely didn't take him too seriously. So for him to be surrounded by people who actually admired him must be a nice experience. Or so she tried to tell herself. The lines were hollow even in her own mind, and it seemed that even without her past history, he wasn't impressing everyone. The other Marshals, who most likely knew what had actually happened, did not look awed by the Guardian. It was difficult to tell what the warriors thought, as they remained impassive, but many of the law enforcement personnel looked thoroughly impressed by Radrean. Of course, they would also be swapping stories of how he had held a group of Seacast monkeys with his magic earlier in the day, letting the warriors and law enforcement officers kill the beasts.

Settled at the back of the room along with the other Marshals, Max practised some breathing exercises around her meal, searching for a way to keep her temper under control and to stay quiet.

Once the conversation had died down, the wild tales of Radrean's exploits getting more exaggerated as they were shared, she managed to get a quiet word with Vanko to let him know about the lights she had seen in the distance. Too far to be a threat, she thought, but the others still needed to be aware. To her frustration, she hadn't been able to give him more than a vague direction. Vanko had taken the information and promised to alert those keeping watch that there might be other people out in the Wild, however unlikely that seemed.

By then, Radrean had stopped his performance, and the building was settling in to quiet for the night. There was nothing for Max to do apart from try and sleep in the cot bed she had been assigned. She lay down, her dogs nearby, and stayed stubbornly awake. And not just because of her annoyance with Radrean.

She hated sleeping in communal spaces. It reminded her of the orphanage, crammed into narrow cot beds with the other orphans in touching distance, lying on her bed with the covers pulled over her head while a voice whispered out of the dark, heard only by her. The voice had given her nightmares enough as a child, before she had even heard of the underworld. Now she knew that it had been Queran murmuring to her, even if she didn't know why he had singled her out. She didn't know of anyone else unlucky enough to have a demon paying them close personal attention, and wished she knew why she had been targeted. She wanted to find a way to convince the demon to leave her alone.

Besides that, she rarely got through a night without violent dreams, and hated the thought that someone else might see or hear her nightmares. She tried turning onto her side, the cot bed far more yielding than her normal, firm mattress, and scowled into the dark. She couldn't get comfortable. Cas and Pol were apparently fast asleep on the blankets she had put down for them beside her bed. And from the sounds all around her, everyone else was managing to sleep, including some impressive snoring.

With a silent sigh, she got up, sliding her feet into her boots and holstering her gun before she headed out of the room. She had been sleeping in her clothes, all her other weapons in place, which might have been why she was so uncomfortable, but she hadn't felt safe getting undressed knowing that she might need to get up at any point. Almost the entire party that wasn't on duty was sleeping together in this large room. The injured man and Faddei had been given cot beds in one of the building's offices, away from everyone else, to let them rest more soundly. Faddei was worn out from using his healing magic. The injured man would live, Max had heard, even though he hadn't woken up yet.

She left the main room as quietly as she could, heading for the dining room. It was probably quieter, and she might manage to get a bit of sleep sitting on one of the benches with her head on one of the tables.

Cas and Pol joined her just as she left the sleeping area and she paused to give each of her dogs a pat. They had done good work earlier in the night, clearing the building. They accepted her fussing, staying by her side as she kept walking.

Before she reached the dining room door, a whisper of magic tugged her senses. It had a familiar taste to it. Queran. He had interfered with the convoy twice already. She did not want to find out what he might have planned for a third try.

She hesitated, glancing over her shoulder into the canteen, wondering if she should go back for her shotgun and more ammunition. She would risk waking other people up, and having put half a magazine into Queran earlier that day, with no apparent effect, she wasn't sure that extra ammunition would do any good. The gun she carried and the extra magazines tucked under her jacket would have to do. If he got close enough, she could always try stabbing him with one of her knives. She hadn't done that yet.

She turned again, following the trail of magic as it led her out of the building's front entrance, still open to the elements. The night had been lit by a few powerful spotlights which were mostly aimed at the trucks. The trucks were still empty, but they were going to be guarded around the clock. Not only were they needed as vessels for the oil that the convoy was due to take back to the city, they were also the group's only reliable means of transport out of the Wild.

She saw a pair of shadow-hounds on patrol with their handler. Sirius, she thought, as she would most likely have recognised Aurora or Ben even from this distance. There was a pair of law enforcement walking their patrol on the other side of the space, weapons ready.

The trail of magic was coming from somewhere in the Wild, somewhere back along the road they had travelled to get here. With a sigh, Max turned and headed in that direction, her movement hampered by her sore leg. She hadn't found time or privacy to apply any ice to the bruises yet, and had forgotten to take painkillers before she lay down to sleep. She had hoped she might manage to get some rest and let her leg heal a bit. She should have known that rest would be in short supply.

As she moved out of the shadow of the main building, soft footsteps sounded to one side, resolving into Bryce.

"Something wrong?" he asked her. It seemed a genuine question.

"The demon I found earlier is back," Max said. "I'm going to see what it wants."

Bryce's expression changed to sheer surprise. "On your own?"

"I have my dogs," Max pointed out.

"Let me get some back-up," Bryce said, slowing down.

"Do as you wish," Max said, and kept walking. She felt her face heat up as she replayed the words in her head. She had sounded sharp and ungrateful, and hadn't meant it that way. But she was worried about why the demon was here, and what he might be planning.

She heard Bryce's voice, speaking quietly, and then he caught up with her, matching her stride for stride.

"Sorry," she said, not looking at him. "I didn't mean to bite your head off."

"No problem," he said, sounding as if he meant it. "So, the same demon as earlier? You've met this one before?"

"Yes. Queran. He tried to kill me with a dark magic shadow-hound a few weeks ago," Max said. "And he put up some kind of concealment in the building which hid the first mammoth spider from view," she added.

"And earlier today he was dressed as a priest," Bryce added.

"Yes," she said, not looking at him, remembering Radrean's scorn and disbelief. The Guardian thought he knew more about magic than Max. He was probably right. But he had failed to sense the demon earlier in the Wild, and hadn't appeared yet. She glanced at Bryce. "Did you call for Radrean?" she asked.

"No," he answered, seemingly amused by the idea. "He's sound asleep, and doesn't like to be disturbed."

Max almost snorted with laughter. It sounded like a perfectly reasonable explanation, except that she could hear the hint of mischief in Bryce's tone. He hadn't wanted the Guardian with them.

But he was walking through the night with her, she realised, warmth creeping through her. Bryce had believed her about the demon, and he was coming with her. She wondered why. It could be as simple as the fact that the Order's purpose was to stand against dark magic and the underworld. Or it could be that he hadn't wanted her to go alone. Perhaps he felt responsible for her, somehow, as she had once been an apprentice in the Order. That didn't seem right, though.

Rapid footsteps behind her drew her attention before her mind could come up with more questions. She glanced over her shoulder, somehow unsurprised to find Khari, Joshua and the unnamed warrior who had faced the mammoth spider joining them, all wide awake and armed to the teeth.

"Max, I don't think you've been introduced to Osvaldo," Bryce said.

"Not formally," Max said, and nodded at the warrior. "Thank you for your assistance earlier. Thanks to all of you, in fact."

"It's been a while since we faced a genuinely tough opponent," Osvaldo said. There was no bravado or glee in his voice, he was simply stating a fact. "What are we doing now?" he asked, addressing the question to Max and Bryce.

Max looked at Bryce. He lifted a brow, waiting for her to speak.

"I sensed the demon out here. I want to find out what he's up to. He's done enough damage already," Max told them.

"Lead the way," Osvaldo said.

Max still hesitated. The last time she had been on her own surrounded by warriors of the Order, the warriors had died swift and terrible deaths. The weight of the nine warriors' deaths was almost unbearable at times. She opened her mouth to dismiss the warriors around her and hesitated. Something about the way they were standing, and the quiet determination on Bryce's face, told her that they weren't going to simply leave. But she didn't want to put them in danger.

"Can you stay a little bit behind me, please?" she requested.

To her surprise, they did as she asked as she turned and started walking again, heading in the direction that she had sensed the demon magic. Cas and Pol spread out to either side without being asked.

"You're injured," Khari said a moment later. "Did that happen earlier?"

"No," Max said, glad that the darkness and the back of her head would hide the heat in her face. She had been trying to hide her limp, and it seemed she had failed. "It's an older injury. Being thrown by the Darsin and trampled by the spider aggravated it."

No one said anything in reply, but her face still burned. She hated to feel vulnerable.

Just as she reached the edge of the concrete, the trail of demon magic vanished. She spat a curse, halting and drawing a deep breath, trying to find some calm to see if she could catch the trail again. Nothing. She cursed again.

"There's something there," Joshua said from behind Max.

She glanced back at him and saw he was pointing his weapon off to one side. Following the direction, she saw a faint gleam in the undergrowth.

Cas and Pol went ahead at her gesture, but didn't seem alarmed by whatever they found, so she drew her small torch out and shone the light on the object.

Beady eyes gleamed out between vibrant green leaves, making her catch her breath. But the eyes didn't belong to anything living. She carefully peeled back the branch to reveal, of all things, a teddy bear. It was difficult to tell its colour even in the light from her torch, but she thought it might be lilac. It looked familiar, even if she couldn't place it right now. She reached down and picked up the bear, careful to handle it by one of its ears, finding it light in her hands. It was also dry and clean, so it had not been there long enough to collect moisture from the leaves or dirt from the forest floor.

"A child's toy?" Osvaldo said, sounding astonished.

Max didn't blame him. It was not what she had expected to find, either. "I know this bear," she said, running her torch over it, worry and apprehension curling through her. This bear had been in the pictures that Alonso and Elicia had shared with her of their granddaughter, Ynes. "It belongs to the missing child," she told the others, hearing a sharp intake of breath.

"What's it doing out here? We're a long way from the city, or anywhere else a child might wander," Khari said.

"I don't know," Max said, answering the question. The faintest trace of demon magic slid off the bear as she lifted it up to better see its face. "I saw lights earlier."

"Yes, Vanko updated us," Bryce said, frowning. Displeased about something.

"They were far off. Perhaps not connected. But the demon was definitely here. I think Queran put it here for us to find," Max said slowly.

"That means he knows about the girl," Bryce said, voice grim.

"And where to find her," Joshua added, equally grim.

Max silently agreed, staring at the soft toy dangling from her hand, the long day finally catching up to her, pressing her shoulders down with exhaustion. She couldn't think straight. The bear was here. That didn't mean that Ynes was here. But Queran had put it here. Which meant he somehow knew about the girl, and Max's connection to her.

Max wanted to march into the jungle, find Queran, and demand answers from him. What was his connection to the missing girl? Why had he left the bear here? And not least, why was a full-fledged demon so interested in her? He had singled her out for torment as a child, and now he had found her again, seemed determined to ensure she didn't forget about him again.

"We need to alert the patrols to keep an eye out for the demon and the girl," Osvaldo said to Bryce. It was a sensible, practical suggestion and Max's tired brain could not have come up with it.

"Yes. We can't search in the dark," Bryce added. Another sensible, practical observation. Even with magic to provide additional light, it wasn't the same as daylight. "We'll do a wider sweep when it's daylight. In the meantime, we should all get some rest."

Although he addressed his comments to everyone, Max had a feeling he was speaking to her more than the others, and her face burned again. The warriors didn't look tired, or weary. They looked as if they were more than capable of setting out right now to search the entire Wild if they had to, to see if they could find the missing child. Whereas Max wasn't sure she would make it back to the building.

Chapter Twenty-Two

Max woke slowly, reluctantly, aware of space and gentle movement around her. It took a moment to orient herself. She was in what had been the canteen of the oil field's main building, tucked into a narrow cot bed. At least she had remembered to take off her extra ammunition and her knives before she had lain down to sleep this time. There was nothing digging into her ribs. And her leg felt better. She'd taken painkillers and applied an ice pack over her trousers the night before, not wanting to strip in the communal space, and the diffused cold seemed to have helped ease the ache.

She sat up, rubbing her hands across her face, opening her eyes to find the soft toy staring back at her from its place on top of her pack. She had put it into an evidence bag to preserve any scent on it, but through the clear plastic she could tell it was the toy she had seen in the photos of Ynes, down to the mended tear across its stomach. Even with the evidence bag around it, she was a little surprised that it had survived the rest of the night with both Cas and Pol nearby.

Still not fully awake, she looked around the space. Only about a quarter of the beds were occupied, forms huddled under blankets with the covers pulled over their heads to try to shut out the daylight from the floor-to-ceiling windows that ran along one side of the room. The windows looked out onto the Wild, and part of the oil field. From what Max could see, none of the machines seemed to be working. A chill ran through her, wondering if it was even going to be possible for the oil crews to get the machines working and extract the crude oil that they needed to fill the tankers outside.

There were a few people moving around the space, taking care to be quiet and slow, trying not to disturb the sleepers. Max stretched, feeling the protest in her muscles. She needed to move. She got to her feet, putting her weapons back into place and slinging the ammunition bag across her body, tucking the bear into the bag. She didn't want to leave it behind.

Cas and Pol were silent shadows as she moved across the room, heading for the makeshift dining room. They should have coffee there, if nothing else.

As she settled with coffee and a plate of hot food, she glanced up at the clock and paused, the coffee halfway to her mouth. She had slept far longer than she had planned, and she was due to be on watch in about half an hour.

Even as she thought that, Faddei settled onto the bench opposite her. He had his own coffee and plate of food, steam rising into the chill morning air.

"You look how I feel," he commented, voice gruff. He had dark circles under his eyes. The healing gift extracted a price for its use, draining him of energy. She was surprised he was up.

"That bad, huh?" Max asked, starting on her food. She paused almost at once to appreciate it. The very good cooks who were part of the science team and oil crew had outdone themselves with this morning's offering.

"Feel like I've been hit by a truck," Faddei grunted in reply.

They didn't say much else while they finished their food.

"How's the injured man?" Max asked.

"He woke up early morning," Faddei said, grim expression lightening for a moment. "He'll be up on his feet in a day or two."

"Well done," Max said, meaning it.

"Vanko told me about the mammoth spiders," Faddei said, nose wrinkling in distaste, "and something about demon magic and lights in the distance?"

Max nodded, putting her coffee down and giving Faddei an update on what had happened. She paused before telling him about her sensing the demon the night before, after everyone had settled to sleep, then brought out Ynes' lilac bear to show him.

Faddei stared at the bear, face grim. "So, this demon is playing games with us. You think the girl is nearby?"

"I don't know," Max said. "I mean, I can't think how that's possible. We're a long way from the city and as far as I know neither Nati nor Ynes have the magic or skills to survive this long in the Wild." There was the other, awful, possibility that one or both of them were dead already, but Max didn't want to think about that. She would much rather believe they were alive until she had proof otherwise. Alonso and Elicia deserved to see their daughter and granddaughter again.

"But we can't rule it out," Faddei said and nodded, once. "Alright. I'll pull you off the watch rotation. Take Cas and Pol and see if you can find a trail. I assume they can track scent?"

"They can," Max confirmed. "I'll need to check in with Bryce, though. I think he might have been sending out a search team at first light." She grimaced. "I didn't mean to sleep so late."

"Vanko gave orders that everyone was to be allowed to sleep as long as they needed," Faddei said, the suggestion of a smile crossing his face. "He's turning into a fine leader, that one."

"He did a great job yesterday," Max agreed.

Bryce was easy to find, as he was coming into the main building as she was heading out. He stopped as soon as he saw her, sweeping her with a cool, professional gaze. Max had seen him look at other students like that. Measuring their capabilities. Whatever he saw seemed to satisfy him as he gave a small nod.

"We've gone a few paces into the Wild all around the perimeter, but haven't found anything," he told her. "I was just coming to see if we could use your shadow-hounds to track."

"Faddei suggested the same thing. We're ready," Max said. She had swapped out her ammunition bag for a backpack, stocking up with water, food, blankets and a basic first-aid kit. She had her shotgun and spare ammunition strapped to the backpack, and was as ready as she would ever be to head out of the comparative safety of the perimeter. Ynes' bear was dangling from her backpack, still in the evidence bag. Bryce had a vest over his body armour that looked to be stocked with ammunition and a radio, but she was sure he was also carrying basic supplies as well. Order warriors liked to be prepared.

"Alright," he said, turning and walking with her out of the building into the weak sunlight.

As they made their way across the concrete, heading for the spot where they had found the bear the night before, a great groaning sound split the air. Max tensed, wondering if they were under attack, then a ragged cheer went up and she turned to find that one of the machines was working, its movement stop-start at first, then easing up into a smooth motion. She paused to watch for a moment, relief coursing through her. If the crew hadn't been able to get any of the machines working, the entire convoy would have been a failure. More cheers erupted from the people outside as the machine kept working. She didn't blame them.

"Finally, a bit of good news," she said.

"Indeed. Let's hope they can get some of the others running as well," Bryce said, and started walking again.

There was a group of warriors waiting by the edge of the concrete. Osvaldo, Khari and Joshua, along with three less welcome faces. Killan, Hop and Gemma. Max had first met them when she and Zoya had been assigned to repair a breach in the Wild not that long ago. Hop and Killan had done their jobs, but Gemma had been openly scornful about Max, somehow recognising her from her past life within the Order.

"We're here to help," Bryce said in a low voice, not meant to carry to anyone else, as they came closer to the others.

Max stiffened, then tried to ease the tension in her shoulders. She hadn't realised her reluctance was so obvious. "Alright," she said. She couldn't quite manage enthusiasm, but she could manage some basic manners.

As they stepped off the edge of the concrete, she pulled the lilac bear out of the evidence bag, careful to handle it by the ear again, and called Pol then Cas over to get whatever scent might be left on the fabric.

She stood, waiting with the warriors, while her dogs went straight to the point where the bear had been the night before. Max wouldn't have recognised the precise spot in the daylight, but her dogs had no hesitation. They worked out in a spiral from where the bear had been left, then Pol gave a low bark, pausing and looking back over his shoulder.

"He's found a trail," Max said to the others, stowing the bear again before she walked after her dog, skin tightening. He had found something to follow. Something that might lead them to Ynes.

Pol led the group on a more-or-less straight line through the Wild. Cas had appointed himself as lookout for the group, ranging from one side of the group to the other, careful to keep behind Pol so as not to interfere with the scent trail his brother was following.

Max trusted her dogs, following their lead without hesitation through the densely packed jungle that was the Wild. She was no tracker, but even she could see that some branches had been bent back and broken. Someone or something had forced their way through the undergrowth, heading to the edge of the concrete platform to leave the bear for Max to find. If she had to bet, her first and only suspect would be Queran, even if she didn't understand why he had done it.

She kept her speculation internal, saving her breath for trying to keep up with her dog. Pol was going slowly, for him, but it was still a struggle to keep him in sight from time to time as Max had to navigate around giant tree trunks and tangled plants on the ground. With her recent injury, she hadn't been doing as much exercise as normal and was embarrassed by how quickly she was out of breath. Still, she did not want to stop. There might be a little girl and her mother somewhere ahead of them.

Pol scrambled up a sharp incline and came to a halt on the top, letting out another low bark. He had found something that she needed to see.

Max drew her weapon on instinct, the warriors all around her readying their own guns in response.

With Cas beside her, Max made her own way up the incline, with far less grace than either of her dogs managed, reaching the top feeling sweaty and red-faced.

Once there, she stopped and stared. The incline hadn't been natural, but was in fact the side of what had once been a road. She could see it stretching out to either side, the once-clear surface now covered in short, tough plants.

By a quirk of the land around them, they were high enough to see a bit further ahead than the next tree trunk, and Max squinted, spying a hill in the distance with what looked like the remains of a building on it. It wasn't that unusual in this part of the Wild to find old buildings. It had been inhabited by humans for a long time before the Wild reclaimed it. The building looked large, even from this distance, and had somehow survived in good enough condition to have many of its windows intact, from the way she could see light bouncing off glass. She remembered the lights from the night before and glanced back in the direction they had come. She couldn't see the oil field from here, but the building might be more or less where the lights had been. Possibly.

Pol made a low sound, catching her attention. He hadn't been looking at the building, but at something much closer.

On the ground not far from where he was standing were strips of fabric. They looked as if they had once been white but were now stained with a reddish brown substance that might be blood. There were three strips, arranged in a crude arrow sign, pointing in the direction of the building. Max stared down at the fabric, jaw tight. First the bear, now this. Someone was playing games, and she didn't like it. Not one bit.

Cas paced forward, sniffing delicately at the fabric before turning away, snorting and shaking his head.

"It's not from Ynes," Max said, reading her dogs' body language.

"Did the demon leave it here?" Bryce asked.

"I don't know. I can't sense any trace of him," Max said, hearing the frustration in her voice. She rubbed a hand over her face, dragging her fingers through her hair. Her scalp was sweaty. Her whole body was tired. "But it looks like someone wants us to go that way," she said, pointing in the direction of the arrow.

"I don't like it," Khari said, and Max could see the unease reflected on Joshua's face, the married pair in perfect agreement.

"Me neither," Max agreed, tilting her head to try to ease the stiffness in her neck. She'd forgotten just how uncomfortable it could be to carry a backpack for any length of time, particularly with all the other bits and pieces of equipment she had stashed around her person.

"It's fresh," Killan offered, surprising Max. He'd taken a step forward, crouching down to get a better look at the fabric. "The blood doesn't look all that old. It's not been here long. Since daybreak, perhaps."

Max glared at the fabric strips. Daybreak made sense. Whoever had left it here had meant for it to be found by whoever was following the toy bear's trail through the Wild. Even though it was just fabric, the scent of blood would almost certainly have drawn predators to it if it had been in place overnight. As it was, the position was exposed. Even predators in the Wild didn't want to be out in the open this much during the day.

"We'll take a break here," Bryce said. He had taken a long, frowning look from the crude arrow to the building, then back along the roadway.

"We don't need a rest," Gemma protested.

"That's because you had a full night's sleep," Khari said, the sharp edge to her tone surprising Max. "Some of us were up all night. A few minutes being still would be nice," she added, glancing across at Max and sending her a wink, out of sight of Gemma.

Max ducked her head to hide a smile, and shed her backpack, settling herself on the ground with a sigh of relief. The only thing she could be grateful for was that she hadn't had any episodes of displacement during the day. Perhaps being truly exhausted was the key to stopping them. She had lost far more fitness than she had thought possible. As much as she hated running, she might need to start jogging again to build up her stamina when they got back to the city. The dogs would enjoy that, at least. They found her running pace laughably slow and usually entertained themselves by running in circles and loops around her.

Cas came to settle beside her, lying down, his tongue lolling out. Keeping an eye on her, she realised. He might have sensed Gemma's hostility, or just be reacting to Max's tiredness. Pol was a few paces away, also taking the chance to lie down. Her dogs wouldn't need much of a rest, she knew, but they would stop as long as she wanted. She reached out and stroked Cas' silky soft ears. He tilted his head, silently demanding a scratch behind each ear. She complied, smiling. It didn't matter what was happening in the world, her dogs would always make her feel better.

She drank some water and ate half a protein bar, still reasonably full from the excellent breakfast, but knowing she needed to keep taking in food and water.

Just as she had cooled down and was beginning to think about moving, Cas and Pol both lifted their heads, ears pricking. They turned as one in the same direction.

Max scrambled to her feet, along with the others.

"What is it?" Osvaldo asked.

"They've heard something," Max said. "Sorry, I can't be more precise than that."

"Dangerous?" Joshua wanted to know.

Max looked at her dogs' postures. Alert, but not worried. "I don't think so. Not right now, anyway."

Gemma muttered something under her breath that Max didn't hear, but from the sharp sideways look she got from Killan, it hadn't been a nice thing. No surprise there. When they had first met, Max had understood Gemma's hostility. The only thing Gemma had really known about Max was that Kitris blamed Max for the death of nine warriors. Anger had seemed entirely appropriate. But as time went on, Max couldn't help but wonder if there was more to Gemma's reactions. The warrior seemed extraordinarily bitter.

"I hear something, too," Bryce said. Osvaldo, Khari and Joshua agreed. "Sounds like something coming towards us. Let's take cover."

They must have far sharper hearing than the others, Max thought, as none of the others seemed to be able to hear anything. Still, Max trusted her dogs and Bryce, and grabbed her backpack before following the group as they went further along the old road to a place where a pair of giant old trees formed a natural arch over the road surface. Tucking themselves under the spreading branches of the trees should keep them from view of whatever was coming, rather than being out in the open on the roadway.

It was only as they gathered under the trees that Max realised that Bryce and the others were looking up, towards the sky, as were her dogs.

No sooner had she realised this than she heard it, too. The low thump-thump-thump she associated with the helicopters that were used to ferry tourists on their visits over the Wild. A dark speck formed against the pale, washed out sky, growing larger until she could see that it was, indeed, a helicopter. It was a black shape against the sky, whether painted dark or just shadowed against the bright sunlight, Max couldn't tell.

"Single rotor," Osvaldo commented, "looks like a ten- to fourteen-seater. Landing skids, not wheels." He was peering into the sky. Max looked again, but could barely make out the detail he had seen apart from the single set of rotor blades.

"Did Faddei call for a medical evac for the injured man?" Bryce asked Max. Like everyone else, he was crouched in the shadows of the trees, keeping still.

"He didn't mention it, but we were told at the briefing that there would be no rescue. We're on our own," Max reminded him. "And if we'd been able to use helicopters, we wouldn't have needed to bring so much equipment on the trucks."

"We have no assigned air support," Osvaldo confirmed. He was crouched next to Bryce. "We checked when we realised the Guardian had stowed away."

Max was glad she was facing away from the others so they couldn't see her expression. Of course the warriors would have tried to get the Guardian back to safety. Of course they would. Guardians were precious resources, and the warriors were charged with their safety.

"As if he would have gone. He's too busy playing a hero," Khari said, an edge to her tone that made Max like her even more. The warrior seemed to have as low an opinion of Radrean as Max did, although Max suspected for quite different reasons.

"It's not going towards the oil field," Max noted, eyes following the helicopter as it cut across the sky. She could see more details as it got closer. It looked as if it was painted a dark, matte colour. It was flying low, too, she noted, almost brushing the tops of the trees it was passing.

"It's heading for that building," Joshua concluded. He was settled next to his wife. "I wonder what's so interesting about it."

Now that, Max thought, was an excellent question. She glanced back at the path they had made through the undergrowth, and the makeshift arrow formed of bloody bits of fabric that had been left on the roadway. "It does seem like someone wants us to go there," she noted.

She saw frowns on a few of the warriors. As unhappy about the arrow as she was. It could only have been left for them. This was not a place that anyone would simply stumble across, and the strips of fabric were too small to be seen from the air.

"The mission is to follow the tracks and find the girl," Bryce reminded them. "Os, call back to base and let them know there's a helicopter in the area."

Max watched as the helicopter rose up the side of the hill that the building was on, and circled around it, disappearing from view. She could still hear it, though, until the sound gradually died away. She frowned, wondering if it had landed there or just gone out of her hearing range. Then she looked at her dogs. They shook themselves, as if dismissing something unpleasant, and turned to her, with expressions she had no difficulty in reading as asking her: *what next?*

So the helicopter's engines had been cut off. It had most likely landed by that building. Max wanted to go there and find out what was happening. There shouldn't be anyone flying into the Wild and landing. It wasn't strictly forbidden. Probably because the city's law makers didn't think anyone would be foolish enough to just venture into the Wild. A few supernatural creatures - like the forest ogres that occasionally visited Malik's bar - did go between the city and the Wild, but they were born to it, and the Wild left them alone, as they belonged. Anyone needing to fly a helicopter in almost certainly didn't belong.

She got Ynes' soft toy out of her pack to let her dogs refresh the scent again, and stared at the lilac fabric and beady eyes before looking up at the building again. Nati and Ynes couldn't have made the trip from the city on foot. But if someone had flown them here, that was a different story. It meant they might be alive. They had to be, Max told herself, refusing to consider any other options. She would rather face the underworld again than have to tell Alonso and Elicia that their daughter and granddaughter were dead. And if Ynes and Nati were alive, the building was the obvious place to go looking for them. There was no time to waste.

Chapter Twenty-Three

Even wanting to head for the building, Max knew that they needed to follow the scent trail. Just in case there was anything else to find. Still, she didn't think anyone was surprised when Pol's nose led them in an almost straight line through the packed undergrowth towards the hill and the building. In the same direction the fabric arrow had pointed.

As they walked, Max's apprehension grew. There was no good reason for someone to have brought Nati and Ynes from the city to the Wild. No good reason why anyone would land a helicopter in the Wild. No good reason why there was a demon somewhere in the jungle around them. From time to time she thought she caught flashes of Queran's presence, but they were brief and gone almost before she realised what they were. The brief flickers of his presence confirmed that he had been through the jungle, and in her mind also confirmed that he had left the bear and the arrow. He hadn't been trying to help her, that much she trusted. He had a purpose of his own. She also had the feeling of being watched, a crawling sensation between her shoulder blades.

The feeling of being watched might have been owing to the hard looks that she was getting from Gemma from time to time. The other woman hadn't said anything direct so far, just contenting herself with stares. But her lip curled when Max stumbled over a hidden root and stopped short with a muffled cry as the jolt woke up the pain in her leg. Max kept going, eyes stinging, and the pain dulled again, although she had to grit her teeth when the ground started rising under their feet. They must have made it to the hill where the building was, as Max couldn't remember seeing anywhere else with this much of an incline when they had stopped on the road. The rise in the ground set off more pain in her leg and she slowed down, unable to keep up with the others.

After a little while, Bryce called a halt. Gemma happened to be in Max's line of sight, and Max saw the warrior rolling her eyes in disgust. If it had been up to Gemma, Max was sure that the warriors would simply abandon her and her dogs and keep going.

Max flopped down on the ground, not caring that Gemma was sneering or that anyone else saw how tired she was. She shrugged off her backpack again and just focused on breathing. She was more worn out than she could remember being in her life before. The weeks of enforced rest and a day trekking through rough jungle keeping pace with the warriors had drained her energy almost entirely. Cas and Pol settled on the ground beside her, and she gave each a quick pat, too tired to do more.

"We're stopping again?" Gemma asked. "Really?"

"Take Hop and Killan and scout ahead. Quietly," Bryce said, voice stern. "We don't know what kind of traps might be laid or what kind of defences there might be."

"An abandoned building in the Wild," Gemma said, scorn dripping from her words. "You think there are defences?"

"The helicopter could have brought in weapons, and don't forget there's a full-fledged demon out here somewhere," Bryce reminded her.

"Oh, really? The only one who's seen this demon is her. You believe her?" Gemma asked, chin jutting out.

"Well, I do," Osvaldo said.

"And me," Joshua added.

"And me," Khari said.

Max's heart swelled, eyes stinging. She hadn't expected any of the warriors to voice their support, let alone so readily. When she had been dismissed from the Order, she had never thought that anyone there would want to have anything to do with her. Not after whatever tale Kitris had spun of her failure and cowardice.

"You know who she is, don't you?" Gemma said, voice rising in pitch. "She's the bitch traitor who got our brothers and sisters killed. Nine of them. Nine of our best. And they are all dead because of her."

Max stayed where she was, sitting on the ground with her elbows resting on her knees, still breathing too hard. She wasn't sure she could have got to her feet even if she had wanted to. The warmth of a moment ago faded into prickling ice along her skin. Gemma's hatred and contempt hung in the air.

Next to Max, Cas lifted his head, eyes fixed on Gemma and a low, displeased sound emerged from his throat. Pol shifted his weight, closer to Max, his eyes also on the warrior.

"You've said enough," Bryce told Gemma. He was standing a few paces away from Max, between her and Gemma. "You have your orders. Go and carry them out."

"How do you know she's not leading us into a trap?" Gemma demanded, taking a step towards Bryce, fury in her face, body tight. "If we turn back now, we can make it to the perimeter by nightfall. If not, we're stuck out here overnight. With her."

"Turn around if that's what you want. I would prefer it if you weren't here. All of you," Max said, voice harsh. It was the bare truth. She sensed and saw surprise around the group. "If you want to go back, then go. I'll keep going on my own." Her face heated up. She sounded sulky and ungrateful even in her own ears, but she couldn't find nice words to explain herself. And Pol had followed a scent this far. She wasn't leaving until she had answers.

Gemma glared down at her, then back at Bryce. "Why did you bring us here? Why are we following the traitor?"

"You volunteered for a mission out of the perimeter," Bryce reminded her, voice low and soft and dangerous. "And we're here because there's a child missing. We're not turning back until we've got answers." Max's brows lifted at hearing her own thought so clearly expressed. She hadn't imagined she had much in common with Bryce. It seemed she had been wrong.

"How do we even know that's true?" Gemma protested, not backing down.

"You don't want us here?" Khari asked Max, ignoring Gemma. "Why?" She sounded puzzled, and seemed genuine in her curiosity, rather than insulted when Max glanced at her, so Max drew a breath, trying to find the right words to answer her.

"Nine warriors died trying to protect me," Max said, her voice harsh. "That's nine too many. I don't want anyone else to die." She stared at the ground, not wanting to look up and see condemnation on the faces around her. Her face was wet, and she brushed the tears away impatiently, wishing she had the strength to get up and stride away into the jungle. But right now she wasn't sure she could get to her feet, her middle hollow, body heavy and tired. She rummaged in her backpack for some food. It also helped her avoid looking at the others.

Movement in front of her drew her attention. Khari was crouching in front of her, the woman's expression serious as she stared back at Max. Max couldn't help but notice that both her dogs were calm and relaxed in Khari's presence.

"We know the risks. We swear the same oaths as the Guardians and the apprentices," Khari said, her voice low. "And if nine of my brothers and sisters died protecting you, they must have thought you were worth protecting."

"I wasn't. Not then. Not now," Max said, throat tight, more tears on her face. "Kitris lied to them. Lied to me." Her throat closed up and she couldn't speak. Couldn't tell them that Kitris had meant for her to die, and hadn't really cared about the warriors he had sent with her.

"He does that," Khari agreed, mouth curving into a smile at Max's astonished look. "What? You thought we all believed he was perfect? Oh, no. He's arrogant. Always thinks he's right. He will lie, cheat and steal if he thinks that will get him what he wants."

"Khari!" Gemma looked and sounded horrified. "You should not speak about the master like that. Bryce, tell her. It's not right."

Max looked across at Bryce, wondering what he thought. He was standing with his arms folded across his chest, frowning. As if he was hearing things he didn't like, but didn't necessarily disagree.

"Kitris is the head of the Order," Bryce said at length. "We owe him our respect. That does not mean we have to be blind to his faults." Kitris had refused to investigate the potential for dark magic at the docks, Max remembered. Not perfect, indeed.

Gemma's gasp of shock and outrage seemed genuine. "I can't believe you would go against him like that," she said.

"I didn't do that," Bryce said, still frowning. "As I said, we owe him our respect." He glanced up at Gemma. "And you have your orders. Go."

Gemma's expression would have looked more at home on a three-year-old, Max thought. But the woman turned on her heel and stalked away up the hill, Hop and

Killan following. The pair had stayed quiet, watching and listening what went on. Max couldn't help wondering who they would agree with. Gemma, Khari, or Bryce.

"Good riddance," Khari said, not quite under her breath. She had moved away from Max and was standing next to Joshua.

"One of the nine who died was Gemma's cousin," Bryce said, his voice neutral. "And she's young enough, still, not to fully understand the dangers we face."

Khari's expression didn't change. "She's only three years younger than me," she said to Bryce. "And she's been in the Order nearly as long. I don't think you can keep making excuses for her."

"You are wise beyond your years, though," Joshua said, putting a hand on Khari's cheek, a fond smile on his face as he looked at his wife.

"Oh, stop it you two. Save it for your quarters," Osvaldo said, with mock-disgust. From the grins Joshua and Khari sent him, he had said something similar before. More than once.

Max watched the exchange with hurt blooming in her chest. She had never been loved like Khari was, or had a circle of friends who would tease her like Osvaldo was teasing Khari and Joshua. The Marshals were colleagues, but they were not friends. She had not *let* them be friends. She looked down at her hands, realising that she had eaten one and a half protein bars in the time she had been sitting on the ground. She took a drink of water, feeling some of her exhaustion lift. It might be possible for her to get off the ground soon.

Even as she was thinking that, a sharp crack sounded further up the slope, following by a brief cry. Too short to identify if it was pain or surprise.

The warriors around her went from relaxed to combat ready in the blink of an eye, weapons lifting as they looked up the slope. Cas and Pol were on their feet, as alert as the warriors.

"Go check it out," Bryce ordered. "I'll follow with Max."

"I don't-" Max started to say, wanting to protest that she didn't need a babysitter, cutting off her words as Bryce lifted a brow at her. Heat rose in her face.

Khari, Joshua, and Osvaldo hadn't waited for her permission, though. They were already disappearing into the trees up the slope, moving far more quickly than she had at any point during the day.

She got to her feet, wincing as her leg protested, and dug into her pockets for a conventional painkiller. It wasn't as effective as the magical patches, but it would take the edge off and hopefully let her focus. She swallowed the tablets with more water, then headed up the slope after the others, Cas and Pol on either side, Bryce a pace or two in front of her, keeping watch. She wanted to protest again, to tell him that she didn't need looking after, that she could manage, and that she didn't want him to be hurt because of her, that he should go after his people and make sure they were safe.

He was unlikely to listen, though, so she saved her breath for the climb.

Chapter Twenty-Four

Max's breath was harsh and rapid in her ears as she followed Bryce up the steep incline. She could tell he was moving slowly to accommodate her, but she was struggling to keep moving upwards.

He stopped and she almost ran into the back of him, so focused on putting one foot in front of the other. She opened her mouth to say something, and stayed silent as she looked past his shoulder, seeing what had made him pause.

There was a break in the ground ahead of them. What looked like a narrow fissure exposing a chasm of dark soil and roots, stretching out to either side. It completely blocked their path up the hill.

Through the undergrowth and trees ahead, Max could see the brighter daylight that indicated open space. They must be nearly at the top of the hill, she realised. No wonder her legs were tired.

There was no sign of the other warriors at all. Max frowned, thinking that she should be able to see them, then wondering just how good they were at hiding themselves. There were bushes along the edge of the daylight ahead of them, but the slope they were standing on was mostly tree trunks and low, tough ground cover.

Bryce lifted his weapon and took a step forward.

As he moved, Max felt magic stir around them. She grabbed hold of his backpack, trying to pull him back. She might as well have tried to stop a runaway truck. "Stop. There's magic around us," she told him.

He froze at once, turning his head towards her. "What is it?"

"I'm not sure," Max said. "Give me a minute. And, if you can, don't move."

He didn't say anything, but he didn't move, either.

She drew a deep, ragged breath, willing her heartbeat to slow and her body to settle its various aches enough that she could focus. It didn't help much.

She didn't recognise the magic. It wasn't Queran, which was something of a relief. And it was subtle, woven into the trees around them.

"It's some kind of perimeter," she told Bryce eventually. "I'm guessing that the others tripped the spell when they came up here."

"So, where are they?" Bryce asked.

An excellent question. Six fully trained, armed warriors of the Order would not simply have disappeared. Max tried concentrating on the area, to see if she could sense anything out of the ordinary or any concealment, getting nothing for her efforts other than a stab of pain behind her eyes. Apart from the faint trail of magic, there didn't seem to be anything else unusual in the jungle around them. But she knew that couldn't be right. They had seen the building on top of the hill, and the helicopter that seemed to have landed there. The jungle around them was quiet, as it had been for most of the day. Plus, the fissure in the ground ahead of them looked fresh. As if it had just been made.

Cas and Pol were crouched low to the ground, ears back, noses twitching. They weren't alerting to any particular threat, just generally unsettled. It took a lot to make her dogs nervous.

She took a careful step forward, and another, until she was shoulder-to-shoulder with Bryce. The ground trembled under her feet and the fissure in front of them widened. She looked down and saw the ground actually shaking, bits of soil and plants tumbling into the fissure.

"We should move," she said to Bryce. She glanced up the hill. "I really wanted to get up there. We'll need to find another way."

"No need," Bryce said. "We can get across here." He put his arm around her waist, under the backpack, lifting her off her feet before running the few steps forwards up the slope to the gaping gap in the ground. Before she could protest or wonder what he was doing, he had jumped.

His leap was finely judged, taking them across the gap, to a landing on the other side where he somehow managed to put Max back on the ground lightly enough that she didn't jolt her injured leg. Cas and Pol landed beside them, both dogs showing white around their eyes.

"Move," Bryce suggested, urging her on up the slope.

She blinked at him, wondering what had just happened. She had known he had non-human blood in him, but had had no idea he was so physically strong. He had just picked her up and carried her across the gap as if she weighed next to nothing. He let her go, perhaps judging that she could move on her own, and started up the slope. The ground on this side of the fissure seemed solid. The trap had most likely just been laid for unwanted visitors, not anyone coming down the hill from above. But she didn't want to stay here, close to the gap, to test her theory. She found a bit of energy from somewhere and went after Bryce, scrambling up the slope until she reached a point where the trees thinned and the ground flattened, reminding her of the roadway they had stopped on earlier in the day.

Bryce tucked himself behind a large-leafed shrub that should conceal them from view. Annoyingly, he didn't seem in the slightest bit out of breath or tired from the scramble up the slope, or the trek they had made during the day. Max could hear her heart thumping in her ears, breath harsh and rasping with effort, her shoulders and hips aching from the weight of the backpack she carried. She had barely noticed it when they had set out, but it was a constant pressure now, her back sticky with sweat under the pack and her leather jacket.

"Would the others have been able to jump across that gap?" she asked, kneeling on the ground next to Bryce. She kept her voice as quiet as possible.

He frowned as he looked across at her. She tried to control her breathing, not sure if he was worried about being discovered or about his missing warriors.

"Yes, easily," he told her, speaking equally softly.

"But they aren't here," Max pointed out. "Or are they, and I just can't see them?"

"No, they're not here. We can't make ourselves invisible," Bryce said, a touch of humour in his voice. The laughter faded as he went on. "There were no signs that anyone else had come up that slope today, so they must be somewhere else."

Max nodded, trying to shift her weight to be more comfortable. The pack slid a fraction on her shoulder, metal frame digging into her hip and she muttered a curse, releasing the clips and shrugging it off.

"Good idea," Bryce said. "We need to be able to move lightly."

Max couldn't help noticing that he didn't shed any of his equipment. But then, he had just carried her and her backpack across a yawning gap in the ground with as much effort as he carried his weapons. Which was to say, none at all.

As her breathing slowed, sweat beginning to cool now that the backpack was on the ground, she took a closer look around. The light was fading, night fast approaching, but there was still enough daylight to see that the helicopter had, indeed, landed here. It was settled on the flat, open ground, held up by landing skids. It was bigger than Max had expected and she remembered Osvaldo's assessment of it being a ten- to fourteen-seater. It certainly looked big enough for that, not including the pilot and co-pilot. She couldn't see any logos or other insignia anywhere on the vehicle. That made sense when flying over the Wild, as bright signs or sharply contrasting colours might draw attention from the predators. But this didn't look like a tourist vehicle, not to her eyes. It was painted in a matte finish, absorbing the light, and looked more like something law enforcement or the Order might use.

Beyond the helicopter, she could see the building that they had spotted earlier in the day. This close, it was far larger and more impressive than she had imagined. It had solid stone walls that rose three storeys above the ground, with high, arched windows and a pitched roof. The roof was missing a number of tiles and the walls had trails of vines growing over them, but it still looked like a reasonably solid structure. It was in far better condition than she would have imagined for something that had to have been abandoned at least a decade before, when the Wild had last expanded.

"That's an odd structure," she commented. She couldn't remember seeing anything else like it in the city. For some reason, it made her think of a temple, even though it was a completely different design. It had the same sense of serenity and purpose, standing alone and on a prominent spot. Easy to see from a distance, even with the Wild having sprung up around it.

"It looks like an old meeting hall," Bryce said.

"A community building?" Max asked, startled. She couldn't imagine what it was doing here, out on its own. Even when the Wild hadn't advanced this far, the building had been placed on a hilltop with no signs of other structures round about it.

"This was very fertile land. There were probably lots of small farms around here originally," Bryce said. "The people would have wanted somewhere to gather, and this hill was probably too steep to farm."

And the stone walls and simple, pitched roof would have been a relatively easy construction project, at least compared to the formal temples or more ornate public buildings that Max was used to seeing in the city, she realised.

A soft rushing sound behind her made her turn. In the fast-gathering shadows of the jungle, she saw the fissure that Bryce had jumped over widening, the ground seeming to fall away, leaving an enormous gap. Far too big for him or her dogs to leap over.

"I hope there's another way down," Max said, still speaking softly. She couldn't see anyone around, but that didn't mean much. Apart from the open space where the helicopter was, they were surrounded by jungle.

"There's the helicopter," Bryce pointed out.

"Assuming we can find a pilot," Max said.

"That's true," he agreed. "Do you need to rest a bit more?" he asked.

There was no judgement in his tone. It was a simple, direct question.

"A moment," she said, trying not to feel embarrassed anew by her weakness. She grabbed more food out of her pack, searching blindly in the dark, the rich, sweet taste of chocolate surprising and welcome. At least chocolate was not being rationed in the city. Not yet, anyway. The energy from the snack spread more quickly than the protein bar had and she nodded. She tucked the backpack more securely under the shrub. It had a matt black finish, so shouldn't be easily found. She hoped. And she had plenty of ammunition on her person. Hopefully. "Ready."

Bryce didn't question her, just rose from his crouch and led them along the edge of the trees, heading for the building. As they moved, Max could sense another trail of magic. It didn't seem to be near them, and didn't bear the demon's signature, so she just noted it and kept moving.

The helicopter appeared to be unguarded, which surprised her. Even if the pilot and passengers hadn't expected to find other people this far out into the Wild, there were still predators around that would find the foreign object interesting.

Nothing moved as they crept past the helicopter, the scent of the metal, oil and fuel harsh and unappealing after being surrounded by the Wild for the day.

Max stopped again at the last set of dense undergrowth before the building, crouching down into the shadows and grimacing as her leg protested. There was no daylight left now. The moon had risen, though, and there was enough open space around them for her to be able to see fairly well. Closer to the building, she could sense magic laced into its walls. There were different layers. Old magic, which felt benign. The sort of magic she might use on her perimeter wards around her house. Then newer magic, more like the power that she had sensed coming up the hill, that had caused the fissure in the ground.

"Someone has been adding spells to the building," she told Bryce. "If we try to go in, we're going to get noticed." Whoever had used the helicopter was most likely inside the building.

"Let's watch and wait for a while," he said. He had settled beside her, seemingly prepared to stay there all night.

Max shifted her weight, taking pressure off her injury, and tried to adopt the same patience as Bryce. She failed. She wasn't good at waiting. Almost none of a Marshal's job involved sitting still.

"I want to do a circuit if I can," she told Bryce, straightening, still within the shadows of the undergrowth. The shrubs here were taller than Bryce, easily high enough to conceal both of them.

He didn't say anything, just followed her as she started making her way along the side of the building, keeping to the shadows and the trees and shrubs.

There was a strip of ground all around the building that looked like it had been cleared recently, jagged ends of plants sticking up from the ground. Whoever was in the building would have a clear line of sight to the outdoors and Max could all-too-easily imagine someone standing behind one of the windows, a gun ready to fire.

Before they got too far along the first side of the building, a sharp cry split the night. It sounded like someone crying out in pain. And came from inside the building.

Max left the shelter of the undergrowth, forcing herself to an uneven run across the open space, tucking herself against the side of the building, back pressed against the stone wall, her dogs with her, Bryce a pace or two behind.

"So much for waiting," Bryce muttered.

Max didn't apologise. The cry had confirmed that there was someone else in the building. Walking around it wouldn't tell them who that was.

She crept back to the end of the building where the helicopter was. There had been a doorway there, and she hadn't seen any other way of getting into the building.

The front entrance of the building had two double-height doors that were partially open. She put out a hand towards the entrance but, to her surprise, couldn't feel any magic in the gap. The air was cool, but it was just air. Whatever protections had been placed on the walls hadn't extended to these main doors. Either that, or the spells weren't active when the doors were open. Whatever the reason, it meant that no alarm would go off when they went inside.

Max drew her gun, creeping along the side of one of the doors, listening for all she was worth. She couldn't hear anything. She glanced down and found Cas and Pol alongside her, shifted into their battle forms. Her dogs went through the door at her gesture, Max following, Bryce her shadow.

It was darker inside the building, even with the high windows. Despite the great height of the building, there was just one floor, no upper levels. Max moved along the doors, pressing her back against the wall beside the great hinges, glad she had removed the backpack as it made her a less bulky shadow. She paused, letting her eyes adjust to the poor light. Even then, she couldn't see much. As well as no upper floors, there didn't seem to be any formal rooms inside the building. On the side of the building where they were there was a series of wooden partitions that were taller than she was, but still far shorter than the main walls, dividing that side of the building into makeshift rooms. They had open fronts, a couple of them with what looked like heavy curtains pulled to one side.

Apart from the makeshift rooms and some thick stone pillars to support the roof overhead, the building was just one vast, open space.

In the centre of the building the available light had pooled, whether by accident or design, and was supplemented by a few old-fashion lanterns, the sort that burned oil and provided a muted, steady light, all of which gave Max a clear view of a group of people. All but one were wearing floor-length, dark robes with the hoods pulled up, hiding their faces. The last figure was dressed in a beautifully fitting black suit, black hair gleaming in the faint light. She thought she knew him. Max frowned, wondering if she was mistaken. Then the man turned, his movements stiff, and she saw his face. Lord Kolbyr. One of the most powerful vampires in the city, and an authority on dark magic. When they had first met, she had almost been overwhelmed by the aura of power he carried around him, but she couldn't sense him at all in this space.

She forced herself to look away from the vampire and continue her scan of the building. On the other side of the doors from her and Bryce, she could see a small, square table with a pair of men sitting at it. There was a lantern on the table, letting Max see that its surface was covered in beer cans and cards, and that the men were dressed in the one-piece coveralls she associated with pilots. The pair might have flown the helicopter in, but it looked as if they had been drinking and gambling for a while. Max took a moment to be thankful that she had moved away from that side of the building when she had crept inside. If she and Bryce had run into the drinkers, they would have been spotted at once. As it was, it didn't seem that anyone in the building had noticed her and Bryce.

He touched her arm, pressing slightly to urge her forward. She looked along the wall, and saw that they were close to one of those makeshift rooms. This one had its curtain mostly intact, shielding half the opening in deep shadow. It would be a much better place to hide than in the shadows by the wall.

She moved, as quietly as she could, her dogs absolutely silent beside her, Bryce following.

The air in the more enclosed space was stale and smelled of mould, as if something had been stored there and gone off a long time ago. Still, it seemed empty, and Max discovered as she turned to the curtain that there were various tears in the fabric that would give her a partial view of the building without needing to stick her head around the end of the fabric and risk being seen.

As she and Bryce settled in to wait, she wondered how it was they had not been spotted. Someone had gone to great lengths to protect the building with magic, and yet the pair of them and her dogs had managed to sneak in the front door and into their current hideout without raising any alarm. As she was wondering what she had missed, a voice cut through the air.

"Really, how many times do you need to be instructed?"

That was Kolbyr's voice, sounding faintly bored. He had an extraordinarily high opinion of himself, Max knew from her limited experience. She also knew that the confidence was justified.

"We've done precisely as you asked," another voice answered. It must be some quirk of the building's design, but the words spoken in the middle of the space carried perfectly around the building.

"For a third time," another voice said. It was faintly familiar, but Max couldn't place the speaker. Not yet.

"If you had done it correctly, it would not need to be redone," Kolbyr said, his tone one of forced patience. As he spoke, he moved further into the centre of the building, into the light, and Max saw the gleam of something metal around his throat. She remembered her impression that his movements were stiff, and wondered what device he was wearing.

"He's lying to us," one of the robed figures said. With them all wearing identical outfits, and having their faces covered, Max was having difficulty telling them apart. She didn't recognise this voice, though. It had a hard edge to it. A man used to getting his own way and not afraid to use violence.

"Don't be so ridiculous," a female voice spoke. The speaker dragged her hood back off her head, revealing a familiar face. Shivangi Raghavan. Which meant that her brother Hemang was probably one of the other robe-wearers. "We've bound the creature so it has no choice but to do our bidding," she said, addressing the others, all but ignoring the powerful vampire a few paces from her.

Max's brows lifted. She had seen first-hand how arrogant the twins were, but provoking Lord Kolbyr seemed reckless, even for Shivangi. There were no armed guards around to protect either of the twins if Lord Kolbyr decided to make an example of them.

To Max's further surprise, Kolbyr did nothing. He didn't react to the insult, simply staying where he was, that metal device catching the light again. Shivangi had said they had bound the creature. As far as Max knew, metal had no particular effect on vampires, but the collar Kolbyr was wearing seemed to have him confined.

"He's still tricking us. Somehow," a male voice said, also pulling back his hood to reveal a face that Max had not expected to see. Evan Yarwood. The chief of detectives.

"Perhaps he is not a true servant of our lord." The voice was silky smooth and familiar. Queran. Max knew him even before the demon removed his hood. The rest of the circle drew their hoods back, too, revealing Hemang and two males that Max didn't recognise, but who both possessed the sharp glitter in their eyes she associated with the Huntsman clan.

She blinked, wondering for a moment if she was imagining the whole thing. A demon, the Raghavan twins, the chief of the city's police detectives, and two members of the Huntsman clan. And one of the city's most powerful vampires, apparently bound by some kind of metal device. She could not imagine how they had all come to be here.

"After all, things have been quite comfortable in this world for him," Queran said, dragging Max's attention back to the demon. "I can well imagine the prospect of bending a knee to our master is not all that appealing."

Max's brows lifted again. She remembered having a similar thought not long after she had met Lord Kolbyr. He studied dark magic and rituals, many of which were dedicated to Arkus. But the vampire bowed to no one in this world, and if someone actually succeeded in opening the Grey Gates and bringing the dark lord into the daylight world, Kolbyr would lose his position.

"You are ridiculous," Kolbyr said, scorn in his voice. "Little watcher demon. You forget your station."

"I forget? I?" Fury made Queran's voice boom around the building, rattling the windows. "I am not the one who has insisted we set out this light-blighted ritual three times already."

"Don't you want our dark master to be satisfied with your work?" Kolbyr asked, turning to Queran. "Or do you think He will be pleased when the ritual fails because of your incompetence?"

Silence as loud as Queran's shout rang through the building.

The demon was still, the promise of violence hanging in the air. Then his lips curled into what might have been a smile.

"I live at His pleasure to service His will. If it is not perfect, we will do it again," Queran said, taking a small, deliberate step back from the vampire. "Secure him in his pen while we clean the space to start again," he told the others.

"You don't get to give me orders, demon," Shivangi said.

Queran rounded on her, flinging out an arm, and the joint head of the Raghavan family flew across the room, slamming into one of the pillars. Max winced in reflexive sympathy. Hemang let out a cry of outrage and went to his sister's aid. Not challenging the demon, Max noted. Very wise.

The two Huntsman clan members seemed to have no issue with taking orders from the demon. They each took one of Kolbyr's arms and steered him away from the centre of the building, coming towards the place where Max and Bryce were hiding. Not directly, she realised after a panicked moment. They were heading for the next partitioned space along the wall.

All the same, Max held her breath as the two clan members escorted Kolbyr into the space beside the one she was standing in. She heard the clink of metal, a snap which sounded like something closing, and then the two clan members headed back to the central space, leaving Kolbyr behind.

The rest of the robed figures had already picked up brushes from somewhere and were beginning to sweep the floor. It seemed far too menial a task for them, in particular the twins, and Max didn't have a good angle to see what precisely they were clearing away. Some kind of powder, it looked like, from the way it lifted into the air.

"Enjoying the show?" a low voice asked from somewhere close by.

Chapter Twenty-Five

Max jumped, clamping a hand over her mouth to hold in a cry of alarm. The voice had sounded so close. Almost next to her ear. She looked around to find Bryce glaring at the wooden partition next to them and the room where Kolbyr had been chained.

"I know you're there," the voice said again, and this time she recognised the speaker. Kolbyr. He was speaking in a normal tone, and as her shock subsided, she could feel a trace of his magic in the air. It was not the powerful force she remembered. Whatever had been done to him had weakened him. After a pause, he said, "You may answer. I'm concealing our conversation and your presence from the others."

Max took a long, deep breath and moved closer to the wooden partition. "How did you know we were here?" she asked, keeping her voice low, not entirely trusting his word. It had looked like he was being held prisoner by Queran and the others, but she could not imagine how even Queran had captured the powerful vampire.

"You are just delightful," he said, reminding her of the demon. "It was my magic that got you inside without being seen. Or did you think that everyone in here is deaf and blind? Now do come and free me, there's a good girl."

"Not until you tell me what's going on," Max said, setting her jaw. If Kolbyr was telling the truth, he could be a powerful ally. If.

"Come now, you can't be that stupid," Kolbyr said.

"Dark magic is your expertise. Not mine," Max said grimly. It looked as if the robed people were trying to perform some kind of ritual. All in the service of the dark lord Himself. Beyond that, she didn't want to speculate, not even in her own mind.

"Child, we don't have time." Kolbyr's tone of forced patience set her teeth on edge.

Max was about to challenge him when Bryce shifted his weight beside her. "I hate to say it, but I agree with him. Explanations can wait." She looked at him in the poor light, unable to make out his expression. "Go and free Lord Kolbyr. I'll cover you. Just in case," he said.

In case Kolbyr's magic wasn't as effective as the vampire claimed, Max assumed. She trusted Bryce far more than the vampire, so she put her gun away. Bryce put something metal into her hand, apparently not having any difficulty in finding her in the dark.

"That should cut through anything," Bryce told her.

Moving very carefully, she used her fingertips to explore the object. A metal handled knife in what felt like a metal sheath. She could feel magic in it, and decided not to unsheathe it to test the blade. At least not near her fingers.

With the blade tucked by her side, she signalled to her dogs to stay and crept along the outside of the curtain. The robed figures had finished their sweeping and were now washing down the area with mops and buckets. In any other circumstances, that would have held Max's attention. She couldn't imagine that Shivangi and Hemang regularly used any kind of domestic cleaning equipment. Whatever they were doing must be important to them. As it was, she concentrated on keeping to the shadows and creeping along the outside of the curtain until she reached the opening of Kolbyr's cell.

With the better light of the building at her back, Max could just make out the vampire standing close to the wooden partition that now separated him and Bryce. Kolbyr turned slightly as she approached, and she saw that the metal collar he was wearing had a loop in it, and a chain had been attached to the loop.

Unsheathing Bryce's knife, Max set the blade against the last link of the chain. She couldn't see the detail of it, but she could feel the knife sliding through the metal. Careful to keep hold of the chain so that it wouldn't crash to the floor and alert anyone else, Max separated the chain and the collar. She crouched, slowly, and put the end of the chain on the ground, straightening back to her feet to find the vampire looking at her with a fixed expression, eyes glittering in the poor light. He was focused on her neck.

"How long has it been since you fed?" she asked him.

"They've had me here for three days," he told her, voice and posture stiff.

Most very old vampires, like Kolbyr, didn't need to feed every day. It was one of the few popular myths about vampires that was actually true. But they did need to feed regularly, and more frequently if they were put under stress. Just like humans. And Max could imagine that having a collar put on him and being chained to the wall had been an unpleasant experience, to say the least, for Kolbyr. It had probably been centuries since anyone had been so openly disrespectful.

"I have excellent self-control," Kolbyr murmured.

"Bryce, my dogs and I are not on the menu," Max told him, meeting and holding his eyes. Even subdued by the collar, he was still powerful.

His lips peeled back, revealing sharp teeth. "I am not so far gone that I would feed on your dogs." He sounded revolted by the idea.

"Good to know," Max said. "How about Bryce and me?" she asked.

Kolbyr was practically vibrating with impatience, his teeth descended far enough to be visible under his top lip, but he inclined his head slightly. "I will not feed on you or your warrior," he said.

It was more than she had expected, and exactly what she had asked for, so she took a step towards him, frowning at the collar. "I'm sorry, I'm going to need to touch you to get this off," she said.

"Very well." Kolbyr held himself stiff and straight while Max reluctantly worked her fingers under the collar, lifting it away from his skin enough that she could get the tip of the blade under the metal. She couldn't help noticing that his skin was cooler than a human's, his pulse strong and rapid.

Bryce's magic knife sliced through the collar as easily as it had the chain. Whatever magic had been in the collar warmed the metal until it was too hot for Max to keep holding. She had to let go, dropping the cut collar onto the ground. The metal was molten by the time it hit the ground, pooling on the floor rather than striking with a clang.

With the collar gone, Max took a couple of steps back from the vampire.

He was standing quite still, the skin of his neck reddened where the collar had been, eyes closed as he drew in a long, deep breath. As he breathed out, he opened his eyes and his aura, the powerful, dark presence that Max remembered, rolled out from him, coating her and everything else in its path.

"That's better," he said, smile revealing his fully descended fangs. He had changed from his human appearance, his face now in its more natural form. Beautiful and deadly. Vampires preferred to seduce their prey, not fight for their next meal. Max felt herself drawn towards the vampire. It would be so easy to just take the steps back, to stand beside him and let him do what he wanted. So easy. She closed her hand around the knife Bryce had lent her, the solid weight of it in her hand providing an anchor that she held on to. Vampires disguised themselves so well that it was easy to forget what master predators they really were.

"You smell quite delicious. And you've been spending time with Audhilde, haven't you?" he asked, in a gentle murmur that made her want to lean closer. It was a soothing tone, promising warmth and comfort. "Are you sure I can't have a sip?" he asked her.

She could feel the pull still there, but forced herself to take a step back. Not too far, as she didn't want to stray into the open space. Just enough to put a little bit more distance between her and the predator.

"I'm not on the menu," she reminded him. She still had the blade in her hand. If it could cut through metal, she was sure it could cut into a vampire and do some damage.

To her surprise, he smiled. A much more genuine smile, it was shockingly attractive on his vampire face. "Well done, my dear. Not many people can resist me. If you will excuse me, I'm hungry. And I have a score or two to settle."

That was an understatement, Max saw. Despite the magic that made him almost irresistibly beautiful, he looked feral. She wasn't sure if any of the robed figures would survive his wrath.

"Wait," Max said. "The helicopter outside. Do you know how to fly it?" It could take them back to the oil field in a fraction of the time they had taken to get here.

"No," Kolbyr said, a frown gathering. "Very well. I will leave the pilots and the offerings untouched."

"The offerings?" Max asked, but she was speaking to empty space.

Kolbyr stalked out of the shadows and into the light at the centre of the building, leaving Max to tuck herself hastily into the shadows, not sure he would remember to conceal her as he left to seek his revenge.

Chapter Twenty-Six

Shivangi saw the approaching vampire first, pausing with her mop held mid-air, water dripping onto the stone floor.

"How did you get free?" she demanded.

"What?" one of the Huntsman clan asked, whirling. He had called Kolbyr a creature when the vampire had been restrained, Max remembered. And she had a feeling that Kolbyr had not forgotten, either.

Evan Yarwood pulled a gun out from under his robes and fired at the vampire. Max watched his bullets strike home, travelling through the vampire, leaving ragged tears in his clothes. Kolbyr didn't stop moving, and barely reacted to the bullets.

Low cries from further along the wall dragged Max's attention away from the group in the middle of the building. She sheathed the knife, tucking it into a pocket, then left the shadows and looked around the other side of the wooden partition, breath catching as she saw the *offerings* that Kolbyr had referred to. People. There were people huddled together on the floor of the room, perhaps half a dozen in total, pressed back against the stone outside wall and wooden partitions, all of them wide-eyed and terrified.

Max's stomach turned. The robed group had been preparing for some kind of a ritual, and had been going to use these people as *offerings*. Sacrifices to the dark lord, for some purpose she didn't yet know.

"Marshal's service," Max said to the group of terrified victims, pulling her badge out from under her jacket. The seven-pointed star was gleaming in response to all the magic in the air. "Sit tight for a bit, and I'll get you out as soon as I can." She scanned the faces. "Are there more people here? More like you, I mean?"

"In the n-next one," a man close to the front said.

"Are you really a Marshal?"

"Are you here to help us?"

"Can we go home now?"

The questions tumbled out on top of each other. Max lifted a hand, asking for quiet. Behind her, she could hear sounds of a struggle, and an ugly snarl which suggested Kolbyr was not getting everything his own way. That was dangerous.

"Yes, I'm a Marshal. I'll get you out. Stay here for the moment," Max said, and moved on.

The next room was the same. A huddled mass of terrified people pressed back as far as they could get from the centre of the building. With an important difference. In the midst of all of the adults was a small figure, arms wrapped around a too-thin woman with a fearsome bruise on one side of her face.

"Nati? Ynes?" Max asked, crouching down so she wasn't so intimidating to the child. "My name is Max. I'm a ... well, I know your parents, Alonso and Elicia."

"Max?" Nati said, astonished. "What are you doing here?"

"Your parents asked me to look for you and Ynes," Max said, throat closing up. She could hardly believe that she had found them both. Together and alive. Not safe, not yet. But alive. It was more than she had dared hoped for.

Rapid movement behind her brought her up on her feet and turning, just in time to see one of the robed figures slide across the floor to come to a rest at the base of the nearest stone pillar. Hemang. From the way he flopped on the floor, he seemed to be unconscious.

Shivangi let out a scream of rage, drawing Max's attention back to the centre of the room. The two Huntsman clan members were on the ground, their throats torn open but with very little blood around them. It looked like Kolbyr had found his meal.

The rest of the conspiracy were proving harder to kill, which surprised Max. Kolbyr was locked in a hand-to-hand struggle with Evan Yarwood. Max blinked, sure that could not be right, but it was. The supposedly human chief of detectives was grappling with a vampire, and not yielding.

Queran was standing back, watching the show with every appearance of enjoyment. Max wondered if he was somehow helping Evan. She couldn't think of another way that an ordinary human could hold their own against any vampire, let alone one as powerful as Kolbyr. Unease crept through her as she wondered what she had missed in Evan Yarwood's make-up, and what else she might have overlooked.

Shivangi charged at Kolbyr, wielding her mop like a weapon. The vampire must have sensed her approach as he turned, putting Evan in her path so that Shivangi's wild swing thudded into the side of Evan's head and not Kolbyr's. Evan dropped to the ground, unconscious. At least for the moment. Leaving Shivangi facing off with Kolbyr. The vampire straightened his suit jacket, despite all the bullet holes, and faced the Raghavan twin.

"You know, if you had asked nicely, I might have helped you," Kolbyr told Shivangi. "We do serve the same master, after all." It sounded oh-so-reasonable, and Max did not believe a word of it. Kolbyr had his own agenda.

"You hurt my brother," Shivangi answered, teeth bared.

"He got in my way. And he enjoyed putting that collar around my neck a little too much," Kolbyr answered.

Shivangi screamed in fury again, lifting the mop.

"Stop," Queran said. A trail of his power leaked out into the air. Whatever he had done, Shivangi was held motionless, still furious. "I see we have guests," the demon said, looking past Kolbyr, his eyes meeting Max's across the room. "Miscellandreax. How delightful. Do join us."

There was a compulsion built into his words, a trail of magic sliding around Max's body, encouraging her to move forward. Either by accident or design, the magic wasn't strong enough to force her to move. She stayed where she was. Out of the corner of her eye, she saw her dogs moving through the shadows, coming to stand near her. Bryce was still hidden, which was good. It might give them an advantage.

Looking past the demon, she could see that the pair of drinkers had got to their feet, although they didn't seem to have any weapons, which was something.

"How could I resist, after you invited me here? That was you with the stuffed toy and the fabric strips made into an arrow, wasn't it?" Max asked. She tried to keep her tone light, to show no weakness to the demon.

"Oh, how clever of you to put it together. Yes. I had hoped that the Behemoths and Seacast monkeys would send you running, but after that didn't work, what was a demon to do apart from invite you further into the Wild?" Queran said, exposing too-white teeth with what looked like a pleased grin. "I didn't think you would make it this far, but I did enjoy thinking of you floundering around in the jungle. So many dangers out there. And now you're here, I'm sure we can find a use for you," he added, the grin still in place. His eyes slid past her to the shadowed areas where the kidnapped people were still huddled together, making it clear to Max just how he thought she would be useful. Her stomach turned at the idea of being used as an *offering* for the ritual that Queran and his accomplices had been preparing. Then anger rose, a welcome wash of warmth through her body. He thought he could use her. She had no intention of being used.

"And the spiders?" Max spat at him, remembering the sheer terror of the creatures surging towards her.

Queran chuckled, the low, rich sound filling the air. "Oh, they did like their nest. And the shield was a little joke. Was it you who found it? How lovely. I'm afraid I couldn't resist. But you did very well," he assured her, in a patronising tone that set her teeth on edge.

"What are you doing here, Queran?" Max demanded. Now that he wasn't forcing her to move, she walked closer to the central space, careful to keep her steps small and even. She didn't want him to see she was injured.

He just chuckled again, and didn't answer. Her temper spiked. She was tired of the demon playing games with her.

As she got closer to the centre, she could see the remnants of the ritual that had been laid on the floor, despite the sweeping and the mopping. It looked like a series of squares, all set slightly off from each other so that the outer edge looked like a multi-pointed star and the inner part was almost circular. Her temper faded, breath catching in her throat.

"That's a portal spell," she said. She might not know much dark magic, but what was etched on the ground was one of the simplest forms of magic. Far simpler than the magic used by Kitris and the Guardians, but still effective. Or so the Order teachers had told their students, a sneer in their voices.

They hadn't got around to mopping the centre of the markings and the faint outline of a familiar symbol lay on the floor near Queran's feet. Arkus.

Max's mouth was dry, her fingers itching to reach for her gun. She held herself still. She had put half a magazine into Queran the day before to no effect whatsoever. Bullets weren't going to help.

"Well done," Queran said, as if she was a very stupid child who had just learned something incredibly basic.

"A portal spell," Max repeated, and had to swallow before she could continue. "To open the Grey Gates and bring Arkus Himself to this world?"

"Not as dumb as you look, are you?" Queran said, a pleased smile on his face.

Max ignored the insult, turning to Shivangi, who was the only one of the other conspirators still standing. "Are you insane? Do you have any idea what would happen if the Grey Gates were opened and Arkus and his demons were let loose on the world?"

"Well, we were preparing it at the docks, but your interference there forced us to change our plans," Shivangi said, voice flat and displeased. Closer to the woman, Max caught the trace of a familiar scent, rich and vibrant. Some kind of perfume, she guessed, and abruptly remembered where she had come across it before. Not just on the docks, when she had first met Shivangi and her brother, but before then, in the police station, when she had been forced to pass close to Evan Yarwood. Which meant that Evan had been spending time with the twins, or at least Shivangi, before their trip into the Wild. Doubtless helping them with whatever preparations that had been underway at the docks.

"You were using the Darsin to keep people away from your little plot, weren't you? And it leashed the Galdr for you?" Max guessed, a trail of disgust and fury running through her. If the twins had been preparing a space for a portal spell at the docks, no wonder they had wanted it guarded. And with them up to their necks in dark magic conspiracy, it made sense that they would turn to a Darsin, rather than any of the far more legitimate magicians who could be found in the city. Magicians who might ask questions about what the twins were up to.

"That was my brother's idea," Shivangi said, a sharp edge still in her voice. "But at least he made himself useful here. Did you like the little surprises he left outside? The explosions sounded quite good."

Max pressed her lips together. She hadn't realised Hemang was a magician, but if he had set the traps in the ground around the hill, then he had a decent amount of power and skill. "And all of this to try and open the portal? Are you crazy?" she asked.

Shivangi's mouth curved up in a smile and her whole body relaxed. "We will be favoured above all others for assisting in our master's return," she said, voice lilting and soft, a far cry from the screaming fury she had displayed earlier. "We will have a place at our master's table and rule our own kingdom."

"You are insane," Max said, voice flat. "You already rule your own kingdom, more or less. What could you possibly want with more power?"

"The docks? A filthy bit of useless land that no one else wants," Shivangi said, scornful. "We barely see daylight unless we go into the city." The woman shuddered. "We used to have real power, you know. This land was ours."

"This land," Max repeated, eyes widening. "You mean, this building and the land around it used to belong to your Family? Before the Wild expanded?"

"It was beautiful. I still remember it. We had a palace. An actual palace," Shivangi said, eyes unfocused as she looked into the past. "We kept our honour with our dark lord, and now He will reward us."

Max couldn't help but remember the fine clothes that the Raghavan twins had been wearing when she had first met them, and the soldiers that had surrounded them. Shivangi might think the land her Family now occupied was filthy, but it had been the operation of the docks, and not this stretch of land now taken over by the Wild, that had made her family wealthy beyond the imagining of most of the city's residents. And the woman still wanted more. More power. More wealth. More everything. The Raghavan twins had grown up as the favoured children of one of the most powerful families in the city. They had been given every privilege possible. Max was not impressed with how they had turned out. Their ambition and greed had made them stupid, though.

"You think that you are going to get your palace back and see more daylight if Arkus comes to this world?" Max asked, incredulous. "Don't you remember the old legends? When Arkus escaped His realm before, there was a decade of darkness and ruin in the world. Thousands died. The world only survived because the Grey Gates were formed and closed, sealing Arkus away."

"Ah, good times," Queran said, a happy smile on his face.

"Don't quote legends to me," Shivangi said, ignoring the demon, her lip curling back. "Useless old things. This will be different."

"She is right, though," Kolbyr said, voice mild. "No, my dears, I was not alive at that time, but I have heard first-hand accounts. It was a remarkable time. There were no rules." He glanced at Max.

"And no Marshals, either, I would guess," Max said, sarcasm heavy in her voice.

"Quite," Kolbyr said, a faint smile on his face. He had returned to his human form, the beauty set aside along with his fangs, but he was still somehow compelling. Recently fed, and with his power intact, he was at least as dangerous as Queran, in Max's view.

"Well, there are Marshals now. And I'm here now. And I am not going to let you idiots open a portal to the underworld to bring the dark lord out of His realm and into this one," Max said, her voice firm and certain. She just hoped no one asked her how she was going to achieve that.

Chapter Twenty-Seven

"You think we didn't anticipate resistance?" Queran asked, teeth showing in a smile. He tilted his head to somewhere past Max's shoulder, towards the front of the building. She resisted the urge to follow his glance, not wanting to take her eyes off him.

Kolbyr had no such hesitation. He looked and his mouth curved up in a feral smile that looked utterly wrong on his human face. "Oh, my, more snacks? You really are spoiling me, little watcher."

"Don't call me that," Queran hissed.

It was the second time Kolbyr had referred to the demon as a watcher, and both times it seemed to have gotten under Queran's skin. Max made a mental note to ask Kolbyr about it later. Assuming they survived and there was a later.

"Snacks?" Shivangi hissed. "Is that all we are to you? Food?"

"Do you really want me to answer that?" Kolbyr asked, a dark undertone to his voice that raised the hairs on the back of Max's neck.

"You aren't on our side at all, are you?" Shivangi asked, in a tone which suggested she had only just realised that.

"As I told you, I might have helped you if you had but asked," Kolbyr said. He sounded distracted, most of his attention on the space behind Max.

Skin crawling, Max looked over her shoulder in what she'd intended to be a quick glance, but stopped, frowning, at the sight that met her eyes.

A group of at least twenty people had come into the building without her noticing. They were standing between her and the door. All of them looked ready to fight. And all of them had the familiar glitter in their eyes of members of the Huntsman clan. *Snacks*, Kolbyr had said.

"He's lying. Kolbyr wouldn't have helped, even if we'd asked," Queran said, voice sharp and unlike his usual tone of absolute confidence. "No matter. We will succeed without you. Once the Huntsman clan has dealt with you." The demon flicked his hand at the clan members. "Kill the vampire and the Marshal. They are annoying me."

"You really are too, too kind," Kolbyr murmured. Max didn't have to look at him to know he'd shifted into his vampire form. "Do allow me to deal with this inconvenience, my dear," he said to Max.

"Go ahead," Max said, taking a step to one side, away from Queran and Shivangi and Evan. She was quite certain that there was no way she could deal with all of the newcomers, even with her dogs.

A groan from the floor distracted her. She glanced down to find that Evan Yarwood was, somehow, moving. The blow that Shivangi had hit him with should have at least cracked a human skull. Max had not expected him to wake again. But he was moving, putting a hand to his head and attempting to sit up, the folds of his robes getting in his way as if he was not used to wearing them. Max's fingers twitched and she checked an impulse to reach for her gun. Evan's face was swollen, bruises forming from the strike, but he seemed to be breathing and alive. And he wasn't threatening her just now.

Kolbyr moved past Max, ignoring Evan and focusing on the Huntsman clan, who were waiting for him with weapons raised. The vampire moved almost too quickly for her to track, sending the nearest clan member off his feet with an almost casual swipe of his arm. The clan member flew across the building, thumping into one of the stone pillars. There was an ominous crack and not from the impact of the body. Max glanced up at the roof. The building had been abandoned for at least a decade. Despite looking intact, it might have some flaws. The last thing they needed just now was the roof falling in.

There was no time to worry about the state of the building as the clan swarmed forwards, half surrounding Kolbyr, the remainder heading in her direction. She stiffened, raising her gun and starting to fire before they could reach her, Cas and Pol surging forward, seizing a leg each and dragging two clan members off their feet.

Max's bullets hit home, but the charge forward didn't stop. She shoved her gun away and drew her longest knife. Her least favourite weapon. She ducked under the first, wild blow of the nearest clan member. The second was more cautious, grabbing hold of her knife arm and squeezing her wrist harder and harder until she dropped the knife, the blade clattering to the floor amid furious growls from her dogs and the sound of more gunfire. Bryce.

Bryce's bullets hit home, as Max's had. Spurts of blood erupted into the air along with grunts of pain from the clan members. But they didn't stop. Not human, her panicked brain reminded her. She had never been sure what kind of non-human they were, but whatever it was seemed oblivious to pain.

Max struggled to get free from the clan member's hold. The man didn't even bother to make it seem like an effort to hold her, raising his arm until her feet were off the floor. She tried hitting at him with her free arm but couldn't connect and twisting in his grip only made his fingers tighten until she thought he might break a bone. Or two.

Dark shadows converged from either side, Cas and Pol in their attack forms. They grabbed the clan member around his legs, tearing him down to the floor, Max with him. She landed badly, flat footed, the shock of striking the floor jarring her all the way to the top of her skull. The grip finally eased enough on her arm that she could twist free, only to find another pair of clan members ready to try to tackle her.

She scurried backwards across the floor, stumbling as she tripped over Hemang, who was still unconscious on the floor. Her back hit the stone pillar that Hemang had landed against and she stopped. Cas and Pol came to join her, shifted into their attack forms, standing in front of her, snarling at the clan members, daring them to approach. The clan members didn't seem to care, still converging on her. Max reloaded her gun and fired again, aiming for head shots this time, insides turning into knots. She didn't want to kill them. But she didn't want to die, either.

A tall, heavy weight slammed into the nearest clan member. Bryce. He had abandoned his automatic weapon in favour of a long, gleaming blade that he wielded with almost casual expertise, slicing through the first three clan members he encountered before they knew what was happening.

Max stopped firing, afraid of hitting Bryce. And her one attempt to use a knife had ended up with the weapon on the ground. So she stayed where she was, back pressed against the pillar, dogs in front of her, gun ready to use if she had a chance.

Watching Bryce move in battle was extraordinary. He didn't seem to rush or hurry and yet he was always just a fraction ahead of whatever blow the clan members sent his way. He flowed through the greater number of enemies as if he knew precisely where each of them was and what he needed to do not only to stay ahead of them but to stop them in their tracks. Huntsman clan members fell all around him, hitting the ground with thumps until there was only Bryce left standing. He looked over at Max, breathing hard, and raised a brow.

Max realised that her gun was pointed at him and lowered it, heat rising in her face. She had been so caught up in watching him she hadn't been paying attention to what she, or anyone else, was doing.

"An excellent display, if I may say so," Kolbyr said, his voice sounding loud in the hush that had fallen over the room. "We should spar sometime."

Max dragged her eyes away from Bryce to see that the vampire was standing in his own field of fallen enemies, although there was far more blood, and all the fallen clan members around Kolbyr looked to be dead, whereas Max thought that most of Bryce's opponents were incapacitated but still breathing.

"I don't spar," Bryce said tersely. He bent down at the side of the nearest pillar and retrieved his main weapon, pointing it towards the centre of the room. "Stay where you are," he ordered.

Max had all but forgotten about Queran, which was extraordinary in itself. She had thought that the demon was the most dangerous thing in the building, and now wasn't so sure. She looked across to find Queran glaring back at Bryce, the demon's face tight with displeasure, the hint of his other nature showing through the too-tanned skin.

"I don't take orders from you," Queran said, flicking a hand. Power shot across the room, slamming into Bryce. Whereas Shivangi had been flung off her feet, Bryce slid back across the ground, remaining upright, weapon still pointing at the demon.

"That's impressive," Kolbyr said, still speaking to Bryce. He didn't seem to be in the slightest bit bothered by Bryce's refusal to spar with him. Instead, he was straightening his clothing, grimacing as he found more holes and tears in the fabric. "Really, this is a handmade jacket. Impossible to replace. Ruined," he complained. He sounded genuinely annoyed by that, and his face was tight with irritation as he looked across at Queran. "Are you done with your stupid scheming, little watcher?" he asked.

Queran's face shifted, as if the bones were moving, showing more of what lay underneath the innocuous human form. "Do not call me that," the demon said, voice deep and full of hate.

"It is your nature," Kolbyr said. "And you have exceeded your instructions."

"As interesting as this is, how do we bind this demon or send him back to his master?" Bryce asked, voice terse. He had not taken his eyes off Queran.

"You can do neither," Queran said, his human façade back in place. His too-white teeth gleamed in a predatory smile. "Do you think bullets will stop me?"

"I am willing to try," Bryce told him.

Bullets might not stop him, Max thought, but the magic knife that Bryce had given her might well do the trick. She put her gun away, as casually as she could, and shoved her hands into her jacket pockets, fingers closing around the hilt of the knife. She just needed to get close enough to Queran.

"You seem to be under the false impression that you are in charge," Shivangi said, with all the arrogance of a head of Family. She looked between Kolbyr and Bryce.

"As do you," Kolbyr said, voice silky soft and full of the promise of hurt.

Shivangi lifted her chin, reaching under her robes and producing a black velvet pouch. It looked very like a nullification pouch, and Max's attention shifted to it as the woman reached inside, drawing out a glimmering black stone. As the stone left the pouch, its aura spread through the room, as dark as the stone itself. It was the most powerful object Max had ever seen in her life.

"Little girl, put away that ridiculous artefact and surrender before you get hurt," Kolbyr said, in that same soft voice. If Max had been holding the stone, she would have obeyed without hesitation. Shivangi did not.

"It kept you subdued before," Shivangi said, taking a step towards the vampire, the stone held out in front of her. "I'm sure it can work again."

"You took me by surprise before," Kolbyr said, the admission startling Max. But it did explain how the Raghavan twins had been able to put a collar on one of the most powerful vampires in the city. He was still looking at Shivangi and the stone. "But you have lost that advantage now."

"Oh, really? You think now you know about the stone, it won't have any effect on you?" Shivangi said, taking another step towards the vampire.

The stone's power pulsed, and an ugly stirring in the air made Max's skin crawl. "That's a stone from the underworld, isn't it?" she asked Shivangi.

"Yes," Shivangi said, not taking her eyes off Kolbyr. "It's been in my family for generations."

"And none of your ancestors were stupid enough to use it," Kolbyr said, "certainly not in the careless way you did."

"Careless?" Shivangi's mouth curved up in a smile. Another step forward. There was a whisper of magic in the air, sticky and static, raising the hairs at the back of Max's neck. Shivangi was at the centre of what had been the ritual space, Max realised, and wondered if the woman knew where she was. Frowning at the faint lines of where the ritual had been set out, Max thought she could see the lines moving. "This ridiculous artefact, as you called it, worked, didn't it?" Shivangi taunted.

"Dark calls to dark," Kolbyr told her, taking a step forward, closing the distance between them. "Objects like that don't like being away from their home."

A frisson of power trailed across Max's skin. The lines of the ritual space had definitely changed, growing more solid from the faint impressions that three failed attempts had left. The frisson came again, stronger this time, and the ground trembled. She didn't recognise the spell-caster but whoever was wielding the magic was powerful, which suggested either Kolbyr or Queran.

Shivangi was still in the middle of the ritual space, stone held in front of her. She looked around, brows lifting. "What are you doing, vampire?"

"Me? Nothing. I told you that you are meddling with things you don't understand," Kolbyr said. Max believed him. He hadn't seemed all that keen on helping the others create their ritual.

"Queran. Demon. What are you doing?" Shivangi demanded, turning towards Max.

Queran was standing a few paces away from Max. She started. She had not seen or felt him move, but there he was. Cas and Pol had shifted to stand between her and the demon. As she realised just how close the demon was, she felt a trail of his power in the air.

"I have done nothing. But I think that the vampire was lying to us," Queran said. "We did mark the ritual correctly. And we did that at least three times. Enough to leave a mark."

Shivangi looked down and seemed to realise for the first time just where she was standing.

"What? You mean that the ritual is active?" she asked, voice rising to a shriek. She moved, or tried to. Her feet seemed to be stuck to the ground in the centre space of the ritual. "You! You did this," she screamed at Kolbyr.

The vampire was standing several paces away from the edge of the ritual, mouth tilted in a half smile. "I told you, more than once, that you were meddling in things you did not understand. And I also told you to put that stone away. What's the matter, little girl, don't you want to meet your master?" His tone was mocking, his eyes watchful.

Chills ran across Max's skin at the implication of his words. The ritual was a portal spell. Designed to bring Arkus here, to this place and to this world. And it was becoming active.

"We didn't finish the ritual," Shivangi protested. "No offerings were made."

Kolbyr's faint smile grew. He was definitely enjoying Shivangi's discomfort.

"That's true," Queran said in Max's ear. She jumped. She had been distracted by the magic spilling into the air and the conversation between Shivangi and Kolbyr. She had lost track of the demon. Again. And of Evan. "Go get some of the offerings," Queran said to someone past Max's shoulder.

"Do you think it will work?" Evan's voice said behind Max.

"I am not sure, but I'd like to find out," Queran answered, a hungry look in his eyes.

Before Max could guess his plan, the demon had seized hold of her arm. It happened to be the one the clan member had been gripping earlier and she cried out as the demon's hard fingers dug into her already-bruised flesh through the layers of her clothing. There was a gleam of metal at the edge of her vision and a blade came towards her. Her blade. The one she had dropped earlier.

The realisation that Queran was trying to stab her with her own weapon gave her extra strength to turn away from the strike in time for her dogs to seize hold of the demon's robes, growling as they pulled him away from Max. He still had hold of her arm, though, and gave her a hard shove as he let go, sending her staggering, off balance, across the floor until her feet stuck and wouldn't move.

She looked down, horrified, to see that she was also in the centre of the ritual. The ground was wavering under her feet, the magic changing it from solid and real to something else. She tried moving but couldn't free her feet from the floor. As she watched, the toes of her boots sank into what had been solid stone. When she tried to pull her feet out of her boots, she sank in farther, up to her ankles. She stopped moving and stayed where she was, the surface of the stone rippling in a way that made her feel sick.

Stuck in a dark magic ritual. Her heart was hammering in her throat. She scrabbled in her pocket. Salt. She had salt. It should work to counter the magic.

She drew out the small pouch of salt. It looked far too small and insignificant next to the size of the ritual space, but she spilled some of it anyway, hoping it might at least weaken the magic holding her. It had no effect. She shoved the pouch back in her pocket, fingers trembling.

Cas growled nearby. He was at the very edge of the space, Pol just behind them. As creatures of magic, they knew something was wrong.

"No! Stay back. Stay away. Go and guard Nati and Ynes," she told her dogs, trusting that they would be able to work out who she meant. Queran had sent Evan to get the offerings, which meant gathering people from the makeshift rooms.

"Take my hand," Bryce said, appearing in place of Cas as her dogs headed away.

"No. The magic is too strong. When I try to move, I sink in further. You'll get pulled in too," Max said, her voice too high and too fast, breathing rapid. She was caught in a dark magic ritual which was supposed to open a gate to the underworld. "The people," she said to Bryce, mind and brain disconnecting for a moment so that she couldn't produce any more words.

"They'll be fine," Bryce said, frowning at her. He still had his hand held out.

"No, they won't. Evan was going for them," Max said, looking past Bryce. Her dogs were standing in the opening of one of the rooms, snarling at Evan, who was standing a few paces away, not seeming to be intimidated by the shadow-hounds glaring at him.

"Don't move," Bryce told her, and strode across the floor to deal with Evan.

"Such a pity," Queran's voice said, too close for Max's comfort. He was back on his feet, the great tears in his robes repairing themselves as Max looked at him. He was just outside the spell markings, eyes gleaming as he looked at her. "You were showing such promise. But I am sure that my master will be pleased with you as an offering at His altar."

"I doubt it," Max said through clenched teeth. "Are you really so desperate to get back to the underworld that you were going to kill all those people?" she asked.

"I've been here longer than you could possibly imagine," Queran said, his human faced slipping again, showing the wrong angles of something else. "I've been a good demon, doing my duty. I am sure He will reward me."

"Your duty?" Max questioned, partly out of interest and partly to keep Queran distracted. Beyond the demon, she could see Bryce and Evan locked in what looked like a wrestling match where neither was winning so far. She wanted to tell Cas and Pol to help Bryce, but didn't want to alert Queran that one of his allies was in trouble.

"He's a watcher," Kolbyr said.

"I don't know what that means," Max said, trying to keep hold of her temper. It was difficult. She was ankle-deep in stone in the centre of dark magic and couldn't work out a way to free herself, and both Kolbyr and Queran knew far more than they were saying.

"You insult me again," Queran said, lips curling back from his teeth.

"Not at all. That is what you are. A watcher, my dear, is a demon who watches," Kolbyr told Max.

Max had a moment of being glad that she was stuck in the floor. Otherwise she might have been tempted to do something very stupid, like take a swing at Kolbyr. He was looking at her as if he expected his words to be the enlightenment that she had been seeking.

"Watches what?" she asked, after a long breath.

"That is a most insightful question," Kolbyr said.

"Stop your blabbering," Shivangi said from near Max, "and get me out of here. I command it."

Max looked across at the other woman and saw that the floor was up to her calves. She must have been struggling for longer than Max had. Shivangi was still holding the black stone in front of her as if it was her last hope.

"I don't think so," Queran said, voice turning thoughtful. Whatever was under his voice made Max's skin twitch in revulsion. "The master is always looking for new talent, and He will doubtless want to reward your service to Him."

"I serve Him here," Shivangi said, fury in every word. "Here, in this world. Not in the underworld."

"But what did you think would happen when He was free of his prison?" Kolbyr asked, head tilted slightly. "This world will become the underworld as well. So it's really no different." He shook his head and looked at Max, giving her a wink that she wasn't sure how to interpret. "Honestly, the youth these days. No concept of devotion or service."

Max stared back at the vampire. There was something in his words. Something important. If only she could get her brain working long enough to work it out. Think, think, think. Dark magic that was supposed to open a portal to the underworld. Ritual prepared by the dark lord's worshippers. In service to Him.

Her mouth dropped open. In service to Him. But He had an equal and opposite counterpart. The Lady. If the ritual was meant to honour the dark lord, perhaps something honouring the Lady could counter it. Or at least let Max get free of the stone that was slowly and steadily creeping up her legs.

But what could she do, with her limited magic and-

The Darsin. Light and the Darsin. Now, if only she could remember what she had done. Her mind went blank, refusing to cooperate. *Think, think, think. What had she done?*

Some kind of magic. Some kind of spell. Alright. She could start that, at least.

She placed her hands on top of each other in front of her, palms horizontal to the floor. There was a spell for light. A long and complicated spell that would call on the Lady's light. But she couldn't remember it. And she hadn't used it around the Darsin, either. Instead she had sent out a silent, instinctive prayer.

Lady of light, I pray that you will hear me, she thought. Hopefully that was the right start to a prayer. It had been a long time since she had formally prayed. *Lend me some of your blessed light that I may keep this world safe from your adversary.*

Nothing. No spark of light between her hands, no well of magic. Nothing.

She glared at her hands, willing light to form. Still nothing. And the floor was halfway up her shins now. Shivangi must be up to her knees.

Do you want Arkus to take over the world? Max yelled in her mind. *Because that's what will happen if you don't lend me some of your dark-blighted light right now.*

The space between her hands warmed, a blinding light forming. Max gasped in astonishment. Prayer hadn't worked, but shouting had?

There was no time to think of that now. She poured more energy into the light. The ground rippled under her feet, not enough to send her off balance but enough to fracture her concentration for a precious second.

"What are you doing, Miscellandreax?" Queran asked, teeth bared. "Stop that at once."

"Make me," Max snapped back, looking down. The floor had shifted under her feet and she was being slowly ejected from the stone. Her salt had had no effect. But this was working. The dark magic didn't like the light, which was hardly surprising.

There was still blinding light pooled between her palms, and she realised she had no idea what to do with it. She couldn't read the lines of the spell that Queran and his conspirators had used to make the portal. The lines on the ground were too faint for that. But it was dark magic, and she had light magic in her hands.

She lifted her hands in front of her, turning them so that each of her palms cradled a pool of blinding light. She tipped her hands sideways and the light spilled down, towards the stone floor and the active dark magic. As the light touched the stone surface, it surged, enough that she lost her balance, almost falling sideways. Then the dark magic recoiled and spat her out, away from the ritual space.

Max landed on the stone floor and slid across the hard surface, aware of more bruises forming. She came to a stop close to where her dogs were still guarding Nati and Ynes.

Behind her, Shivangi screamed. Looking over her shoulder, Max saw the other woman being pulled further into the floor, her body covered with a cascade of light too bright to look at and dark too black to see. Max scrambled to her feet, her whole body ringing with the after effect of the dark magic, the skin of her hands tingling. She looked down to find trails of light sparkling along the backs of her hands and little motes of brilliant white light gathered in her palms when she turned them over.

"What have you done?" Queran hissed close to her ear. He grabbed her arm, fingers tight enough to bruise. He was furious, his demon self clearly visible through his human skin. Max saw sharp angles and flat planes that she had glimpsed in the underworld, remembered terror catching her breath. He took a step back towards the ritual space, dragging her with him. Back towards the portal.

Max shifted her feet so that she was better balanced, and put her hand on his where he was holding her. The light slid across her skin, pouring onto the demon's hand.

Queran let out an unearthly shriek, letting her go and stepping away from her, shaking his hand. "What have you done?" he cried again. There was smoke rising from his hand, the skin charring as Max looked at it. "I can't go back like this. Not with this taint on me." He glared at her. "What are you?" he demanded.

The question hit Max like a blow, almost sending her off balance. She opened her mouth to tell him she was human, that was all, but no words came out.

"Demon! Get me out of here!" Shivangi looked absolutely terrified. As well she might. She was almost up to her waist in the stone floor.

"There's nothing I can do," Queran said, baring his teeth at her. "Be sure to tell our master about my good service. I am sure your gift will please Him."

Shivangi screamed in response, struggling to move and only succeeding in pulling herself further into the ground. "Kolbyr. Vampire. Help me. I command it."

"I'm afraid that the ritual has been badly compromised," Kolbyr said. He was standing a few paces outside the central space, at what he perhaps considered a safe distance from the rippling floor. "And this is the consequence of meddling in things you don't understand."

Max watched, both horrified and morbidly fascinated, as Shivangi slid further into the ground until she was up to her chin. Somehow the woman managed to look across the room at Max, her face full of hate. "You. You did this. You've killed me."

"Not me," Max said, voice flat and hard. The light was fading from her hands, but she could still feel it inside her. "I didn't make you form an alliance to perform dark magic or to bring Arkus to this world. You did this all to yourself."

"Sister." Hemang was sitting up against the pillar he had struck earlier, looking shaken and confused, staring at Shivangi's head in the middle of the rippling stone. "What has happened?"

"You must avenge me, brother," Shivangi said. The stone around her twisted and she sank further, her screams of fury cut off by the stone closing over her head, a sight which Max just knew was going to give her more nightmares.

Chapter Twenty-Eight

As Shivangi disappeared from sight, the stone floor cracked across its length, breaking through the faint lines of the ritual. A wave of magic rolled over the ground, almost sending Max off her feet again. One of the pillars near the centre of the building cracked, huge chunks of stone falling onto the floor, followed by a wooden beam and a section of the roof. The ground shook again and more tiles from the roof crashed onto the floor, cascading on top of the bodies lying there. Kolbyr's victims, and the ones Bryce had defeated.

Looking around the rest of the room, Max saw Hemang struggling to his feet, unsteady and uncoordinated. Queran was cradling one hand to his stomach, glaring at her. Kolbyr was standing quite still, looking at the cracked stone floor with a thoughtful expression. Max wasn't sure what he was thinking, but the sight of him so still and contemplative in the midst of chaos sent a chill across her skin. The pilots were pressed back against the wall near the table, which surprised her. She had thought they might have taken the chance to run away while the arguments and fighting were happening. They were pilots, after all. She frowned, wondering why they had stayed.

And there were other things she needed to tend to. Max headed across to the rooms where Queran and his conspirators had gathered their *offerings*, seeing Evan on the ground with his wrists tied together and linked to his feet with what looked like strips of fabric torn from his robes, which were in tatters around him revealing an ordinary pair of jeans and t-shirt underneath. The chief of detectives seemed to be unconscious again. Bryce was standing near him, automatic weapon in hand, looking as if he was ready to shoot Evan if the man so much as twitched.

"We need to get out of here," she said to Bryce as the ground shook under their feet again. "This building feels like it's going to come down."

"Agreed. There are ten hostages," Bryce said. "They don't seem to be badly injured, but they won't get far on foot."

"The helicopter outside looks large enough to hold them," Max said.

"Yes. We just need a pilot." Bryce's hard glare shot across the room to where the drinkers were still standing by the wall. "Let's just hope they are sober enough to fly."

"Is it over?" Nati asked. She had got to her feet and come to the front of the room, Ynes tucked in beside her. "Really over?"

"The dark magic part is done," Max said, "but we need to get you out of here. Can you walk to the outside?"

"Yes," Nati said, with no hesitation, then glanced over her shoulder. "But there are a couple of people here who were badly beaten. They might need some help."

Before Max could reply, the doors of the building were flung open and half a dozen warriors appeared, weapons raised. Khari, Joshua, and the other warriors. They were covered in dirt and bits of leaves and looked around the building in astonishment.

"You had the fight without us?" Osvaldo said, spotting Bryce across the room.

"What happened?" Khari asked.

"No time for that now. Khari, Joshua, Hop, Killan, Gemma, over here," Bryce said. "Os. Those two are pilots. Get them outside and get the helicopter started."

"On it," Osvaldo said, and turned to where the drinkers were huddled against the wall.

Max watched as Khari and the others gathered around the hostages, as Bryce had called them, getting them to their feet and heading towards the doors. A few of them needed help. Hop, Killan and Joshua provided support without any complaint or hesitation while Gemma brought up the rear, scowling.

Osvaldo brought the two pilots across the room to Bryce, careful to skirt around the vampire. "They say that one of the people with robes has the keys to the chopper, and they can't fly without the keys."

That would explain why they hadn't left, Max thought, and had to credit Queran and his co-conspirators with a bit of cunning, at least.

"Hot wire it," Bryce said tersely. "We've no time to search this lot, and if the woman had the keys, I'm not going into the underworld to get them."

"It's been a while since I hot wired a chopper," Osvaldo said, eyes gleaming in anticipation. He turned the pilots around and nudged them out of the building at the end of his gun, leaving Max blinking and wondering just when he had had to hot wire a helicopter before.

Bryce joined Max, watching the hostages and his fellow warriors leave, then tilted his head to the demon, vampire and remaining twin. "What about them?" he asked her.

Max looked around the faces that were all now turned to her, with a variety of expressions. "Lord Kolbyr was brought here against his will. If there's space, we should offer him a place in the helicopter. The others can make their own way back," she said.

Queran peeled his lips back from his teeth. "Full of surprises, aren't you? No compassion for a poor, hard-working demon?"

"None," Max confirmed. "You got yourself into this mess. I'm quite sure you can get yourself out of it. That goes for you, too," she added to Hemang. "And Evan, when he wakes up." She spared a glance for the unconscious chief of detectives. She had a vague idea that she should try to arrest them. Evan and Hemang, certainly. She was quite sure Queran would evade any attempt to arrest him. But she had a group of terrified people to get to safety first, and didn't want Hemang or Evan anywhere near the people they had gathered as *offerings*.

The ground shook again, and another pillar cracked.

"Time to go," Bryce said.

"Yes," Max said, and headed for the door, her dogs with her. As she crossed the room, Kolbyr moved to join her.

"My dear Marshal, I am touched by your concern for my welfare," he told her, managing somehow to bow while he was walking.

"Don't be. I like fairness, that's all. Can you get everyone loaded while I get my bag?" Max asked Bryce. She could leave without her pack, but she didn't want to leave the equipment behind. And it also contained a very special soft toy that she thought Ynes might like to have back.

Not waiting for his reply, she stalked away across the open space, strides hampered by the shaking ground, and ducked into the undergrowth, finding her bag untouched. By the time she had retrieved it and was making her way back to the helicopter, Osvaldo had got the engines started and Khari and the others had got the hostages loaded. The pilots were involved in an animated discussion with Bryce outside the helicopter, though, suggesting they weren't quite ready to leave.

Max came up to them to hear the words "overloaded" and "fuel allowance" from one of the half-drunk men.

"What's the problem?" she asked.

"The helicopter can fly, we just don't have enough fuel to get back to the city with the extra weight on board," Bryce told her.

"Get to the oil field, you can refuel there," she told the pilots tersely.

They looked rebellious, yielding under Bryce's glare.

"Os, will you sit as co-pilot?" Bryce shouted over the helicopter's engines.

Osvaldo simply nodded and settled into one of the pilot's chairs. Bryce pushed one of the pilots towards the free seat, and dragged the other one to the back of the helicopter. There were a few rows of seats which were crammed full of the hostages, Lord Kolbyr having the row at the front all to himself as Max came up.

"Get inside," Bryce told Max, "you and your dogs."

"What about you and the others?" Max asked, shouting to be heard over the blades whirring overhead.

"We'll ride on the landing skids," Bryce said, an unexpected grin crossing his face. "Haven't done that in a while. Don't worry, we'll manage. Up you get," he said. He shoved the pilot in, next to Kolbyr, and then offered a hand to Max. She accepted, not wanting to fall flat on her face with the combination of the shaking ground and the pain running up her leg. His hand was warm and firm under hers, anchoring her to the here and now after all that had happened. As she took her place, shoving her backpack under her feet, Cas and Pol leapt in, crowding against her, the whites of their eyes showing. They hadn't travelled by helicopter before.

The doors shut, cutting off some of the noise, and the vehicle lifted into the air, less smoothly than Max had expected. She leant towards the windows, seeing Bryce, Khari and Joshua settling themselves on the helicopter's landing skids on her side as the vehicle lifted.

And not before time. As they rose into the air, Max saw enormous cracks appearing in the earth below, fissures disappearing into the depths of the world. And a small figure staggering out of the building, something in his hand. Hemang. And it looked like he was holding a weapon of some sort.

There was a flat crack from somewhere close by and Hemang fell back. Max started, then saw that Bryce had his weapon up on his shoulder, Khari and Joshua each holding on to him. Max closed her eyes, rubbing her hands across her face. There had been too much death today. Far too much. She had tried to give Hemang a chance to survive. A slim one, but a chance nonetheless.

She scrubbed the tears away, conscious of the people crowded around her. They were alive. They had been gathered together in that building for the purpose of being used as offerings in the dark magic ritual, and they were still alive and free. That was a victory she could hold on to.

Chapter Twenty-Nine

Faddei and Vanko were both standing on the old concrete apron of the oil field when the helicopter descended in the first light of day. From what Max could see, they barely blinked as Bryce and the other warriors jumped off the landing skids as the helicopter slowly descended to the ground, but they did gape in astonishment as the doors opened to reveal not just Lord Kolbyr but also ten exhausted, filthy people and a child clinging to her mother so tightly that Nati struggled to get down from the helicopter, her fellow captives lending a hand.

As the former hostages got out of the helicopter, Max dug into her bag and pulled out the lilac bear, holding it out to Ynes. The girl grabbed it and started crying. Then Nati cried, and most of the rest of the former hostages joined her as Faddei barked orders, which resulted a few moments later in people pouring out of the main building with blankets and bottles of water, taking the hostages in hand.

Max watched some of the Marshals, oil crew and scientists escorting the captives into the building, not surprised to find her face was wet again.

"Looks like you've had quite an adventure," Faddei said to Max, voice loud as the helicopter engines were finally shut off.

"Yes," Max agreed.

"Was that the girl you were looking for, and her mother?" Khari wanted to know, stopping nearby, Joshua beside her with his arm around her shoulders.

"Yes," Max said again, smiling. "They seem to be in one piece, at least. Thank you for your help," she added.

"Does this have anything to do with the hill collapsing?" Faddei asked. "Half the crew was up on the roof watching it fall at first light."

"It's gone? Good," Max said, sounding more fierce than she had intended. She pushed aside a slight twinge of guilt remembering that Hemang, Evan and Queran had still been in or near the building when they had left it. If anyone could survive, it would be Queran. And she wasn't sure how much sympathy the Raghavan twin or former chief of detectives deserved, as they had been planning to sacrifice people and bring Arkus into the daylight world.

"I'll want to hear all about it," Faddei said. "After you've had a shower and some rest."

"Shower?" Max said, mind sticking on that one word. "You got the showers working?"

"And hot water, too," Vanko confirmed.

"Oh, my," Max said, almost crying again. After her trek through the Wild and the awful night, the idea of a hot shower and being truly clean was a miracle.

When she made her way out of the shower room and into the dining room, light-headed from the heat of the shower and the luxury of clean clothes, she saw more miracles all around her. Some of the rescued hostages were sitting at tables with bowls of soup in front of them, still huddled in the blankets that they had been given on arrival. Others had clearly made use of the showers and were in clean clothes, more bowls in front of them, settled at tables with members of the oil crew and a couple of the scientists, looking around with slightly dazed expressions. Nati and Ynes had been among those getting clean and Ynes was sitting tucked against her mother's side, the lilac bear hugged close. Max's mouth curved up as she saw Cas and Pol nearby, lounging oh-so-casually on the floor. Clearly, they had not given up their guard duties. Or perhaps they were simply hopeful for some scraps from the nearby diners. Max thought they would be out of luck. From the way the former hostages were eating, she would guess that they hadn't been properly fed in their captivity.

The pair of pilots had been settled at their own table, on the other side of the room from the hostages, and there was a pair of armed law enforcement officers keeping a casual watch on them. Max wasn't sure how involved the pilots had been in the dark magic plot, but it seemed no one was taking any chances with them. She approved.

Aurora came through the door beside Max and paused, looking her over. "You look dead on your feet," the older woman commented.

"I feel it," Max said. She had taken the opportunity when she was in the shower room to look over her bruises. The ones on her leg, across the pink scars, were the worst, but she had plenty of others, including several impressions of fingers on her arm. She needed rest. Badly. "I'm just here to get some food, then I'm going to find a place to sleep."

"Ben and I have been bunking down in one of the offices. We're used to a lot more quiet than fifty other people around us. We're on day shift, so it's empty right now. You're welcome to use it," Aurora said. "If you don't mind the dog hair."

Max laughed, her chest lightening. She hadn't been looking forward to sleeping in the communal room. She had a lot of fresh memories that would almost certainly disrupt her sleep for weeks and months to come. "Thank you, that's really kind."

"No worries. If you're wanting some food, better be quick. That soup is amazing," Aurora said, and headed out of the room again.

Max looked after her, heart swelling as she realised that Aurora had simply come to check in on Max and make the offer of a quieter place to sleep. For a long time, she had believed that she didn't have any people she could truly call friends, telling herself to be content with her quiet life. She had a job, she had Cas and Pol, and colleagues that she respected, and who respected her. That should be enough. More than enough. And now, standing in the doorway of the makeshift dining room, she realised she had far more than that. True friends. She might not see them that often, but Aurora and Ben, Alonso and Elicia, and Malik, were all friends. Far more than she had ever had in her life before, and her quiet, empty life suddenly felt very full indeed.

Then Nati spotted Max and lifted a hand to wave. Ynes saw her, too, and detached herself from her mother, running across to Max to hug her legs, looking up with a face covered in breadcrumbs and butter. "Thank you for finding Polly," she said.

"You are most welcome," Max said, guessing that Polly was the bear. She gently unwound Ynes' arms from her leg, trying not to wince as her bruises ached. Ynes tucked one of her hands into Max's instead and tugged her across the room to Nati.

Nati looked as exhausted as Max felt, but her eyes were bright.

"Thank you, Max," she said. "I thought we were going to die there."

"How did you come to be there?" Max asked, curious.

"It was stupid," Nati said, ducking away from Max's eyes.

"I know about Ivor," Max said. "I went to see him."

"Oh," Nati said, colour rushing into her face. "I'm sorry."

"Don't be," Max said, taking the free seat at the end of the table, next to Nati. She saw a couple of nods of agreement from Nati's fellow former captives.

"You're not the first one to fall for a charming smile," an older woman said, her voice low and rich. Her mouth tilted up in a wistful smile, eyes distant as if she was remembering the past. "And he gave you a beautiful daughter, so it's not all bad."

"That is true," Nati said, hugging Ynes closer to her. She managed a smile, eyes bright with unshed tears. "Well, to your question, I was trying to find the warehouse. I didn't think he would look for me there. But there was something awful in the mists. I couldn't see what it was. Not exactly. Looked a bit like a man, but I knew it wasn't." That sounded like the Darsin, Max realised, chills running across her skin as she realised how close Nati and her daughter had been to the predator.

"Big monster," Ynes confided, looking up from her mother's side. "Bad monster."

"Yes, there was a very bad monster on the docks," Max confirmed gravely. "But it's gone now."

"Thank the Lady," the older woman said, putting the two fingers of her right hand onto her heart. "I could hear that thing at night. Hunting."

"It's not going to hunt anymore," Max said.

"Dead monster?" Ynes asked, eyes bright.

"Very dead," Max confirmed.

"Well, we heard that thing prowling around, and then we saw the helicopter and a few people getting into it. It was stupid, but we hid in there," Nati said.

"We got promised all sorts of things to get in the helicopter," one of the men said. "Jobs. Food. Clean clothes. We were told it was dangerous."

"But we're used to dangerous," the older woman finished for him, shaking her head. "It sounded too good to be true. Should have known it was a trap."

"Who made the promises? Shivangi and Hemang?" Max asked.

"No, not them. The other fellow, the one with the orange skin and white teeth," the older woman said.

"You seemed to know him," the man said, a touch of hardness in his face as he stared at Max.

"Queran. He's a demon. Not a friend," Max confirmed, nose wrinkling in distaste. "I'd really prefer not to know him at all."

"By the time we realised we were being kept prisoner, it was too late," the man said, shoulders slumping. "We were in the Wild, and none of us knew the way home."

"We'll get you back to the city," Max promised.

"And back to the warehouse," the woman said, face and voice grim. She didn't seem to be looking forward to the prospect. With winter approaching, Max could understand that.

"We'll see," Max said. Shivangi and Hemang's actions couldn't go without some kind of punishment, she thought, and the Raghavan family holdings included a lot of wealth and housing. Something could surely be done to provide for the homeless people.

Two long days later, they were all back in the city, the convoy returning through the Wild with no more interference from the demon. The helicopter had left the day before, taking the former captives, pilots and Lord Kolbyr back into the city along with Radrean, who had been almost forcibly escorted to his seat by Bryce. Max couldn't help but wonder what stories Radrean would spin when he got back to the Order, not just of his own heroic deeds, but also of her - the Order's most infamous former apprentice. She tried to tell herself that she didn't care. It was partly true. She didn't care about his opinion of her. Not in the least. But she found she did care, quite badly, what Bryce thought of her.

Between wondering what lies Radrean was telling and keeping watch from her position in truck five, Max found plenty of time to wonder how Nati and Ynes were doing. They were being taken back to Alonso and Elicia, and Max could only hope that Nati's former boyfriend would be discouraged from looking for them there by the knowledge that the Marshals' service was taking an interest in them. That was assuming that Ruutti hadn't already found a reason to arrest the boyfriend.

Max had far less pleasant things to turn over in her mind, too. Whether Audhilde had managed to identify the victims in the Darsin's nest. The fact that Queran seemed to have found willing co-conspirators to open a portal to the underworld. The question that Queran had thrown at her, in the middle of the struggle. *What are you?* A question that Max had turned over in her mind a thousand times since then. The only answer she had to give - that she was human, and could use magic - didn't quiet the echo of Queran's voice.

And then there was the girl she had failed to protect. Just one of several that the Huntsmans had killed, according to Audhilde and Ruutti. The weight of responsibility settled on her shoulders. She hadn't prevented the girl's death. She wanted to do what she could to prevent other deaths, and the chief of detectives wouldn't be there to interfere with her any longer. Audhilde and Ruutti might not welcome outside questions, but she didn't think they would turn her away, either.

After the almost anti-climatic journey back, the full tankers arrived back at the city's refinery, which had been their starting point. All their personal vehicles were there, along with more heavily armed members of law enforcement. The protection was in place to keep watch while the crude oil was refined into usable fuel. It seemed that the tension in the city had only grown in the few days they had been gone. Max wondered how long it would take for the city to calm down again, now that the fuel reserves were restored. Or even if the city would calm down.

The main part of their jobs done, there was just the clean-up to do. Removing the guns from the trucks, making sure that they collected all their belongings, hampered by the excited chatter of the scientists who seemed to have spent their time in the Wild gathering almost impossible amounts of samples, which all had to be checked by the warriors and Marshals to make sure that there was nothing dangerous. One of the scientists had, apparently unknowingly, brought back a sapling of one of the carnivorous plants and Vanko and Faddei between them had to wrestle the plant away from the scientist, who insisted that it wouldn't hurt anyone. The plant returned the scientist's dedication by trying to chew his arm, and at that point he let Vanko and Faddei take the plant away. Max was quite sure that Raymund and his team would find a use for it in the Marshals' own science facility.

Eventually, it was over. The scientists left, heading back to their labs and their daily lives. The oil crew was being given the night off to rest, but they would be back on shift at daybreak to work on the refining process. The law enforcement officers who had been in the Wild exchanged nods of respect with the warriors and Marshals, before heading home to their loved ones. Max couldn't help but wonder how many tall tales would be spreading around the city's police force about what had gone on in the Wild.

Aurora and Ben came over to give Max fierce, warm hugs and extract a promise to join them for dinner soon. Max had already found several messages from Alonso and Elicia on her phone, delighted to have their daughter back and also insisting she join them for dinner soon, too. Her normally empty social calendar seemed to be filling up.

As the warriors and Marshals began dispersing, Bryce made a point of shaking Faddei's and Vanko's hands, a visible and potent symbol of respect and cooperation that Max was sure didn't go unnoticed by any of the Marshals or warriors.

She made her way back to her pick-up, shoving her personal bag and ammunition bag onto the passenger seat. The ammunition bag was far lighter than it had been and she tried not to think about the lost resources. Even Leonda wouldn't send the Marshals back into the Wild to gather their spent ammunition. Assuming that the bulk of it could be recovered from the corridors where they had faced the mammoth spiders.

Cas and Pol settled into the back of the pick-up, nestling into the blankets with great sighs, as if they had each just worked a long, hard day. Even though she was aching with tiredness, she smiled and gave them both a pat and some dog biscuits. They had more than earned their keep these past few days. They lifted their heads, alerting her to someone behind her.

She turned to find Bryce approaching. The rest of the Marshals and warriors had either left, or were in the process of leaving, so there was space and quiet around them.

"Bryce," she said, and stopped, her tired brain not coming up with anything else to say.

"Max," he answered. He didn't seem to be laughing at her. He had shed the outer vest he normally wore, stuffed full of extra ammunition and other bits and pieces, stripped down to close-fitting body armour over a long-sleeve t-shirt. He looked almost vulnerable without his automatic weapon, although Max knew that was deceiving.

"Sorry, did I forget something?" she asked.

"No. I did." He dug into his pocket and pulled out his mobile phone. "I wanted to ask for your number."

It was a straightforward request, but Max stared at him, shock coursing through her. "Sure. I mean, yes," she said, and dug into her own pocket for her phone, staring at the screen as if she'd never seen it before. "Sorry. I can never remember the number," she said, heat blooming in her face as she scrolled through her contacts to find her own details.

"Me too," Bryce said, smile lifting his mouth. The smile chased some of Max's embarrassment away.

Max read off the number and watched him add it to his phone, then send her a text so she had his number. The text just had his name: *Bryce*. It made her want to laugh, as it was so in keeping with him.

"I've got to go and debrief Kitris, which will probably take most of tomorrow, but how about a drink in the evening?" he asked her.

She blinked, wondering if she had misheard. But no, he had just suggested a drink. Together. More warmth coiled through her and she found herself wanting to smile again. Then realised that she hadn't answered him.

"Sure. Yes. Let me know when and where," she managed to say, feeling heat in her face again.

"Great. It was nice working with you," he added before he turned away, heading over to where Osvaldo was waiting next to one of the warriors' sleek vehicles.

Max turned to her own pick-up and nearly dropped her phone as she fumbled for the handle, shoving it back into her pocket as she got behind the wheel. She drove home with a lighter heart and a smile on her face. The convoy had survived its journey into the Wild. The city's fuel supply was sorted for the foreseeable future. And she could look forward to some good company. She would get to spend more time with Aurora and Ben, as well as Alonso, Elicia, Nati and Ynes. And Bryce wanted to have drinks.

When she had left the Order, she had mostly wanted to hide and keep out of sight, building a quiet, careful life. Now that life was growing, expanding and the possibilities filled her with hope. She was looking forward to seeing what might happen next.

THANK YOU

Thank you very much for reading *Called*, The Grey Gates - Book 2. I hope that you've enjoyed continuing Max's story and spending more time with her and her hounds.

It would be great, if you have five minutes, if you could leave an honest review at the store you got it from. Reviews are really helpful for other readers to decide whether the book is for them, and also help me get visibility for my books - thank you.

Max's story continues in *Hunted*, The Grey Gates - Book 3, also available on Amazon.

Meantime, if you want to be kept up to date with what I'm working on, and get exclusive bonus content, you can sign up for my newsletter at the website: www.taellaneth.com

CHARACTER LIST

(Note: to avoid spoilers, some names may have been missed, and some details changed)

Alexey T'Or Radrean - human, male, twin to Sandrine and apprentice to Radrean

Alonso Ortis - human, male, married to Elicia

Arkus - dark lord, lord of the underworld

Audhilde (Hilda) - vampire, medical examiner

Aurora - human, female, shadow-hound trainer and handler, married to Ben

Ben - human, male, shadow-hound trainer and handler, married to Aurora

Bethell - lady of light

Bryce - partly human, male, one of the warriors of the Order

Cas - one of Max's dogs

Connor Declan Walsh - human, male, head of one of the city's most powerful families

Damayanti Raghavan - human, female, matriarch of Raghavan Family

David Prosser - human, male, councilman for one of the city districts

Ellie Randall - human, female, senior police officer in the city

Elicia Ortis - human, female, married to Alonso

Evan Yarwood - human, male, chief of detectives in the city

Faddei Lobanov - human, male, head of Marshal's service

Forster - family name of one of the powerful families in the city

Gemma - human, female, one of the warriors of the Order
Glenda Martins - human, female, nurse at the city clinic the Marshals use
Grandma Parras - human, female, Leonda's grandmother
Grayson Forster - human, male, owns the Sorcerer's Mistress, member of Forster family
Hemang Raghavan - human, male, Shivangi's brother
Hop - partly human, male, one of the warriors of the Order
Huntsman clan - one of the Five Families
Ivor Costen - male, member of Huntsman clan
Jessica Walsh - human, female, niece of Connor Declan Walsh
John Smith - human, crime scene technician (dead at the start of *Called*)
Joshua - male, one of the warriors of the Order, married to Khari
Killan - partly human, male, one of the warriors of the Order
Kitris - male, magician, head of the Order of the Lady of the Light
Khari - female, one of the warriors of the Order, married to Joshua
Kolbyr - vampire, male, master of dark magic
Leonda Parras - human, female, chief armourer for the Marshals
Lukas - vampire, male, part of Audhilde's household
Malik - male, owns the Hunter's Tooth
Max Ortis - female, Marshal
Nati - human, female, Elicia and Alonso's daughter
Nico - human, male, magic user
Orshiasa - human, male, Guardian in the Order
Osvaldo Martinez - male, one of the warriors of the Order
Pavla Bilak - human, female, one of the Marshals, married to Yevhen
Pol - one of Max's dogs
Queran - outwardly a human male
Radrean - human, male, Guardian in the Order
Raymund Robart - human, male, lead researcher and scientist for the Marshals
Ruutti Passila - female, detective
Sandrine T'Or Radrean - human, female, Alexey's twin and apprentice to Radrean
Sean Williams - human, male, police Sergeant

Shivangi Raghavan - human, female, Hemang's sister
Simmons - human, male, member of police specialist unit
Sirius - human, male, shadow-hound handler
Therese - human, female, dispatcher for the Marshals' service
Tina - female, truck driver for the city
Vanko Tokar - human, male, one of the Marshals
Walsh - family name of one of the powerful families in the city
Yevhen Bilak - human, male, one of the Marshals, married to Pavla
Ynes - human, female, Nati's daughter, Alonso and Elicia's granddaughter
Zoya Lipka - human, female, one of the Marshals

ALSO BY THE AUTHOR

(as at February 2024)

The Grey Gates (complete)
Outcast, Book 1
Called, Book 2
Hunted, Book 3
Forged, Book 4
Chosen, Book 5

Fractured Conclave
A Usual Suspect, Book 1 – expected to release early May 2024

Ageless Mysteries (complete)
Deadly Night, Book 1
False Dawn, Book 2
Morning Trap, Book 3
Assassin's Noon, Book 4
Flightless Afternoon, Book 5
Ascension Day, Book 6

The Hundred series (complete)
The Gathering, Book 1
The Sundering, Book 2

The Reckoning, Book 3
The Rending, Book 4
The Searching, Book 5
The Rising, Book 6

The Taellaneth series (complete)
Concealed, Book 1
Revealed, Book 2
Betrayed, Book 3
Tainted, Book 4
Cloaked, Book 5

Taellaneth Box Set (all five books in one e-book)
Taellaneth Complete Series (Books 1–5)

ABOUT THE AUTHOR

Vanessa Nelson is a fantasy author who lives in Scotland, United Kingdom and spends her days juggling the demands of two spoiled cats, two giant dogs and her fictional characters.

As far as the cats are concerned, they should always come first. The older dog lets her know when he isn't getting enough attention by chewing up the house. The younger dog's favourite method of getting her attention is a gentle nudge with his head. At least, he would say it's gentle.

You can find out more information online at the following places:

Website: www.taellaneth.com

Facebook: www.facebook.com/taellaneth

Printed in Great Britain
by Amazon

46118255R00148